D0208543

"I want the truth, you sonafabitch," I snarled into Luciano's mottled face, "and if I don't get it, I'm going to throw you into the river."

"I can't—" he said, but I shook him until his eyes rolled.

"Wait, wait!" he cried. "Tell me what you want."

"I want to know why someone blew up my house last night," I said. "I want to know why an innocent woman had to die last night. I want to know what you're not telling me, Luciano, and I better hear it damned soon."

THE
BLACK MOON

by
Robert J. Randisi
Loren D. Estleman
W.R. Philbrick
L.J. Washburn
Ed Gorman

Edited by
Robert J. Randisi and Ruth Ashby

A Byron Preiss Book

LYNX BOOKS
New York

The Black Moon

ISBN: 1-55802-125-6

First Printing/June 1989

This is a work of fiction. Names, characters, places, and incidents are either the product of the Authors' imagination or are used fictitiously. Any resemblance to actual events, locales, or persons, living or dead, is entirely coincidental.

Copyright © 1989 by Byron Preiss Visual Publications, Inc. Cover art copyright © 1989 by Byron Preiss Visual Publications, Inc. "The Black Moon" is a trademark of Byron Preiss Visual Publications, Inc.

All rights reserved. No part of this book may be reproduced or transmitted in any form or by any means electronic or mechanical, including by photocopying, by recording, or by any information storage or retrieval system, without the express written permission of the Publisher, except where permitted by law. For information, contact Lynx Communications, Inc.

This book is published by Lynx Books, a division of Lynx Communications, Inc., 41 Madison Avenue, New York, New York, 10010. The name "Lynx" and the logo consisting of a stylized head of a lynx are trademarks of Lynx Communications, Inc.

Printed in the United States of America

0 9 8 7 6 5 4 3 2 1

Cover painting by Paul Rivoche
Cover design by Dean Motter

THE
BLACK MOON

BLACK MOON

by
Robert J. Randisi

He was as out of place in my Black Moon Saloon as I would have been at the ballet.

Greenpoint, Brooklyn is not exactly the heart of tourist country in New York. You're more likely to find blue-collar types sitting at my bar: cops, sanitation workers, gas company employees, even the neighborhood mailmen stop in for a beer—but when this guy walked in he stood out so much that everyone there—all eight of us—couldn't help but stare.

He was tall and slender, wearing a silk suit that was worth more than all of our clothes *and* everything we had in our pockets combined. His silver hair was razor cut to perfection, as were his mustache and beard, and his cologne reached me before he did, making me wrinkle my nose and almost causing my eyes to water.

When he bellied up to my bar between old Harry Walsh and my mailman, Ben Simmons, I could see that his eyes were the same gray as the suit. I was almost sure that the suit had been bought to match the eyes, and not vice versa.

He looked at me and said, "Vodka martini, please," with an Italian accent. I knew the accent because my name's Sal Carlucci, and he sounded like my Uncle Vinnie—as well as some of my other relatives—sounded when I was a kid.

"Comin' up."

7

I was more used to serving beers and shots, so it was an interesting change of pace to be able to make something else, for a change.

If the guy knew he was being looked up and down by Walsh, Simmons, and the rest of the guys—and the one lady—he didn't show it.

Finally, Harry couldn't resist. He leaned over and nudged the guy with his elbow.

"You lost?"

The guy turned his head and said to Harry, "I beg your pardon?"

"Lost," Harry said, moving his network of wrinkles and broken blood vessels closer to the guy, "are you lost?"

"I don't believe so," the guy said, looking at the martini I put in front of him.

"Uh, no," he said.

He couldn't kid me. I knew I'd breached some little known law of etiquette because I didn't have an onion or an olive to put in the martini, and I'd probably made it worse by adding the cherry as a last thought.

"This is the establishment called the Black Moon, is it not?" he asked.

"Sure is," I said, leaning on the bar.

The guy smiled at Harry "the Map" Walsh and said, "Then I am not lost."

Harry had come by his nickname "the Map" because that was what his face looked like with all the wrinkles and broken blood vessels—and his big red nose was like a great mountain sticking up from the center of it. The wrinkles had deepened as he'd gotten older, and the blood vessels and nose had come from all the booze he'd consumed. I couldn't take all the credit for that, but he *had* been drinking at my place since I'd opened fourteen years ago, so I guess some of it was my doing—maybe one quarter, if I was any judge of a man's age.

Ben Simmons, on the other side of our Italian visitor, touched the sleeve of the silk suit and said, "Nice."

The guy took it well.

"Thank you," he said, moving that arm so he could lift his drink.

Down at the far end of the bar Myra was leaning over to give the guy a good look-over, and then back, probably checking out his ass. Myra always said she was an ass woman. She always said, "The tinier the butt, the tastier the bite."

Mad Myra must have been a looker years ago, before the booze got to her. Now she was pretty fair looking for a "bar bimbo"—her words, not mine—dark haired, blowsy, full-breasted. Her face had sagged some, but her body was still pretty solid, and she usually didn't have to go home alone. Of course, none of the regulars ever went home with her, so as soon as a stranger walked in she would start checking him out.

"What do you think, Myra?" I heard Artie Dietz asked her.

"Looks pretty good," she said over her beer, "but what's he drinking?"

"A martooni," Dietz said. It was about five p.m., and Artie had been in since noon. He was an ex-sanitation man retired on disability.

"Excuse me," the guy said to me.

"Yeah?"

"Are you the proprietor?"

"Yeah, that's me."

"Then . . . you are Salvatore Carlucci?" He pronounced my first name "Salvator-ay." I hadn't heard that for years, not since my Uncle Vinnie died.

"I'm Carlucci."

"In that case," he said, "allow me to introduce myself." He reached across the bar with his hand to shake mine and his sleeve rolled up, revealing his Rolex.

"Go ahead," I said, ignoring his hand.

"Excuse me?"

"Go ahead and introduce yourself."

"Ah, yes . . . my name is Victor Antonio Luciano."

"Luciano?" Harry the Map asked. "Hey, you any—"

"No, my friend," Luciano replied, as if he'd done so countless times before, "no relation."

He still had his hand out and now that I knew his name, I shook it.

"I understand you are a private inquiry agent."

"A what?" Harry asked, squinting as if that would help him hear better.

"A private detective, you dope," Simmons said.

"Yes, of course," Mr. Luciano said, "a private detective." He looked at me and said, "This is true?"

"Sometimes."

"I am sorry," Luciano said. "Sometimes?"

"Ol' Sal likes staying behind the bar," Harry the Map said.

"Is this true?" Luciano asked.

"Sometimes."

Luciano looked at the others, as if he suspected he was the butt of some sort of joke.

He looked at me and tried again.

"I would like to speak to you about the possibility of employing you."

"I made you a martini," I said.

"I do not mean as a bartender—"

"Tell me the truth," I said.

"About what?" he asked. Had he been taken aback by the word "truth"?

I pointed to the martini he hadn't touched yet and asked, "Does the cherry really change the taste that much?"

"I am sorry—" he said, sort of helplessly. "You *are* Salvatore Carlucci."

"He sure is," Harry the Map said.

"He's Carlucci," Ben Simmons said.

"That's him," Mad Myra said from the end of the bar. "That's Carlucci."

Luciano finally looked like he thought he may have stepped through the looking glass.

"All right," I said aloud, "show's over. Mr. Luciano, would you like to come with me to my office?"

"Please," Luciano said, with some relief.

"Harry," I said, "you're my relief bartender."

"All right," the Map said, leaping off his stool. Relief bartenders get to drink for free. It's an incentive plan.

I limped around from behind the bar and said, "This way, Mr. Luciano."

Luciano slid off his stool, looked at the others sitting at the bar, and then followed me.

Ever since that TV show *Cheers* came on the air I've always wanted to have a square bar like they do, but all I could afford to have was the conventional straight bar. I also didn't have *room* for a *Cheers* type bar—or much else. What I really would have liked was to have the whole place be a copy of the *Cheers* bar, but there was about as much chance of that as there was of Kirstie Alley walking into my place. Believe me, I'd settle for Kirstie Alley. (I never liked Shelley Long. Kirstie is more my type.)

In the Black Moon, space was at a premium. Just the bar, a juke box, and a fun poker machine that nobody played because who wants to play poker for fun?

Except for the back room. When I bought the place the previous owner used to rent out the back room for parties, and he used to cater them. Since I don't cook and I hate parties, I discontinued that practice. Now I used it as an office—and it makes a *big* office. I've pushed a desk off into one corner, with a lamp on it and a chair in front of it, and I handle both of my businesses from there—the bar, and my investigative business, such as it is.

It's a gross waste of space, but it's my space to waste.

There's a curtain across the doorway separating the back office from the bar, and as we walked through it Luciano stopped.

"It is dark," he said.

"I'll get the lamp."

I knew my way in the dark and hell, there wasn't anything to bump into, anyway. I turned on my desk lamp and the sixty watt bulb did its best to light the entire room. It failed, of course, but it did light up my desk, which was why it was called a desk lamp.

I eased myself behind my desk and lowered my carcass into the leather chair I cherished. My bulk and my bad leg made it look like a chore, but I finally settled in and waved Luciano forward.

He walked across the empty room and sat in the old wooden chair I supplied for clients—and liquor salesmen.

"Your leg—" he said.

"I got shot."

"I see. The war?"

"No," I said, "I was a cop."

I didn't have to explain about being shot in the leg in 1972, which put me out to pasture on a disability pension, getting my PI license in 1973, and buying the bar and renaming it the Black Moon in 1975. I didn't have to explain that I'd named the bar the Black Moon, because cops are always talking about how things go crazy when there's a "full moon." Well, I had always put the really crazy nights down to a "black" moon. I'm clever that way.

But I didn't have to explain all of this to him because he only wanted to hire me, he didn't want to marry me.

So while he sat there waiting for me to elaborate, I sat there waiting for him to get tired of waiting.

Which he did.

He cleared his throat and said, "Yes, uh, well—"

"You said something about wanting to hire me," I said, prompting him.

The truth of the matter was that no one had tried to hire me as a PI for months. The effect of the sudden interest was like a drunk who's been off booze for a while finally getting to take a sip. I'd gone a little sappy.

Now I was trying to play it straight, before he changed his mind.

"Mr. Carlucci, I understand that you were in Italy after World War Two, during reconstruction."

"I was," I said. I was just a kid, then. I'd used my older brother's ID to get into the Marines. He didn't need it. He'd gotten himself killed in a gang fight the year before I enlisted.

"Do you remember an incident involving an art work that was stolen from the Italian museum you were guarding?"

I leaned back in my chair and took a deep breath.

"Incident" was putting it lightly.

2

When I was a wet-behind-the-ears soldier in Italy during reconstruction one of the more boring assignments I pulled was standing guard over a valuable art collection in a museum in Salerno. There were three of us assigned, me, Ralph Parnell and Jim Wyman. Somehow, three thieves managed to break into the museum and make off with a collection of paintings, at the same time killing Jim Wyman. The funny thing about Wyman was that, although Parnell and I weren't buddies and didn't particularly like each other, we were both very friendly with Wyman.

That had to be why Luciano had come to see me.

"I remember the . . . incident."

"Quite a few valuable pieces of art were stolen from that museum," Luciano said, "but none more valuable than a collection of five paintings called 'Ladies in the Cathedral.'"

"I don't remember them," I said. All of that artwork had been way over my head at the time.

"They were painted in 1920 by Giacomo Giordano. Giordano was lying on his deathbed at the time of the theft, which might explain why they were stolen."

"Because somebody figured they'd double in value when the artist died."

"Exactly. The paintings depicted a shadowy woman in a long gown. There was an almost supernatural eeriness to the style, which could best be described as gothic surreal."

Some artwork is *still* over my head.

"Why are we discussing this?" I asked.

"That is the interesting part. None of the five paintings—there were five separate pieces, although they are considered part of the same work—have been seen since, but the Italian government is still very interested in getting them back."

"And you represent the Italian government?"

He smiled, inclined his head and said, "I have that honor."

"Don't tell me, let me guess. The paintings have surfaced."

Luciano seemed to grow excited. "An elderly convict in a Texas prison claimed to have been one of the original thieves. Before he died he disclosed their current whereabouts."

"What was this con's name?"

"Uh . . . I believe it was Bagetta, Antonio Bagetta."

"And why was he being so vague about the whereabouts of these paintings? If he was confessing on his deathbed, why not give their exact location?"

Luciano shrugged. "Perhaps he did not know. Unfortunately, he is dead and we cannot ask him. In any case, we know the cities."

"So," I said, "go and get them."

"Unfortunately, he did not disclose their *exact* whereabouts, just the cities that they were in—except one. Apparently one of the paintings was purchased at some point by a man named Del Gato, in Miami, but it has recently been reported stolen."

"Where did you get that information? That it's been stolen, I mean?"

"We, ah, did some preliminary investigating before coming to you."

"And exactly why have you come to me, Mr. Luciano?"

Luciano leaned forward and said in a conspiratorial whisper, "We would like to hire you to go and find them."

"Why me? I'm a broken down ex-cop turned PI and bar owner. Surely the Italian government can do better than that."

"We believe you have a personal stake in this, Mr. Carlucci."

He kept saying "we" and I wondered if he meant he and the Italian government, or if he was using the royal "we." He seemed to have the ego for the latter.

"None that I'm aware of."

Luciano smiled, as if he knew something I didn't—or something that I did.

"We understood that you and Jim Wyman were good friends."

"So?"

"Even after all this time, Mr. Carlucci, you must still wonder who killed him. You must still desire . . . justice?"

I had a feeling that he had intended to use another word—like revenge—and then changed his mind.

He had a smug look on his face, too, one that I would have liked to have slapped off, except for one thing—he was right. I still remembered Jim Wyman's great booming laugh, and would very much have liked to find out who killed him.

"Tell me exactly what you want, Mr. Luciano."

"We would like to hire you to go to Texas, Michigan, Iowa and Florida, and find those paintings."

"Iowa?" I asked. "What the hell would a valuable painting be doing in Iowa?"

"There are collectors all over the world, Mr. Carlucci," Luciano said, "even in places as mundane as Iowa."

"I suppose so," I said. "Finding these paintings doesn't necessarily mean I'd find the thieves, or the killer, you know."

"Staying here gives you even less of a chance."

Damn his smugness, he was right again.

"I still don't see why you don't contact the FBI, or someone in the United States Government to do this job for you."

"If we did that, word would get out. It would have to. One of the people who has the painting might hear that we were looking for it. You, on the other hand, can operate on a much more discreet level."

What he meant was that any government intervention would kick up some dust, but it would take somebody inside to notice it. That meant that he felt that somebody who had one of the paintings had an in somewhere in the U.S. government.

"Are you telling me that one of the paintings might be owned by someone in the government?"

Luciano struggled.

"Collectors," he said, "come in all shapes and sizes—and occupations."

"How could a government employee afford such a painting?"

"It would not have to have been *bought*," he said, and of course, he was right.

Some high ranking—or low ranking—government official might be in possession of a very valuable—and "hot"—painting.

All the more reason why I should have said no.

"If I butt heads with the United States Government on this—"

"At that time we would then intervene on your behalf."

Sure, I thought.

"You just mentioned four cities, but you said there were five paintings."

"Yes, I did," Luciano said. "This is the fifth city, Mr. Carlucci. One of those paintings is right here in New York."

I walked him to the curtained doorway after he gave me everything I'd need to know to go to work—including a retainer check, the name of his hotel, which was the Wellington, and the name of the insurance Carrier in Miami.

"Your fee will of course be paid by the Italian government," he said, "but I am empowered to give you a small retainer."

The "small retainer" was more than I'd ever made for a case before.

"If I have to use some outside help you'll cover that, right?"

"We will, uh, cover all debts that you accrue on our behalf."

"Who has the painting here in New York?" I asked him on the way to the door.

"Alas, we do not know that. Do you have any contacts in the local art world?"

It was funny, but I did.

"I'll look around."

As he walked out through the bar Mad Myra started checking out his butt. Again. She leaned so far back on her stool that she almost fell off—and would have if Artie Dietz hadn't caught her.

Harry "the Map" gave me a look, but I waved at him to stay behind the bar a while longer. That was like giving a kid another twenty dollars and telling him to stay in the arcade.

I went back to my desk and left the bar in the capable hands of Harry Walsh while I decided just how the hell me and my game leg were going to city hop looking for those paintings.

And why?

3

Believe it or not there are certain similarities between working as a PI and running a saloon. The major similarity is that both jobs can be done from behind the bar.

I had to get Walsh out from behind the bar before he drank me into bankruptcy—or himself into an early grave. Once I was back of the stick I picked up the phone and called a guy I knew who worked in a government office. What office he worked in doesn't matter—except that it *wasn't* the FBI or the CIA. Still, because he *did* work in a government office as a computer operator, he was just the guy to check out Mr. Luciano for me.

"Luciano?" he said. "Is that on the level, Sal?"

"No relation, Kid."

His name was Andy Hawkins, and he was twenty-nine years old. The fact that he *was* twenty-nine had a lot to do with why he agreed to run the name through the computer for me. I was walking a beat when his mother went into labor in an alley in the Bronx, and with nobody else around it was up to me to deliver him. In three years on the job, he was the first baby I delivered. There were others after Andy, but ask any parent—there's something special about the first one.

So I kept in touch with Andrew *Salvatore* Hawkins, even while he was going through college, and even after he got his job in a government office.

He'd had his job for about seven years now, and I don't think

I asked him for a favor more than three or four times.

Make that five.

"I was just getting ready to call it a day, Sal, but I'll run it and get back to you. Okay?"

"Thanks, Kid. I owe you one."

"Who's counting?"

"Say hello to your mom for me."

"When you gonna come and see her?"

Never, I thought.

"Sometime," I said.

Jeannie Hawkins had been a real looker back when Andy was born. She'd been abandoned by her husband during her fifth month, and I had big shoulders back then. We saw each other for a few months after that, but when she started getting that look in her eye, I stopped coming around.

"She asks about you."

"Tell her what an old man I am."

"Hell, you're only ten years older than her—"

"Get back to me as soon as you can with that info, will you, Kid?"

There was a pause and then he said "Sure, Sal. Tonight."

"Thanks."

I hung up and dialed another number.

When you've lived as long as I have—fifty eight years, five months and sixteen days—and you've spent as much time on "the job" as I did—only my injury kept me from putting in my twenty—you meet a lot of people, and you never think that having met some of them will ever come in handy, but it does.

There was a break in at an art gallery in Soho the last year I was on the job. I was still just a patrolman—I never liked taking tests—and me and my partner responded. The owner of the gallery was a man named Edward Wells. Edward was as queer as a three dollar bill, but he was all right. He gave us a very calm report of the items that were missing, and when I saw a kid trying to peddle a small statue on the street in Little Italy I turned it into a full recovery of the items. The kid had a big brother, the brother had a couple of friends, and the younger brother had managed to swipe the little statue when none of them was looking.

Anyway, Edward was real pleased, and he'd been sending me invitations to art shows ever since then. I never went to any of them, but that didn't stop him from sending them.

"Wells Gallery," a man's voice said.

Edward had managed to keep his gallery small, handling only certain artists, and the only help he employed was whoever his main squeeze was at the time.

"I'd like to speak to Edward, please."

"And who shall I say is calling?" the man asked. There was an unmistakable note of jealousy in his voice, probably because I had asked for "Edward" instead of "Mr. Wells." He sounded very young, also—too young for Edward.

"Tell him it's Sal Carlucci."

"Ooh," the voice said, "the cop."

"Ex-cop, friend. Could you put him on the line, please. It's kind of important."

"Hold on."

I waited a few minutes and then Edward came on the line.

"Salvatore, my friend."

"What are you doing with one of those, Edward?"

He knew what I meant.

"Can't be choosy at my age, old boy. I'm not the chicken hawk type, you know."

"I know." Edward was a contemporary of mine, perhaps a few years younger.

"To what do I owe this pleasure?" he asked. "When are you ever going to come to one of my shows?"

"Art's over my head, Edward. You know that."

"You knew enough to recognize it on the street, didn't you?"

"You gave us very good descriptions."

"Yes, we were both wonderful. What can I do for you, Salvatore?"

"'Ladies in the Cathedral.'"

There was a long pause and then Edward whistled low into the phone.

"For a man who knows nothing about art—where did you ever hear about the ladies?"

"I had a very close relationship with them once."

"What?"

"Never mind, Edward. It's a long story. What can you tell me about them?"

He proceeded to tell me everything that Luciano had told me, and I let him go on to the end.

"What else can you tell me?"

"That's all I know, Salvatore," Edward said. "What else—"

"Where are they, Edward?"

"Oh, don't I wish I knew—and what makes you think I would?"

"I understand they've surfaced."

In a deadly serious tone he asked, "Where did you hear that?"

"Never mind, Edward. Is it true?"

"I hadn't heard that—Salvatore, where—"

"In New York."

"What?" There was genuine shock in his voice.

"Edward, are you all right?"

"Yes, yes, I'm—I can't believe—Salvatore, are you sure—"

"It's something I've been told, Edward. I'm checking it out with the best art source I have."

"I can't believe—look, how much time can you give me?"

"To do what?"

"To *find* them, damn it."

"It, Edward, not them. If it's true, only one of them has surfaced in New York."

"If that is true, Salvatore," he said, "I will find it for you. I promise."

"I'll appreciate whatever you can find out for me, Edward. Take whatever time you need."

"If this is true," Edward said. "If one of the ladies is truly here in New York, it won't take me long. I will be in touch."

"Thanks, Edward."

"This will cost you, you know."

I smiled and said, "I know."

I hung up, realizing that I would finally have to go to one of his art shows.

4

There were four of them and I knew they were out to hurt me, not rob me.

They were waiting after I closed. There's an alley behind the bar and I usually go out the back door when I close up. They had to have known that in order to be waiting there for me.

They flanked me in the dark and I said, "I haven't got much money, but you're welcome to it."

"We don't need money, man—" one of them said, but he was cut off violently by one of the others.

"No talking!" The one who was apparently the leader said. He had a shock of unruly blonde hair and a very pale complexion. "Let's just get it done."

It went real fast, and it's only in this kind of fight—four against one where the four are amateurs—that my bulk really comes in handy. I'm six feet and two forty when I should be two hundred. I'm also fifty-eight years old, which in some circles makes me an old man.

The four of them were kids and they thought that if they cornered me and hit me a few shots I'd go down. Once I was down they would have stomped me.

I didn't go down, and then they weren't sure what to do.

My belly may hang over my belt, but my arms are still pretty hard and my hands are big—which means I have fists like hams.

I started slinging the hams and they started going down, one by one, until only the leader was standing.

"You're going down, man," he said, and took out a switch-blade to show me how. I noticed a tattoo on his wrist, but it didn't really register right then.

"Come on, you little fucker," I said. "I'll shove that blade right up your ass."

I could see the whites of his eyes gleaming as he tried to make up his mind. If he hadn't been high on something—there was *that* much white showing—he might have turned and ran.

He feinted at me a few times with the knife and I was about to take it away from him when I tripped on one of his fallen comrades. He caught me with the knife then, tearing open my side, but then I grabbed his wrist and very deliberately broke it. He screamed and went to his knees, clutching his wrist. I was lining up a kick to his head when something hit me from behind and I went down, but not out. By the time I got back to my feet, they were gone.

I guess they figured a second round was out of the question.

I knew the boys from the nine-four precinct who responded

to my 911 call and one of the detectives—Carl Devlin—came into the emergency room as the doctor was sewing me up.

"I would have thought you were too old for this kind of thing, Sal," Devlin said.

Carl Devlin was about forty-two, a tall, sandy-haired man who lived alone, dressed well and drank a lot. He'd been on the job twenty years, the last ten as a detective, the last four in the nine-four, which was literally four blocks from my place. We had never met on the job, but only made each other's acquaintance when he started stopping into the Black Moon for drinks after his tour.

"I am."

"Did they get anything?"

"They weren't after anything," I said. The doctor finished stitching me and told me to put on my shirt. She said she had a little boy's arm to set and that I should take care of my bill at the cashier.

"What do you mean? They were trying to rob you, weren't they?"

"No."

"No? Here, let me help you with that."

He held my shirt while I slipped into it. The bloody rent in it flapped as I started to button it and I finally gave in.

"Come on, I've got to settle my bill."

"Don't you have Blue Cross like normal people?"

"Too damned expensive. Besides, I don't have to get sewed up but once or twice a year."

We walked to the cashier's window and he stood by while I settled up and then gave me a ride home.

In the car he said, "Why don't you think they were just four punks trying to rob you?"

"Several reasons," I said. "One, I offered them my money and they didn't want it."

"So they wanted to stomp you first and then take it themselves."

"Number two, one of them said they didn't *need* my money."

He didn't have an answer for that one.

"They were out to hurt me, Carl," I said, "either that, or kill me."

"Why? What did you do to them, refuse to serve them?"

"I never saw them before in my life."

"So, what did they have against you?"

"That's a good question," I said. "Maybe you can ask them when you find them."

"If you give me good enough descriptions maybe I will."

"I doubt that," I said, but I told him what I knew. It was while I was giving him the descriptions that the tattoo worked its way from my subconscious to my conscious "alleged" mind.

"It looked like a bird, or a dragon of some kind."

"Well," he said, writing in his notebook, "that's distinctive enough that we might get a lead on him."

He dropped me in front of my house, about five blocks from the Black Moon. I'd lived there for almost twenty-five years because I hate apartments. I feel more . . . solid living in my own house.

I leaned into the open passenger window and asked, "Do you want me to come in tomorrow and make a report?"

"Naw," he said, "I'll type it up the way you told it to me. If you think of a reason why they went after you, gimme a call, huh?"

"Sure, Carl," I said. "Thanks for the ride."

"Take it easy."

He drove away and I let myself in carefully. I catwalked through the house but there was no one there waiting for me. I took a bottle of Wild Turkey from under the sink and poured myself a stiff one.

Victor Luciano hires me to find five valuable paintings for the Italian government, and that same night four punks try to carve me up.

Some coincidence, huh?

In a pig's ear!

5

I woke up the next morning with a dead soldier, a hangover, and various aches and pains, not the least of which was that tear in my side. I staggered to the bathroom and took some aspirin, ignoring the empty bottle as it fell off the bed. I went into the kitchen and put some water in the coffee maker. While it was working I put in a call to Luciano at the Wellington.

"Do you know what time it is?" he asked when I identified myself. It was nice to see that the upper crust asked the same question when their phone rang early in the morning.

"As a matter of fact I don't," I said, truthfully. "I haven't looked at my clock yet. I generally don't until after my first cup of coffee."

"How nice for you."

"I'll tell you what isn't nice for me, Lucky," I said.

"I told you there was no relation—"

"A few punks tried to carve me up last night."

There was a moment's hesitation and then he said, "How terrible for you. I hope you're not badly hurt."

"Let's just say they took a piece out of me."

"I hope you are not hurt so severely that you will not be able to continue, uh, working for us."

"The question is not am I able to continue to work for you,

Mr. Luciano," I said, "but will I."

"I do not understand."

"Who knows I'm working for you?"

"I—no one."

"You're a representative of the Italian government, and they don't know I'm working for you?"

"You must understand . . ." he said, trailing off lamely.

"Oh, wait," I said. "I haven't had my first cup of coffee yet, so I'm a little slow, but I think I understand now. They *don't* know I'm working for you. *They* think *you're* doing all the work."

No reply.

"Is that it?"

After a moment he said, "Yes."

"Well, Lucky," I said, "I have to tell you, I think that stinks. That's like getting someone else to do your homework for you." And I used to do that all the time, but I wasn't going to tell *him* that.

"Does—does that mean you will not take my case, Mr. Carlucci?"

"No," I said, inhaling the aroma of the coffee, "it means I think it stinks. I'll still work for you, Mr. Luciano, but if I find out that I was cut because you told somebody—"

"I swear to you, Mr. Carlucci, I have told no one."

"Is it possible someone found out, anyway?"

"I do not see how. As I said, I have told no one."

"No one at all?" I asked. "Not even as part of a little pillow talk?"

Now he got annoyed, which effectively turned the tables on me.

"Mr. Carlucci, I have already said several times—"

"All right, Mr. Luciano, all right. I'll get in touch as soon as I know something."

I hung up, poured myself a cup of coffee, sipped it, and

looked at the clock.

Six A.M.?

No wonder he was pissed.

I poured the coffee down the drain and went back to bed.

I woke up four hours later. I still felt like shit, but I dragged my sorry, overweight ass into the shower and tried not to get my stitches wet, rebandaged my side, then tried another cup of coffee. It tasted better at a more sensible hour of the morning.

Now that I was awake I seriously considered whether I should continue working for Luciano. Points in favor: the fee and the possibility of finding out who had killed Jim Wyman forty years ago. After all this time I still thought of Jim as a friend, and I didn't have that many that I could forget that one was murdered.

Points against: I was at an age where it was imprudent to dance around with punks, like I did last night. There was a time when I would have come out of a fracas like that without a scratch—but that time was long gone. Still, there was no proof that what had happened last night had anything to do with the "Ladies in the Cathedral," and until there was, I figured I might as well earn my fee. If things got hairy I could always pull out.

If I was going to get started on this art thing, I was going to have to make some calls.

The locations of the other four painting were supposedly Cedar Rapids, Iowa; Houston, Texas; Miami, Florida and Lake Superior, Michigan.

What I needed was some help, because my globe-trotting days were over.

I went to my beat up desk, sat in my beat up chair and pulled the phone over.

Cedar Rapids would be easy. Ralph Parnell was about my age and used to be a cop. That wasn't all we had in common. He was also about as successful at being a PI as I was. In addition to that, he was in Italy with me when the theft went down, and when Jim Wyman was killed. Jim Wyman was the main thing we had in common, and Ralph would want his killer—even after all this time—just as much as I did.

Also, it wouldn't hurt that he'd be able to use the money.

On the other hand, Jim Bailey in Houston *was* a good P.I. and a successful one. He'd take the case from me more out of friendship than from a need for the money, but then again, he *was* in business. Unfortunately, the phone call told me that Jim Bailey had died some time ago. I talked to the man who had taken over his agency, and he agreed to help. After I hung up I gave Jim Bailey's memory a few moments of silence.

Miami would be a little harder. I knew a PI there named Tony Mack, who used to be a New York cop. He quit young, went down there, and got married to a Cuban woman with ten kids or something like that. We weren't exactly pals, so I might have to do an end run to get him to take the job. I decided I'd have Andy plant something in the computer at the Miami insurance company that carried the policy on the painting. After that all it would take was a phone call, passing myself off as a colleague and suggesting Tony Mack for the job.

As for Lake Superior, I was stumped there. I decided to call a Manhattan PI named Miles Jacoby who had himself a phone book filled with names, addresses and phone numbers of PI's from other states. He'd inherited it from Eddie Waters, the PI who taught him all he knew. He taught him so well that when Eddie was killed, it was Jacoby who found the killer.

All he had to do for me was find *me* a PI in Lake Superior.

THE HUNGRY PERSIAN

by
W. R. Philbrick

The faces always change. You get used to the perky brunette at reception and the droll Hispanic behind the frosted glass partition and then they're gone, moved up through the ranks, or out the door. Disappeared by actuaries, a fate that transcends mere death.

"You're new," I said to the blonde receptionist. "Tell Juarez that Mr. Mack is here. Tony Mack."

"Mr. Juarez is out," she said. Very neutral. She had crisp orange lips and the large, decorative eyes of a tropical fish.

"When will he be back? We had an appointment."

"Out as in gone. Resigned. Mr. Crowell has taken over as caseload manager."

I sighed. It had been one of those mornings. Dueling the heavy traffic all the way up from Key Largo, only to find that the South Florida Mutual Life parking garage was full. I'd walked ten blocks in stunning heat through a section of town that might as well have been in Caracas. Fending off crack-dealing urchins, hoping that Juarez had a no sweat assignment for his not-so-old pal. A whiplash deal, say. I needed the money—I always need the money—but there was a heatwave stalled in Miami. Too hot for a scramble.

The receptionist smiled faintly. "Mr. Crowell is expecting you," she said. "Third partition on the left."

Those were the only constants at South Florida Mutual Life. Partitions and desks. Crowell was a skinny guy with pink-framed glasses. He had a brown skin cancer on the fleshy part of his nose. I tried not to notice.

"Mack, Tony? Let me just pull the file," he said, staring at the computer screen as he punched a few keys. "Right. The other guy left a flag. Gave you his top rating for a freelance investigator."

"Juarez," I said.

"Who?"

"The other guy. The one before you. Caseload manager."

He nodded. The spot of cancer went up and down.

"Got any whiplash?" I asked hopefully. "I kind of make a specialty of photographic surveillance jobs. Stills, videocam, whatever it takes. Juarez may have mentioned that."

"He did. You're an ex-cop, right? New York?"

"Mostly Brooklyn," I said. "Crime scene photographer. Did two years as a patrolman, playing hopscotch over the winos on Flatbush. I said get me out of here. They had this slot open for darkroom tech, I grabbed it. Stayed with Photo until I took the early retirement."

Crowell shrugged. Just being polite. He didn't care what planet I came from. "This one's a little out of the ordinary. Doubt you'll need a camera, or much surveillance."

"Not liability, then," I said, disappointed. The liability cases, particularly auto involved, are the cleanest jobs for a freelance investigator. Gimme that whiplash. The month before I'd gotten some beautiful footage of a claimant playing raquetball with his neck brace on. Oscar material. He won the set and lost the suit.

"Theft," Crowell said, tearing a print-out from the machine. "Private collection, high ticket item."

I glanced at the print-out. "An art object? You're kidding."

I knew from my years with the cops that art theft was a highly specialized field on both sides of the law. Aside from shooting a few burglary scenes, the closest I'd come to an expertise in art was meeting Carol at MOMA for a cafe lunch. Picasso and pasta salad.

"I don't know from art," I said. "Maybe you better try someone else."

Crowell tapped the screen. "Got a request filed for Mack, Tony."

I sat back in the chair. Who was he trying to kid? No one requests an insurance investigator. You take who they give you.

"There's a couple of kinks," Crowell said. "The painting was reported stolen a day or two after it made the Carrier hot sheet. And according to the Carrier the provenance is in dispute."

I was baffled and said so.

"Read the file," Crowell suggested, indicating the print-out in my hand. "The painting was purchased at auction six months ago by a Mr. Arturo Del Gato, of Coral Gables. Last week he was notified of the provenance dispute—apparently the piece he bought is one of several related works claimed by the Italian government."

"It was hot when Del Gato bought it?"

Crowell nodded. "That's a distinct possibility. He's pressing the claim, of course."

"Sounds messy. I suggest you bring in an expert."

Crowell tapped the screen again. "They want you," he said. "Special request from the New York office, filed through the police liason."

It made me dizzy, just listening to him. Or maybe it was trying not to watch the spot on his nose that did it.

"Let me get this straight," I said. "You're laying this off on me because someone on the New York cops mentioned my name?"

Crowell nodded, his gaze impassive through the pink frames. "That's what it boils down to, yeah."

I said, "Beautiful, who needs enemies?"

The city shimmered in the heat. The sidewalks were molten.
Even the crack dealers had crawled back under their rocks.
Urban scorpions waiting for dusk. When I got back to my car, a
leased Plymouth sedan with tinted windows, the hubcaps had
been pried off. Not stolen, just left in a careless heap beside the
curb. Too hot to carry away. I managed to get them into the trunk
without scalding my hands.

I headed for nearest air-conditioned public building. A
branch library. After a couple of deep, cool breaths I fed my
charge card into a payphone and set up an appointment with
Arturo Del Gato. He was, his male secretary implied, an extremely important gentleman who, might, if I presented myself at
the appointed hour on the following morning, grant me a few
moments of his precious time.

"Muchas gracias," I said.

You want to get ahead in this business, you have to know
when to toady. In Spanish if necessary.

Before checking out the illustrious Señor Del Gato—assuming he was grand enough to rate a few entries in the *Miami Herald*
microfilms—I settled into a fiberglass chair in the Reading Room
and studied the file Crowell had given me. The first item was
culled from the Agency hot sheet.

NEW YORK CITY. REQUEST ANY ALL INFOR-
MATION REGARDING LOCATION OF FOLLOWING
WORKS OF ART, ITALIAN ORIGIN, DISPUTED
PROVENANCE.
'LADIES OF THE CATHEDRAL,' GIORDANO,
GIACOMO. OILS ON SIZED PANEL. A SERIES OF
FIVE SCENES, NUMBERED SEQUENTIALLY UN-

DER ARTIST'S MARK, LOWER RIGHT OF PANEL.
    NOTIFY CARRIERS.

'Carriers' being interested parties such as South Florida Mutual Life. There was a half-million dollar rider on Del Gato's policy to cover the cash loss value of the little painting. The appraisal noted that current market value was estimated to be twice that amount. Apparently the value of a signed Giordano was on the rise.

A color transparency had been included in the file. I held it up to the light. The shot was a tight exposure, professionally lit and focused. The scene was a moonlit night inside a ruined, gothic-looking structure. The cathedral, I supposed. The woman, who seemed to be fleeing, was dark, beautiful, and dressed in a diaphanous gown. There was something about the luminous, encroaching shadows that gave the little scene a nightmare quality. It made me wonder what compelled the dark lady to flee.

I slipped the transparency back into the glassine envelope. 'Ladies of the Cathedral No. 3' was not something I would want to hang on my bedroom wall. Not if I wanted a good night's sleep.

2

"So what's the big deal problem?" Maria said. "You don't like what they want you to do, just say no."

With her black hair, olive skin, and large dark eyes, Maria is almost a negative image of Carol, who was blond and fair. Carol and I married the year I went on the cops. Both of us nineteen, dumb as rocks. All we knew was each other. For twenty years that was more than enough.

We had it all planned. After putting in twenty-five I'd take an early retirement, Carol would cash in her annuity as a municipal librarian. We'd still be in our mid-forties, prime of life. We were going to head for Florida, live out of a camper for a while, pick the place we wanted to settle. Somewhere on the Gulf coast, maybe, where Carol could set up her rare book business and I could freelance as a photographer. Enjoy our middle years in paradise.

It was a good plan, something to look forward to. We were congratulating ourselves on the finer points over champagne cocktails on my fortieth birthday—the big four zipper, Carol called it—when she mentioned a slight headache and marched off to the ladies. Where, a few minutes later, she slumped to the floor and died of a cerebral hemorrhage.

The doctor who performed the autopsy said the aneurysm had probably been there since birth, always a heart-beat from rupture.

"All the years she did have were a gift," he said. "Try to think of it that way."

I was too busy trying not to think. Not thinking got me all the way to Sarasota, driving mostly drunk. It got me into barroom brawls and county lock-ups. It was stupid, self-destructive behavior. A damn poor way to mourn the love of my life, but for six months I was out of control, unable to cope. I was starting to come out of it, slow and shaky, by the time I landed in Key Largo.

Figuring that some good hard physical labor would help clear my head, I signed on as mate for two Cuban shrimpers, the Cordova brothers. Ray and Eddie. Being the first Anglo crewman they'd ever hired. It was something less than an honor. They'd heard me braying at a tiki bar about being a big city cop, neglecting to mention that I was more adept at snapping pictures than catching criminals, and the Cordova brothers thought I could help out with a little problem they had. The problem was named Pedro Rapaz, part-time smuggler and full-time psychopath. The

DEA boys called him Sneaky Pete. I never got the chance to help out the Cordova brothers because Sneaky blew up Ray and Eddie and Eddie's pretty wife Teresa before the boat ever left the dock. I was asleep in my camper at the time, and the hot wind of the explosion sobered me up for good.

When the DEA and the Monroe County Sheriff's Department shrugged it off as just another crazy Cuban drug killing, Ray's widow persuaded me to bring Pedro Rapaz to justice. Cuban women have this thing about revenge. So do Cuban men, for that matter. For a while I thought the whole culture was based on getting even. It suited me, suited my urge toward self-destruction.

Then I fell in love with the widow. Found a new reason to live—actually eight excellent reasons. Maria and her three kids and the four who were orphaned when Eddie and Teresa died. Eight reasons to get up in the morning and go to work and get through the rest of my life in no particular hurry.

"I hear of this man Arturo Del Gato," Maria said. "He's a big political *exilio*. Raises money for *la causa*, the fight to rid Cuba of Castro. He won't miss one little thing stolen from his house. He probably got two, three houses, rich *hombre* like that."

"Five," I said. "Not counting the apartment buildings and the motels. And the radio station and the newspaper."

Maria whistled. When she whistles her white teeth show over sunset red lips and I tend to lose my concentration. She was standing at the kitchen counter, dicing bell peppers with the same knife she'd used on Sneaky Pete. The windows were open and the mingled scents of salt water and backcountry mangroves wafted in through the screens. The kids were out on the porch watching cartoons. Thank god for television.

"Anyhow, I can't decline the assignment," I said. "If I turn it down, Crowell will write me off."

"Crowell? What happened to Juarez?"

"What always happens when I get tight with a caseload manager," I said. "He moved on."

Maria shook her head. The knife went clunk! through the heart of the pepper. "I don't like it. Political man with *dineral* like that, he's gonna be dangerous, you don't process the claim like he wants."

The thought had occurred to me, and it was troublesome. Since hooking up with Maria and the kids I've developed a thing about risk-taking. I loathe it.

"Don't worry," I said, slipping my hands around her waist. "First sign of trouble, I quit."

"Promesa?"

I promised.

Del Gato's primary residence was a modest, five-acre spread in Coral Gables. That's the equivalent of fifty acres in the best part of Westchester, New York. The Del Gato estate was enclosed by a ten-foot-high, poured-concrete wall tricked out in ceramic tiles so as not offend the neighbors. Hispanic security guards cruised the perimeter. The crisp white uniforms made them look like yacht club waiters, were it not for the semi-automatic weapons. It seemed that Arturo Del Gato had a private army, electronic sensors, doggie patrols, the works.

I was impressed. A burglar who could get by all that could walk out of Fort Knox with a gold bar in his pocket.

"Spell the name please."

The security honcho looked a bit like Ernie Kovaks in *Our Man In Havana,* except he had better English and lacked the cigar.

I spelled my name. I showed him my driver's license and a South Florida Mutual Life ID card. Just to jazz him I showed off a snap of Maria and the seven samurai.

"Cute, eh?" I said. "The smallest one bites. You could use him on patrol."

"Very nice," he said, glancing at the photo, not reacting to the puzzle of my obviously Cuban family. "You may enter. Leave the car here at the gate."

"You mean I have to walk in?"

He was appalled. "Of course not."

What was I thinking. An electric golf cart, piloted by one of the guards, delivered me to the appropriate entrance of the main *hacienda*. A willowly number by the name of Tomas was waiting just inside the door. He escorted me into a glass-enclosed court-yard. It was Miami ersatz-grandee style, overlooking a canal and the landscaped acreage of an abutting estate. Palm trees planted along the water's edge looked like candles on a lime-green birthday cake. A big impressive Rybovich fishing machine was parked at the dock, varnish gleaming. A stack of large, plastic fish crates caught the light, green as emeralds.

"Buenos dias," Del Gato said, not rising from his chair.

"Good morning," I countered, establishing the language. My Spanish, though improving steadily, would have left me at a serious disadvantage. With a specimen like Del Gato you have to play every angle.

"You have my check?" he asked. He was a slender man of fifty or so with large, active hands and a long, knife-blade face. His thick black hair, combed straight back, had just a few wisps of gray at the temples. Handsome in a stagy way. The black hair, I decided, was a dye job.

"Check?" I asked, genuinely puzzled.

"Ah," Del Gato said. "Perhaps I am mistaken. I assumed your company had decided to process my claim."

I nodded, helping myself to a cup of coffee from an enameled tray. "You're not mistaken. The claim is being processed. Unfortunately no check can be issued until the investigation is complete."

Del Gato watched me drink his coffee. "There's very little to investigate," he said. "The *pintura* was stolen. My policy covered theft, did it not, Mr., ah, Mack?" he added after glancing at the card his assistant had dropped on the tray.

"Just Tony or Mack," I said. "Sure, you're covered for the cash value. The dollar amount you paid at auction. I understand the piece is actually worth considerably more."

Del Gato shifted on his rattan chair and sighed. "So I was told. If I'd known that I would have increased the coverage. Naturally."

"Bad luck," I said. "Also, they asked me to mention the question of provenance. Make sure you're aware of the counter-claim that has been filed. The question will have to be settled before the check is released."

I wasn't sure if Del Gato was going to spit or smile. The smile, when it came, had a kind of crocodile charm. All teeth and confidence. A smile that said Arturo Del Gato had insurance investigators for breakfast whenever he had the urge.

"The *pintura* is *mala suerte*." he said. "As you say, bad luck. That is what I told Mercedes, but she insisted on having her way."

I said, "Excuse me, Mercedes?"

"My wife. She is artistic. It was she who wanted to own the little *pintura*. Myself, I had no affection for the thing. There is something disturbing about that picture. I think perhaps the artist was insane."

I smiled and shrugged, finding it easy to play the part of Philistine flatfoot.

"My lawyers have told me of this Italian claim," he said. "They say it has no affect on my policy. Your company is obliged to pay. Later the Italians can sue me, if that is their decision, and of course I will respond by suing those who issued the certification of authenticity. The 'question of provenance' as you call it."

I shrugged. "I'm sure you're correct, Mr. Del Gato. I'm merely conducting the investigation of theft."

"Paperwork?" he responded.

"Mostly," I said, wanting to sound agreeable. "Just routine stuff."

The painting had been displayed in the *galeria*, a long cool room adjacent to the big salon where the Del Gatos entertained. It had a quiet, churchy feel. The lighting was indirect. The effect was pleasant and soothing, although I didn't recognize any of the paintings on the walls. Then again I'd never heard of Giacomo Giordano or 'Ladies of the Cathedral' until they handed me the file.

"Very impressive," I said dutifully.

Del Gato said, "There are those who think so, yes. Myself, I could care less. Truly. Mercedes, she has the passion for art. I merely agreed to let her acquire this collection as an investment."

Mercedes Del Gato. Had a nice ring to it, like the chimes on a cash register. I asked if the lady herself was available for an interview.

"Perhaps later," he said. "When she returns from La Paz."

"La Paz?"

"My wife is a Bolivian, " he said. "She is visiting her family in La Paz. The painting was stolen after she left, so she knows nothing useful."

I checked out the blank spot on the wall, a little surprised to see that a half-million dollar miniature was hung from an ordinary ten-cent hook. The wall area had been recently plastered. There was a distinct odor of fresh paint.

"How did it happen?" I asked.

"No idea. One day it was there, the next it was gone."

We went around on that for a while but Del Gato stuck to his story. He seldom visited the *galeria*. The missing *pintura* was reported by a member of the domestic staff. Yes, I was welcome to speak with the maid, although she had no English. How had the security been breached? Had there been a break-in?

"Of course not," Del Gato said. "As I told the police, a break-in is impossible."

I glanced at the file. I knew what was in the file; it was just an excuse to gather my thoughts, maybe catch Del Gato off balance. "Ah, yes," I said. "According to what you told the police, you had something referred to as a 'social festivity' the night before. Is that correct?"

Del Gato nodded. "A fund-raiser. More than a hundred guests."

"And was the gallery open to the guests?"

"Of course," he said. "If they wished to enter."

"And you think one of them pinched the painting?"

"Pinched?"

"Swiped. Filched. Stole."

"I have no idea who took it. Nor do I care," Del Gato said. "Now, when do I get my money?"

3

I was handed over to Tomas, Del Gato's assistant. He was slender, languid, and slightly effete in a thoroughly Latin manner, and unfailingly polite in the way he refrained from divulging information. It was a major effort to get him to comment on the weather.

Crossing to the cabana that served as the office, I said, "Heat's a bitch, hey?" and got a serene smile, a slight nod.

Complaining about the heat was an amusing gringo habit, apparently. Tomas looked like he might, just might, break a sweat as he was being immersed in a live volcano.

"Keep out of the sun," he advised. "Drink plenty of liquids."

"Really?" I said. "I never heard that."

But he was impervious to sarcasm. No way to rattle his cage.

"How long have you worked for Señor Del Gato?" I asked as he unlocked the cabana door.

"Quite some time," he replied.

"What's Mercedes like?"

Tomas said, "She is Señor Del Gato's wife."

"I mean what's she *like*. Give me your impression. Is she young, old, what?"

He hesitated. Thinking it over. Deep thinker, was Tomas. At last he said, "The señora is neither young nor old."

"Take it easy," I said. "Don't go out on a limb."

Eventually I persuaded him to show me a picture of the boss's wife. Pretty. Lively dark eyes hinting of mischief. When I was done looking he put out his hand, took the picture back, and returned it to a drawer.

"Now for the list," I said.

"List?"

Tomas was supposed to provide me with a list of all those who had had access to the *galeria* the night before the painting was reported stolen. He approached this mission with all the enthusiasm of a cat contemplating a swim across the Atlantic.

"It was a typical charity function," he said, staring up at the motionless blade of an overhead fan. He was seated at a small desk. There was a computer, filing cabinets, three telephones, a pre-Castro Cuban flag—all the comforts of capitalism brought home to the *barraca*.

I perched on the corner of the desk and lit up a cigar, hoping it would irritate him. I had to do something to get under his skin, make him react.

"Your boss said more than a hundred people attended. Where did they park all the cars?"

Tomas opened a drawer, removed a ceramic ashtray in the shape of a sea turtle, and placed it within my range. "Most of the guests come by limo," he said. "It saves the trouble of parking."

Silly question. I puffed at the cigar and tried a different tack.

"Does Del Gato often host these functions? What charity was it, exactly?"

Tomas watched me flick an ash. I got the impression that had I missed he would have reacted quickly enough to shift the ashtray and make it right before the ash hit the desk. "Señor Del Gato is one of the leading fund raisers in Miami," he said. "In all of Florida."

"And what was he raising funds for that night?" I asked.

Tomas shrugged. "Some organization or other. There are so many."

We both watched a perfect smoke ring wrap itself around the fan blade. "Maybe we should do it this way," I suggested. "I'll pick a name out of the phone book and you tell me if that person was in attendance."

"I don't understand."

"A list, Tomas. If your boss hosts fund-raisers all the time you must have a mailing list to work from. Good citizens who can be counted on to dig deep, cough up a few bucks."

"Ah," he said, eyes flicking to the blank computer screen, "A list."

"Invitations were sent out, correct?"

Tomas shook his head. It was very slight. You had to concentrate to catch it. "It was, how do they say it, an *impromptu* affair. Organized at the last minute."

That didn't sound right. "An impromptu fund-raiser? Come

on, Tomas. You don't leave something like that to the last minute."

"A need arose," he said, nesting his fingers together and resting his chin there, as if weary of all the difficult questions. "Sometimes, in this community, a need arises rather quickly. For money, you understand. Then Señor Del Gato, he makes a few calls. People come."

People come. As simple as that, gringo.

I fared slightly better with the two cops assigned to investigate the theft. Detective Sergeants Ben Valera and Dominick DiMambro, the former a Miami native, the latter a transplant from Providence, Rhode Island.

"Well, well, another ex-flatfoot come south," Valera said, offering his hand. The partners had agreed to meet me at the Neon Flamingo, a trendy new Brickell Avenue cafe. The assumption being that South Florida Mutual Life would pick up the tab.

"I heard of you," DiMambro said. "A snap-shot artist, right? Camera, lights, action?"

I admitted to a special interest in photographic surveillance and followed with a brief resume, heavy on the Brooklyn brotherhood, wanting to establish our mutual copness. Dom DiMambro was a big, beefy specimen with a bulldog chin and an affable disposition. After five years in Miami he still retained a thick, adenoidal Rhode Island accent. Ben Valera was a portly, darkly complected Cuban with a gold incisor that flashed whenever he smiled.

They both had the look of serious trenchermen.

"I got an urge for veal," DiMambro said, smacking his lips. "They got a veal they do here with truffles that will knock your socks off."

I checked my wallet to make sure my charge cards hadn't

stampeded at the mention of truffles. DiMambro grinned at me as he eyeballed the menu.

"You're a snap-shot specialist, how come they threw you an art theft?" Ben Valera wanted to know.

"Enemies in high places," I said, shrugging. "Somebody mentioned my name to the New York office."

"And you being on the Brooklyn cops."

"Something like that," I said. "It's a raw deal. I know nothing about art heists, or exile politics. I'm hoping you guys can point me in the right direction."

DiMambro blinked at that. He was pouring a Corona beer; inexplicably fashionable with the trend-setters, considering its resemblance to infected tap water. "Politics?" he said. "What politics?"

"I'm not sure. All I know is Del Gato was raising money for one of his pet political projects the night the painting was lifted. The damn thing was small enough to slip into a purse."

Valera nodded. The conversation was halted while the lunch was ordered. The two gourmands decided the best way to deal with the diversity of offerings was to leave no morsel untasted.

"Calamari?" Valera chided. "You don't like calamari."

"You gotta keep trying in this life, right?" DiMambro responded. "So today I'll taste the squid. They got it here with mole sauce. Who knows it might be a whole new experience."

Valera was visibly moved. "Calamari with mole? Are you serious?" he said, eagerly re-examining the menu.

That was how it went. Crime-stoppers in Miami, hearts aflutter over a high-tech luncheon. After coffee—*con leche* for DiMambro and French roast for Ben Valer —I managed to steer the conversation back to the night the painting went missing.

"Yeah, the fund-raiser," Valera said, puffing contentedly at a thin cheroot. "Arturo is a genius at raising money. Legendary. Fought with Castro, you know, in the Sierra Maestra."

I hadn't known, and said so.

"Yeah, well, that was then, this is now. Now Arturo Del Gato is a professional patriot. *La causa* this *la causa* that. In some ways he's typical for top-ranked exile. Served as a captain in the brigade for the Bay of Pigs fiasco. Then businessman and CIA consultant in the sixties. That's how he got the FCC approval for WGAT, what I heard. Which in case you're unaware is a very big influence in the *exilio* community."

Maria had told me about WGAT. Fifty thousand watts of endless *la causa* rhetoric. *La causa* being the exiles' dream of ridding Cuba of Castro, communism, and the intervening thirty years. A time machine of wishful thinking that had held the Cuban community in thrall for decades. Most of the exiles, now a million strong, listened to the prime-time talk show hosted by Ricardo Blades, himself a former Castro commando notorious for his skill in demolishing Batista's bridges. Many of his fellow *exilios* called in to express opinions and promulgate rumors. I had tried listening to the station, just to get the flavor, but the Spanish was too fast and impassioned. Too angry.

"The station is Del Gato's power base. I mean if Arturo wants to reach out and touch someone, all he has to do is give the word to Ricardo Blades and within hours everybody in the community knows what Del Gato is thinking—and more important, what *they* should be thinking."

The waiter slipped me a small enameled tray. The bill. I glanced at it and shuddered. "You don't sound like a member of Del Gato's fan club," I said to Valera.

DiMambro looked at his partner and chuckled. "You got that right," he said. "You gonna tell him about your cousin, Ben?"

"Nah," Valera said, glaring at his cigar. "You tell 'im."

DiMambro folded his hands over his ample tummy and leaned back in his chair. "Ben had this cousin, see. Nice little guy, ran a bakery. Name happened to be Emilio Vasquez. It was right

47

up there on the bakery, over the door. So what happens, Del Gato is pissed at a crony of his, also happens to be named Emilio Vasquez. They had a difference of opinion over some matter, probably involving money. Anyhow he gets his mouthpiece Ricardo Blades to go on the air and denounce Emilio Vasquez as a traitor to *la causa* and early the next morning someone fire-bombs the bakery. Ben's cousin was in back, checking the ovens or whatever, and he got roasted. Case of mistaken identity. Somebody got enthusiastic."

"Unbelievable," I said.

"Believe it," Valera said, interrupting. "The irony is that Del Gato and the other Emilio made up. Now they're the best of friends."

"So what do you think," I said. "Is Del Gato the type to rip off an insurance company?"

Valera shrugged. "Why bother? The man is super rich already. Also it brings down too much heat. What must have happened, one of the guests slipped the thing in a briefcase or maybe a purse, like you say, and just walked out with it."

I nodded. "That's the angle I'm working. Except I can't get a list of the guests."

Valera stared at me, then glanced at his partner. They both broke up.

Laughing so hard that Valera almost choked on his cigar and tears came to DiMambro's eyes.

"Hey man, excuse us," DiMambro wheezed. "We didn't know, honest."

"Didn't know what?" I asked. Provoking giggles among working detectives was not the best way to establish my credentials with the burglary unit of the Metro cops.

"That all you wanted was a guest list," Valera answered. "Hell man, it was printed next day in *La Causa.*"

"What?"

"Take it easy, man. In *La Causa,* Del Gato's newspaper. Right there in the society column, like they always do after one of his fund raisers."

Leave 'em laughing, that's my motto. The two detectives were still grinning happily when we parted just outside the restaurant. As it happened, their unmarked cruiser was parked on the same block where I'd left my sedan. So I was close enough to feel the wind burn when the bomb went off.

4

Homicide passed me around for a few hours. There wasn't much I could tell them, beyond describing the last meals of Detectives Valera and DiMambro.

"So what you sayin', Mr. Mack, you met with the officers to discuss theft and recovery of a missing object, is that correct?" This came from a squinty-eyed individual who introduced himself as Sergeant Leland Snyder.

"Just the theft," I told him. "We didn't get to the recovery stage."

"They mention any threats? Any problems with their investigation?"

"Nothing like that," I said. "I got the impression the case was no big deal, a low priority. Hell, it was just a free lunch for those guys."

The homicide dicks left me with the impression that Valera and DiMambro were about the last two cops likely to be targets of an assassination. They were not involved in vice or drug-related crimes, nor did they have an important cases pending trial.

"What a freaking mess," Snyder said, grimacing. "A goddamn mess. Valera had been cleared for vacation time starting next week. It just makes me sick, something like this happens."

"Vacation, huh?" I said. "That's tough. Where was he going?"

"Bolivia," Snyder said, squinting at me. "Who the hell would want to vacation in Bolivia?"

The advent of twilight hadn't done much to relieve the heat. After leaving Homicide I stopped at a Cuban grocery on the wrong end of Twenty-second Avenue, intending to get a cold beer and a newspaper. It was the kind of place where they never throw anything away. Not even the heavy sheets of plywood that had been nailed over the storefront during the riots. Inside it was so dark the bare lightbulbs glowed like low-watt stars in a painted sky.

A sign over the counter announced, in both Spanish and English,

The owner is armed and dangerous.

I stared at the sign for a while, holding a sweating beer bottle against my cheek, until the grocer emerged from a back room. He seemed to be a small, jovial fellow, despite the revolver clipped to his apron, but I decided to keep my hands in full view while negotiating the purchase of the beer and a week-old newspaper.

"Ever hear of Arturo Del Gato?" I asked when I had the newspaper in hand.

The grocer shrugged. "Of course. He is a famous patriot."

"How about his wife?"

"I know nothing of his wife," he said evasively.

"So it's only Señor Del Gato who's famous, not his wife?"

The grocer sighed. "A wife is not supposed to be famous. A wife is a wife."

With that settled, I found my way to the South Dixie

Highway and headed for home, where a wife can be a whole world of things.

Maria got a kick out of the society column in *La Causa*.

"It's not enough to be mentioned," she commented, sipping from a tall glass of iced tea. "They put how much you donated right after your name."

We were on the front porch. The children were playing outside, ranging over the patch of Bermuda grass that faced the gulfside lagoon. Bob and Eduardo, the two oldest boys, were fishing from the dock. They looked, in the lingering twilight, like smaller editions of their late fathers. Anna, Ruthie, Teri, and Carly, the four girls, were playing tag with a palm frond. Whoever got tagged picked up the frond and chased the others. Jorge, the youngest, was faced with a three-year-old's dilemma: whether to join in the noisy fun with his sisters or nag his big brothers into letting him hold a fishing pole. As a result he spent all his time running back and forth between the dock and the shore.

An old Brooklyn acquaintance, on hearing that I'd married into an instant family of seven kids, had expressed dismay. Was I crazy or what? The children weren't my own, were barely even American. The reaction was typical—people tend to forget that no one owns children, least of all the biological father. And as to the quantity, well, seven just happens to be my lucky number.

The luck was holding. I might just as easily have walked the two detectives to their car, a fact that wouldn't have escaped Maria's attention had she been aware of the circumstances. Luckily none of the media reports had mentioned my name, and while I never lie to Maria about my work, or about anything, for that matter, I thought it prudent to delay the truth for a bit, until I had a handle on what had happened. We needed the money; for that and a couple of other reasons backing off the case simply wasn't an option.

"Does it mention what organization sponsored the fund raiser?" I asked.

"Something called Triumpho del Dos Rios. It says here they were raising money for a new wing at Children's Hospital. So perhaps they are a charity organization," Maria concluded.

"What," I said, "like the Shriners? Remember who hosted the thing. Somehow I can't see Arturo Del Gato wearing a funny hat, or marching in the Orange Bowl parade."

"OK, smart guy, *you* figure it out."

"Triumph of Dos Rios," I mused "Dos Rios, that was the battle where Jose Marti was killed. The great Cuban revolutionary, right? So anything calling itself Triumpho del Dos Rios has to be a political organization."

Maria scowled at me over the top of the newspaper. "You're such a suspicious person," she said. "Even donating to a hospital makes you suspicious."

It was true. Nineteen years on the cops had made me suspicious. Before taking early retirement I was mostly suspicious of other cops. The behind-the-scenes maneuvering for promotion, the endless games with departmental budgets, the minor feuds. You couldn't take anything at face value, you had to figure out the motive. I'd thought it was symptomatic of life in New York, that big city tension monster, but things weren't much different in laidback South Florida. Different people, different motives. The same old suspicion.

"You recognize any of the names?" I asked.

"Sure. Let's see. Ramon Suarez, he's on the city council. Ran for mayor and lost. Elena Prio, she's from a very important family, own a chain of seafood restaurants. Her brother got himself killed, maybe two, three years ago. Assassination, I can't remember if it was political or drugs. Maybe both. Now I hear her all the time on the radio, she introduces the records, mostly salsa and sometimes the old patriotic songs. And here's Ricardo Blades, he gave two hundred fifty dollars. You know about him."

"Host of the radio show on WGAT. That Ricardo Blades?"

Maria nodded, brushing back a lock of glossy black hair. "Yeah. I wouldn't be surprised if Elena Prio is his girlfriend. I think I hear something about that." She returned to the newspaper. "Luis Calzon, artist. Oh yeah, I read about him in the *Miami Herald*, the Spanish edition. Say he's going to be famous painter someday soon. I remember because they have his picture and he's very handsome."

"Handsomer than me?" I asked.

"Different kind of handsome," she said evasively.

"Right," I sighed. "The kind that's young, popular, soon to be famous."

The telephone rang. I went inside, picked up the receiver, and got an earful of Brooklyn.

"Slow down," I said. "Who the hell is this?"

I could hear a noisy jukebox, the clink of glasses, someone shouting for a drink, and an oddly familiar voice.

"It's Sal, you schmuck," the voice growled. "Sal Carlucci."

You can run, I thought, but you can't hide. Not even in Key Largo.

The thing I remembered best about Salvatore Carlucci was that he always had an angle. When I first got on the cops he was already a senior precinct detective, a tough as nails guy who was, from my rookie perspective, hotwired into that special cop network. Later, when Sal had his troubles in homicide and we became better acquainted, I came to realize he was almost as much of an outsider in the department as me.

We never got to be friends, not in a meaningful way. I was a cop with a camera; he was a ranking detective. Two different worlds.

"It was you," I said. "You put in the word, had the New York office recommend me. Am I right?"

"What's a matter, kid, you don't want the work?"

Nevermind that I had just turned forty-one; I would always be 'kid' to Salvatore Carlucci.

"I'm a surveillance expert," I said. "A damn photographer. I don't know from art theft."

Sal wasn't interested in hearing excuses. He had his angle, as usual. What he wanted was information, anything I could give him about the location of the painting.

"All I can tell you is where it's not, Sal. It's not hanging on the wall in Del Gato's gallery. Someone pinched it. I've got it narrowed down to a hundred or so possible suspects. Including the owner's wife, who happens to be conveniently out of the country. Also there's another small detail. The two cops who were investigating the theft were just blown to pieces."

Carlucci swore. I'd gotten used to being cursed in Spanish. His Italian oaths were a welcome change of pace.

5

I headed back into *la bestia* first thing the next morning. *La bestia* meaning the beast, which is Maria's word for Miami. The way Maria sees it, the man who murdered the father of her children came out of that Miami. Therefore the city is at fault, and no trick of logic is going alter her mindset in that regard.

Personally I have great affection for the place, in all its improbable extremes. The stark contrasts of wealth and poverty, beauty and vulgarity are more stimulating than the cornucopia of drugs available on the molten streets. Give me a whiff of that crazy town and my head clears and my eyes sparkle. Maybe that's why my instincts were keyed so high that morning.

Or it could have been the memory of a sudden, searing wind on Brickell Avenue.

Working on the assumption that a talk show host might be willing to talk, I found my way to the WGAT broadcast facility, located a few blocks north of Calle Ocho, in the heart of Little Havana. The station was housed in a low, cinderblock building painted in alternating blue and gold stripes. The intention, no doubt, was to suggest the Cuban flag. The sun-bleached reality was a stuccoed cakebox with a bullet-proof door.

"All sales persons require an appointment."

This was a new one on me, a radio station with a security guard. I was barred from entering by a slender youth in a white *guyaberra*, chinos, and Reeboks—a kind of melting-pot fashion statement if you ignored the holstered pistol on his hip. His solemn brown eyes regarded me with indifference until I dropped the magic name.

"You work for Señor Del Gato?" he said as indifference hardened into suspicion. "Why have we not been informed? Perhaps you are mistaken."

"I don't exactly work for him," I said. "It's about an insurance claim he's filed. I need to sort a few things out, starting with Señor Blades."

"Insurance claim," he said doubtfully. "Very unusual."

"Five hundred thousand," I said. "I guess that's pretty small change in this neighborhood, huh?"

"I will make a telephone call. Wait here."

I waited. I cracked my knuckles. I sighed and wondered just how hot it would get by the time the sun was directly overhead. Already heat was blurring the pavement, charring the air. The inescapable truth of Miami is that paradise is just a few degrees shy of Hell.

When the guard returned he had a new attitude.

"Mr. Tony Mack? Follow me, please. Señor Blades will see you as soon as he gets off the phone."

The guard escorted me to an air-conditioned reception area, and brought me a cup of coffee and a plate of *churros*. I drank the coffee, munched the sweet cinnamon pastries, and glanced through a glass plate window into the broadcast studio, where an attractive young Hispanic woman was cuing up turntables. Gold hoop earrings glittered as she worked. A low-key salsa tune trickled from the monitors. Latin elevator music.

I was licking sugar from my fingertips when Ricardo Blades emerged from his office and beckoned me inside.

"Would you like more coffee?

"I'm fine, Señor Blades."

"Ricardo, please. Or even 'Rick' if you like. We are informal here at 'GAT. That was Arturo I had on the phone. He requests that I make you welcome, answer any questions you may have. It is an insurance matter, correct?"

Blade's English was flawless, with a slight nasal intonation that suggested an Ivy League education. He looked like a neatly groomed, graying version of Che Guevara except that if you closed your eyes you heard Harvard or Yale. The effect was disconcerting and possibly intended that way.

"Tell me about the party," I asked. "The night the painting was stolen."

"I was merely one of many guests," he said, leaning back in his chair. "There was nothing special about that particular evening."

"You attend a lot of Del Gato's functions?"

He shrugged. "Almost all. Part of my job. If some person or organization in the community wants to raise money for a good cause, they go to Arturo. He comes to me, we get the word out."

"What was the good cause, exactly?"

"I believe it was for a hospital. A building fund."

"Not a political function, then?"

Blades smiled slightly. "Everything is political," he said. "Especially for Arturo and myself. It is our business to be political. But no, it was not a political function per se, although one of Arturo's organizations may have been sponsoring it. More a social event. Among the *exilios* it is considered an honor to be invited to these events."

I got the impression that Ricardo Blades was an exceedingly cautious man. He knew the value and power of words and meted them out accordingly.

"It would be helpful to know who was there, what took place. Perhaps if you started at the beginning."

He seemed faintly amused by the request, as if I was another of those earnest Anglos with a aggravating proclivity for detail. "The beginning? Okay. I am at the gate, they let me in."

"You arrived by limousine?"

He chuckled. "No. Most of the others, yes, but as it happens I live only a few hundred yards away. Next place down the canal. So I walk over."

"You came alone?"

He sighed. The Anglo was so literal minded. "No no, Elena is with me."

"Elena?"

"Elena Prio. She works here at the station, the morning music slot. You may have seen her in the studio. Like me it is part of her job to attend these kind of functions. Community relations, you understand?"

I nodded, made a show of scribbling in my notepad. "Go on. You and Elena arrive at the gate."

"Okay. Arturo says you have been to his house, so you know how it works. Heavy security. Invitations are checked, identity verified. It's a little game they play, those guards, to make themselves important. You really want all the boring details?"

"Please."

"Okay. Next thing is we wait our turn. The houseboys come on the golf carts, drive each group of guests up to the hacienda, the big house. We go inside, then out to the courtyard, where the bar has been set up. A few cocktails, then dinner." He paused. "Do you want to know what I was drinking, what I ate?"

"I want to know your impressions. This was a charity function. Had it been a long time in the planning stages? Was it an elaborate affair? What?"

Blades shrugged. It was a gesture that rippled upwards from his shoulders to his eyebrows. "Not so elaborate. Arturo put it together on short notice. The hospital discovers it needs an infusion of money, he obliges. I promote the affair on the air. It was successful."

"Last minute?" I asked.

He responded with another full-body shrug. "You know how it is. A need for funds develops, Arturo obliges."

"He's an obliging fellow."

"Exactly," Blades said.

"Did you know everyone at the party?"

He thought about it before replying. "Almost everyone. There may have been a few newcomers. Fresh blood," he added, smiling. "Friends of Mercedes."

"I thought Señora Del Gato was in Bolivia."

Blades stirred, suddenly ill at ease. "Correct," he said. "I just assumed that the new faces were acquaintances of hers. The señora is well-known in the artistic community."

"So I keep hearing," I said. "I understand that most of the collection was purchased at her direction. Any idea when she'll be back from Bolivia? I'd like to ask her how she happened to buy that particular painting."

"You'll have to ask Arturo."

Just one more in a growing list of things to ask Arturo, if I could keep from being fobbed off on his underlings.

"The gallery," I asked. "Was it open?"

"It's always open, I suppose," Blades said. "I didn't bother going in."

"You're not an art lover?"

"Let's say it's not one of my areas of interest. I have been in the gallery many times, of course. That night I did not bother."

"So you didn't see the painting that night?"

He shook his head, glanced at his watch, waited for the message to sink in. He was a busy man and I was wasting his time.

"Just a few more names, Ricardo, if you don't mind. Let's start with Luis Calzon."

"What about him?"

"He's an artist, a painter, supposedly quite handsome and popular. I take it he's a protege of Mercedes Del Gato. I wonder if you saw him that night, spoke to him, whatever."

Blades chuckled again. "Luis is a suspect, huh? You must be joking. I don't think he was even there. No, I'm pretty sure he wasn't."

"That's odd," I said. "His name was in the paper. They even made a note of how much he donated."

"So I was mistaken," Blades conceded, making a point of consulting his watch again. "I just didn't notice. Perhaps he was in the gallery. Can we wind this up, do you think? I've got to prepare for my show."

There was something about Ricardo Blades that made me want to shake him up, find a way to get under that Ivy League veneer.

"Two more names," I said. "Ben Valera. Dominick DiMambro."

He shook his head. Absolutely no reaction. Not even curiosity.

"Detectives," I said. "Burglary detail. They were killed

yesterday. A car bomb."

"Oh, yeah. I read in the paper."

"Del Gato didn't happen to mention it?"

"Why should he? What's the connection?"

"The connection," I said. "Is that Valera and DiMambro were investigating the theft of the painting. And now they're not."

"So what has this to do with Arturo?"

"I thought maybe you could shed a little light on how an explosive device got wired into their vehicle. I mean, you *are* an explosives expert, right? That was your specialty when you and Arturo were fighting in the mountains."

Blades stood up and opened his office door. "Pardon me, but I still fail to see any connection," he said, waiting for me to move. "Your function is to check out a reported theft for the insurance company, correct? This thing with the car bomb is police business. Now if you'll excuse me."

I handed him my empty cup on the way out.

6

The most important tool of the claims investigation trade is not a gun or a camera, but a telephone.

"This is Sergeant Leland Snyder of Metro P.D.," I said, "May I speak to the editor please?"

Misrepresenting yourself over the telephone is against the insurance investigator's code of conduct, but it's only a violation if you get caught.

"Ruiz speaking. How can I help you, sergeant?"

I invented a plausible story about needing to contact several of those in attendance at the Del Gato residence the night the painting went missing.

"Just a routine follow-up on the reported burglary," I added assuringly, then dropped a question that was anything but casual. "We'd like to know if you assigned a reporter to cover the event."

"Hang on, let me check it out."

I hung on, and kept my fingers crossed. Most newspaper editors are too harried to question the veracity of incoming calls. Ruiz was no exception.

"Sergeant? No reporter. The article we printed was in the nature of a PR release. Our contribution to a worthy cause."

"I see," I said. "So how did you determine who attended the function?"

"I assume they phoned in the information. That's the usual practice for our society page. If you want to be sure, I suggest you check with Señor Del Gato."

I wasn't in a mood to check with Señor Del Gato, but thanked him for the advice anyway. Just doing my part at maintaining cordial relations between the police and the media.

There was a bare-assed girl roller skating through Coconut Grove. Challenging middle-aged male drivers to keep their eyes on the road as she showed off the latest in sub-minimal swimwear. Not that I'm complaining, mind you; I've always had a keen appreciation for the fine art of roller skating.

On St. Gaudens Road, green trees intertwined with palms to form a canopy of dappled shade. I had to slow to avoid a sleeping dog. It lifted up a yellow head as I passed, as if in reproach. Had I no respect for the dog days? For sleepy streets?

I found the artist's garage apartment with a minimum of fuss because Luis Calzon had thoughtfully lettered his name above the mailbox on the downstairs door. The garage and the overhead apartment were set back from a sprawling, ranch-style house that had been tricked out with the gingerbread trim so typical of older homes in the Grove. I stood at the bottom of the outside stairs and rang the apartment bell. Got no response, then tried knocking on the garage doors.

Nobody home.

The main house was closed up tight. Shutters down, doors bolted. A sticker on each shutter warned me that the property was kept under continual surveillance by a security service. I wasn't convinced. The owners had fled the oppressive heat, no doubt, along with half the neighborhood, relying on their tenant's presence to discourage thieves.

That was my supposition. A calculated guess. I went back to the garage and tried the chimes again. Maybe young Luis was up there in his air-conditioned loft, not answering the bell because it amused him to torment an overheated ex-flatfoot.

I had no intention of breaking in. It was the cat made me do it. The animal must have sensed me trudging up the steep steps because it was in full frenzy by the time I rapped on the door.

"Meow yourself," I said to the locked door.

Meow didn't cover it. More of a panicky feline howling. It was a dreadful noise, worse than fingernails on slate. I went back to my car, opened the trunk, and found the set of bent-wire lock picks I keep under the spare tire, along with my surveillance gear.

I was out of practice and it was a high quality dead-bolt lock. Took almost five minutes of fiddling with the pick, stroking the pins, before the bolt slid back. By then the cat was trying to scratch its way through the panel.

For future reference:

When attempting to enter an apartment containing a half-starved Persian, don't forget the chair and the whip. The scrawny cat went right up my pant leg and hooked its needle claws in my belt. That made finding and opening a can of cat food an exercise in awkward hysteria.

"Nice kitty," I lied as it leapt from my belt to the counter and burrowed into the can.

I think of painters as bohemian types, prone to living in squalor. Luis Calzon's loft didn't adhere to the stereotype. It was elegant, severely modern, and very tidy if you ignored the claw marks in the kitchen cabinets. I had expected to find the place strewn with filthy capes, ratty berets, and candles in Chianti bottles. No candles, no Chianti. Just matching Bauhaus furniture, a well-stocked bookcase, and a couple of large, impressive paintings displayed so as to take best advantage of the northerly skylights.

The paintings were seascapes, or at least they gave the impression of green gulf waters and sunbleached shores. The colors were translucent, charged with light, and dreamlike.

"Way to go, Luis," I said, just to hear the sound of a human voice.

The cat was purring like a small tractor as I checked out the bedroom. A double-sized futon, with bed linen folded into crisp hospital corners. The closet was in order, shirts, trousers, shoes, all high quality and arranged with care. Either Calzon had a maid service or he was obsessively neat. The bathroom was fitted into an nearby alcove. A sink, a commode, and a simple shower stall with a steady drip and a lot of recent pawprints on the damp tile.

I wondered how many lives the Persian had used up, surviving on faucet drippings.

An inside stairway led down to the garage, where Luis Calzon painted his pretty pictures. By now I was not surprised to discover an orderly workplace, more like a surgeon's theater than a studio. An array of brushes was fanned out on a clean glass serving tray; rolls of canvas tightly furled and stored in overhead slots; tubes of paint arranged by hue. Even the faint scent of mineral spirits was clean, clinical.

I'd been expecting to find one of Calzon's surreal seascapes in progress. Instead I was confronted by a lovely nude woman with gold-tipped breasts. She seemed to be emerging from the canvas, like a swimmer breaking through the surface tension of the water. The painting was not strictly realistic—there was a mirage-like distortion at work—but I recognized the lush and lovely eyes of Mercedes Del Gato.

I stared into those eyes for quite some time, until the Persian padded down the stairs and purred, "Wow!"

My sentiments exactly.

7

I fiddled with the radio on the drive back through Coconut Grove, scanning stations until I found a voice I recognized.

"Give 'em hell, Ricardo," I said, trying to decipher his rapid Spanish. Near as I could make out he was addressing Fidel, as in how do I loathe thee, let me count the ways.

Blades had plenty of company. The phone lines were open. Other, equally impassioned voices joined him. It was the daily bash Castro party. I'm no fan of the dictator, or of tyrants of any stripe, but there was something equally disturbing about Ricardo Blades' brand of venom. He made noises about *democracia* and *libertad* but his underlying message was a simple four-letter word: hate.

Put hate together with its eager understudy, paranoia, and you have a winning combination. Put the right spin on hate and you can elect presidents or depose them. Hate has sizzle. It sells. Arturo Del Gato had learned that dirty little secret and, with Blades' rhetorical skills had used it to construct a small, deadly empire.

I listened to the harangue all the way into Coral Gables,

easing my way through stop-and-go traffic. Ricardo Blades remained exactly where I wanted him, tethered to a live mike in the Calle Ocho.

The Blades hacienda was within easy walking distance of the Del Gato estate, but it was mere proximity. In size and stature the modest bungalow was worlds away. There were, surprisingly, no guards or servants to intervene. And best of all Elena Prio, Ricardo's girlfriend and co-worker, answered the door. She was shaded by the screen, but I recognized the pretty profile and the hoop earrings.

"Yes?"

I'd considered various deceptions and decided not to veer too far from the truth.

"Tony Mack. Representing South Florida Mutual Life."

"I don't believe in life insurance."

"I feel the same way about UFO's."

You never know what will get you through the door. This time a feeble joke did it. Elena Prio laughed, and after being assured there would be no insurance spiel, and that the interview was sanctioned by Del Gato himself, she agreed to a brief discussion about a certain missing painting.

"Come on in," she said, leading me into an air-conditioned sitting room. Knife cuts of sunlight pierced the drawn blinds and spilled over the carpet. The blades of an ceiling fan turned sluggishly. "What'll you have, a coke, a beer, what?"

I opted for a beer, playing the relaxed, ever-casual insurance flack. Just going through the motions, ma'am, filling in the blanks on this here long form. Miss Prio found me amusing.

"You really think one of Arturo's guests stole the thing?" she asked, sipping soda pop through a straw.

"That's the main thrust of the investigation," I said. "Narrows it down to a hundred or so suspects."

"Am I a suspect?" she asked, sounding positively delighted at the idea.

"If you like," I said. "Actually I had someone else in mind. Handsome young dude named Luis Calzon."

Elena had a pleasing, musical laugh. "Luis? Are you kidding?"

"Either him or Mrs. Del Gato. It's a tossup."

"Mercedes? You *are* kidding. Or crazy," she said, her smile fading. "It's a cute idea, but I wouldn't share it with Arturo. He's got no sense of humor. None."

"Mrs. Del Gato is out of the country," I said. "Mr. Calzon is not at his studio. I sort of put one and one together and got two."

"My God. You're serious."

"Just a theory."

Elena leaned forward in her chair. "Hey, it's a theory that could get somebody killed."

"Maybe it already has," I said. "Of course that's just another theory."

I reminded her that two of the detectives who had been investigating the theft had been blown up on Brickell Avenue.

"Yeah, Ricky mentioned that, but I'm sure there's no connection," she said uneasily. "What you're saying is impossible. Do you know Mercedes?"

"Never had the pleasure."

Elena nodded. "I thought so. We've had our little differences, but basically she's a classy lady. I guess Arturo married her for her looks and her poise—being married to an activist like Arturo is a full-time job, a little like being married to royalty. Lots of social obligations, you know? Anyhow, Arturo probably got more than he bargained for, because Mercedes has brains. This is one smart lady, okay? She knew exactly what she was doing when she hitched up to Arturo's star. She has a special place in

Miami society, and she likes to use it to full effect."

"Like encouraging artists?" I said.

Elena smirked. "Yeah, wise guy. Like encouraging Cuban artists."

"Indications are that Luis Calzon has been duly encouraged."

"Forget it," Elena said, shaking her head. "Mercedes would never abandon Arturo, not for Luis Calzon, not for anybody. I know they've had their problems, but it's never been more serious than a temporary separation. If it ever came to divorce Arturo would cut her off without a dime."

"Oh?" I said. "Could he do that?"

She shrugged. "Hey, he's an old-fashioned kind of guy. The wife is the wife, you know? He's got everything in his name, you can be sure of that. And if Mercedes was cheating on him he'd figure a way to keep every penny. That's the way they do it."

"The way who does it?" I asked.

"Cuban men," she sighed. "The rule of machismo. The husband can have a mistress, that's okay, but if a wife takes a lover, forget it. Big disgrace. So what you say is impossible."

"Impossible that Mercedes would take a lover?"

Elena's face was in shadow, so it was hard to read her expression. I thought I detected a certain wariness in her posture. "Impossible that she would abandon Arturo," she said carefully. "She likes the life. Likes to have her own importance in the community. Likes spending Arturo's money."

"What if she had money of her own?"

"But she doesn't," Elena insisted. "She came here from Bolivia without a dime. That's, uh, why she so often returns home. Her family depends on her. On whatever little money she brings them."

"Getting back to my theory," I said. "The market value of the missing painting is a million dollars. That's more than enough to buy a new life in Bolivia, or elsewhere in South America."

"What a crazy idea."

"Hey, love can be crazy. So I've hear0."

"Maybe you better have another beer," Elena suggested. "I gotta straighten you out on this or you'll get yourself in big trouble."

She meant well. I got the impression Elena Prio was genuinely worried that anyone foolish enough to rock the Del Gato boat risked life and limb, not to mention peace of mind.

"I'm not saying you should cheat your insurance company," she advised. "All I'm saying is, be careful what you say about Arturo and Mercedes. Also, you got to understand there is no way Mercedes would run off with *anybody*, never mind a poor boy like Luis Calzon."

"His family lose everything to Castro, too?"

Elena chuckled. "No way. Luis, he's a *campesino*, a peasant, you understand? He's got looks and talent, but it takes a lot more than that to keep Mercedes happy, believe me. Also he happens to be a pretty smart guy. Too smart to steal from Arturo."

"You don't think he took the painting that night?"

"Not any night. Especially not the night of that party."

"Why not?"

"Because," Elena said triumphantly. "Luis wasn't there."

"You're sure about that?" I said, trying to sound disappointed.

"Sure I'm sure. I was going to ask him about an interview we had scheduled for Ricky's show. The influence of folk art or something. I was going to do the prep work, then something came up and the interview got canceled. I heard Luis is up in New York."

"So I'm barking up the wrong tree?"

"You're in the wrong forest, that's how wrong you are."

"Okay," I sighed, "scratch that little theory. Now I'm back

to square one. Did you happen to go into the gallery that night?"

Elena shook her head. "Couldn't," she said.

"Why not?"

"Didn't Arturo tell you? The gallery was being repainted or something. He had the doors locked."

"Oh yeah," I said. Hoping that she couldn't see the wolfish grin on my face. "I think Ricardo mentioned something about that."

8

Maria answered on the seventh ring.

"Scuze me, Jorge got loose, I had to fetch him back."

"Where was he going?" I asked.

"Jorge, he want to climb that coconut palm. Can't get no further than hugging his arms around it, not so far. That *bambino* is very affectionate to everyone, including the palm tree. Right now he wrapped around my leg. I guess you calling to say you'll be late for supper, *si?*"

"Very late," I said.

"Too bad, I got yellowtail Eduardo caught off the dock. He fillet the fish himself, do a pretty good job. And Teri and Carly been making a big salad, all kind of fresh stuff like you like."

"Can't be helped," I said. "I've got all this paperwork to catch up on. Also I need a little help. Telephone type help."

Maria laughed. "Well, *mi querido,* you always say I give good phone."

"Get a pen," I suggested, "write this down."

I gave her the spiel, had her read it back. She did it with style and verve. Very convincing.

"Don't sound like no paperwork you're up to," she commented.

"Okay," I said. "A little surveillance. I intend to keep my distance."

"You do that. *Promesa* ?"

"I promise."

I did keep my distance. As it turned out, considerably more distance than I had anticipated.

The plan was simple. It was a ruse I'd worked before: While the subject is under surveillance, have a confederate call with a message that startles the subject into action. Then watch what happens. The truly innocent will do nothing very interesting. Those with something to hide will frequently react unpredictably, out of pattern.

Later Maria told me how she'd muffled her voice with a pair of panty-hose, a touch she knew I would appreciate. This was the gist of her call:

"Listen carefully. We have the missing painting and are prepared to return it to you for a price. Three hundred thousand in small bills. Get the money ready and we will call again with details. Repeat, we have obtained the painting. If you want to avoid embarrassing publicity, get the money ready."

Maria rattled that off in Spanish. She told it twice. Once to Del Gato's male secretary, Tomas, and again to Del Gato himself. Tomas, cool as always, had no response. Del Gato said only this:

"You are lying," and hung up the phone.

Very interesting. He was right, of course. Maria *was* lying. But how did he know that?

At the time of the call I was staked out two blocks away, parked in a area that left my Plymouth effectively hidden, but with a fairly good view of the estate and the various motor vehicles Del Gato owned or leased. The view was considerably enhanced by a pair of eight-by-forty extra-wide-angle Minolta binoculars. Bird-watching field glasses, although I've never actually used them on birds. Not flying birds, anyhow.

So I sat there, watching and waiting. Expecting to see Del Gato or his secretary come tearing out of the big house, select a car, and take off. Whereupon I would follow, keeping a discrete distance.

Del Gato knew a lot more about the theft—if it was a theft — than he was letting on. He had been lying consistently, trying to give the impression that someone on his extensive guest list had been responsible. It seemed likely that Ricardo Blades had been recruited to underscore that impression. Why bother? And how did Mercedes figure in, or Luis Calzon? I was still juggling a lot of jagged little details, trying to make everything fit.

It all hinged on the Agency report relayed from New York. The sudden question about provenance that seemed to have kicked off the reported theft: Del Gato is informed that a painting his wife recently purchased may actually belong to someone else, and a few days later he says it has been stolen and files a claim to that effect. A coincidence so blatant it was bound to alert any insurance investigator. Or any police detective, for that matter. Which made it a rather stupid crime.

The key question. What would make a man like Arturo Del Gato act stupid?

To get an answer, merely jangle his nerves, see how he reacts. Follow the car when he makes his move.

Nerves got jangled, all right, but the reaction did not involve a motor vehicle. I had both garages and the exit gate covered with the binoculars. Nothing went, nothing came. Time passed. I watched, waited, rediscovered my patience. Maybe I had it all wrong. Maybe Del Gato wasn't involved. Or maybe he had taken the thing himself, hidden the painting on the premises. Slipped it into a shoebox in the closet, or under a bed. Or maybe Mercedes and her loverboy really had taken the 'Ladies in the Cathedral' to Bolivia to make a new life for themselves.

I was debating the wisdom of entering the estate unannounced when I noticed the canal bridge going up. Just the tip of the bridge appearing in the hazy distance over the white tile roofs. I stared at it like a fool, uncomprehending.

Sonovabitch. *The boat.*

I got out of the car, ran part of a block, and found an angle that gave me a shot at Del Gato's dock. The big, varnished Rybovich was gone. And the bridge was still going up.

So all I had to do was follow the boat through the canal, see where it went. A couple of problems with that little plan. The first being that I didn't have a boat handy, or any prospect of getting one on the quick—try to steal a boat in that section of Coral Gables and trigger-happy security guards will perforate your body with automatic weapons before you get an oar in the water. Also the sun was setting and visibility was going to hell.

I put the car in gear and headed for the bridge, hoping to catch sight of the boat as if passed through, just to make sure Del Gato was really aboard.

It soon became obvious that my knowledge of Coral Gable streets was far from complete. The canal curved through the heart of the suburb, southeast to Biscayne Bay. And when George Merrick laid out his little fantasy city he decided that a winding confusion of streets would make the place charming. So there was no easy way to drive parallel to the damned waterway.

I got hopelessly lost. The first stars of the evening were starting to glow in a sky of airbrushed blue as the bridge descended behind the palm trees and the over-priced real estate that lined the canal. The only recourse was to try and find the next bridge before it opened. Easier said. Doing it involved terrifying several innocent residents unused to dodging a rapidly reversing automobile.

I made it on the third bridge, or maybe the fourth. More than halfway to the bay. I got to the intersection just as the last bridge was going down, in time to see the wide, powerful stern of the Rybovich as it passed through. Del Gato was up on the flying bridge, driving the boat. Tomas was on the rear deck, stripped to the waist and checking out scuba-diving gear.

Right about then I'd have traded my late model sedan for a leaky dinghy or an inner tube. Anything to get into the waterway and follow their wake. I'd been expecting Del Gato to bolt for a safe deposit box or a bus station locker, not head for the briny depths. He wasn't following the expected pattern. Shooting my theories all to hell.

The big boat glided into the twilight and disappeared around a bend in the canal.

Out of sight, amigo.

It was pure luck that a full moon came up over Biscayne Bay about an hour later. Good luck for me, bad for Arturo Del Gato. I had pretty much given up on finding the boat anywhere near shore. It was a big ocean out there. I ended up cruising Old Cutler Road, knowing it would head me in the direction of Key Largo, eventually. Mostly I was just wasting time, trying to figure out what had gone wrong.

That's when I stumbled upon the estuary. It was more of a backwater, really, an area of saltwater marsh that had, according to the signs, been protected before the developers got around to paving over the bullrushes. This was, I suddenly realized, what the canal emptied into before spilling out into the moonlit bay. That oddest of anomalies: an undeveloped cove within a few miles of downtown Miami.

And there was a boat anchored out there, not more than a hundred yards from shore. A big fishing machine with a flying bridge and outrigger whips. Seen in silhouette with the estuary glittering around it. Pretty as a postcard.   Moon Over Miami.

I pulled the sedan up against a chainlink fence and got a Nikon SLR and matching three-hundred-millimeter nightscope lens out of the camera case. I fed in a roll of high-speed film. One thousand ASA. Not really fast enough for action shots, even on a moonlit night, but if I saw anything interesting I could push the film, maybe pick up faint images on the negative.

Click click, my specialty.

Steadying the cumbersome lens against a fence post, I brought the boat into focus. Much better. It wasn't exactly crisp daylight, but the dude with his butt planted on the stern was Arturo Del Gato, no doubt about it. Alone, it seemed, as he puffed on a cigarette.

Click.

"M-m-moonlight becomes you," I crooned softly, holding the shutter open for a half-second. The snap would be blurred but possibly identifiable in court, if it ever came to that. Not that there was any crime in taking a boat out into a moonlit estuary.

Click.

Del Gato smoked four more cigarettes. I was beginning to think he'd driven that monster boat through all those bridges just to put a little tar and nicotine in his lungs when he jumped, as if startled.

I shifted the lens. Something was coming out of the water at the stern. The creature from the deep lagoon. Mask, scuba tank, flippers.

The creature was holding onto something as Del Gato helped him onto the dive platform.

Click. Click.

It was a mesh diving bag. Bulging with whatever it held.

Something the creature had scooped from the muddy bottom.

I waited, hoping Del Gato would open the bag and take the damn thing out. Examine it in the moonlight. It was only human nature to want to check it out, right?

Wrong. The bag disappeared into the cockpit unopened. I got some lovely shots of Arturo helping Tomas slip off the scuba tank. Then the two chums winched up the anchor and headed back into the canal, serene as you please.

9

Maria woke me with a kiss.

"Man on the phone," she whispered.

I crawled from the bed, pulled on a robe, and took the call in the kitchen. Seated at the table, I pushed aside the blinds and saw the sunlit lagoon, bright and mirror flat. Mid-morning in paradise. It was hot enough so the palm fronds appeared to droop like weary ballerinas. Hot enough to make the air shimmer.

"Have you got it on tape?" I asked, cradling the receiver with my shoulder as Maria handed me a glass of juice, a cup of coffee.

Crowell hemmed and hawed. The anonymous caller had not specifically asked for the executive in charge of the Del Gato claim. So the message had been taken by the switchboard.

"No tape," I said.

"Is it important?" Crowell wanted to know.

He sounded uneasy. I remembered he was new on the job. South Florida Mutual Life had a way of moving executives along pretty quickly—sometimes right out the door.

"Probably not," I said. "I want to check this out myself."

"Sure thing," Crowell agreed. "You don't sound surprised."

"I've been out all night, setting this up," I said, fully prepared to exaggerate my influence on the situation.

"Should I notify the police?"

"Let me do that," I said. "There's a homicide detective I need to impress."

Miami International Airport is the air-conditioned subconscious of Latin America. It is there, under the scream of descending aircraft, that the dreams of gold, greed, and love intersect with the lines of power and finance, producing a kind of hallucinatory super-state. Shrieking children with hair the precise color of raven wings race through steel-glass terminals, hurling oranges and hand grenades. Toy hand grenades, usually, and real oranges, although the sequence is sometimes reversed.

Anything can happen at Miami International. A Panamanian banker can drink cyanide in his thimble-sized cup of *molido* expresso and die with a foamy smile on his lips. Rocket launchers can be openly exchanged for five gallon buckets of uncut cocaine while CIA operatives look on through reflecting sunglasses. The famous wife of a famous dictator can board a large jet as the sole passenger, accompanied only by two hundred and eight pieces of luggage and a three-ton pallet of one hundred dollar bills.

Life, death, birth, marriage, murder—everything is possible. Shattering poverty, unspeakable wealth. I think of it as an endless, airborne caravan circling a concrete oasis. The first Latin American outpost on the shores of North America. Somehow it made sense that the missing painting would turn up as unclaimed baggage.

It took a while to find the appropriate clerk. I knew I had the right guy when he flatly refused to turn over the package without a claim ticket.

"Look," I said, laying out a row of identification cards. "I represent South Florida Mutual Life. The package is, I believe, addressed to South Florida Mutual Life."

"Still need a claim ticket. That's the rule."

"Check the package," I suggested. "I'll bet it doesn't have an invoice or a claim number. It was left here early this morning."

The clerk went away. I had time for a coffee, read Edna Buchanan and the *Herald* sports section. The clerk came back. He looked happy.

"You're wrong," he said. "It's not a package. It's a suitcase."

"No bullpen," I said.

"What?"

"Why the Mets are on a losing streak," I said, rattling the newspaper. "The relief pitching went south."

"You'll have to fill out a lost baggage claim form," the clerk said, staring at a spot several inches to the right of my head. "There's a thirty-day waiting period."

"Very reasonable, I'm sure," I said, "if the bag happened to arrive on one of your airplanes. It didn't."

"Oh? How do you know that?"

"Because whoever put it on your carousel called South Florida Mutual Life to report, anonymously of course, that a stolen work of art had been left here. We insured the work of art, a painting, so naturally we'd like to have it back. Now."

"I'll need a claim ticket. That's policy."

This went on for a while. Eventually we were able to determine that the clerk would settle for the facsimile of a claim ticket, namely a hundred dollar bill.

"Only because the bag doesn't actually have a claim receipt," he explained, handing over the piece of luggage. "Otherwise I'd never go along with releasing it."

"Of course," I said, giving him the bill. "You're an honest man."

On the way out I was accosted by a squinty-eyed individual in a cheap suit.

"What have we here," he said, putting his hand on the bag.

"Sergeant Snyder," I said. "What a pleasant surprise."

"Come off it. You called me, right?"

"Did I? Just kidding, Sarge. Of course I called you. This is a homicide investigation now. And I don't screw around withholding evidence on a homicide case."

"Glad to hear it," Leland Snyder said, tugging at the bag.

"Promise not to put your sticky fingers all over it?"

"Don't be a jerk," Snyder said.

"I'm serious. If this is what I think it is, it needs the deluxe treatment at Forensics. Maybe put the FBI lab on it if your boys can't handle it."

"They can handle it. All I want is a look, make sure I'm not wasting my time."

I let go of the bag. Snyder balanced it on his knee, ready to hit the locks.

"There's another consideration," I said.

"Yeah?" he said, pausing.

"When we open the bag it might go boom."

"Jesus," Snyder said. Freezing with his knee up in the air, the bag wobbling slightly.

"I mean look what happened to Valera and DiMambro." I said. "We're dealing with someone who likes to make things explode unexpectedly. Someone who's willing to risk taking out a couple of cops."

Snyder gave me his squintiest squint. "You said it was the missing painting. Anonymous call announcing a drop off."

I shrugged. "Maybe they were fibbing."

Detective Sergeant Snyder proved to be a quick thinker.

"Here," he said, handing me the bag. "Follow me. And if you don't mind, keep back about ten yards."

He had me spooked. I'd been kidding, sort of, about the possibility of a bomb. Now the thought lingered.

"Maybe we should get a Sky Cap," I suggested. "We could give him a big tip."

I more or less chased Snyder to the nearest security checkpoint. When I got there he was already flashing his badge, ordering the line of passengers to step back.

"This'll only take a minute, folks. Just a precaution."

"I'm sorry, officer, you're not supposed to do that."

"Go ahead," Snyder said amiably. "Call in your supervisor. Meantime we're putting this bag on the conveyer, we'll just have a little look, be on our way."

"Whataya mean 'we'?" I said, heaving the bag up on the conveyer belt.

Snyder had the necessary air of authority and succeeded in convincing airport security to let him pass the bag through the x-ray inspection. He stopped the conveyer, had a good long look at the contents.

"How big was that painting?" he asked me.

"Bigger than a bread box. Smaller than the suitcase."

He nodded, grabbed the bag, and walked back through the metal detector, setting off the alarm.

"'Scuse us," he said to the line of cowering passengers. "Must be the keys in my pocket."

Homicide threw a party and I was the guest of honor. There were no candles or cakes. Refreshments were limited to coffee and doughnuts.

The game of choice was pin the tail on Tony Mack. Sergeant Snyder started it off.

"Tell it to these gentlemen like you told it to me," he instructed.

About half the squad had crowded into the interrogation room. It wasn't a very friendly gathering, considering that I was volunteering information.

"Don't ever let this guy buy you lunch, Sarge."

"Hell, he didn't even have the decency to sell Ben 'n' Dom any life insurance."

"Somebody crack a window," I said. "It stinks in here."

"Windows are sealed. 'Course if we had something to *throw* through the window, smash it open . . . whadda they call it, defenestration?"

"Look it up," I said. "But why the aggravation? I'm here of my own free will. I want to nail the bastards, just like you do."

"Which particular bastards?"

"The cop-killing bastards."

"Oh, *those* bastards. Sarge, let's get frosty with this smart-ass goon."

I appealed to Snyder. He gave me one of his polygraph squints and then cleared the room of extra personnel, retaining the stenographer.

"This case has caused a certain amount of anxiety within the department," he said.

"No kidding."

"Two senior detectives blown up in the line of duty, their fellow officers tend to get a little frustrated if they think a civvie is withholding information, screwing up the investigation."

"I was a cop," I said. "I don't forget."

Snyder nodded. The cheap suit looked like the glued seams were about to dissolve. In Brooklyn the ranking homicide officers had dressed like princes, as a point of honor. So did most of Snyder's colleagues, who still favored the flashy *Miami Vice* look. Silk shirts and chains of gold. I decided Snyder was an outsider type and wanted to look the part.

"Let's start over," he said. "Make a new beginning. Just tell the story, okay?"

"Sure," I said. "That's why I'm here."

"And don't get cute, try leaving things out."
"You've got me all wrong, sergeant."
"Fine," he said. "Convince me."

1 0

It was cocktail hour in Coral Gables by the time I concluded negotiations with homicide. This time I was cleared through the gate with a minimum of fuss. After all, I was the harbinger of good news.

"Come in, Mr. Mack, come in and be welcome."

Del Gato met me at the door. He put his hands on my shoulders and squeezed. For a moment I thought he was going to kiss me. Then he noticed the briefcase I was carrying. The sight of all that potential paperwork seemed to sober him up.

"You have time for a drink?"

"Sure thing," I said. "I could use a stiff drink. It's been a rough couple of days."

Drinks were out on the glass-enclosed courtyard, overlooking the canal and the dock. Tomas was tending bar. Ricardo Blades was dancing with Elena Prios to piped-in salsa music. Elena smiled and waved and continued dancing. As Blades whirled her expertly around I could see the empty glass flashing in his hand, the canny, confidant smile on his face.

"As you see, the recovery is a cause for celebration," Arturo said, leaning close as Tomas handed me a drink. His eyes were slightly glazed. I could smell the olives on his breath. Too many martinies for Señor Del Gato. I wasn't sure that was a good thing. Alcohol tends to make things get bumpy when you're conducting the kind of carefully orchestrated duplicity I had in mind.

"Your wife must be relieved," I said.

Del Gato's eyes clicked into focus. Sober again, just like that.

"Mercedes is very happy, yes."

"So she's back from Bolivia?"

He picked up a fresh martini. Touched his glass to mine. "Cheers, my friend. And no, to answer your question, Mercedes has not returned yet. An illness in her family, a cousin, I believe. I called her in La Paz with the good news."

I smiled, sipped the cool gin.

"Ricardo, say hello to our friend Tony Mack. He's some investigator, hey? Top notch."

Blades said, "Hello Tony Mack," and kept on dancing. Considering who he had in his arms, I didn't blame him.

"So," Del Gato said. "How did you recover the painting? Tell me everything."

I set the briefcase under a deck chair, central to the little gathering, and smiled over the rim of my glass. "Nothing to it," I said.

"It was all a matter of surveillance."

"Surveillance?" he said, as if uncertain of the meaning of the word. "How do you mean surveillance?"

"Specialty of mine," I said. "A certain way of looking at things."

Del Gato chuckled. Amused, apparently, at the over-confident gringo. He settled into a chair beside me. The low slant of light picked up a glint of white in his hair, strands the dye job had failed to cover. His knife-thin face was even more gaunt, as if the bones were straining to come through.

"Your company must be very happy," he said. "Now they will not have to pay the claim. So you have saved them a half-million dollars."

I shrugged. "They're a big outfit. Takes a lot to make them happy."

"And a half-million is not enough?"

"Hey, a half-million would make me positively giddy. To South Florida Mutual Life it's small change. A drop in the ocean."

Del Gato gulped his martini, signaled for another. "You mean 'drop in the bucket.' Is that not the correct phrase?"

"Sure," I said. "What was I thinking?"

Elena broke away from Ricardo and flopped into a chair. From the way Del Gato reacted I got the impression she wasn't particularly welcome, but that he had no way of politely excluding her from the gathering.

"You bring that silly painting back?" she asked, indicating the briefcase.

"Uh, no. There's a slight problem with the painting. A couple of slight problems."

Del Gato said. "It will be returned to me, of course."

"Possibly," I said. "The police have it now."

"Of course. A formality."

There was the sound of breaking glass. Blades had crushed his empty glass under his heel. It seemed to make him happy.

"It's a legal matter," I said. "A question of provenance. You'll want to consult your attorney. Also the painting was damaged. Rather seriously."

Blades veered in, sat down next to Elena. "What sort of damage?" he asked. "Is it ruined?"

"Apparently it was immersed in salt water. Also a section of the panel has been removed. Looks like it was cut out with a hacksaw. The police have it at the forensic lab now, checking it out."

"Immersed in salt water?" Ricardo said, sounding puzzled. "How strange."

Tomas arrived with a tray of fresh drinks. The only taker was Del Gato, who reached for a glass and said, "And what do they hope to find with this, uhm, forensics?"

"Who knows?" I said. "They might not find anything interesting. Or they may be able to determine where the painting has been since it disappeared. And why the thief cut out a section of it."

"Since it was stolen," Del Gato corrected. "It didn't 'disappear.' It was stolen."

"Of course. Stolen. You never know what they'll come up with, these modern lab boys. The spectography they do is amazing stuff."

Ricardo made a face. Clearly he thought the gringo insurance flack was talking through his hat.

"I kid you not," I said. "It's like science fiction. They can identify individual molecules, trace elements. A hair follicle so tiny it won't even show under a microscope. A flake of dandruff. The ghost of a speck of blood. Amazing."

Elena smiled. "What does it matter?" she said. "You've got the painting back. That's all that matters."

Del Gato cleared his throat. "What is this talk of ghosts and blood?"

I shrugged. The big amiable flatfoot. "Beats me. Something to do with the way blood affects oil paint. Chemical interaction or something. Anyhow, they can tell if even a tiny drop of blood every touched the surface of the panel, no matter how long it was immersed in salt water."

Del Gato sat back, his eyes lidded. "That is, I think, pretty far-fetched, no?"

"That's what I told 'em," I said, pretending to gulp at my drink. "Probably a waste of time. And even if they can determine that the painting was spattered with blood, so what? I told them they were better off looking for fingerprints and you know what they told me? That the thief would probably have worn gloves."

Elena got a kick out of that. "I don't remember anyone

wearing gloves to the fundraiser. Not in this heat."

"Elena," Ricardo said in a warning tone.

"Boy," I said. "If looks could kill."

"What is that supposed to mean?" Ricardo responded, showing me his teeth. A wolf cub grin.

"Just a phrase. It's not looks that kill. Everybody knows that. It's bombs. You'd agree with that, wouldn't you Ricardo?"

There was silence for several heartbeats. Blades picked up an empty glass, set it gently on the terrace tiles, and crushed it underfoot. "Arturo, I think this one is abusing your hospitality. He is making jokes."

Del Gato was sitting up straight. His expression was blurred but his voice was clear enough. "Perhaps you could be more specific," he said. "Then we would understand the joke."

"No joke, Arturo," I said. He reacted to the familiarity as if he'd smelled something distasteful. "It isn't only the painting that was damaged. Lives were damaged. Suspending the investigation could be expensive. Very expensive."

Del Gato forced himself to smile. I was starting to get through the haze of unadulterated gin. "Elena," he said. "Do you mind? It would be better if you excused yourself."

"I'd rather she stayed, Arturo," I said.

"What's the big deal," Elena said, looking puzzled. "I thought we were having a party?"

"I think Mr. Tony Mack is trying to make a point. Is that correct Mr. Tony Mack?"

"Could be," I said. "Like I was saying, the cost of suspending the investigation, writing up a satisfactory conclusion. It's not easy to assign a dollar value to the cost, but if you really give it a lot of thought—and I've been giving it a lot of thought—you just might arrive at a hundred and twenty-five thousand dollars for each life that was lost. Multiply that times four and you get, correct me if I'm wrong, five hundred thousand. Which by coincidence happens to be exactly the amount the painting was insured for."

"This one has been out in the sun too long," Ricardo said. "His brain has fried. He makes no sense and his jokes are very bad."

"Relax," I said. "We can settle this amiably. Arturo is a very astute businessman, right Arturo?"

"Make your point, Mr. Tony Mack."

"My point is we can all be friends here. I happen to have come across some information that might, if it became public knowledge, be inconvenient. I think you know what I'm referring to, Arturo."

"I haven't the faintest idea. I think perhaps Ricardo is right. You've been out in the sun too long."

"Not the sun," I said. "The moon. It was a lovely full moon last night. I'm sure you and Tomas noticed."

"Tomas?" Del Gato growled. "What does Tomas have to do with this?"

I was watching Ricardo. He looked genuinely puzzled at the reference to Tomas and the events of the previous night. As if Del Gato hadn't bothered to clue him in. Which made it interesting. Maybe I could play them off against each other. The immovable object against the irresistible force.

"Tomas did the diving," I said. "He's the one who recovered the painting for you, Arturo. Your bad luck *pintura*. Out there in the estuary, under the full moon."

Ricardo said, "What is he talking about? Tomas, is this true?"

"I got some real pretty shots," I said. "Took me most of the night in the darkroom, souping the negatives just right, but I got a nice sequence of Tomas coming out of the water with that net bag in his hand. And you checking it out. You were smoking a cigarette, Arturo. I even got the little puffs of smoke. I blow it up enough, you could tell the brand."

Del Gato was starting to look a little green around the gills. All that icy gin in his blood. Ricardo was hunched forward, his face a mask. The bits of glass under his heels made little bright noises.

"You have these photographs?" Del Gato said, glancing at the briefcase.

"Not with me. They're in the mail, as a matter of fact. To various locations. Not to worry, though. No one will open them so long as I'm there to pick them up."

"Photographs mean nothing. We often go night fishing, right Tomas?"

Tomas was waiting attentively by the bar. He nodded, expressionless.

"You're right, of course. Photos mean nothing by themselves. They only mean something if they are part of a chain of evidence. For instance if you put certain photographs together with certain tapes of certain telephone conversations. In particular a brief conversation you had last night."

Del Gato's eyes looked like black thumbprints in soft clay. He sighed heavily and said, "An illegal tap is not admissible. That much I know, even without consulting an attorney."

Ricardo stood up. He went to the bar, reached behind the shelf, and turned around with a gun in his hand. A Beretta 93R machine pistol. I got a good look at it when he placed the barrel against the tip of my nose.

"Tell me all about it," he said.

11

Del Gato sobered up for the second time. His thin neck

trembled with the effort and the sunken eyes burned. "Ricardo, put the gun away. It is not necessary."

The Beretta drifted, hovering somewhere between myself and the ground.

"I want to know what this man knows," Ricardo said. "You owe me that much."

Del Gato stared at the machine pistol and shrugged. Elena held herself utterly still, as if afraid that Ricardo might decide to include her in the gun pointing.

"You," he said, swinging the barrel like a rude, scolding finger. "No more cute talk. Tell me why you think you can blackmail Arturo."

Hostility tends to make my throat dry. I asked if I could have a drink. "Just a beer," I said. "These martinis make me dizzy."

Tomas uncapped a bottle. "Glass?" he asked.

"Just as it is," I said. "You're running out of glasses."

"Talk now," Ricardo said through clenched teeth. "Before you have time to think up more lies."

The thing about running a stunt, you have to be willing to improvise. I had neglected to factor in the possibility that Ricardo Blades might be in the dark regarding the painting and why it had gone missing.

I'd been intending a simple enough deception—pose as an extortionist, coax the guilty parties into incriminating themselves, then let the cops and the prosecutors put together a jury-proof case. Ditching the script left me with a naked feeling. I would have to rely on the truth, always a risky business.

"This may take awhile," I said, glancing at the canal and playing for time. "You're asking me to describe my state of mind."

"I'm telling you," Ricardo insisted, "to tell me. Everything."

"Fine, you got it. I wonder, could you back off that trigger just a little? Those Berettas are kind of touchy. Okay, first thing got my attention, the burglary didn't conform to the normal profile."

Ricardo said, "Plain English, my friend. I know you can speak it if you try."

"Well, it's like this: Mrs. Del Gato, Mercedes, she buys the painting at auction. Her husband, naturally, insures it. Fine, that's normal. Then a few months later we get an inquiry, raising the possibility that the painting actually belongs to the country of origin, in this case Italy. So the provenance is in dispute. Which is not, by the way, all that unusual, the way art is bought and sold in the marketplace. What *is* unusual is that a couple of days after being informed of this problem, Del Gato reports that the painting has been stolen. It's no longer in his possession."

"A coincidence," Del Gato interjected.

"Let him talk," Ricardo said.

"Well," I said. "It *could* have been a coincidence. But ripping off insurance companies is a national pastime, so my first assumption is that, faced with the possibility that he might lose this very valuable work of art in a court squabble, Arturo here decides to stick it to South Florida Mutual Life. So he pretends the painting has been stolen. For your average millionaire that wouldn't have been difficult. Just fake a break-in, file a police report. But Del Gato is not your average millionaire. He's got a small army guarding his happy little home. State of the art security. A break-in, to be convincing, would have to be some kind of *Mission Impossible* scene. Very difficult to fake, right Arturo?"

"You have a vivid imagination, Mr. Tony Mack."

"Goes with the job," I said.

"There was no break-in," Ricardo said, staring at Del Gato.

"No," I said. "Arturo decided to keep it simple. Throw a last minute fund-raising party. That allowed him to create the impression that any of a hundred or so guests could have walked out with the painting. Guests who are influential members of the *exilio* community. People not inclined to cooperate with any investigation. People who have the poise to know how to make a cop's job almost impossible. It was a smart idea, that party. And we should take note of that, because it was the last smart thing Arturo did."

Del Gato sighed. "See how he insults me, Ricardo?"

"What proof have you?" Ricardo demanded.

"Circumstantial evidence," I said. "A lot of little things were wrong."

"Tell me these little things."

"Well, one little thing that made the deal look phony is that we never heard from the thief."

"Explain," Ricardo said.

"Theft of fine art is a specialty, okay? Has its own rules. The more valuable or well-known the piece, the more difficult it is to dispose of. Best you can do is ten or twenty percent of the market value. So the professional thief will frequently attempt to shop the artwork back to the owner or cut a deal with the insurance company. Our policy, which again is typical, is that we'll pay up to fifteen percent to recover, no questions ask. And when that didn't happen, when nobody contacted Del Gato or the company, it helped convince me of what I already suspected. That the owner was implicated in the theft."

Ricardo nodded solemnly, gestured with the machine pistol, urging me to continue.

"So what I do, my technique when I have a little suspicion like that, I try to put myself in the suspect's shoes. See it from his point of view. If I was Arturo Del Gato, what would I do with the painting? Assuming I couldn't bear to burn something I'd paid half a million bucks for. The safest thing would be to get it out of the country. That's where Mrs. Del Gato comes in, or so I thought."

"Mercedes," Ricardo said, his eyes flitting nervously. "What does she know of this?"

"Maybe you better ask Arturo that."

"I'm asking you."

"Hey, easy with the pistol, please."

"Talk."

I obliged him. "Well, this was pure speculation, but I thought there was a pretty good chance she'd taken the painting to Bolivia. As a native she'd be aware of the fact there's a lot of unwashed money floating around Bolivia right now, because of the drug cartels. Some of the cartel *gamberros* live like feudal kings. Vast estates, fabulous collections of art—and they're not fussy about little details like provenance, or whether a work of art is stolen. So if I was Arturo, I might arrange for my wife to take the painting to Bolivia, get what she could for it. And maybe the wife, a little nervous about the enterprise, she decides to take along a friend, a young painter she knows. Anyhow, that was my theory."

"You don't believe this theory?"

"Not any more," I said. "Not when I found the hungry Persian."

I described my visit to Luis Calzon's studio. Finding the starving cat, the unfinished canvas.

"That gave me a couple of new things to think about. Such as would a neat, totally organized perfectionist like Calzon abandon his pedigree cat like that? Even if he didn't care about the animal, would he risk letting it damage his apartment? All that precious furniture? And what about this painting he was working on, this sensual nude of Mercedes Del Gato? How did *that* figure in?"

Ricardo glanced at Elena. "Mercedes and Luis?" he asked. She looked at Arturo, then nodded, ever so slightly.

"Right," I said. "If Mercedes and sweet Lou were an item,

that raised all sorts of interesting possibilities. And motives. All of a sudden the other thing made sense."

"What other thing?" Ricardo asked softly. The pistol, I was happy to note, had drifted back toward Arturo, who glanced it it with profound contempt.

"The thing nobody wants to talk about," I said. "The explosion on Brickell Avenue. Why was it necessary to kill two Metro detectives? Can you shed any light on that, Ricardo? Did he tell you it was in the line of duty, all part of *la causa?* Did you really think that blowing up Ben Valera and his partner had something to do with fighting the Castro menace?"

That's when I made my first big mistake. I glanced at my briefcase. Just the merest flicker, but Elena caught me. I could see it click in her eyes. She knew.

"Ricky," she said. "Don't talk to this man. It's a trick."

Then things got very quiet. Ricardo, smiling again, put his finger to his lips and rested the business end of the Beretta against my neck. Elena reached under the chair and retrieved the briefcase. It was locked, of course. Ricardo went through my pockets, very deft and confident, and found the key. Less than a minute later Elena handed the tape cassette to him.

He crushed it under his heel. Elena tossed the tape recorder in the swimming pool. It barely made a splash.

So much for incriminating testimony.

"I think that will be all," Ricardo said, stroking my neck with the barrel. "Do you agree, Arturo?"

"Just let him go," Elena said. "Without his cassette he can accuse you of nothing, Ricky. It was all a bluff."

"Arturo?"

"I'm thinking."

I cleared my throat. "May I say something, please?"

Ricardo shrugged. I got the impression he didn't much care.

"Ask him about Mercedes. Ask him what he was doing out

on the estuary, diving for soggy paintings."

Del Gato said, "Maybe you better shoot him."

"Go on," I urged. "Tell us what happened to Mercedes. And Luis Calzon."

"Give me the gun," Del Gato said, putting out his hand. "I'll fix this. You and Elena can leave it to me."

Ricardo hesitated, considering the request, tempted to turn me over to Del Gato and leave, just pretend nothing had happened.

It was a now or never type of situation. I went for the now.

"He killed them," I said. "Mercedes and her lover were already dead when Arturo arranged the fund-raising party."

Ricardo tightened his grip on the pistol. "That's not possible," he said.

"It was all backwards," I said. "That's what confused me. He didn't steal his own painting to collect the insurance. The painting was already gone. Already damaged. You'll have to ask him exactly how it went down, but my guess is he happened to stroll into the gallery at the wrong moment and caught his wife and her young painter friend in the clinch."

"The gun, please, Ricardo. You are, remember, a guest in my house."

"I don't think it was premeditated," I said. "If it had been, Arturo would have done a much neater job. No, I think he shot them in a jealous rage. Just reached for a weapon and I'll bet he didn't have to reach far in this place. Shot them where they stood. And that's where the bad luck started, right, Arturo?"

Elena said, "I don't believe it. He's still trying to trick you. Arturo, tell him you didn't do it. Tell him Mercedes is in La Paz, visiting her family."

Del Gato was contemptuous. "Why should I tell this *maricone* anything?"

"The bad luck," I said. "That's what made the whole thing so complicated. One of the shots penetrated the painting and lodged in the wall. Check it out, Ricardo. If you look close you can see the plaster repair and the new paint job. And then there was the problem of blood. Blood spattered all over the painting and the wall. What a mess, huh?"

Elena said, "This is a bad dream. A *pesadilla*. Ricky, *mi querido*, tell him you had nothing to do with those two cops. Let Arturo handle his own affair."

"Whose idea was it to ditch the painting with the bodies, Arturo?" I asked. "Was it you? Or Tomas? It was a panic situation, I assume. Clean up the bloody mess, get the bodies into the boat. Yes *that's* what you had to concentrate on, the bodies. How'd you manage it, Tomas? Did you load the fair Mercedes and her lover into one of those big plastic fish crates, wheel them down to the dock? Huh? Arturo, I've got to hand it to you, this is one resourceful *hombre* you got working for you. I'll bet he was the one took charge. Calmed you down. Went out and got the crates and the dolly. Maybe he even handled the plaster repair himself. A regular Señor Fix-it."

Elena said, "Ricky, I think we should leave, right now. You notice how he keeps glancing at the canal? Huh? He sees something out there. Come on, *mi querido*, let's go."

That Elena, what eyes she had. She noticed everything. The briefcase. My concern for the canal. The darkness that seemed to be settling over the Del Gato fortunes. Elena knew, but she couldn't budge Ricardo.

"We can settle this, Arturo," he said. "Get Mercedes on the phone. I don't care about Luis, do you understand? I don't care if you killed that smug little bastard, but let me speak to Mercedes."

I said, "So you took the bodies and the bloody clean-up rags and the ruined painting—everything that was incriminating—and you loaded them into the boat and took them out to the estuary and weighted everything down and slipped them over the side. One thing that puzzles me, Arturo, you went that far, why didn't you go offshore? Out into the really deep water? Afraid you might run into a Marine Patrol? Or did you just get spooked? Is that what happened, Tomas, the boss get spooked and decide he didn't want to go any further, the estuary would have to do?"

"Tomas!" Ricardo said. "Bring us the phone! *Rapido!*"

Tomas did not respond. You had to admire his cool, the way he stood poised by the bar, as if the only thing on his mind was making the perfect martini. Shaken, not stirred. Just a kiss of vermouth.

"Arturo, you must show this *maricone* that you and Mercedes have merely separated, like two civilized people. Like you told me. That she has gone to stay with her family in La Paz. Call her for me, *amigo* let me hear her voice."

"Why all this concern for my wife, Ricardo?" Del Gato said contemptuously. "You have this new, beautiful girl, this lovely Elena. So you no longer need to make love to Mercedes, *correcto?* Look how your eyes drop! You think I did not know?"

Elena said, "There's a boat out there, Ricky. See how slow it's moving?"

Those big brown eyes never missed a trick. A Marine Patrol boat was coming around the bend, gliding ever so slowly into view. That was my cue to push things along.

"Must have been a hell of a shock when you were notified that the provenance was in dispute," I said. "That was more bad luck. You had to produce the painting or explain why it wasn't in your possession. So you went through the motions, invented an excuse to have the house filled with people—a hundred wealthy and powerful suspects, what a nightmare for the cops! But the bad luck kept coming, didn't it Arturo? What rotten luck to draw Detective Valera, who had good reason to hate and distrust you. Most cops would just have gone through the motions, filed the report, but not Ben Valera. He was persistent. Heard the lady of the house was on an extended vacation and he started checking it out."

Del Gato spat. "A *campesino,* you understand? A peasant. In Cuba his people lived like animals. They owned no land. They had nothing. This is why he hated me."

"Maybe," I said. "I think it had more to do with the fact that you inadvertently got his cousin killed. Emilio Vasquez the baker, remember? You had Ricardo drop his name on that sweet-talking show of his, somebody blew him away. All a terrible misunderstanding, but Valera never forgot."

Out on the canal the Marine Patrol boat began to circle, presenting itself in profile, gliding slowly toward the dock. When Del Gato saw it the light seemed to dim in his eyes.

"Valera intended to go to La Paz to check out your wife, Arturo. That's what the homicide boys finally told me. He thought she and her boyfriend had taken the painting, split the country. Never suspected you'd really killed them, that the bodies—and the painting, too—were sinking into the muck of the estuary. When you heard Valera was going to Bolivia—he'd had to buy his own ticket, the department wouldn't finance such a long-shot venture—you panicked again and arranged to have him eliminated. The quickest way possible. No time to arrange for a discreet accident."

Elena said, "What's that boat doing, Ricky? Why has it come?"

I said, "Tell your boyfriend he better look out for himself, Elena. Arturo's ship is finally coming in."

Ricardo was confused. The pistol wavered. "Arturo? What's going on here? Who are those people?"

Del Gato closed his eyes. Maybe he thought that would make the world go away. His nostrils twitched as he breathed heavily.

"Marine Patrol," I said. "They've been out there dredging

since dawn. And now it looks like they're bringing your wife back home where she belongs, Arturo. Or what's left of her."

"Madre de dios!"

Good cops tend to be good actors, able to play a variety of convincing roles, and Detective Sergeant Leland Snyder had a provocative flair for the dramatic. He had placed the two body bags high up on the stern, in full view. They kind of jumped out at you, those body bags. I know they made an impression on Ricardo Blades.

"It's true," he said, "you *did* kill her."

My chief concern at the point was deciding where to duck. Snyder and his boys, working under the assumption that the tape was still rolling, were giving me plenty of time to get everything down on cassette. So the cavalry, in that sense, was destined never to arrive. I was on my own.

Ricardo had let the Beretta droop. His attention was on the Marine Patrol boat and its somber cargo. His anger seemed to have dissipated. The edge was gone. I think it might have played out that way, a sad, dejected tableau of old friends and lovers, resigned to giving up without a struggle, if Arturo hadn't opened his big mouth.

"I made a mistake with Luis," he said, blinking his eyes open. "Luis was just a foolish boy. How could he resist a woman like Mercedes? But you, Ricardo, you were a man. You ate at my table, took my money, slept with my wife. You dishonored me."

Ricardo reacted as if he had something stuck in his throat. As if physically revulsed by the mere proximity of Del Gato. He, too, had a flair for dramatic provocation. He let the Beretta fall to the ground and stood up, turning his back. The ultimate *machismo* gesture.

"Come Elena," he said, holding his hand out for her. "I want to have a word with the police."

That's when things got noisy and confusing. I wasn't really

able to sort it all out until after the shooting stopped. When Del Gato made his move for the gun I very prudently threw myself under the chair and tried to cover my head with a cushion.

Maria would have approved of my caution. When you have seven mouths to feed you play it safe. So I never actually saw Del Gato shoot his old pal Ricardo Blades in the back and I never saw Tomas, cool and calculating, go under the bar and come up with a Smith & Wesson .38 revolver and put a slug dead in the center of Arturo Del Gato's heart, thereby eliminating a potentially damaging witness at his own trial, if it ever came to that, and probably saving Elena's life and mine, too, for that matter.

It was Leland Snyder who came in and lifted the cushion off my head.

"What a goddamn mess," he said. "I hope you got it all on tape."

1 2

They never did recover the bodies of Mercedes and her handsome young lover. Maybe they drifted out on the tide, or were consumed by crabs. Maybe they're still down there, sinking deeper into the mud, becoming part of the life cycle of the estuary.

The stunt Snyder and I had cooked up, with the body bags stuffed with life jackets, didn't work out the way we'd expected. I had nothing on tape and Del Gato never flat out admitted he'd killed anyone. Not that it mattered in his case, but it would have been nice to bring Tomas to trial as an accessory and see how well he could keep his cool.

The way it worked out, Tomas was never even indicted. At the inquest into Del Gato's death it was decided that his use of deadly force was justified, considering Del Gato's unstable state of mind, which yours truly had to testify to under oath. So Tomas got off. Last I heard he was managing a restaurant on the Calle Ocho.

Sal Carlucci gave me a hard time about that.

"Son of a goddamn bitch," he roared, drowning out the juke in the background. "The bastard was involved in a cop killing. Couldn't you lie a little?"

Maybe I should have. But the way I look at it, I had a hand in making sure two out of three bad guys can't do bad things anymore. Check out the latest criminal justice statistics—two out of three ain't bad. And if you agree, maybe you could drop into the noisy joint Sal Carlucci runs and tell him to get off my case. The guy is *never* satisfied. Even returning that deadly painting didn't make him happy.

As to WGAT, it's still on the air under new ownership, although the format is pretty much the same. Salsa and politics. Elena Prios took over the Ricardo Blades' show. She tries hard, but she just can't seem to muster up the same level of venom. Nobody's been blown up lately. Assassinations are down. Life goes on.

And we've got another mouth to feed. I surrendered to a weak impulse and brought the white Persian home to Key Largo. The kids were delighted, of course. Maria gave me a dark look, but secretly she's pleased to have another lady in the house.

We haven't settled on a name yet. Any suggestions?

DARK FLIGHT

by
Ed Gorman

    I should have known better than to ask Bannion for his car. I'd forgotten about the seat cover speech that always goes along with it.

    Frank Bannion is a man of my age and my fortunes, which is to say he's retired, doesn't feel he hears often enough from his son, and spends most of his time down on Fourth Avenue at the Legion Lanes or across the street in Greene Square Park, which was were I found him that bright Tuesday morning last April.

    Because it was lunchtime, the park was filled with young people from the downtown office buildings, dining from sack lunches or the hot dog vendor's cart on the corner. I imagined that Don, my son who lived in Denver and worked for IBM, probably looked a lot like the kids here, well groomed, well behaved, and in much better physical condition than my generation had ever been. As I walked toward the center of the park, which now sits across from a three-story parking garage but which once sat across from a sprawling and splendid railroad depot, I even felt a few vague longings for some of the young ladies flicking back blond hair or taking delicate bites out of sandwiches. Nobody will ever take the place of Sharon, my wife who died in the winter of 1981, but loneliness gets formidable sometimes.

    Bannion is bald and round. He's usually dressed in wrinkled blue trousers and a wide brown western belt with a buckle the size of a hubcap that reads Frank and a wrinkled permanent press white shirt with the sleeves rolled up so you can see a fading dragon tattoo beneath ginger hair on his left forearm. He sat on a park bench and when he saw me, shook his head and nodded toward a lone black man under a tree to our left. "Colored guys," he said when I sat down. "That's all we get in this park any more. Colored guys and drug addicts."

I smiled. "You know something Frank?"

"What?"

"If I'd had two heart attacks the way you have, I don't think I'd let myself get so worked up over stuff like that."

"He's probably a drug addict, too"

The young man wore a gray three-piece suit, a blue-and-white striped shirt, and a maroon necktie. He was the color of creamed coffee and was one of the most presentable people in the park.

He'd never done anything to irritate Frank personally; it was just that Frank put him in the same category as Japanese, non-Catholics, republicans, and military vets who bowled out at Westdale or Lancer Lanes instead of at the Legion, "us WW2 guys have to stick together, Parnell," he always said.

"You want a hot dog?" I said.

"What's this?"

"Huh?"

"You asked if I wanted a hot dog?"

"Right."

He frowned. He is a past master at frowning. When Frank Bannion frowns the whole world should reach for a bottles of Pepto. "You want my car."

"Well, yeah, I guess."

He looked at me with a harsh blue gaze. "Your goddamn heap in the garage again?"

"Fan belt."

"When the hell are you gonna get a new car?"

"When you gonna loan me the money?"

"So why you need it?"

"I got a job."

"A job? we're retired."

"An investigation job."

The frown again. "Hell, Parnell, you put all those years in with the Linn County Sheriff's Department. Isn't that enough?" He took a sip of his Diet 7-Up. "Anyway, you got a job. Managing that apartment house."

"The Alma isn't always real exciting, Frank."

"You want excitement, watch the fights."

This was part I hated about Bannion. Whenever he did you a favor, he made you crawl for it. You had to tell him all the details. It was like being twelve years old again and pleading with your old man to sleep over at somebody's house.

So I sat there and talked. As I talked I looked around at the Cedar Rapids Gazette building on one corner, the beautiful spires of First Presbyterian on the other, and then at the railroad tracks that divide the downtown area and mark the business district proper from the Iowa Electric Building that dominates the skyline to the skywalk system that connects all the major business and shopping buildings. Greene Square Park was first plotted in 1849 and sometimes, particularly on warm spring nights after Sharon's death, I came down here and sat on a bench and smoked a dozen or so Winstons and wondered what it would have been like to just have been sitting here since the day the park was opened. I would have seen the countryside giving way to the city, then the emergence of the railroad, the spirited noise of World War I, then the silver streak of airplanes against the blue prairie sky and the darkness and screams of World War II, and then at last the new city here, as calculated to please as downtown Kansas City only more pleasant because of the warm breezes off the nearby Cedar River and the refurbishment of buildings that date back to the late 1800's.

"So who's Carlucci?"

"I've mentioned him, Frank." Bannion doesn't like to admit his memory is going. But then none of us do. "Salvatore Carlucci. We were in the war together, in the occupation forces in Italy."

"Oh yeah, that's right." He still didn't remember but he was making a good show of pretending otherwise.

"One of our duties was to guard a museum outside of Salerno."

"Sounds like dangerous work."

Did I mention that Frank can also be a wearying wise-ass?

"Anyway, during our museum duty, the place was robbed and one of our best friends—a kid from Idaho named Jim Wyman—was killed."

"Why the hell would somebody stick up a museum?"

"This particular museum had a series of small paintings called 'Ladies in the Cathedral.' Very beautiful things. If you're into that. Anyway, there were five of the paintings and they were all stolen."

More 7-Up. Another frown about the young man under the tree. A glance up at an especially sweet-looking woman in an especially nice-looking peasant skirt and white blouse. "Hell, Ralph," he said, "that was what—forty-some years ago?"

"Right."

"And you're going to start working on the case now?"

"Carlucci called yesterday morning. He said that the Italian government has hired him to get the paintings back. This old Italian who was dying told the government where the paintings were. He was one of the thieves who took them. He wanted to settle an old score with one of the other thieves. Anyway, it runs out one of the paintings is supposed to be here, in Cedar Rapids.

So the Italian government wants them back—five paintings in five different American cities. So I called a local art dealer named Frederick Davies and thought I'd go talk to him. I've got a one o'clock appointment." I reached in my pocket and took out a Winston. The first drag tasted like the sulphur of the match. "I'm cutting you in for ten percent of whatever I get."

"What if you get nothing?"

"Then I pay for the gas and pay for one of those fifteen dollar auto shines you get up on First Avenue?"

"Really?"

"Really."

He took out the keys and looked at them. They might have been his son and he might have been sending him to war. Some more frowning. "I want to tell you about the seat covers."

"Oh, no. Frank. Not the seat cover speech." I was grinning.

"I bought those special clear plastic kind so the original seats I got from the used car lot wouldn't get all messed up. So you know the rules, right, Parnell?"

"Right."

"No smoking, no drinkin' anything, no Dairy Queens, nothin' like that, anywhere near the interior of the car."

"Right," I said, watching a robin strut across a patch of vivid green grass toward a perfect golden circle of warm sunlight. The air was sweet with violets, roses, and appleblossoms.

"And use that cushion I've got for your butt so in case the bottoms of your pants are dirty you won't get nothin' on the seat covers."

"I got it, Frank."

"And one more thing."

"What?"

"Don't change the radio dial. It doesn't work so good and it's a bitch to use. I've got it set on WMT AM and I don't want you to do what you did last time. That rock and roll station."

"I kinda like rock and roll," I said.

"I know," he said, handing me the keys. "But I like you anyway."

2

The names are beautiful, Indian Hill Road, White Eagle Road, and High Stable Road, and so are the homes that are hidden in the deep woods on either side: clapboard, cedar, and red brick glimpsed through the budding trees and heavy green foliage. When you live near the downtown area, the lives lived out here are almost unimaginable. You wonder what's it like to go for a sunny morning walk when the grass is golden with dawn sunlight and the mint leaves heavy with moisture. You wonder what it's like to get into your Mercedes and go to work. You wonder what it's like to unthinkingly hand over your American Express Gold for whatever whim strikes you. Of course, this was also the kind of neighborhood paperboys like to tell stories about—at least the poor ones do—how there are two Caddies in the driveway but never enough cash to pay their paper bill.

Frederick Davies lived down a twisting piece of blacktop at the head of which was a No Trespassing sign. I angled the Pontiac down a steep turn and five minutes later pulled into a horseshoe-shaped driveway in the middle of which sat a large Georgian-style house with siding and shutters painted a warm brown with gray tint, accented with a paler gray trim. The front door, almost a shock, was a high-gloss and dramatic red.

I parked and got out, lighting a Winston as I shut the car door. I'd kept my word to Bannion. I figured with my luck, I'd light up and a stray piece of ember would float down and put a pustule in Bannion's seat.

I stood by the car a minute. The sunlight was hot. The surrounding woods—shortleaf pine, silver maple, quaking aspen—pitched steeply to a ravine below. It would be chilly in the shade of the woods and sweet with goldenrod, spiderwort, and wild hyacinth. There would be barnswallows, yellow warblers, and prairie falcons, and I supposed that's why I liked living in the Midwest so much. Fifteen minutes from downtown, you could be deep into nature.

I got about six drags from my Winston—so quick it burned especially hot—and then I went up the three broad steps to the fine red door and knocked. In the silence, the knock sounded rude.

I tried three times before I went over to the adjacent two-stall garage and peeked in through the window of the closed overhead door. Inside, show-room clean, sat an antique red MG and a new tan Jeep Wagoner. A plump calico cat sat on the trunk of the MG watching me. He did not seem impressed. He yawned a pink disdainful yawn and fell immediately asleep.

Unless Mr. Davies had gone out for a walk, or unless he'd gone for a ride in somebody else's car, he was inside his house.

Assuming that he might have been taking a late shower and hadn't heard me, had been on the john with a magazine, or deep into a phone conversation upstairs, I went back to the red door. This time I got serious. I used the knocker and the doorbell, the chimes bursting with cheer, and finally I used my fist the way I always had back in my days with the sheriff's department, without social poise, just banging to get noticed. And still Mr. Davies did not reply. Instinctively, I tried the knob and let myself in.

When you're a law officer as long as I was, you get nervous when you don't have a piece with you. There are certain times that are always dangerous and walking into a house in this fashion is one of them. You start to remember other men you knew who walked into houses in these circumstances. Briney, who was shot point blank by a husband who had just killed his wife. Zitek, who was surprised by the burglar he'd been looking for and stabbed eight times in the chest. Carney, who come upon three members of a street gang doing a drug deal. For some reason, the gang thought it would be neat to kill him execution style, complete with a bag over his head.

The living room was startling in its drama, with coral walls, eighteenth century furnishings including an antique settee in the bay window, and a beautiful cream-colored fireplace with gold candelabra at either end of the mantle. Easy enough to imagine a professor who fussed with the problems of students, retreating here at the end of day to smoking jacket, pipe, slippers, his book and a wife, beautiful and compliant beyond imagining. I wondered if Davies had a life like that.

My footsteps creaked across the parquet floor as I called out Davies' name and worked myself across the room behind the couch, which was where I found him. Louder than the jays on the patio, louder than the oaks creaking in the spring breeze, my heart started hammering. I sighed, feeling exhausted as I saw the soggy hole in the back of his head.

3

"So you never talked to him?"

"Just that once on the phone."

"You used to be a detective with the sheriff's department, right?"

"Right."

"Mind if I ask why you were talking with Mr. Davies?"

"I had some questions for him. About a piece of missing art work."

"Missing art work?"

"A private investigator in New York asked me to check into the art scene out here. He'd heard rumors that a painting he was looking for was in Cedar Rapids."

"Cedar Rapids? I mean, with all due respect to the founding fathers, Cedar Rapids isn't Paris."

"Or even Chicago."

"But your guy in New York thinks it really might be out here?"

"That's what he says."

"You've got a license, of course?"

"A license?"

"A state-issued private investigator's license?"

"I was kind of hoping you'd ask," I said, smiling. "I've had this thing four years and nobody's ever asked to see it."

You have your homicide investigator and you have your criminalist. Then you have your coroner. In addition you've got at least two other detectives and maybe a half-dozen uniformed men but you don't see them tramping around the premises the way they do on TV and for a simple reason. Because if they do go tramping around, they're likely to destroy everything from footprints to tire marks. So the homicide investigator has to keep strict control of his whole team, just as Powers, the man in charge here, was doing now. In addition to asking me for my license, he was dispatching people to certain parts of the house the way a basketball coach makes key substitutes at a critical point in the ballgame.

"You didn't see anybody?" Powers said, handing me back my laminated license. Powers was in his fifties, with a strong if not handsome Irish face, thinning white hair and a blue pinstripe suit that almost made him seem white-collar. The rough hands with traces of oil beneath the nails, said otherwise. He'd be one of those guys who worked on cars in his spare time.

"Nobody," I said.

"Hear anything?"

"Nope."

Powers touched a finger to the tip of his nose. "You assuming his death had something to do with this painting."

"I'm not assuming anything."

Powers looked around the house. "Some place, huh?"

"We probably won't be living in a place like this."

"You see the upstairs?"

"No."

"You should see the tub. Looks like a lap pool."

"I assumed he had money."

"He also had something else, apparently."

"What?"

He reached over to an end table and turned a gilt-framed photograph up. "You see this?"

"Huh-uh."

"There are six pictures of her throughout the house and every one of them looks like this."

She was in her early thirties, blond, sad-eyed, and fragile as a leaf fluttering to earth. The gravity of her eyes said that she wasn't nearly as weak as her soft erotic mouth might mislead you into believing. There was more than a hint of destructive madness in those eyes, the kind her air of fragility would disguise fetchingly. She was both the kind of woman you wanted instantly to help and the kind of woman who could get you into a great deal of trouble helping. The glass on the photograph had been smashed. You had to look behind the shards and splinters to see her. The smashed-in effect only enhanced the quality of her eyes. She seemed smashed-up, too.

"Six photos of the same woman. All the same photo," Powers said.

"Wonder if he did it?"

"Shattered all the frames?"

"Yeah."

He set the photograph down carefully. "That's what I was wondering." He glanced down at where the corpse had been. Now there was a chalk outline and ruts of dark blood on the Oriental rug. "Bad enough you and I have to die, Parnell." He pointed out the spectacular living room again. "He had to die and give all this up."

"Yeah," I said, "I know what you mean."

4

I called Bannion and told him what happened so he'd let me keep his car, then I drove back to the Alma but before I could open the door, a plump elderly lady called down from the tier of apartments above. Mrs. Sizemore was having trouble with her cat again.

She wanted me to check the vomit and see if I could find hairballs in it. A few years earlier, one of Mrs. Sizemore's other cats had died of a disease I still did not understand. That cat had thrown up a lot but there had never been hairballs. Hairballs were a sign, apparently, that a cat was just being a cat. So now when this one, Timothy, threw up, Mrs. Sizemore always got very anxious, spending most of her day in one of the front pews of Immaculate Conception, which is four blocks from the Alma, the eight-plex apartment building I manage in return for free rent.

Now, I knelt next to a dried chunk of kitty vomit in the middle of Mrs. Sizemore's tiny living room. She had thoughtfully given me a piece of paper towel. I scooped the stuff up and took it into the bathroom. Mrs. Sizemore is one of those people who believes that bathrooms should never smell like bathrooms. She's got candles; she's got Air Wick; she's got blue stuff in her toilet bowl. I clipped on the light, there being no windows in the bathrooms of the Alma, and had a good long look at the gray mess in the paper towels.

"Hairballs," I shouted back to Mrs. Sizemore, who was pacing around the living room, clutching the oversized tomcat to her frail bosom. "Definitely hairballs."

"Oh, thank God, Mr. Parnell. Thank God." At which point, working her arms around the big ball of Timothy, she managed to make a sign of the cross.

I dropped the paper towel and its contents into the small metal wastepaper can with the portrait of the beautiful 1920's girl in profile on its side, and went back into the living room.

The Alma's apartments are laid out this way: You have a walkway leading to your front door, said door opening on to your living room, then a small hallway to the right, leading abruptly to the bathroom on the left and abruptly to the bedroom on the right. You find the kitchen in back of the living room, behind louvered doors. The man who owns the place, a Mr. Albrand who spends most of his time in Florida, was not happy the day that I suggested we advertise the apartments as "efficiencies." He said don't be ridiculous, don't be stupid, don't be moronic, these are not efficiencies. These are full-size apartments. But of course full-size apartments don't have four-feet deep kitchens behind louvered doors.

Mrs. Sizemore's living room always reminded me of the Catholic store I passed every day on my four-mile walk. Every kind of religious object imaginable was hung, draped, nailed, or taped to the wall. Palm, for example, lay across a painting of a beatific Jesus whose brown gaze seemed slightly cross-eyed. The thing was, I was Catholic myself and yet all this stuff vaguely embarrassed me and I wasn't even sure why.

Mrs. Sizemore was one of those fortunate few whose weight seemed to help. She was maybe five-three and perhaps one-eighty, but somehow her fleshiness made her seem much younger than her seventy-some years. Timothy, resentful that he'd been held so long, growled and jumped from her arms. "We still should let them play someday."

"Herman and Timothy?"

"Yes."

"I'm not sure Mrs. Sizemore. Last time we tried it, remember, Timothy took a big hunk out of Herman's side." Herman is my Russian blue, a feline as big as Timothy but not anywhere near as mean.

"Timothy gets rambunctious is all." She had caught my tone. Her gray perm, dark eyes, and thin lips all seemed very tight right now. She had a disposition not unlike Timothy's. "Anyway, you should have heard Herman this morning. He was really raising Cain."

Mrs. Sizemore lives in the apartment directly above mine. After last year, when her husband died, she began taking an undue interest in my affairs. Easy enough to imagine her with a glass pressed to the floor, trying to hear everything that was going on in my apartment.

"He was?" I said.

"Most definitely, Mr. Parnell. He knocked several things over." She nodded to the TV. "I even heard him over *The New Dating Game.*"

"That doesn't sound like Herman. Most of the time he just lies around in the sunlight and sleeps. He's getting pretty old." Fifteen years old. I dreaded his loss. I prepared for two things when that grim day came—missing Herman himself and having to keep my grief to myself. People just don't understand when you mourn cats. They really don't.

But I was curious now. "When did you hear this noise?"

"Let's see. *The New Dating Game* is on right after *The New Price is Right*. . . . Hmmm, I suppose around one-fifteen."

"You sure?"

"Yes." Her eyes had narrowed. Something's wrong, isn't it, Mr. Parnell?"

You have to be careful with Mrs. Sizemore. Give the slightest hint that something is amiss, and everybody in the apartment complex is coming up to you with advice or sympathy. I had a bad cold once which Mrs. Sizemore had decided was something far more sinister. Several of the residents had virtually put me in my grave until I finally relented and went to the doctor and he told me I had bronchial pneumonia. The odd thing is, I sort of appreciate Mrs. Sizemore's concern. It's nice to have somebody care about you; it's just that it gets oppressive at times.

I patted Timothy on the flat of his head. He bared one long tooth that hung down like an icicle. Apparently he was too tired to get mad. Timothy doesn't like being touched.

"Well, Mrs. Sizemore, everything's fine here, so I guess I'll go back to my apartment."

She nodded, but it was obvious that she had one more thing to say to me. "I saw Faith and Hoyt today. Hoyt was in his stroller. He looked so cute." She paused, knowing what the pause would mean to me. "Faith asked me how you were doing."

Faith Hallahan is a thirty-six-year-old who lives across the street. A year and a half ago, following a split with her live-in stockbroker, Ken, we had what you would probably call a thing. It hadn't been a big thing, running four weeks max, but it had been intense—me, because I was so lonely, she, because she was so scared. She had never been dumped before. According to Faith, the result of our "thing" had been the birth of a child she'd named Hoyt Patrick Hallahan. Hoyt is not my favorite name. But since I've never been quite sure that the kid is even mine—though I pay her a quarter of my Social Security a month and give her all I can besides—I don't want to hassle her about names. If "Hoyt" is fine by her, "Hoyt" is fine by me. Anyway, Faith, one of those slight, freckled redheads whose fragile beauty can be almost punishing in its splendor, is given to tears, and I'm still not good around tears, mine or anybody elses'.

"Thanks for telling me Mrs. Sizemore," I said.

"She's such a nice girl. Such a nice girl."

I nodded and went down to see if I could find out who had burglarized my apartment.

5

When I got back to Cedar Rapids after the war, Third Avenue up to Nineteenth Street was still fashionable. On Sundays you saw shiny new Packards, shiny new Buicks, and shiny new Cadillacs parked in the driveways of the big three-story houses with the Victorian gingerbreading, cupolas, and widow's walks. I'm not even sure when it changed, exactly. You never are. It happens block by block and then suddenly eleven blocks have been converted into apartment houses and a few small businesses appear and then you don't have so good a neighborhood any-more, at least not by real-estate standards. I didn't have any idea, when Sharon and I would Sunday-drive down this block, that someday all these palaces would be frayed apartment houses.

The biggest problem these days is the crime rate, which has to do directly with drugs. Within the past four years there have been four major busts at the Cedar Rapids airport—connections from Florida as well as Central America. So in case you have the idea that my city is little more than green pastureland, you're wrong. Metro population, which is everything comfortably reached by Route 1-380, is about 200,000 and an alarming proportion of that number seems to be involved with drugs, either as users, pushers, or both.

So I expected to find my apartment had been tossed by a druggie.

After leaving Mrs. Sizemore's, I went downstairs and out to the garage in back where I picked up a garden shovel, something that makes an excellent weapon because of its weight and its sharp edges.

The Alma is constructed of concrete blocks that get spraypainted a different color every four years. When the owner tore down the previous house, he had the grace and sense to leave two big oak trees, on one of which you can find carved a lover's heart dating back to 1942. It reads "KJ Loves RL." I wonder if one of the initials might not have belonged to a soldier, it being 1942 and all, and if the soldier made it back all right.

I was thinking about this as I passed the oak and headed to my apartment.

I had just put my hand on the doorknob when the door of the adjacent apartment swung open. It was Mr. Dodds and as always he wore K-Mart house slippers, gray work pants, a blue work shirt, and a cardigan sweater that looked as if moths dined on it regularly. He always reminded me of an astigmatic Captain Kangaroo. "Morning, Mr. Parnell."

"Morning, Mr. Dodds,"

"Beautiful day."

"It sure is."

"Got my checkup this afternoon."

Six years ago, doctors had discovered a small trace of cancer on Mr. Dodds' nose. They removed it and everything seemed fine but he never missed his checkups. He was a sweet old bastard, maybe as old as eighty-five; I wasn't sure.

"Wish me luck, Mr. Parnell."

"You know I do, Mr. Dodds." He reached down and picked up his Gazette and started back inside. He paused. "Say, is everything all right?"

"I don't follow you, Mr. Dodds."

"Just a minute or so ago I heard this noise from your apartment."

"Just a minute or so ago?"

"Yep. Terrible noise, too. Terrible noise."

"Thank you, Mr. Dodds."

"Everything all right?"

"Everything's fine, Mr. Dodds."

"See you, then."

"See you, Mr. Dodds."

By now whoever was in my apartment obviously knew I was coming in. I wondered if the burglar had a knife. A gun. Certainly he would be just as afraid as I was.

I took out my key, unlocked the door, and then pushed it back abruptly, so that it slammed hard against the opposite wall.

What I was looking at was my ancient twenty-one-inch black and white RCA console. It had mahogany veneer and we got it for Christmas in 1966, one of those joint presents people without undue money always give each other.

The rest of the stuff in the apartment had to be just as dispiriting to an enterprising thief. The operative word was old. Not as in antique but as in worn. There was an oak veneer drop leaf table with one of those big white knit tablecloths that looks like a huge doily. There was an overstuffed couch with throwrugs tossed over the back to cover up the worst of the worn spots. There was a small bookcase crammed with paperbacks—my taste running to unlikely tales of crime such as those by Agatha

Christie and Max Brand, whom I think is a lot better than Louis
L'Amour, despite the fact that you can't escape Louis these
days—and a pea green recliner where I sit at night in the darkness
and listen to the Larry King show on radio, with matching
ottoman and floor lamp. Once in a while, getting nostalgic, I play
one of the old radio tapes, "The Shadow" with Orson Welles,
Fibber McGee 'n Molly, or my favorite Jack Benny, and sometimes there in the darkness, it's 1952 again and Sharon is alive.
Red-haired, blue-eyed, and laughing, and very much alive.

But now it was daylight and I was standing here with a
garden shovel in my hand and there was somebody in my
apartment. I said, "You can make this easy for both of us. You
can just come out." I moved a few inches closer to the door. My
heart raced. I wasn't sure what inspired it. Fear or excitement.
Maybe both. "You here me? This is a ground floor apartment,
there's only one way out and that's through this door. You
understand?"

Cars went by in the street and trucks went by and on the
sidewalk poor young mothers pushed strollers.

From inside the bathroom. I heard a scraping noise. The
burglar had accidentally pushed against something. I took a few
more steps into the apartment. I had the shovel ready to go.

"Darn."

Probably it was the tone of voice that made me smile. I was
all ready to meet some street punk—black or white, didn't
matter—high or wanting to be high, mean out of necessity if not
malice, wanting nothing more than to knock me down and beat
it out of here.

I wasn't ready for the girlish, forlorn "darn" that came
floating from behind the partially closed bathroom door. The
sound reminded me of my niece when she lost at jacks or when
the dress on her doll wouldn't quite fit right.

  I wasn't sure hardened criminals said "darn." At least not in that tone of voice.

  "You coming out?" I said.

  "I guess I don't have a lot of choice." Pause. "You don't have a gun or anything, do you?"

  "Why don't we decide when you get out here?"

  "You're not a sadist, are you?"

  "What?"

  "A sadist? You're not going to beat me up. are you?"

  By now I had fixed her, in my ex-cop's way, as in her early twenties, well-educated, and very nervous. I sighed. "Why don't you come out here?"

  "Are you going to call the police?"

  "Maybe."

  "This isn't what it seems."

  "What does it seem?"

  "Well, you know."

  "No, I don't know."

  "Like I broke in or something."

  "Were you invited in."

  "Well, no."

  "Did you have a key?"

  Irritated pause. "You know I don't have a key."

  I said, "Then I'd have to say that sort of sounds like breaking and entering to me."

  "You're enjoying this, aren't you?"

  "Why don't you come out."

  The bathroom door squeaked open and there she was. You noticed two things about her immediately—she was very beautiful and something long ago happened to her right ankle. She was crippled.

  Oh, yes, there was one other thing I noticed about her. She

was the same woman in the smashed picture frame back at Frederick Davies' house.

6

She kept her eyes low and that told me how painful it was for her to have others watch her. It wasn't a bad limp but it was certainly one you noticed. In the war I'd known a man with a harelip and when he was drunk it was all he talked about.

She wore a white spring dress with fancy blue hose and dark blue ballet shoes. Her golden hair was caught up with tiny red barrettes. She had wonderful wrists and a sad gorgeous mouth and somber brown eyes that always seemed about to smile but never quite succeeded.

"You going to tell me how you got in?"

She just sort of shrugged. "That'll explain it." She nodded to a small white envelope on the drop leaf table.

"You could save me the trouble of reading."

For the first time she laughed. "Gee, are you kind of like a tough guy or what?"

"Not that I'm aware of."

"Well, you sure sound grouchy."

"You just broke into my apartment."

"That's why I left the envelope. Because I had to break the window near the door and then reach in and let myself in. I left a check for twenty-five dollars in the envelope to cover the cost of the glass. My name's on the check and everything."

I went over and picked up the envelope and tore it open. Just as she said, there was a check inside. The check gave her name as Emma Croft. I put envelope and everything in my front shirt pocket.

"I assume you're going to explain."

"You mind if I smoke while I explain?"

"I'll join you."

"You mind if I sit down?"

"You must really be afraid of me."

"I just don't want to impose."

"You don't consider breaking and entering imposing?"

She fluttered a smile toward me. "I guess I see what you mean."

I ended up getting us both Cokes. We sat in the living room, her quite primly on the edge of the couch, me in the recliner with my feet on the ottoman, a Coke in one hand and a Winston in the other, and Herman, my big Russian blue, sitting in a patch of sunlight dozing.

The first thing she said was, "They're going to think John killed Davies. That's why I needed to find out what you had to do with everything."

"I wish I had some idea of what you're talking about."

"Frederick Davies. He was killed because he knew where a certain painting was. Or said he did, anyway. And that's why the police will think John did it."

"Who is John."

She made a little face, then sighed. She had nice small breasts and they moved pleasantly with her sigh. "I shouldn't be dragging him into this."

"If you think the police suspect him of killing Davies, that's hardly 'dragging him in.'"

"That's true." She took a long cigarette from a fancy silver case and said, "I smoke too much." She lighted her cigarette. The smoke was ice blue in the sunlight. Herman's gray nose twitched when the smoke wafted his way. "I need to ask you a question."

"I thought I was asking you questions."

"Why did you go out to Davies'?"

"Now why would I answer something like that?"

"Because I need to get it clear."

"Get what clear?"

"What your part is in all this."

I stubbed out my cigarette. "What's your part in all this?"

"It's simple. John is my fiancé. He and Frederick were business partners in various art ventures. They both heard of 'Ladies in the Cathedral' and how valuable the five different pieces are and then they heard that one of those pieces was here in Cedar Rapids. Somebody at the Downey Gallery supposedly had it. They were going to buy it from this person and then mark it up."

"So what happened?"

"Davies." She made another face. "You could never trust him. He was always putting the moves on me, for instance, whenever John was out of town."

"Is this why he had so many photographs of you in his house?"

She flushed. "He labored under the delusion that he was in love with me."

"I doubt it would be that hard to fall in love with you. You make it sound like a chore."

"My ankle, Mr. Parnell. Men react very curiously to it."

"How so?"

"I realize I'm not unattractive but even better for certain types of men, my ankle makes me seem very vulnerable. They like that a great deal. It makes them feel very powerful—there's this pretty girl they get to protect. It has nothing to do with me. Just with their own need to feel powerful."

"You make people's feelings sound very tidy and knowable. I'm not sure they are."

"Well Davies' were, let me assure you."

I sipped the Coke and wished instantly I hadn't. Some days

the stomach goes bad for no discernible reason at all. I then eat my own weight in Tums. "Why did you break in here?"

"I wanted to know who you were. I wanted to see if you were working with Davies to cheat John out of his share of the profits."

"How did you even know about me?"

"I—I was at Davies' when you called him." She flushed again.

"I though you didn't get along."

"I was—spying, I suppose you'd call it. I pretended I was there because he'd asked me over for a drink."

"I see."

"Then later that night—" She stopped herself.

"Later that night what?"

She shook her lovely head. "You'll find out sooner or later." She blew more smoke toward Herman. "Later that night John came out and they had a terrible argument. John accused Davies of cheating him."

"Cheating him?"

"Ummm-hmmm. John put up half the cash to buy the painting but when he asked Davies who the seller was, Davies wouldn't tell him. Davies wanted to give him his money back."

"Why would he do that?"

"That's how Davies did business. Obviously, he'd already used John's money and bought the piece."

"So he gives John his money back, with a little interest maybe, and doesn't have to cut him in on the real haul."

"Exactly."

"Sounds like a nice fellow."

"He wasn't, believe me. He wasn't."

"How did you know that Davies was dead?"

"I knew you'd ask me that."

"Seems a fair question."

"I was out there this morning."

"And he was dead?"

"Yes." She took a very deep breath and then pointed to the phone. "May I make a call."

"All right."

She stared at me a long moment. "You still don't trust me, do you?"

"Now that you mention it, I guess I don't."

"I just want to make sure that nothing happens to John." She got up and crossed the floor tc the phone. Her walking looked painful again. She was slightly out of breath when she picked up the receiver.

She dialed and said, "Millie, is John there?" She paused a moment and then glanced over at me and said, "Oh, God. Oh, God."

7

"That's Ryan's car," she said, thirty-two minutes later.

"Who's Ryan?"

"John's lawyer. And friend."

She pointed to a red BMW. It had a certain arrogance parked alongside the new three-story Linn County jail, which is located on an island, along with City Hall, in the middle of the Cedar River. The other cars belonged to deputies and people who needed rustproofing, new windshields, and rear bumpers. We had come over here in a rust-brown Porsche. The only time I'd ever been in a Porsche was maybe fifteen years earlier when I'd busted a psychiatrist for possession of drugs. My partner had taken the shrink back to the jail in our car. I'd driven the Porsche. I'd played the radio very loud and generally had a good time.

"What a depressing place," she said.

"Not if you knew how long it took to get this place built," I said, leading her up the steps. For years the county supervisors had been trying to get a combination jail and communications center set up for the entire county to use. The previous jail, which had huddled on the same location, had been best known for the number of sewer rats it housed at any given time. This facility, only a few years old now, was a beauty.

I said hello to at least ten people before I ran into the sheriff. A tall man, with the sort of graying hair and level gaze you like to see in politicians, he put out his hand and listened as I explained why I was here, and who the girl was. Sheriff Robert Lyman said, "Why don't you have her go down the hall with the matron? She can see her boyfriend and his lawyer. Maybe we can talk a minute."

"Sure."

I sent her off and then went inside Lyman's office. His desk was covered with pictures of his grandkids. He could have started and orphanage. On the wall behind his desk was a blown-up photograph of Lyman in his lock-up days. That's how you start out in the sheriff's department. Working lock-up, which, no matter how nice the facility, is not always the most pleasant job. Some prisoners probably shouldn't be in jail, being victims of whatever people become victims of, but others belong in deep dark solitary holes in the ground and it's the proximity to these people that can get you down after a while. After four or five years of lock-up you graduate to patrol. Being out and about never felt so good. Lyman started out in lock-up and then went to patrolman, then investigator, and finally a few years ago he decided to run for office. It was a nasty campaign but then the sheriff's campaign usually is. It so happened that I'd voted for him. He was a good man, bright, dutiful, as even-handed as you can be in a high-pressure job like his.

He said, "They've got him, Parnell. You know that?"

"That was my impression."

"They put him in the residence arguing with the dead man."

"An arguments one thing. Killing somebody's another."

"Then a neighbor puts him driving back there late last night after Davies' other guests had gone home."

I shook my head.

"That's also," he said, "about the time the coroner puts the time of death."

I patted for my Winstons. I was out. "You don't still smoke, do you?"

"Are you kidding? With all those grandkids? They indoctrinate them in grade school these days. You're a real bad guy if you smoke."

"Yeah," I said.

"He must have money."

"So I'm told."

"His lawyer doesn't come cheap."

"I noticed."

"You think it was over her?"

"The girl? No," I said. "At least she says not."

He stared at me with reasonable brown eyes. "You going to tell me anything?"

I laughed. "Technically, I can't. I'm working for her."

"So my name carried a little weight after all."

"A little." I'd used him as a reference for my private investigator's license. In Iowa, if you don't get along with law enforcement, you don't get along at all.

"Well, I guess I'll go see how things are going."

"She's sure pretty," he said as I left his office.

He had one of those patrician faces I don't like because they make me feel sorry for myself. I don't suppose I really wish I'd had all the advantages John Fairbain had. For one thing, I wouldn't have nearly as many good stories to tell over beers down at the Legion. But he wasn't likable, at least not to me. Even in his grief there was a petulance you wanted to smack off his face.

He sat in a small, very clean room at a small, very clean table. There was a single barred window through which came pure golden sunlight. He had been crying. He looked exhausted and confused and angry. His prison coveralls were baggy on him. He had blue eyes, a fine nose, a pink mouth, and lots of curly auburn hair. He looked up and said, "Who's this?"

"This is the private detective I told you about, John," Emma Croft said.

"What the hell's he doing here?" Fairbain snapped.

"Take it easy, John," Thomas Ryan said. He looked like the kind of guy you always caught with other men's wives out on a lonely country road somewhere. A short man with the sharp and pitiless profile of a Roman senator, he was dressed in a three-piece gray suit, a red-and-white-striped shirt, a blue paisley tie and a wide gold collar bar. He had a grip that suggested racquetball or occasional weight lifting. He had blue eyes that never stopped smiling. You learn to do that when you spend enough time in the courtroom. "I'm Thomas Ryan," he said. Obviously he did not mind hearing his own name spoken aloud, even if he was the one who had to say it.

"Hi," I said.

"You going to help us out?"

"Pardon me?"

"The police think they've got a good case built against poor John here."

"Those bastards," John Fairbain said, and slammed a surprisingly formidable fist against the table.

She flew to him and threw her arms around him. "Please, John, you've just got to calm down. Please."

"So will you join us?"

"Doing background work?"

"Yes."

I shrugged. "If I get to ask questions and get some straight answers."

"Well, sure," Thomas Ryan said, sounding surprised. "Why wouldn't we give you straight answers?"

I looked down at Fairbain. "Did you smash up all the photographs in Davies' house? The ones of Emma?"

He glared at me. "Just whose side are you on, anyway?"

I glanced at Ryan. "I thought we agreed to straight answers." Hell, John, answer him."

John Fairbain looked at me and said, "Of course I didn't. Why the hell would you ask me, anyway?"

He was going to be a wonderful client.

8

Over the next few days the following things took place: Mrs. Tomlin's toilet bowl overflowed again and I called the management company and said that I wasn't up for any more of their excuses and that they'd better send somebody out right now, her toilet bowl being beyond the limit of my plumbing skills; I had to put in an appearance at the Social Security office because the man in Apartment 8, Mr. Mendez, had arthritis so badly that he could literally not close his hand around a broom handle and yet the plump people with their big rubber stamps behind the tall ominous desk needed to have me to corroborate what their own eyes must certainly have seen; and Faith Hallahan came by with little Hoyt in his stroller.

I was cleaning my .38, the one I'd carried when I'd been with the sheriff's department, when she knocked. I let her in and of course the first thing she saw was the oil and the rag and the broken down .38.

"God," she said

"The gun?"

"Uh-huh."

"They're not really all that dangerous when you handle them properly."

"They just scare me." In her white blouse, an emerald-green barrette catching up her exuberant red hair, she was fresh and crisp as a high-school girl. She held Hoyt on her hip as he made little pink waves with his fingers.

I went over and knelt, knees cracking, next to Hoyt. He was bundled up in a snow suit—she had an inordinate fear of him catching cold—even though it was nearly fifty outside. Then I leaned over and hugged him. He had cold plump cheeks and they felt cute against my face. He had a snub Irish nose and huge serious blue eyes and a tiny pink mouth that always jerked open a bit to the right. As I held him I allowed myself the luxury of believing he was really mine.

"So why the gun?"

"Case."

"Case?"

"Yeah. I'm working on a case for a lawyer."

"And you need a gun?"

"Yeah because there was a murder involved and because when there's a killing, I don't like to go around naked."

She laughed. "Is that how cops talk?"

"Huh?"

"'Go around naked?' Is that how cops talk?"

"Actually I heard it on *The Rockford Files* once and thought it was kind of funny."

"For real?"

"For real."

She came over and sat next to me on the couch. She smelled good, sweet. She put her finger out to the gun on the coffee table. "They really do scare me."

"They shouldn't."

"Really?"

"Yep."

I took Hoyt and put him on my knee. He loved to play horsey. "So, did you watch PBS?"

"I got busy, hon. Sorry."

"It's the best thing I've ever seen about her."

"Zelda Fitzgerald?"

"Yes."

"You really identify with her?"

"Sure. Why?"

"Well, you've had pretty different lives."

"You mean you think I'm being silly."

"No, I just think you've had pretty different lives is all. From everything you've told me about her, I mean."

Hoyt took my finger and inspected it like a butcher examining a sausage.

Faith sighed. "Well, she got dumped, too, you know."

"Oh."

"There were Kens even in her day and age."

"Oh."

And then she started crying. She wasn't over it yet but there was nothing to say for it. There never is. I kept on playing with Hoyt.

9

Not wanting to pay the Hertz freight for a rented car, I went back to Frank Bannion, endured his seat cover speech again, and agreed to do all sorts of things in the future for the use of his car, including driving him to the Swisher Ballroom where they were having a big band festival in a month. I used to like the big bands very much but somehow the kids who play it today don't have the same feel for it. The world, for good or bad, has not been the same since Elvis Presley.

Anyway, with Bannion's car and a check for three hundred and fifty dollars from the attorney Ryan, I'd spent the last couple days trying to recreate the final forty-eight hours of Frederick Davies' life.

He had been, among other things, a golfer (I talked to people at the Elmcrest Country Club), a shopper (I interviewed a clerk at Clancy's Men's Shop), a drinker (I had two drinks at a downtown bar called The Tycoon), an inveterate renter of video tapes (I spoke to a friend of his at Video Station), a dutiful son (neither his mother nor father, once they knew who I was working for, would talk to me), and a ladies' man (I spoke to three women, two of whom had been with him during the last forty-eight hours of his life).

He had also been, I learned: forty-two years of age, given to hypochondria, vain about his receding hairline, mean on occasion when drunk, father of two girls via three marriages, a fallaway Catholic, a college drop-out whose passion for and understanding of art was nonetheless genuine, terrified of getting AIDS which did not square at all with his inordinate womanizing, a vehement Pierre DuPont supporter in the previous presidential primary, dapper, neurotically neat, physically tough, arrogant, opinionated, without scruples in business dealings, and a total high school boy when the subject of Emma Croft was broached. In other words he made just as much and just as little sense as we all do.

The one place I'd wanted to visit was the Downey Gallery. Emma Croft called three times a day to see if I'd spoken with David Stiles, the man who owned and ran the gallery. I had to keep telling her no because Stiles' secretary told me he was up on the Iowa river fishing, which had shattered another stereotype. For some reason I hadn't thought of art gallery owners as being fisherman.

On a warm Thursday morning, I drove over to Nineteenth and Fourth and pulled into a wide asphalt parking lot on which sat one of those chic two-story glass-and-steel buildings architects are so fond of these days. Sunlight bounced off its severe edges like candlelight off a cutglass bowl.

The receptionist I'd been talking to the past few days turned out to be a somewhat severe gray-haired woman in a very expensive suit, horn-rimmed glasses and a mouth that looked predisposed to disappointment. "You're certainly persistent," she said. She tried to float this at me gently but it didn't work. There was malice in it.

"I'm just representing my client."

"Oh, yes," she said. "Mr. Fairbain." She pronounced it as if she had said the word feces.

"I'd like to see Mr. Stiles now, if you don't mind."

The mouth showed obvious displeasure. Had she expected me to change my mind and vanish? "I'll be right back, Mr. Parnell. Excuse me."

She got up and left. Ten years ago she'd probably been nice to look at. But now her expensive clothes only made her seem all the frumpier.

While I waited, I wandered into the gallery proper. the place had the same effect on me that church does. Intimidating. So what I did was move down along the wall looking at huge garish abstract paintings that I understood not at all. My tastes run more to countrysides and those Cape Cod illustrations that make a Midwesterner like myself long for a mythical sort of ocean life.

The floors here shone like wet black glass. My footsteps sounded lonely in the silent air. The deeper I went into the gallery itself, the less sense of time and place I had. Maybe that's why people like galleries. You can lose yourself in them, even if you can't appreciate the art.

When I reached the rear wall I smelled the whiskey. It was not the sort of scent you expected to find here. Behind a partially open door leading to offices at the rear stood a stocky man in a security guard's blue uniform. He was maybe ten feet away, watching me, even from here I could smell the booze and see by the way he tilted back and forth on his heels that he was drunk. Not falling down drunk, of course, but the kind of drunk alcoholics can coast on for long periods.

As I came over to him, he said, "Fine day."

"Yes. Fine day."

"Beautiful paintings. The Kepners especially."

"Yes. Those Kepners."

"I'm just a little surprised to see you is all."

"Oh?"

"The gallery doesn't open officially till one. It's just—" He made an awkward production of shooting his sleeve to glimpse at the Timex. If I hadn't known he was drunk before, I knew now. He was close to my age but with jowls and thick glasses. Beneath his hat you could see that he'd recently had a short haircut. He wore a lot of Old Spice but it wasn't doing him any good. Nothing can cover up cheap whiskey.

"You've worked here a long time?" I asked.

"Ten years."

"Really?"

"Good job. Nice insurance and things."

"You ever know a man named Frederick Davies?"

I would have loved to play poker with this guy. He looked as if I'd just stepped hard on his instep. "Oh. Sure. Terrible thing."

"You know him well?"

"He—came here a lot. Him and Mr. Stiles were good friends."

"You ever see them argue?"

Inside his uniform, he shifted his whole body. "Not really. Why?"

"'Not really' means you did see them argue?"

"Well. Everybody argues."

"You see them argue recently?"

"Who the hell are you?"

I showed him my license. He was not the least impressed. "Hell, you ain't got any more authority than I do."

I decided to keep moving. "You ever hear anybody talk about a group of paintings called 'Ladies in the Cathedral?'"

He said it too fast. "No." Then, knowing that I knew he was lying, he said, "You tryin' to get me fired?"

I sighed. "No. No, I'm not. I'm just trying to help out a client."

"Well, I can't help you, bub. I really can't."

I laughed. "I haven't heard 'bub' since the 1940's."

"Sometimes I wish it was those days again."

"Where do you usually eat lunch?"

"Why?"

But before I could answer, I heard someone moving quickly down the gallery toward me, and a voice meant to interrupt whatever we were saying called, "George, I want you to go check out that breaker system. This is the third time I've asked you to do it, and it still isn't done."

"Yes, sir, Mr. Stiles." the way he'd said it, so hangdog, I wondered if Stiles ever made him come to work in blackface.

"So you're Parnell."

"That's me."

He put out his hand. He had one of those small hands that sometimes surprise you with their ferocity, like a Pekingese that suddenly turns killer. The rest of him suggested the same kind of ability to startle. He wore a conservative blue suit, white shirt, and yellow tie. His haircut, which any young corporate executive would envy, looked like it cost at least one hundred dollars. His teeth were so white you knew they had been bleached and his eyes were so dark you knew he was wearing contacts. he was very handsome and he had a red mouth and black hair. He appeared to be, in all, a contemporary version of Dracula and you just sensed, despite how country-clubby he looked, that he was capable of anything he needed to be capable of.

"So," he said.

"So," I said.

"You're here asking about poor John."

"Yes. And about a painting in the 'Ladies in the Cathedral' series."

You would have expected him to be a lot better than poor drunken George but he wasn't. He tried to play it the opposite—rather than looking evasive, he looked right at me, with the earnestness of a TV minister effecting a cure—but a tiny tic appeared in the corner of his right eye and ruined the whole show. "Vaguely, I've heard of it. Vaguely."

"I think John Fairbain was killed because of it."

"Really?"

"Yes." I looked around the gallery. I decided to get him as nervous as I could. "And I've been told that somebody at your gallery was involved in obtaining one of those paintings."

"You may be too old for this kind of thing," he said. A nasty gleam had come into his porcelain eyes.

"Pardon me?"

"Too old, Pops. Hell, you're older than George."

"I guess I'm not getting your point."

"The point is," he said, and before he finished the sentence he did a dumb thing. He took my elbow the way the nuns used to take my elbow and while there were many things I liked about nuns, the way they manhandled me was not one of them. I jerked my arm so violently free of him, his face got red and sweaty.

"The point is what, Mr. Stiles?"

He'd had just time enough to clear his throat, and find, if not the source of his dignity, at least the cool clear center of his wrath. "The point is, Pops, you're too frigging old. You are, in frigging fact, a joke. John-boy wasn't killed because of some goddamn painting. He was killed because he had this adolescent crush on his best friend's girl and finally his best friend got pissed off enough to do something about it."

"And the painting wasn't involved?"

"Not a goddamn chance."

"Meaning you're not going to help me find out about this?"

"Meaning I'm going to call George and he's going to take out his gun and throw your medicare ass out of here. You understand?"

"Don't call George."

"You afraid of him?"

"No. I don't want to hurt him, that's why."

"George may look like some old wino but he has his moments, believe me."

I stared at him, noticing the edges on his incisors. Easy enough to imagine them gleaming.

"I'm sure we're going to see each other again, Mr. Stiles."

"That means you're leaving, Pops?" He had taken to

smirking, which is never pleasant in man or woman, but especially not in a man.

"That's what it means, Mr. Stiles," I said. "For now."

The receptionist made certain she was gone when I reached the lobby.

10

Right at noon George came out of the Downey Gallery and made his way east down Fourth Avenue. If you watched him carefully, as I did, you noticed the slightly drunken sway. Otherwise he was just a middle-aged man in a blue security uniform intent on getting somewhere quickly. He walked against three different yellow lights, once coming closer to getting knocked down than perhaps he realized.

On First Street, he went into a large, brick-faced restaurant all fussed up with French Quarter wrought iron on the front and a name I couldn't pronounce written in gold script on its doors. Six months earlier the place had been Lebanese and six months earlier than that Chinese.

I gave him five minutes and then went inside. The French approach seemed to be doing better than the previous toasts to international brotherhood. Women in ties and men in ties and women in suits and men in suits packed booths, cocktail tables, and long tables. Nearby was a big data processing company, not to mention Ma Bell and several advertising agencies. This had apparently become the place of choice for many of them.

I had a hamburger. The college kid dressed up like a taxi dancer looked vaguely irritated that I didn't try to pronounce any of the French words on the menu. Maybe you got a discount if you got them right.

George sat in the back. His lunch companion looked both unlikely and somehow familiar. He was a big man with iron gray hair. He had the unctuous manner of a TV anchorman. He flirted with his cocktail waitress and got gruff with the server and when he spoke to George, it was with an obnoxious mixture of scorn and anger.

George, in his blue uniform, didn't belong here. George, with his whipped blue eyes, just kept shaking his head. He had obviously done something very disappointing to the gray-haired man.

Halfway through my apple pie a là mode, I remembered who George's friend was. Carl Sedgewick. Fifteen years ago, I'd worked a stakeout in which he'd been a principal. At the time, the county attorney was convinced that Sedgewick was one of the prime movers in the local porno market, which then consisted of very profitable outcall massage parlors as well as bookstores, films, and prostitution. The county attorney had also felt that Sedgewick was the conduit between the mob out of Chicago and all the local action. Sedgewick would have been a good choice. Son of a local millionaire whose fortunes had dwindled over the past two decades, Sedgewick was educated, well-traveled, urbane, and psychotic. He was notorious among local police for beating his women rather badly, and at the last minute getting them to recant and drop all charges. Now, in his forties, he had put on fifty pounds and his hair had gone completely gray and he showed the wrinkles of middle age. But he was imposing, there was no doubt about that, and all I could do was sit there and watch him alternately make time with the cocktail waitress and then ream out George some more. You had to wonder why they were having lunch together.

"Do you know a man named Carl Sedgewick?" I asked Emma Croft over the phone twenty minutes later.

"I don't think so."

I described him.

"He sounds a little like the man who came to a party at Frederick's last Christmas."

"Is John there?"

"He's on the couch watching TV. Since he got out on bail, that's all he does. It's clinical depression. I read that in *Cosmo*. That when you sit and watch TV all the time it means you're clinically depressed."

"How about asking him?"

"About Sedgewick?"

"Yes."

"Okay. Just a minute."

While she was gone, I stood across the street in a phone book and watched the front door of the French restaurant. Happy young people floated on the soft spring air. Across the river on the island, in the small park in front of the municipal building, somebody had sent up red, yellow and green balloons against the cloudless blue sky.

"He says he thinks that Frederick and Sedgewick had some kind of business dealings once but he isn't sure what."

"Is that what you called him?"

"Who?"

"Frederick? Did you always call him that?"

Yeah. He hated Fred. Said it made him feel like that guy on *My Three Sons*. Fred—"

"MacMurray."

"That's it. Fred MacMurray."

"Okay, Emma. Thanks."

"Are you on to something? She sounded young and very excited.

"Could be," I said. "I'm not sure yet."
"Well, call as soon as you've got something, all right?"
I said I would.

Before I went to see Sedgewick, I decided to get some
objective background on the art world which, for me, meant
paying a visit to one of the local colleges. At the Downey Gallery
I'd seen the photograph of a professor who'd recently had a
show there.

The art department took up an entire floor of a vine-covered
brick building that tried very hard to look venerable and would
have made it if some of the refurbishing touches—such as all the
new fire doors—hadn't conflicted with the clinging vines and the
spreading oaks. Outside in the hallway three students stood in
paint-spattered clothes smoking cigarettes. From a door down
the hall I heard a male voice conducting a lecture about the
Impressionists and closer I heard a portable radio without a good
tuner mix static with rock and roll. I knocked on the door where
the music was coming from, glanced in, and saw a man with a
shaved head working efficiently at a desk. I say efficiently
because he was grading a stack of papers in what was record time.
He'd glance at the student's name in the upper right column,
scribble a grade next to it and then go on to the next paper. I knew
something about paper-grading—my wife Sharon had been a
public school teacher—and this assembly-line technique was
impressive, if suspicious. He did not seem to glance at all at what
the students had written.

On the third knock he heard me. When he looked up, I saw
that he had a very fancy little goatee and a gold pirate's earring.

He was probably my age. From the left corner of his mouth dangled a cigarillo. He packed his white shirt and dark jeans with muscles. He looked like the kind of guy who just couldn't wait to tell you all about his workouts.

"Help you?"

I put out my hand, introduced myself, and told him what I needed. With a sandaled foot, he snagged a straightbacked chair, jerked it over next to his desk, and pointed for me to sit down. It was just then I noticed the photograph on his desk. The glossy photo showed Professor Billings, as he'd introduced himself, with his arm around a girl young enough to be his granddaughter. The plump gold ring on his finger told me that she was more likely his wife. You only get plump gold rings the second time around. The first time, at least for most people, there's never enough money, just biological frenzy and all the hope in the world.

"'Ladies in the Cathedral.' huh?"

"Yes."

He took a sharp little pull on his cigarillo. "Actually, I've been hearing about them in the past couple months."

"You mind if I ask where?"

He shrugged burly shoulders. Before he had a chance to speak, a fetching young girl knocked softly and said, "Some of the kids are asking if our term papers have been graded yet."

He thumped the stack with a fist the size of a heavyweight's. "Right here, Alison, Why don't you take them in a pass them out?" He handed the stack over. She came shyly into the room. She was all long blond hair and long skinny arms and long graceful legs. I noticed how he watched her. The one in the photograph had probably been recruited from another batch of Alisons.

When she left, he winked at me and said, "You saw me, didn't you?"

"The term papers?"

"Yeah."

"Yeah, I did."

He leaned back and put his sandals on the desk and his slab hands behind his shaved head. He kept the cigarillo, now dead, tucked in to corner of his mouth. "It's all bullshit, the academic side. Either these kids can paint or sculpt or they can't. Who gives a rat's ass if they know when Michaelangelo's birthday is. You know?"

"I guess."

"Anyway, that's how I look at it."

"So about 'Ladies in the Cathedral.'"

"Oh. Yeah. Right." The feet came down. He hunched forward in his chair. He was going to tell me a secret. "You know a guy named David Stiles?"

"Yes."

"You know a guy named John Fairbain?"

"Yes."

He smiled at me. His gold earring kind of swung back and forth. "Then you're here about Frederick Davies, aren't you?"

"I guess."

"You guess. My ass."

"I'm afraid, for my client's sake, I've got to keep things confidential."

"Well, I'll tell you what happened."

"All right."

Which, of course, is when the phone rang. At first he looked as if he was about to speak openly. Then, recognizing who it was, he turned his back to me and huddled his mouth into the receiver. "Hon, listen, I really was working late last night. I really was. You're just being paranoid. Now I can't talk right now, all right?" He hung up. He had the grin ready for me again. "Young wives. They get real suspicious."

He had a nice racket. He got to sit at a desk and smoke his cigarillo and choose from any number of young lovelies. A very nice racket.

"You were going to tell me what happened."

"Oh. Right. Well, it was Stiles. He found out about the painting and kept it at his gallery. Then somebody stole it."

"What?"

"Right."

"If you don't mind my asking, how do you know this?"

"Because I happen to have had a show going on at the gallery and I overheard some things I shouldn't have. Stiles was arguing with this wino he calls a security man."

"George?"

"Right. George. But it was really strange." His eyes narrowed. "One day I was there and George slapped him. Strange, huh?"

"Very strange. What was Stiles' role in all this?"

"A man named Carl Sedgewick. Carl is—let's say Carl is not unfamiliar with the underworld. And right now the underworld or the mob or whatever the hell you're supposed to call it these days is very interested in stolen art works. There's a great profit in them and you don't get nearly as much heat as dealing drugs."

"All right. Then what?"

"Well, Stiles had the painting and brought Sedgewick in. At least that's how I'd read it. Sedgewick would be able to unload it, given all his connections. But then somebody stole it and I figure either Sedgewick or Stiles assumed it was Davies and killed him because of it."

"You don't think it was John Fairbain who killed him?"

"That lightweight? Not a chance. Davies only hung around Fairbain for an entree into what passes for society in this city."

"The police seem to think it was over a woman named Emma Croft."

He smiled. I was getting kind of tired of his smile. "Good old Emma."

"You know her?"

Doesn't everybody? Back in the days before AIDS, Emma really got around."

I don't know why but it was one of those stories I didn't want to hear. "I see."

"Hey, don't get taken in by her crippled foot. She can be treacherous, believe me. I mean, you don't hang out with Frederick Davies and those people if you're thinking of becoming Mother Theresa."

"You have any idea where the painting is now?"

"Sure," he laughed.

"Where?"

"The killer's got it."

1 2

John Fairbain lived up in the hills off Mt. Vernon Road, near the city limits. Bannion's Pontiac labored up a steep curve and then coasted into a driveway marked Private. The house was a ranch-style stone, wood and glass, tucked deep into a stand of pine. A squirrel sat on the drive watching me. As I got out, and despite the fact that two cars sat in the drive, I had the feeling I was alone with just the wind and the sunlight. It was a nice feeling.

Emma answered the door. "Is everything all right?"

"I just need some answers," I said. I allowed myself the luxury of sounding angry. "Straight answers."

Sensing my mood, she stepped back and let me pass. She led me through a narrow hallway decorated with Indian wallhangings to a vast bright living room with sliding glass doors overlooking the timber below. John Fairbain, in button-down white shirt, jeans and bare feet, sat in the middle of the floor smoking marijuana. He was a contrast to Emma, who was dressed in a starchy white blouse with high collar, a long blue skirt, blue stockings, and low blue heels. I didn't imagine that with her leg she ever wore high heels.

Fairbain said, "You look pissed."

"What I should look is stupid because that's how I feel."

He took some more of the smoke and resins deep into his lungs and said, "I hope you're not offended by such obvious decadence." He sounded like a college boy trying very hard to shock me.

"I want to know about 'Ladies in the Cathedral.'"

He coughed and smiled. "Doesn't everybody?"

Emma Croft glanced at me. I could see the shame she felt for Fairbain. This was how he planned to get through the trauma of being under suspicion for murder. By staying stoned.

"Did you take that painting from Stiles?"

For the first time since I'd come in, he looked straight. "What's that supposed to mean?"

"Just what I said. I just had a talk with a professor named Billings."

"That bastard."

While the line should have come from Fairbain, it came instead from Emma.

I thought of what he'd said about her. How promiscuous she'd been. Her regard for him seemed equally low.

"I take it you know him?"

"I used to date him. Back in my more foolish days. In fact, I probably still would be dating him—and waiting for him to get a divorce—if I hadn't met John. John took me away from a very bad situation and Billings still didn't want to let me go. He always likes to keep something waiting in the wings for whenever he decides he needs a new star in his life. It doesn't surprise me he'd accuse John of taking that painting from Stiles." She walked over and leaned down and took Fairbain's hand. She might have been his mother or sister. "Davies took that piece from Stiles and that's why Stiles killed him."

I smiled. "You've got a nice little group here, Emma. All accusing each other of murder."

"It was Stiles," she said. "It really was. We've been talking about it—and he was the only person with a real motive."

"The painting?"

"Exactly," Fairbain said, taking another hit.

"Do you know a security guard at the Downey Gallery names George?"

Fairbain nodded. "Sure. A drunk."

"Why does Downey keep him on?"

"That's been a source of some speculation for years. The assumption is George knows too much about Stiles and so Stiles can't get rid of him."

"Is there any chance George could be working for Carl Sedgewick?"

Fairbain laughed. "Wouldn't that be great? Stiles likes to fancy himself so clever. And what if somebody on his own staff was selling him out?"

"It's crossed my mind that maybe George stole one of the ladies and sold it to Sedgewick. And it was Sedgewick, not Stiles, that your friend Davies was dealing with."

Fairbain snapped his fingers. "Damn, Parnell, I'll bet you're right. After I put up my share of the money, Davies went out of his way to hint that the person he was dealing with was Stiles. And that's what made me so suspicious."

"How so?"

"Davies was secretive to the point of neurosis. If he really had been dealing with Stiles, he would never have let on."

Emma Croft, crossing over to the leather couch, lighted a cigarette and said, "So where is the painting now?"

Fairbain said, "At Sedgewick's. I'd bet anything on it."

I need a direct answer from you, Fairbain."

"All right, Mr. Parnell."

"Did you have anything to do with stealing that piece from the Downey Gallery?"

For once he seemed guileless. "Absolutely nothing. You believe me?"

"I guess I don't have much choice, do I?"

1 3

Sedgewick lived in an estate house well behind a tall span of brick fence. You pulled up to a gate and announced yourself and were then either buzzed through or cast out into the darkness. A woman who introduced herself over the speaker told me that Mr. Sedgewick was not home.

I hit a drive-up phone next. I was fortunate enough to find one with a phone book still intact. I looked up George Nichols and found an address over on the lower southwest side. By now it was nearly dinner time and he should be home.

He lived in a large two-story house that had been converted to a boarding house. There was a Room For Rent sign thumb-tacked crookedly to a pillar and a Garage Sale sign on the lawn. The house had once been a kind of mustard color; I'm not sure what color it was now. Through a busted-out screendoor came the odors of fried food and beer. I opened the door and went inside the vestibule. Somewhere a kid cried and a harsh woman's voice told the kid to shut up. Upstairs Dan Rather pontificated on the day's news. A chunky woman in a faded housedress opened the parlor doors and stood there, hands on hips, glaring at me. "Yes?"

"I'm looking for George."

"Oh." She jerked her gray head up the stairs. "He's up in his room. Two doors from the left at the head of the stairs." She wiped her hands on an apron. "Sorry if I seemed crabby. It's just that trouble we had the other night when somebody broke into George's apartment."

I went up to see George. Through the partially opened door I could see him sitting in an aged overstuffed chair, his feet in gray worksocks, a cigarette burning in an ashtray. The wallpaper was stained and the window was cracked, and impressed on everything was the shabby air of a poor man dying out his days. The TV was bright with cartoons—*Deputy Dawg* from what I could gather—but George wasn't watching. He was looking through a big photo album he had spread on his lap. When I knocked, he started in his chair and quickly closed the album. "Yeah?"

"George, it's Parnell. I met you at the gallery this afternoon."

"What the hell are you doin' here?"

"I wanted to talk to you."

"About what?"

A small female face peeked out from a door that opened down the hall. She looked irritated.

"George, your neighbors aren't going to like it if I stand out here and keep talking."

He sighed, got up, and let me in. The room was not much bigger than a prison cell. He set the photo album carefully on a shelf before saying anything to me at all.

When he was seated again, he picked up an open quart of Hamms and started drinking directly from the bottle. Finished with his first big swig, he wiped his mouth with the back of his hand and said, "So, what do you want?"

From the sagging daybed where I sat and he no doubt slept, I said, "Sedgewick."

"I don't know no Sedgewick."

"You had lunch with him. Let's not bore each other with any bullshit, all right?"

"What the hell you after, mister?"

"I'm trying to find out who killed Frederick Davies."

"I ain't got no idea and what's more I don't give a damn. I don't give a damn for any of those people at the gallery. They're all snobs and jerks as far as I'm concerned."

"How much did he pay you?"

"Why the hell don't you just get out of here?"

He pretended real hard that he had developed a sudden interest in *Deputy Dawg*. I got up and went over and clipped off the set. I went back and sat down on the daybed and lit a Winston and said, "Here's how I understand things so far. Several months ago word comes that one of the 'Ladies in the Cathedral' paintings is in Cedar Rapids. How it got here I have no idea. But Sedgewick found out about it and wanted it and Davies found out about it and wanted it—and Stiles ended up with it. Whoever bids the highest gets it. Only Sedgewick decides not to play by the rules. He has somebody steal it for him. And that, George, was you. You took it for Sedgewick."

"I don't have to say nothin' at all to you."

"You'd rather talk to the police instead?"

"I didn't take nothin'."

"You know better than that, George."

"I don't even know this Sedgewick."

"You're getting pathetic, George. I sat in a restaurant with you this afternoon and watched you have lunch with him."

"You musta had me confused with somebody else."

"Right."

His eyes had raised to the shelf where the photo album was. For a moment his gaze was peaceful. Living as he did, the album probably brought back memories of better times.

"George," I said, "you're out of your depth in this. Whoever killed Davies may think you know where the painting is. They'd just as soon kill you if they needed to. My impression is they didn't find the painting at Davies', which means they're still looking for it. They might even think you've got it." I paused. "That's why somebody broke in here the other night."

His head jerked up. "How'd you know about that?"

"Landlady."

"Bitch." Then he put his head down.

He wasn't going to say any more. I went over and turned *Deputy Dawg* back on for him.

1 4

When I got back to my place, Faith Hallahan was taking a pizza out of the oven. She buys the Chef Boyardee boxed pizza and then adds all her own toppings. The stuff tastes pretty good. She set out plates for all three of us. After fixing little Hoyt up at the table, she said, "You want to say grace, Parnell?"

"You want me to."

"It'd be nice."

"OK."

The hell of it was it had been so long I couldn't remember the words.

When I finished and picked up my first slice of pizza, she said, "Was that the Catholic version of grace?"

"Sort of."

She smiled around her pizza. "You made it up?"

"More or less."

She tugged a tiny piece from her slice and put it in Hoyt's mouth. He, of course, made as big a mess of his face as he could. There was a soft night breeze through the window. I got sentimental but I wasn't sure about what. Just some kind of memory on the breeze. I thought of George and his photo album. I thought of George slapping Stiles. It didn't make sense, I guess.

"You doing all right?" I said.

"Fine."

"What's up for tonight."

"There's a Fred Astaire movie on PBS."

"That sounds good."

"Put Hoyt on the floor between us and all sort of snuggle up?" She was a perfect little girl sometimes and didn't I love it. She took a tiny, graceful bite of pizza. "Oh. You had a call." She fished into her pocket and brought out a slip of paper. She handed it to me with pizza-stained fingers. "Sorry."

A minute later, from the other end of the phone, Carl Sedgewick said, "I wondered if you could come out here."

Already I could see her following. I wasn't going to join her and Hoyt in that Fred Astaire movie after all.

1 5

This time I was shown right through the gates by a guard in a khaki uniform. He wore a long car coat and cradled a shotgun in his arms. He nodded glumly to me as I drove through.

The place was about what you'd expect for a mansion. In the gloom, windows shone like crazed yellow eyes and the turrets against the night clouds gave the impression I was approaching a castle. When I stepped from my car, I heard viola music on the muggy air. By the time I reached the three broad steps leading past Ionic pillars. I felt the first drops of rain.

A beefy man in a dark suit and sleek black hair who seemed to combine the functions of valet and bodyguard let me in. He mumbled something and stood back to allow me to pass. I went in the direction of the viola music.

The living room was huge and done in Victorian decor. Next to a wide fireplace, the flames blazing behind the screen, stood Carl Sedgewick in a blood-colored smoking jacket. In his massive right hand was a wine glass.

"Good evening, Mr. Parnell."

"Good evening."

"I appreciate you coming out so quickly."

"My pleasure."

His considerable size only added to the theatricality of his gestures. "Why don't you have a seat?" He pointed to a couch next to a Victorian mahogany display cabinet with marquetry decoration in saddlewood. I know something about antiques because they'd been one of Sharon's true passions. The display cabinet was worth well over five thousand dollars. The Persian rugs were not inexpensive either.

"Would you care for something to drink?"

"No thanks," I said.

He came over and seated himself within the confines of a wing-backed chair. "George tells me you followed us at lunch time."

"I assumed you'd heard from George."

"He's a very nervous man. He needs to confide in somebody." He sipped wine. "Would you mind telling me why you followed us?"

"I'm trying to find out who killed Frederick Davies."

"Why would you care?"

"Because Emma Croft hired me."

He laughed out loud. "Emma Croft? My God, you really don't know what's going on, do you?"

He had meant to unsettle me and he had. "I'm afraid I don't follow you, Mr. Sedgewick."

"If you'd care to accompany me in about an hour, I may have a little surprise for you."

"And what would that be?"

He kept his eyes on my face. He was enjoying my reaction to his words. "I'm going to meet the person who has the painting I want so badly."

"They're going to hand it over?"

"For a great deal of cash, Mr. Parnell. For a great deal of cash." He finished his wine and set it down. "Has it ever occurred to you, Mr. Parnell, that none of the players in this little game are what they seem?"

"Meaning what?"

He took out a silver cigarette case and with surprisingly graceful fingers extracted a cigarette. The shape of the case was familiar and then I remembered seeing one just like it the other day, in the hands of Emma Croft.

"You know Emma pretty well?" I said, recalling what Professor Billings had told me about her "getting around."

"This is a small city, Mr. Parnell. In our circles—rich and pretentious as some of the local newspaper columnists likes to call us—everybody knows everybody." He paused, exhaling white smoke. "If you're asking if I've ever had an affair with Emma, of course I have. Most of us have. What made you ask?"

I told him about the cigarette case.

"Very observant. And that's just why I asked you here tonight."

"Why?"

He smiled, "Because I need to be observed this evening."

"What?"

"I need you to follow me to the rendezvous spot out near the bluffs in Ellis Park. Do you know where the cliff overlooks the river?"

"Yes."

"I'm supposed to meet someone there in forty-five minutes."

"I'm already being paid by somebody else."

"But this will only help you, Mr. Parnell. You'll be doing your client a favor."

"I lighted a Winston. "You're telling me that John Fairbain didn't kill Davies."

"That's what I'm telling you."

"You also seem to be telling me that Emma Croft may be involved in Davies' death.

"Yes. Yes, I am, Mr. Parnell."

"Why would she kill Davies?"

The laugh again. "Emma Croft has cheated on every man she's ever been with. Including, unfortunately, myself." He said this with an odd kind of enjoyment. "But she got tripped up with Davies because he not only cheated on her—he used her to help him extract a great deal of money from John Fairbain."

"The money Fairbain put up to get 'Ladies in the Cathedral.'"

"Precisely, Mr. Parnell. Emma and Davies were having an affair while she was supposedly engaged to John. Emma and Davies wanted the painting and needed a way to buy it from Stiles—so Emma went to work on Fairbain and convinced him to put up the money."

"Then maybe Fairbain did kill him."

"I don't think so."

"Why not?"

"Not enough nerve. Not even in anger. Plus which, he's way too much in love with Emma." He laughed again. He wouldn't have wanted to ruin their wedding plans."

"You're sure about Emma and Davies?"

"Very sure." From inside his smoking jacket he took an envelope and passed it over to me. "Two plane tickets. One for Emma, one for Davies. They were to leave for Europe tomorrow. They would have had plenty of cash from selling me the painting and could have started their lives all over again. I found them at Emma's this afternoon while she was out."

"Why are you so interested in the painting?"

He shrugged and made a petulant face. "I don't suppose you've ever wanted to own anything simply because it was beautiful?" His tone implied that he was speaking to a lesser species here. "It's that basic and that profound, wanting to possess something as perfect as 'Ladies in the Cathedral.' There are four, perhaps five paintings in the series and they're among the most haunting of this century. Can you understand that?"

"I can try real hard." I looked again at the tickets in the envelope. I thought of Emma Croft and how she'd broken into my place that day. Now I knew what she'd really been searching for. The painting.

"Things are getting simple, Mr. Parnell. In an hour or so, I should have my painting and you should have a good lead as to the real killer. We will both be happy, don't you think?"

"What about George?"

"What about him, Mr. Parnell?"

"Why did you have lunch with him?"

"George is my spy. He reports what goes on at the gallery and in return I keep him in extra money for alcohol. He told me, for instance, that David Stiles had the painting I wanted and then he told me that somebody stole it from Stiles." He laughed. "We're a nice bunch of people, don't you think?"

He sounded proud.

1 6

It was one of those unexpected spring rains that backs up the sewers and floods lawns for days. Right now it was as blinding as a snow storm on the narrow, curving road that wound along the river. At the appropriate turn, I angled Bannion's Pontiac up a steep road, at the top of which I cut the lights and coasted across gravel to a pavilion. On the grassy slope below, Sedgewick was to hand over the money and receive his painting in return.

I tugged on a disposable plastic rain coat and my fedora and took my .38. I also took a flashlight. I got out of the car and ran through the mushy grass to a tree line that allowed me to see all the way down the hill.

Sedgewick had pulled his dark Lincoln next to a picnic table. He had shut off his lights and now sat in the car. The rain came in silver waves. Occasionally I could see the tip of his cigarette glow red in the darkness.

He had been sitting there for perhaps ten minutes when the shots came. Two of them. Right through the front window.

Instinctively, as soon as I felt the shooting was over, I started running. The shots had come from behind a stand of white pines to the west. But after twenty feet or so, with the ground filled with holes and the rain merciless, I knew I was never going to catch the person who'd done the shooting.

I went over to the Lincoln and found what I expected to find. Carl Sedgewick had been shot once in the face and once in the chest. Checking for a pulse was little more than a formality.

1 7

It looked like the opening of a used car lot. Big emergency lights blasted into the darkness. There were red, blue and white lights. There were plenty of cops and even more press. Everybody stood in the field getting soaked. Carl Sedgewick had been hefted onto a gurney earlier and put into the white box of an ambulance. The rain was more silver than ever. Detective Powers, the man I'd met at Frederick Davies' the other night, said to me, "So he was supposed to get the painting tonight?"

"Yes."

"And you figured that whoever handed over the painting was probably the same person who killed Davies, right?"

"Right."

"Well, Parnell, I wish you would have made my job easier and found out who that was."

If he was joking, it wasn't by much.

1 8

Emma Croft lived in a sedate little brick house on the cusp of a very wealthy neighborhood. I wasn't much in the mood for a formality so I made my knock heavy as I could. I also kept my other hand wrapped tight around my weapon.

If her hair hadn't been wet, she might have made a better show of it. She was without makeup and in a nightgown, and when she came to the door she made a big show of yawning. She she saw me, she tried to look surprised and then made sure to yawn again. But mostly it was her hair.

I came to through the door with the gun pointed directly at her and said, "I want the painting."

"What?"

"The painting."

"But I don't have—"

I grabbed her wrist and twisted once, hard. "I'm too tired to screw around. And I'm sick of your lies. Now get it out here."

"I've been asleep—"

"Your hair's wet. You've been outdoors. Now get me what I want."

So she went and got it. Just like that. It was in a drawer and it was in the bedroom off the living room that was done in stark black and whites, one of those impressive-looking rooms you like to visit but would never want to live in.

Meanwhile, I went to the front closet and dragged out her wet trenchcoat and muddy boots. I'd need to hand them over to the police as evidence.

She came out and set the painting on the coffee table. I'd never seen a canvas that small. Then she went over and sat on the couch and began sobbing.

"You killed Davies, didn't you?"

She shook her head.

"Then how did you get the painting?"

"I went to his house and found him dead. We were—friends. Whether you believe it or not, Parnell, I loved him. But I decided that even if he was dead—"

"Even if he was dead you'd go on looking for the painting."

A whisper. "Yes."

"So you broke into my place just on the off chance that I might have it."

"I wasn't sure why you'd called Frederick's that night. I thought perhaps you were working with him."

"Against you?"

Her dark eyes grew even more somber. "You can't trust anybody completely, Parnell."

"Then you broke into George's?"

She nodded. "And that's where I found it."

Strange how I'd forgotten all about her being crippled. Strange how I'd forgotten all about her beauty. She was a shambles now and in all respects.

"So then what happened?"

"I took the painting and offered it to Sedgewick."

"You were out there tonight. At Ellis Park."

"I was asleep. Here. I—"

I sighed. "I checked your boots and your trenchcoat. There isn't any more sense in lying." I was tired now. Being around people like her always made me tired.

She glanced up, then. She had been crying or trying to, but now she'd given it up. Now she just seemed lost. "Yes, I was out there tonight. Mr. Parnell. But I didn't kill him. Somebody else. In some other part of the woods there. Somebody must have followed me." She shook her head. "I'm not as bad as I might seem right at this moment, Mr. Parnell. I really cared for Frederick—and I'm really worried for John. I don't want him to be convicted. I hired you so you'd find out who the real killer is."

I stood up. "I'm going to call the police now. You'll need to tell them everything."

"I couldn't help falling in love with Frederick. I really couldn't."

I said nothing. There was nothing to say.

19

In the police courses I used to take, it was always referred to as elimination. It's not unlike modern medicine. Maybe a doctor doesn't know what's wrong with you but he can eliminate, through various tests, what's not wrong with you.

When I got up it was nearly dawn and Faith was up with Hoyt who had a rash on his bottom and was crying. The air smelled of baby powder. "You want some breakfast? I said.

"You having some?"

"Yep."

"Sure."

So I made us scrambled eggs and bacon and toast with margarine and grape jelly. We put Hoyt in his high chair and gave him some animal crackers, and then I told her everything that had happened and then she came up with what I should have come up with hours earlier. Elimination.

"It has to be Stiles, I'll bet," she said. "He killed Davies because he knew that Davies had stolen the piece from him."

"That part sounds right. But what about Sedgewick. Why would he have killed Sedgewick?"

But she was busy feeding Hoyt and said, "That part you'll have to figure out."

20

In the rainy dawn, the Downey Gallery seemed drab and not the least fashionable. I swung Bannion's Pontiac into a parking space next to a blue Mercedes I assumed belonged to Stiles.

I had been prepared to pick the lock on the back door but I found it open. I took out my .38 and went inside. My shoes still squished from being wet. The air was stale, the darkness total. I moved on tiptoes down the corridor until I came to his office. Yellow light spilled from inside. I squeezed my weapon tighter.

Easing up to the edge of the door, I peeked inside and there I found him sprawled on his desk. The bullet had been put in roughly the same spot as the one that had killed Frederick Davies. I was just about to go inside when I heard something rustle behind me in the gloom. Before I could turn around, I heard the safety go off a gun and a voice say, "He shouldn't have got involved with them. It happened before on the West Coast and I had to help him out of his jam then. This time it was a lot worse."

As I listened to George, I glanced back in the office and I saw on David Stiles' desk the same photo album that George had been looking at yesterday in his room.

"You were his father?"

"Yes." He sounded terrible. "He promised me out on the coast that he wouldn't ever get in trouble again. Then he starts dealing in stolen goods with people like Davies and Sedgewick and—"

"You killed them so your son couldn't be traced to his part in all this?"

"Yes. He was ashamed of me, no education and everything, and the way the booze got me and—" He paused. "We were supposed to leave this afternoon. Just take off and forget all about the painting."

Everybody had always wondered why David Stiles wouldn't get rid of a drunken washed-out security guard like George. Everybody had always wondered why two murders had been committed that didn't seem to have anything to do with 'Ladies in the Cathedral'.

Now I knew. A father trying to keep his son out of trouble.
"So you had to kill David, too?"

"He wasn't goin' to change any. I saw that and I—"

In the darkness, I could hear him begin to cry. It didn't take a whole hell of a lot to get the gun from him. There wasn't a whole hell of a lot of him left.

2 1

Later that afternoon, after I'd finished giving all my information to the police, I dropped Bannion's car off and then he gave me a lift to get my own. I was just getting out of the door when I stopped and tapped my shirt and said, "Hey, what's this?"

"What's what?"

"There's something in my pocket." I took out two red tickets and handed them over. "There's a ballgame tonight. Why don't you and Malley go and enjoy yourselves?"

"That's nice of you, Parnell."

"Least I can do for you letting me use your car for four days."

"No problem. Not for a buddy."

I had just about closed the door when he said, "Shit."

"What?"

"You changed the station."

"Aw, hell. Did I forget to turn it back?"

"You playing rock and roll?"

"I guess I was, Bannion. I guess that's what I was doing."

He yanked the car down in gear and said, "You should be ashamed of yourself, Parnell. An old fart like you."

Then he took off.

ANCIENT AND DEADLY

by
L. J. Washburn

It was like living in a museum. The walls of the apartment
were hung with medieval weapons. I could glance one way and
see a wicked-looking English war axe from the late fourteenth
century, another way and be greeted by the sight of an elabo-
rately-decorated Rondel dagger from the early fourteenth century. And of course there were crossbows and sabers and, leaning
in one corner, a seven-foot-long German halberd.

Home, sweet home.

I tossed my purse on the table beside the sofa and headed for
the kitchen, for the most part ignoring the weapons. They still
gave me an uneasy feeling at times, but I was getting used to them
after five years of living with Aaron.

Still slightly sweaty from my workout at the martial arts
studio, I got a Diet Coke from the refrigerator, went back into the
living room and sat down. A glance at my watch told me that it
was nearly seven o'clock. I was late getting home, but Aaron
wasn't there to worry about me; he was probably still out at one
of the weekend flea markets, trying to find a good buy on some
old gun or knife.

Most of the weapons Aaron had collected were replicas, of
course, and just as deadly as the originals in most instances but
not nearly as expensive. It would take an actual museum to be
able to afford the real things. There were quite a few swordsmiths

and armorers among Aaron's friends in the SCA, though, who made a living providing weapons for their fellow hobbyists. I had met some of them at the various fairs and tournaments Aaron attended. Overall, they struck me as a bit more normal than the other members of the Society for Creative Anachronism. It was a hobby and a business combined for them, rather than a way to relieve the pressures of everyday life by escaping into the days of yore, days of chivalry and honor and blood.

I sipped the Coke and started thinking about something to fix for supper. Better that than worrying about another long week at the agency staring me in the face.

The sound of footsteps on the stairs outside made me look up. A moment later, the door of the apartment opened and Aaron Wolf came hurrying in, looking even more intense than usual. There was another man with him, and both of them stopped when they saw me.

Aaron said, "Hello, Laura. I was hoping you'd be here. This is my friend Damian Quinn. You've heard me talking about him."

I stood up.

"From the antique store. Of course. I'm glad to meet you, Mr. Quinn."

He put out his hand and said, "It's a pleasure to meet you, Ms. Bailey." He was taller than Aaron, slim-hipped and distinguished in an expensive suit. There were a few flecks of gray in his thick brown hair and neatly-trimmed beard. I put his age at about forty. He was smiling, but the expression didn't extend to his blue eyes. They were worried and distracted.

Glancing at Aaron, I started to say, "You could have let me know that you were bringing company home . . . "

Damian Quinn waved a hand. "Please, Ms. Bailey, don't consider me company. I'm here to see you on a business matter, I'm afraid, although I'd much rather it was a social visit."

I suppose I frowned a little. I knew that Aaron was a customer at the antique store and art gallery that Quinn owned; the man had been able to turn up a few authentic old weapons for Aaron at fairly reasonable prices. But the only thing I collected was books. What could Quinn want with me?

The answer was fairly obvious once I thought about it. And then Quinn said, "I understand from Aaron that you're a private detective."

The words sent a pang through me, bringing back all kinds of memories, both good and bad. I remembered my father and the simple sign on the door: Bailey Detective Agency. Both were gone now. Jim Bailey had died two weeks earlier, and six months before that, he had sold the agency both of us had worked to build up. Now the sign on the door read National Security Services, Inc.

"I work for an investigative and security service," I said to Damian Quinn, not adding that I had a PI ticket of my own as well. Aaron had probably already told him that.

"I find myself needing some investigative work done," Quinn said. "Aaron overheard me talking about the problem with one of my associates, and he recommended that I come talk to you."

That surprised me. Aaron had never seemed overly fond of my profession, not that it was particularly dangerous. But the hours were long and sometimes inconvenient—or at least they had been back in the days when I was an actual operative, rather than a glorified secretary. Aaron had talked a great deal about Damian Quinn in the past; I realized he might be trying to impress the man with the fact that his live-in girlfriend was a private eye.

I said, "I'm not sure I'm the person you need to talk to, Mr. Quinn. The head of the Dallas office is a man named Kenneth Owens. I'd be glad to see about setting up an appointment for you—"

He reached out and put a hand on my arm. The smile he turned on had a practiced charm. "Please, Ms. Bailey. I have a reason for wanting to proceed through you. If we could sit down and talk about it . . . ?"

I wasn't happy with Aaron for roping me into this, whatever it was, but I didn't want to be rude to Quinn. It would probably be quicker and simpler to hear him out, I decided.

"Of course. Have a seat," I told him.

He sat at one end of the sofa, I sat at the other. Aaron hurried off to the kitchen to get a glass of wine for Quinn. Quinn gave me an appraising look, and I didn't imagine he was too impressed with what he saw. I was wearing my sweat pants and a pullover with a Riders in the Sky logo on it. Feeling a little awkward— and a little angry with myself for feeling so—I brushed back a strand of hair from my face.

"You said you had a matter that needs some investigation," I prodded, wanting to get Quinn's attention back on business. It wasn't hard to do. He nodded, a grim look coming over his face.

"As you obviously know, I own an antique store and art gallery on Greenville Avenue," he began. "It's been a successful business, enough so that I'm in the process of opening a second store in Highland Park. But now I'm running into some problems. "

"With your new store?" I asked when he paused.

"Actually, no. The new store won't be open for a couple of weeks yet. All the break-ins have been at the Greenville Avenue store."

"You're having burglaries? You've told the police about them, of course."

Quinn's smile came back for a moment. "The Dallas police department is overworked and in a seemingly constant state of turmoil, Ms. Bailey. They don't get too excited about burglaries anymore, especially when nothing has been taken."

I frowned again and said, "You haven't had any losses?"

"Nothing has been taken."

"Then how do you know someone's been breaking in? Have they left any evidence of forced entry?"

Quinn shook his head.   "There were no signs of forced entry. But I know someone has been in the store on three separate occasions. Things have been moved around. Not much, mind you, but enough for me to notice them. Ah, thank you, Aaron." He reached up to take the glass of wine Aaron brought back from the kitchen.

"Sounds to me like whoever it was tried to hide the fact they had been looking around and just wasn't quite good enough at it," Aaron said. He moved over to sit down in an armchair under a non-working model of a German arquebus. It was an early musket-like weapon, and the engraving on this model was elaborate and beautiful.

"That was my thought," Quinn said with a nod. He sipped the wine, then looked at me again. "What do you think, Ms. Bailey?"

I mulled over what he had told me so far. "If the only thing wrong is that some things have been moved around, how do you know your employees didn't do it?" I asked.

"It's always happened at night, when none of the employees was there."

"Don't they have keys?"

Quinn shook his head. "I always open and close the store myself. Besides, they don't know the security codes to turn off the burglar alarms."

"Then you do have burglar alarms?" I asked.

"Of course. My insurance company insists on it. None of the alarms went off during the last week, when the break-ins have taken place."

"Maybe we'd better not think of them as break-ins, from

what you've told me. What does the security company say?"

Quinn shrugged. "They tell me that nothing can be done unless an alarm goes off. They've tested the equipment thoroughly, and it's all functioning properly, according to them."

His tone of voice said that he wasn't ready to accept their word at face value. In spite of myself, I was starting to get interested. "Why do you sound like you doubt what they're telling you?" I asked.

"I recently changed security services," Quinn explained. "Just before the break-ins, or the incidents, rather, started. I thought I was going to get a better deal." His mouth quirked wryly. "Now I'm not so sure."

"You think someone at the new company could be behind what's going on?" I asked. To me, it sounded like a dubious theory, but I could see how Quinn might be suspicious of the timing.

"I think it's possible, don't you? I'm no expert on burglar alarms."

"What's the name of the company you have working for you now?"

"Protective Associates."

I smiled. "Then that answers that question. I'm well acquainted with the people over at P.A. My father worked with them at times when he still had his agency. They're a very reputable firm."

"I'm still not sure . . . "

I sat back and took a deep breath, thinking about what Quinn had told me. His gaze dropped for a moment to my chest, out of habit, probably. The glance didn't bother me, but it didn't make me any fonder of him, either.

"All right," I said after a moment. "You've had three instances in the last week of someone rummaging around in your store, after hours, like they were looking for something. Right?"

He nodded.

"But nothing is missing, and it doesn't look like anyone has broken in."

Quinn nodded again.

I could see why the police hadn't been very interested in Quinn's story. There was no substance to it, no real evidence of a crime. The cops weren't going to waste their time on something like this.

And I had a feeling Kenneth Owens wasn't going to want to, either. National was a big agency, and this case—if it even *was* a case—sounded like a pretty small affair.

I tried to tell Quinn as much, tactfully. "It seems to me like you'd be better off relying on the security company you're already dealing with," I said. "You're paying them to protect you from things like this, after all."

Quinn shook his head. "I just don't trust them. The agency you work for does this kind of work also, doesn't it?"

I had to admit that it did. Burglar alarms and security guard work were all part of National's operation, although I had little or nothing to do with that area of the company. I said, "Look, Mr. Quinn, to be honest with you I don't see very much to go on with what you've told me. But I'd be happy to set up an appointment with Mr. Owens, as I told you earlier. He might be interested."

Quinn leaned toward me. "I'd really prefer it if you would tell your boss about the situation, Ms. Bailey. I feel that he might be more receptive to taking the case if someone like you, someone within the agency, brought it to his attention."

That was true enough. As I considered Quinn's request, Aaron said, "It sounds to me like Damian's got a real problem, Laura. Don't you think you could help him out?"

I glanced at Aaron, saw the eagerness on his face. Definitely out to make an impression. But I couldn't begrudge him that. Maybe Quinn had some kind of medieval slingshot that Aaron wanted to get his hands on.

"I'll talk to Owens," I said. "But I can't make any promises. I have a feeling he'll just say the same things I've already said, Mr. Quinn."

"But you will have tried, and that's all I ask." Quinn turned on that dazzling smile again. He took another sip of his wine, then put the glass down on the coffee table as he stood up. "Thank you for actually listening to me, Ms. Bailey. That's really more than the police did." He reached into his pocket and took out a card case, slipped one of the cards out and handed it to me. It was a rectangle of heavy paper with gilt embossing on it. "You'll let me know as soon as you find out anything from your Mr. Owens?"

"Of course," I said. I ran my thumb over the letters on the card. Fancy and expensive, like everything else I had seen so far about Damian Quinn.

"Thank you again. Good night, Ms. Bailey."

"Good night."

Aaron went with him to the door, still talking, assuring him that everything would be all right and that I would get to the bottom of everything. I stayed on the sofa, holding that business card.

When the door was shut and Quinn was gone, Aaron turned back to me with an annoyed expression on his dark face. "Dammit, Laura," he snapped. "You could have been a little more encouraging."

"I don't like to lie to people, Aaron. It didn't sound to me like there was anything there to investigate. Quinn's just paranoid, that's all."

"The man is a friend of mine—"

I cut in, "You're one of his customers, Aaron. I wouldn't put any more stock in it than that."

He shook his head. "You're wrong. I want you to do everything you can to help him."

I stood up and turned toward the kitchen. "What do you want to eat?"

My voice was cold and I knew it, even though I didn't want the added burden of anger tonight. Quickly, Aaron moved up behind me, stopping me by slipping his arms around my waist. He put his mouth against the back of my neck and murmured, "Hey, Laura, I'm sorry. I guess I did come on a little too strong there. I just thought you could help Damian out."

I closed my eyes. Aaron had his body pressed against mine, and I couldn't help but enjoy the feeling of it. His lips brushed softly against my neck, and his breath was warm on my skin. I sighed and then let a smile curve my lips.

"Dammit," I said as I turned around in his arms. "You never fight fair, do you?"

"Nope," he said with a grin. "You'll talk to Owens?"

"I'll talk to Owens," I said.

2

I woke up early Monday morning. Aaron was sprawled on his stomach beside me, taking up three-fourths of the bed. His breathing was slow and regular as he slept.

I stayed where I was for a few minutes, studying his face. With his eyes closed, he didn't look as intense as when he was awake. Most people look vulnerable when they're asleep; Aaron was no exception.

He was twenty-six years old; I was twenty-nine. I had been living with him for five years. My father had never liked that arrangement, had liked even less the fact that Aaron was younger than me. I'm sure he wondered sometimes if sex was the only thing Aaron and I really had holding us together, but Jim Bailey wasn't the kind of man to ask his daughter about such things. Aaron was not his favorite person in the world, but he had tolerated him.

I thought back to the day I had met Aaron at one of the conventions of science fiction and fantasy fans that are held fairly regularly in Dallas. He and several other SCA members had been putting on a demonstration in full armor, swinging heavy broadswords that clanged together. When it was over, he had sheathed the sword and pulled off his helmet. Sweat had plastered the dark hair to his head, and he was breathing heavily. Using those broadswords was hard work. But there had been a grin on his face and the fire of a warrior in his eyes. I had immediately felt a surge of attraction to him.

We had gone out several times before he told me that he was one-fourth Cheyenne Indian. His full name was Aaron Running Wolf, but he never used the middle name, only the initial. He preferred to dwell on the other side of his ancestry, the part he had traced back to England in the sixteenth century. That research had led him to an interest in medieval times, which had led, in turn, to his joining the SCA.

I had been unsure what to say or how to feel about all of this. I wasn't bothered by his Indian heritage, but the way he seemed to have turned his back on it threw me a little. It was none of my business, though. We all have things in our lives we prefer not to look at too closely.

I had learned that lesson all too well during the last year.

I sat up in bed, thrusting away the thoughts of my father and his decision to sell the agency and his death. I swung my legs out from under the covers and stood up, trying not to think about the hard feelings that had never been resolved and now never would be.

I stood under the shower for a long time.

Aaron was standing in front of the sink, stretching and

running his fingers through his tangled hair as I stepped out of the shower. He glanced at me and grunted, "Morning."

"Did you sleep well?" I asked as I started to dry off.

"Yeah." He looked at me again. "Are you going to talk to Owens about Damian today?"

"I said I would, didn't I?" My tone was sharper than I had intended, but I didn't feel up to starting that discussion all over again.

"Sure, sure. I just didn't want you to forget. Say, after you've called Damian, how about letting me know how it turns out?"

That was his way of checking up on me, I knew, of making sure that I kept my promise. I felt a surge of anger but didn't say anything. It was just too damned early for an argument.

"I'll call you," I said. "I don't feel much like fixing breakfast this morning."

"That's fine." He headed for the shower himself and added over his shoulder, "I'll grab something on the way to work."

"Okay. I guess I will, too."

I didn't mind the fast-food breakfast. Eating it gave me something to do during the forty minutes it took me to creep along the freeway through Irving, past Texas Stadium, and on to the offices of National Security Services, Inc., on Mockingbird Drive.

National had expanded the operation quite a bit from the single office my father and I had maintained. Several operatives had worked for us on a freelance basis, but we had not had to provide office space for them. National had a suite that took up half the second floor of the building where the offices were located. Kenneth Owens, as the manager of this branch, had claimed my father's old office.

That was another reason I didn't like him.

I parked my Dodge in the same place I had been parking for

the last eight years. The lot was only half-full, instead of being packed like it had been for most of the time I had been working there. Quite a few of the offices in the building were vacant now, a legacy of the slump in the Texas economy. National was still doing well, though, from what I could tell.

I went straight to Kenneth Owens' office. His secretary greeted me with a smile and told me he had already come in. That was no surprise. I didn't particularly like Owens, but he worked as hard as anybody else in the office. I rapped lightly on his door and then opened it.

Owens looked up from his desk and gave me a curt nod. "Good morning, Laura," he said as he turned his attention back to the paperwork spread out on the desk in front of him. "What can I do for you this morning?"

Kenneth Owens was six or seven years older than me, in his mid-thirties. Most women found him attractive. He had thick sandy hair and an earnest smile when he chose to use it. He had also been working for National Security Services for fifteen years, first as an operative, then going on up the ladder until he was in charge of a major branch office. He was smooth, smart and businesslike, not at all the sort of private investigator my father had been. Jim Bailey had been an ex-cop from New York City, part of a hardnosed breed that I didn't think existed anymore.

I sat down in the plush chair in front of his desk that was intended for clients. "I have a possible case to discuss with you," I told him.

He made a note on one of the papers and then pushed it to the side. Leaning back, he regarded me levelly and said,

"Go ahead."

Quickly, I told him about the break-ins that had supposedly happened at Damian Quinn's shop. Owens listened quietly, paying attention at first. But I could see his mind beginning to wander before I was finished.

"Anyway, Quinn wants us to look into it for him," I wrapped up my recital. "I told him I'd tell you about the case and that the decision would be yours whether to take it on."

Owens nodded. "And you already knew what my answer would be, I assume."

"I thought it sounded like something you wouldn't want to bother with," I said with a shrug. "But you're the boss. I figured it was your right to decide."

He laced his fingers together on the desktop and leaned forward. "Would you have taken a case like this when you and your father were running your agency?"

I laughed shortly. "We never had as much overhead as National does. We might have taken the case. We took plenty of others that didn't promise to be very lucrative."

"Oh, we could make this one lucrative." Owens pushed back his chair and stood up to wander over to the window. Downtown Dallas was visible several miles away through the morning haze. "We could put in plenty of hours and charge Quinn for every one of them and then tell him we couldn't find a damned thing. But that's not the way we do business around here, is it?"

I shook my head. I didn't like working for an outfit like National, but I had to admit it was an honest company.

Owens came back to his desk. "You can tell Quinn we're not interested." He sat down and pulled more of the papers back in front of him. Obviously, I was being dismissed.

"All right," I said as I got up out of the chair.

"And Laura . . . next time use your own judgement on something like this. I'm afraid you've wasted your time and mine this morning."

His voice wasn't particularly sharp or chiding, but I still felt my fingernails digging into my palms as I clenched my fists. Kenneth Owens was good at his job, but he was still a jerk.

I left, not really trusting myself to say anything else. When

I got to the office I shared with two other operatives, I pulled Quinn's card from my purse and called the number on it. I didn't know if anyone would be there this early, but after two rings, a pleasant female voice answered, "Damian's. May I help you?"

"I'd like to speak to Mr. Quinn, please," I said. "My name is Laura Bailey."

There was the slightest hesitation, then the woman asked in a sharper tone, "What's this about?"

That was a little rude, I thought, but I said, "It's a personal matter." I didn't know who else Quinn might have told about the problem he was having, and I didn't feel like explaining it to this woman.

"Just a minute," she said coldly. She put the phone down with a thump.

I heard her say something to someone else, and she didn't sound happy. Then, a moment later, the phone was picked up and Damian Quinn said, "Ms. Bailey? Thank you for calling. Did you find out anything?"

"Just what I expected, to be honest," I told him. "Mr. Owens didn't think this was the type of case that would be suitable for National to take. I'm sorry, Mr. Quinn."

I heard the breath hiss between his teeth. "Damn," he said softly. Then he went on, "I'm sorry, Ms. Bailey. I was hoping that your agency could take the job. I appreciate‡you taking the time to present my case. I'd be glad to send you a check for your trouble—"

"That's not necessary," I said quickly. "I didn't do anything to earn any sort of fee. Besides, I didn't accomplish anything for you."

Quinn was silent for a moment, then he said abruptly, "You're a licensed private detective, aren't you, Ms. Bailey?"

"I'm a private investigator, yes," I admitted, unsure what Quinn was getting at.

"How would you feel about looking into this matter for me on your own? Would that be possible?"

The question caught me off-guard. What Quinn was asking was possible, all right; I was licensed under my own name and didn't have any sort of exclusive contract with National. I was just an employee, and there was nothing stopping me from taking on jobs on the side.

Nothing but the fact that I didn't particularly like Damian Quinn and thought his main problem was an overactive imagination.

"I don't think so, Mr. Quinn," I said. "I stay pretty busy with my work for the agency and all . . . "

"I could make it worth your while, Ms. Bailey. I believe in going first class."

"I'm sorry."

I heard the deep breath he took. "I'll tell you what. Why don't you think about it this morning, and if you change your mind you can call me later. Or maybe we could get together for lunch." He named a popular restaurant on Greenville Avenue and said, "That's only a couple of blocks from my place. If you decide you want to take the case yourself, I'll be there around one. We could have a good meal and iron out all the details, then I'll show you the store."

"Well . . . I'll think about it."

I grimaced as I heard the words coming out of my mouth. Saying no has never been one of the things I'm good at. But I hadn't promised Quinn I'd take the job or even that I'd show up to talk to him about it. All I had to do was stay away from Greenville Avenue today, I told myself as I said goodbye to him and hung up, and surely Quinn would get the message.

I never should have called Aaron to tell him about it, I was saying to myself as I walked into the restaurant and looked around for Damian Quinn. It was a few minutes after one o'clock.

Calling Aaron had only been the first mistake. The second and more serious one had been mentioning Quinn's suggestion that I take the case myself. Aaron had thought that was a wonderful idea, and after listening to him try to convince me for twenty minutes, I had agreed to at least talk to Quinn and see what else he had to say.

The restaurant was a trendy place with lots of glass and plants, a leftover from the fern bar boom that had struck Dallas several years earlier. When I was a few steps into the room, a hostess approached me and gave me a questioning look. I said, "I'm looking for Damian Quinn. I was supposed to meet him here."

"Of course," she smiled.

I followed her across the big room toward a row of booths along one wall. The restaurant was busy, and I saw that I would have had to wait for a table if I had not been meeting Quinn. The skirt and blouse I was wearing looked professional enough that I wasn't too out of place among the business-suited women who were there. Quinn was sitting in one of the booths with a woman beside him. When he saw me coming, he smiled and stood up. "Hi," he said. "I'm glad you could come."

"Hello," I nodded.

Quinn gestured for me to sit down and said, "Ms. Bailey, this is my friend and business partner, Jayne Pleshette. Jayne, Laura Bailey, the investigator I told you about."

Jayne Pleshette extended a hand across the table to me. She was about Quinn's age, slender and very pretty with thick dark hair that fell to her shoulders. In a voice I recognized from our phone conversation earlier, she said, "Hello, Ms. Bailey. I'm glad to meet you. Damian hasn't been talking about anyone else all day."

There was only a hint of coolness in her tone, instead of the outright hostility I had heard on the telephone. I shook hands with her and smiled, thinking about the logical explanation of why she would have been upset when a strange woman called and asked for Quinn.

Jayne Pleshette was jealous. Quinn had said that they were friends and business partners, but I suspected there was more to their relationship than that.

I ordered a glass of wine from the waitress who appeared beside the table, then said to Quinn, "I'm still not sure if I can be of any help to you in this matter, Mr. Quinn. If you insist on hiring someone else besides your normal security service to look into it, though, maybe I can refer you to someone."

Quinn gazed intently across the table at me. "I've got a feeling that you're the one I need, Ms. Bailey. Or can I call you Laura?"

"Sure," I said politely, even though I wasn't sure I wanted him calling me anything.

"You're discreet, you're experienced in your work, and Aaron says you can be plenty stubborn when you want to be." He grinned. "What more could a man want from a private eye?"

I glanced at Jayne Pleshette. She was watching me expressionlessly, occasionally casting a glance at Quinn. I had a feeling that she naturally regarded all women as competition. Before I could answer Quinn's question, the waitress popped up again and I had to order lunch from a menu I hastily glanced at. I settled for roasted chicken and a spinach salad, then turned back to Quinn and said, "I'll be very honest with you, Mr. Quinn. I don't think there's really a case here to investigate. There's no solid evidence of any criminal activity."

"Isn't it suspicious, though, that someone seems to be looking for something inside my shop at night?"

I shrugged. "I suppose, if that's really happening."

"I'll prove it to you," Quinn said. "After we've eaten, we'll go back to the store and I'll show you the kind of thing I've been talking about."

I didn't punch a clock at National. There was no reason I couldn't just go by the antique store and take a look at it, I told myself. For one thing, I was curious, having heard Aaron talk about it so much."All right," I agreed. I looked over at Jayne Pleshette. "What about you, Ms. Pleshette? Have you noticed anything out of the ordinary around the shop?"

She shook her head. "No, I haven't. Of course, I'm not there as often as Damian is. I only work part of the time, so I don't know where everything is right down to the inch, like Damian seems to."

Quinn laughed. "A good businessman knows every inch of his operation, Jayne. You know that."

She made no reply, and a moment later our food arrived. I was glad to see it. Not only was I hungry, but I had been afraid from the look on Jayne Pleshette's face that she and Quinn were going to start sniping at each other unless they were distracted.

The food was good, and Quinn stopped talking about the case while we ate. Instead, he told me about the business he and Jayne Pleshette had started several years earlier. Jayne said very little, but Quinn more than made up for her silence with stories about the antiques and artwork they sold and the sometimes bizarre customers who patronized the shop.

"I know Aaron appreciates the help you've given him," I said. "It's not easy finding some of the things he looks for."

Quinn smiled. "Ah, the ancient and deadly weapons of man."

"And woman," Jayne put in.

"Women have other weapons," Quinn said with a laugh. "You don't have any need for a broadsword, my dear."

"I can think of a use for one," she replied, smiling sweetly at him with her lips.

I said, "Do you think we could go look at the store now?" Quinn paid the bill and the three of us stepped out onto the sidewalk, heading down Greenville Avenue, past the old Granada Theater. As we walked, I wondered if Jayne Pleshette had a key to Quinn's shop. He had said that he always opened and closed himself, but if Jayne was his partner, it seemed likely that she would also have a key. Had he even considered her as a suspect?

The store was in an old brick two-story building with an elaborate facade and a sedate sign that read Damian's—Fine Art—Antiques. There were two large display windows flanking the double doors that led into the place. One window featured two paintings on easels and a small piece of sculpture on a black pedestal. The paintings were both abstract, as was the sculpture. The other window was dominated by a huge antique hutch filled with china and Depression glass. I didn't know enough about any of the stuff to even guess how much it was all worth, but from the looks of the store, Quinn's overhead would be high. I was willing to bet his prices were, too.

Quinn held the door and ushered us in. The atmosphere inside was hushed. There was thick carpet on the floor. The front part of the shop was devoted to fine art. I would have enjoyed wandering through it, looking at the paintings, engravings, and sculptures. Quinn led the way toward the rear of the store. I saw that the back half of the building had had the ceiling removed so that it was high and airy. A staircase led up to what was left of the second floor, undoubtedly where Quinn's office and the storage areas were located. The antiques were back here in this part of the building: beds, dressers, tables, chairs, spinning wheels, and more china cabinets. One wall was devoted to weapons, and I saw why Aaron had become one of Quinn's customers. Most of the items were much more recent than the medieval period in which he was interested. I saw several revolvers and rifles from the eighteenth and nineteenth centuries, but there were also some older sabers and knives, even an English pike.

A bell had softly jingled when we came in the front doors. Now a young man appeared at the head of the stairs and came hurrying down them. He was in his early twenties, with tousled red hair, a few freckles, and a quick smile. "Hi, Damian," he said cheerfully. Then he turned to me and extended his hand. He said, "I'm Mark Howard."

"Mark's my second-in-command around here," Damian Quinn said. "General factotum," Mark added as I shook his hand. "I guess I can use an old-fashioned term like that in an antique store."

"Glad to meet you. I'm Laura Bailey."

"Laura's going to try to find out who's been causing the trouble around here," Quinn explained.

"You're going to chase the ghost for us, eh?" Mark Howard said with a grin.

Quinn's voice held a warning tone as he said, "Mark, I told you about that ghost business."

I glanced at Quinn. "This is the first I've heard about a ghost. I thought we were dealing with burglars." As I spoke, I thought, *Damn, I sound like I'm taking the case.*

"Mark is convinced we have a poltergeist living in the store," Jayne Pleshette said. "Maybe he's right, Damian. You should have gotten an exorcist instead of a detective."

Quinn gave a curt shake of his head. "There's no ghost here. Although I'm not sure Eve would stop at bargaining with the devil."

"Who is Eve?" I asked. It was a name I hadn't heard before in connection with this case.

"Eve Rogers," Jayne replied. "And she's a royal bitch."

"Now, she's not that bad," Quinn put in quickly. To me, he said, "Ms. Rogers owns another art gallery down the street. We're competitors. I admit it's been a rather heated competition at times."

"And you think she could be behind your problems now?" As I asked the question, the thought occurred to me that Jayne Pleshette made it sound as if Eve Rogers was more than business competition. I wondered what Eve looked like.

Quinn hesitated, then answered, "I suppose Eve wouldn't be beyond hiring someone to break in here. She'd never do it herself, though. She has too much class."

Jayne laughed shortly. "I'm going upstairs and work on the sales tax report," she said. She hurried up the stairs and vanished down the hall that led away from the landing.

"I'm afraid Jayne and Eve have never gotten along very well," Quinn explained with a smile. "I've tried to at least keep the relationship civil, even if we are business rivals."

Quinn didn't look bothered by the obvious dislike that Jayne felt for this Eve Rogers. If anything, he was probably a little pleased by it. I had a feeling he was the kind of man who thrived on as much feminine attention as he could get, from as many sources as possible.

He was a womanizer, to use another old-fashioned term as Mark Howard had done.

Mark had been standing by quietly. Now Quinn turned to him and said, "Laura is undecided about looking into this mystery for us. Let's show her some of what we've found."

"Sure." Mark moved over to an old trunk and indicated the latch on it. "This was the first thing Damian noticed. The lid of this trunk was closed, but the latch wasn't fastened. We don't keep it locked, but it is usually latched." He moved over to a massive chest. "One of the drawers here wasn't pushed all the way shut. Same thing on that dresser over there."

I followed along behind him as he pointed out the discrepancies that Quinn had noticed. They were all minor, drawers not closed, pieces of furniture shifted slightly, things like that. Things that were certainly easily explained. They didn't look like signs of a break-in to me.

But Quinn insisted that all of the incidents had happened during the night, when the building was supposed to be closed and locked up tight. "I walk through the store every evening just before I close up," he said. "I know how everything is when I turn on the alarms and lock the doors. That's why I'm sure someone has been in here." Quinn sounded absolutely sincere. It was possible he was right, I supposed. I asked, "Why would someone get in here—however they're doing it—and not take anything?"

He shook his head. "I don't know. Unless they're looking for something and haven't found it yet."

"It's a ghost, I tell you," Mark Howard added, still grinning. "Old buildings like this sometimes have them, you know."

While Quinn gave Mark another warning glance, I took a look at the security system. It was a good one. Protective Associates had done their usual fine job.

The bell over the door jingled again as I went back to join Quinn and Mark. We all looked around and saw a woman walking toward us. She was a sleek blonde, expensively dressed, and I had her figured for a customer at first. But then Mark Howard quickly spoke to Quinn in a low voice. "I'll go upstairs and help Jayne with that tax report," he said.

"Thanks, Mark," Quinn breathed. Then he moved forward to meet the blonde woman. "Hello, Caroline," he said warmly. "I didn't expect to see you here today."

"I had some time off this afternoon and just thought I'd stop by to say hello," she replied. She took the hands Quinn extended toward her and leaned forward to give him a quick kiss on the mouth. Quinn slipped an arm around her waist and turned toward me. "Darling, this is Laura Bailey. She's—an accountant who may be doing some work for us. Laura, this is my wife Caroline."

The lie made my mouth tighten, but I forced it into a smile and said, "Hello, Mrs. Quinn."

Caroline Quinn nodded and said, "How nice to meet you." Then she turned back to Quinn, obviously forgetting about me already. "I have to get back to the office and finish up a presentation now, Damian. Will you be home at the usual time?"

"Well, I don't know," Quinn said. "I'll try, but you never know what might come up."

"Of course." She leaned up and kissed him again, nodded once more to me, and walked back toward the front of the store. She was a beautiful woman, all right, just the type you would expect Quinn to be married to.

Except for the fact that I had decided he wasn't married. He certainly didn't go out of his way to give the impression that he was.

A chaser *and* a cheater, I decided. Maybe I wasn't being fair to him, but I had seen his type enough in the past, considering the line of work I was in.

And Mark Howard was upstairs, carefully keeping the mistress out of the way while the wife was in the store. I wondered if that had been part of his job description when Quinn hired him. Whether I liked Quinn or not, though, I had to admit that he posed an interesting problem. Did he really have someone breaking in here at night to look for God knows what?

"Well, Laura," he said as he turned back to me, once his wife had closed the front door behind her. "I'm sorry about what I had to tell Caroline, but I don't want to bother her with my worries about those break-ins. And speaking of that, have you decided whether or not to take the case?"

I found myself nodding slowly. I didn't like Quinn, but I was curious enough about this situation to invest a little time in it.

"No promises, but . . . I'll look into it," I said.

3

How much of my decision to take Quinn's case was motivated, I wondered, by the fact that Kenneth Owens had refused to? Unlikely though it was, if this turned out to be a major case and I solved it, that wouldn't make Owens look too good. That was kind of a petty way of looking at it.

But I was smiling as I called the office and told one of the secretaries that I wouldn't be back that afternoon.

The place to start seemed to be the gallery owned by Eve Rogers. Quinn told me how to find it, and I strolled down the street toward it after stopping by my car to put some more change in the parking meter.

Eve Rogers' place had her name on its sign, too. It was a one-story structure, much more modern than the one housing Quinn's operation. A plain sign over the door announced that it was The Rogers Gallery of Fine Art. There were the usual displays of painting in the windows. I pushed open the door and went in.

She was doing a brisker business than Quinn at the moment. There hadn't been a single customer at Quinn's in the time I had been there. Of course, if the prices are high enough, you don't need much volume. There were three people in Eve Rogers' shop, not counting the striking redhead who was ambling around the place like she owned it—as she undoubtedly did. One well-dressed couple were looking at the paintings, while a middle-aged man in a fine suit was studying a tapestry on one wall.

The redhead came toward me, a business-like smile on her face. I could feel her eyes gauging me as she approached. The smile became a little smaller as she realized that I wasn't likely to be a paying customer.

"Hello," she said in a throaty voice that I could tell was an affectation. "I'm Eve Rogers. May I help you?"

I took a card out of my purse that identified me as a representative of an insurance company that National often worked for. Smiling, I said, "My name is Laura Bailey. My company carries policies on Mr. Quinn, who has the store down the street. He's been having some trouble with break-ins, and I thought I'd check with the other merchants in the area and see if you've been hit, too."

The smile on her face went away and was replaced by a worried frown. "Burglaries? I wasn't aware that Damian was having problems. No, Ms. Bailey, we've had no trouble of that sort here. Of course, it's always a possibility. That's why we already carry insurance."

So she thought I was about to make a sales pitch. That was all right. I kept smiling and said, "That's good to hear. With crime the way it is these days, you can't be too careful. Mr. Quinn would have lost a great deal of money if he hadn't had the foresight to insure his inventory."

Eve Rogers' frown deepened. "That's terrible. That Damian has had such losses, I mean. He hasn't said anything to me—"

"Yes, indeed," I said when she paused abruptly. I snapped my purse shut. "Well, if there's no way I can help you, Ms. Rogers, I'd better be going. I have several other stops to make in the neighborhood."

I started to turn away when Eve Rogers said, "I'll bet that girlfriend of his isn't very happy."

"Girlfriend?" I asked.

"Miss Pleshette." Her voice was very cool.

"Oh, you mean his business partner."

Eve Rogers smiled again and said, "Yes, of course. That's exactly who I mean."

The hostility Jayne felt for Eve was obviously mutual. For the same reason, I wondered? Maybe Jayne had a reason to be jealous of Eve Rogers. Quinn had said that he tried to keep the relationship between him and Eve civil. That "civil" might have an added meaning to a man like him.

Or maybe I was being too hard on Quinn, jumping to too many conclusions. So much of detective work was hunches and instinct. I had learned that over the years. My father had been a good teacher.

I shook my head. "I thought Mr. Quinn was married."

"Oh, he is. That never stopped some men. Some it still doesn't, even these days." Eve looked past me at her customers. "Excuse me, dear, but I think we should both get back to work." It was clear that the short break for gossiping was over.

I said goodbye and left the store, heading next door to a posh bakery. I had told Eve that I was canvassing the neighborhood, so I had to make it look like I had been telling the truth. I suffered through a five-minute chat with the bakery's owner while the smell of the place played havoc with my self-control, then left with a bag of doughnuts.

My act had been good enough to get Eve Rogers to open up slightly. She had looked surprised when I mentioned the break-ins at Quinn's, but that didn't mean her reaction was sincere. If she had anything to do with the incidents, she was probably prepared for someone to eventually show up and ask some questions about them.

She had also confirmed my suspicion that Quinn was probably carrying on an affair with Jayne Pleshette. It was time to go back to Quinn's and ask him if Jayne had a key. He might take offense at the question, but it had to be asked—and answered.

Mark Howard was polishing an antique table when I came back into Quinn's shop. This time there were customers there, too, a couple of elderly women who were browsing through the antiques and looking at the crystal. Mark looked up and greeted me with a smile. I asked, "Is Mr. Quinn upstairs?"

He shook his head. "He and Jayne left a few minutes ago to run some errands. I'm sure they'll be back before the afternoon's over." He grinned. "Damian had better be here. He's got to lock up."

I looked at Mark and said, "Doesn't it bother you that you don't have a key to the shop? What if there was some sort of emergency?"

Mark shrugged. "No, to tell you the truth it doesn't bother me at all. That's the way Damian wants things, and he's the boss. He built this place up from next to nothing, so he likes to keep a firm hand on the running of it. Can't blame him."

"I guess not. What about Ms. Pleshette? Does she have a key?"

"I'm sure she does, but I've never seen her use it. She's always with Damian when I've seen her. But I've heard her talk about coming in at night sometimes to work on the books." Mark frowned suddenly. "You sound like you think Jayne might have something to do with this."

"Why not?" Quinn wasn't here, so I'd just see if I could get his assistant to talking a little.

Mark shook his head. "Why would she poke around down here and not admit it? Damian wouldn't care. Jayne has the run of the place anyway."

"How much money does she have invested in it?"

"You're asking the wrong guy. What goes on between those two is their business." His voice was cooling off a little. I was prodding into areas that didn't concern me, as far as he was concerned.

"That's true," I nodded. "But I noticed you were quick to go upstairs and keep Ms. Pleshette occupied when Mrs. Quinn came in earlier."

"Hey, Damian's my friend." He shrugged again, a hint of a sheepish smile playing around his mouth. "I don't want to cause trouble for anybody."

I changed directions. "What about Eve Rogers? How do she and Quinn really get along?"

Our voices had been pitched low, so that the two customers wouldn't overhear the conversation. Now they had approached closer, and Mark cast a worried glance at them. He angled his head toward the wall where the weapons were hung and said, "Come on."

When we were back out of earshot of the ladies, he went on, "Look, Ms. Bailey—"

"Laura," I said. It didn't hurt to have a friend on the inside of an investigation.

He grinned. "Sure. Laura. But what I was saying was that Damian's personal life is his own business. Maybe he does like the ladies, but he's a good boss and I like him and this job. Understand?"

"Of course. I'm sorry, I guess I'm just in the habit of suspecting everybody and asking a bunch of awkward questions. Offending people seems to be an occupational hazard."

His grin widened. "Shoot, I'm not offended. In fact, I was just wondering . . . "

Suddenly I knew what was coming.

"How would it be if I called you sometime?" he finished. "We could go out to eat or see a movie or something."

He was a little too young for me—that thought would have gotten a laugh from my father, considering how he felt about my relationship with Aaron—but I knew Mark would not want to hear that. So I said gently, "I'm sorry, Mark, but I'm involved with someone right now. Thank you anyway."

He laughed and shook his head. "Figures. I knew a lady like you would probably be spoken for." He paused. "Spoken for. That's a good one, isn't it? I must talk like that because I'm around all these old things all the time. Makes me feel a little like an antique myself."

I laughed, too. "I have to be going now, but tell Mr. Quinn that I'll keep poking around when I have the time. I'll be back in touch with him later."

"Sure. So long, Laura."

"Goodbye." As I left the store, I heard him talking to the two elderly customers, about to make some more money for Damian Quinn.

There was time to head back to National's offices and get some of my real work done after all, I decided. I had been on the case a little over an hour and hadn't learned a damn thing that did any good—which wasn't unusual in the detective business.

I was tied up with work at National all the next day and didn't have a chance to even think about Damian Quinn's case until he called in the late afternoon.

"I'm sorry to be calling you there, Laura, but I guess I was just getting nervous." He laughed, and it did have an edgy sound. "Did you find out anything from Eve Rogers?"

"Not much," I admitted. "She claimed not to know anything about the break-ins at your store. Of course, that's what she would say, regardless."

"Naturally. Eve can be devious, Laura. She's not going to admit to anything."

"Nobody does anything without leaving a trail of some sort," I told him. "If she's involved, a lead will turn up sooner or later."

"Sooner, I hope. This whole business is driving me crazy."

And suddenly I wondered if that was the point of the thing.

If Quinn was the type of man I thought he was, he would have plenty of enemies out there, men and women both. Maybe one of them had decided to even a score with him by driving him into paranoia. It was a far-fetched theory, but I had run across stranger things.

I told Quinn to try not to worry too much and promised him I would stay in touch. Then, as I went back to work, I found my mind wandering as I tried to figure out how to approach this case.

Like most detective work, the best method might be the most tedious one. There's nothing like old-fashioned legwork and surveillance. It was too late in the day to start the legwork— going from shop to shop along Greenville Avenue near Quinn's place and finding out if anyone had seen anything suspicious— but I could spend some time that evening keeping an eye on his store.

Aaron wouldn't like that; he hated it when my work kept me away from home at night. But he was the one who had roped me into this job. I wasn't going to worry too much about how he would react.

To my surprise, Aaron didn't object when I told him I was going to be staked out at Quinn's store that evening. He was anxious enough for me to solve the case that he didn't mind doing without the pleasure of my company for a while.

So a half-hour after dark, I found myself sitting in my Dodge across the street and half a block down from Quinn's. Greenville Avenue was busy at night due to the many restaurants and clubs in the area. I wouldn't be able to stay parked in one place for too long, or I'd draw the attention of the police. I planned to move every half-hour or so. After doing that a few times, I'd call it a night. Quinn wasn't paying me enough to stay up all night watching the place.

I had a good view of the front of the building. I remembered from my look around the place the day before that there was a back door, too, but I couldn't be in two places at once. If anyone got in through the back, I was counting on spotting their movements inside. I had a small pair of binoculars with light-gathering lenses. It wasn't as good as a starlight scope, but it helped.

Even though I was watching the building, I couldn't help but pay some attention to the cars passing me. I noticed a Volvo that went slowly past the store twice, as if the driver was looking for a parking place. On the third try, the driver found one. I was slumped down in the seat of my car, the glasses ready if I needed them, but there was enough illumination from the streetlights for me to recognize Jayne Pleshette as she got out of the Volvo and went to the door of the antique store.

She took a key out of her purse and let herself in.

That answered that question. Jayne had a key, all right, and now she was inside the store with no sign of Damian Quinn anywhere around.

The questions that Mark Howard had asked came back to me. Why would Jayne need to sneak around the store at night looking for something? If she was the one moving things, why not just admit it right from the first?

Unless she was working against Quinn for some reason. That was feasible.

The display windows of the store were softly lit, but that was the only source of illumination for the rest of the place at night. That was enough to let me watch through the binoculars as Jayne Pleshette hurried toward the rear of the store. The control panel of the alarm system was in a small alcove underneath the staircase that led to the second floor. After opening the front door, Jayne had thirty seconds to reach the panel and punch out a six digit code on its keyboard. That would shut down the system and keep it from calling in an alarm to the security company and setting off a siren.

I saw Jayne turn the corner around the staircase and disappear from view.

Ten minutes later, she hadn't come back into sight. I frowned.

She might have been able to go up the stairs without me seeing her, I thought, but it wasn't likely. Of course, she could be somewhere in the back of the store, rummaging around. Or looking for whatever had prompted the series of nocturnal visits to Quinn's store.

She had not paused to lock the front door behind her when she went in. No doubt she had intended to come back and lock it as soon as the alarm system was turned off. I couldn't see her going upstairs to work and leaving the door unlocked like that.

Every instinct in my body told me something was wrong.

I took a deep breath and put the binoculars down on the seat beside me. I picked up my purse. There was a can of Mace inside it, along with a good-sized clasp knife. I worked out regularly at a local martial arts studio, too, if it came to that. I didn't think Jayne Pleshette would present much of a physical challenge, but there was no telling who else was in there.

There was only one way to find out.

I got out of my car, locking it behind me, and waited for a break in the traffic before running across the street. Pausing in front of the store, I looked through the windows and still didn't see anything moving. I put my hand on the door and slowly pulled it open.

The place had not looked eerie at all during the day, but it took on a spooky appearance at night. There were a lot of shadows and dark, hulking forms that turned out to be nothing but paintings on easels and pieces of old furniture. My heartbeat sounded loud to me as I moved toward the back of the store. I thought about calling out to Jayne, then decided against it. Despite the fact that my heart seemed to be thumping so noisily, I knew that in reality I was moving very quietly. Whatever was going on here, I wanted the element of surprise on my side.

I reached the staircase, leaned around it, looked for some sign of Jayne Pleshette.

She was there, all right, lying halfway inside the alcove, her body and her face twisted. She wasn't pretty anymore.

The antique dagger that someone had plunged into her chest had changed all of that.

I stood stock-still, eyes wide, taking in the horrible scene. There was a good-sized bloodstain on Jayne's silk blouse around the blade of the knife. She was the first murder victim I had ever seen. And even in my shocked state, I was sure it was murder. There was no question of suicide, not with the frightened, agonized expression that was frozen on Jayne's contorted features.

Somewhere in the building, a floorboard creaked.

I hadn't been breathing as I stared at Jayne's body. Now, without thinking, I gasped. The killer was still here in the store. I grimaced as I ducked into the alcove, hoping that I hadn't given away my presence.

The lights in the display windows went off then.

My heartbeat got even louder. The killer knew I was here, all right, and he had turned off the lights so that he could sneak up on me. There was no other explanation.

I reached behind me, feeling around on the wall for the control panel of the alarm system. I was familiar with the system and knew it came equipped with a panic button that would immediately summon police, firemen, and an ambulance in addition to setting off the alarm. My scrabbling fingers found the button and started to stab it.

Hands came down on my shoulders, wrenching me away from the panel before I could press the button.

I let out an involuntary yell and lashed out with my free hand. My purse was still clutched tightly in the other hand. My fingers were stiffened, and I got lucky. They jabbed into soft flesh, and I knew I had found the killer's throat.

There was a strangled gasp, and then I heard the hiss of something coming at my head. There was only a split-second's warning, but it was enough for me to jerk my head back. Something clipped it, something hard that made me stagger back against the alcove wall. I felt the keyboard of the control panel against my left shoulder and reached up to slap at it in the dark. I was lucky again.

The system's siren began whooping. I dove for the floor, rolling and bumping into a pair of legs. I kicked up as I rolled, connecting with flesh again. The same thing that had grazed my head slammed down into my back. I screamed as fiery pain shot through me.

I lay there on the floor, gritting my teeth against the pain as running footsteps pounded away from me. I could hear them over the siren, and then the slam of the shop's rear door cut them off.

The killer was gone . . . I hoped. I forced myself to sit up and dig into my purse for the knife there. When I had it in my hands, I scooted backward until my back hit the wall of the alcove. I knew that Jayne Pleshette's cooling body was only a couple of feet away from me, but despite what that knowledge did to my nerves, I decided I should stay put.

So that's what I did, sitting in the dark with a dead woman, waiting with a knife clutched tightly in my hands.

4

The next few hours were a nightmare but nothing compared to the encounter with the killer in the dark. I was safe enough once the cops came storming in with their guns drawn, but I still couldn't stop shaking for the longest time.

No one had ever tried to kill me before—and I was sure that was what would have happened if my attacker had gotten the upper hand for even a minute.

I told my story to the uniformed officers who were the first ones on the scene, then repeated it what seemed like a dozen times for the detectives who followed up. During the middle of one recitation, a plainclothes officer led Damian Quinn into the store and shooed the photographers and technicians aside long enough to show him the body. Quinn paled and said in a choked voice, "That's her. That's my business partner, Jayne Pleshette."

The detective I was talking to drew my attention back to him by saying, "According to your story, Quinn hired you to investigate a series of burglaries, Ms. Bailey?"

"They weren't really burglaries," I said. "Nothing was taken. But you should have all of that in your records. I know Mr. Quinn went to the police before he came to me."

The cop nodded. "We'll check into it." He looked up abruptly, his eyes narrowing as he studied me. "Say, you aren't Jim Bailey's daughter, are you? I heard she was a PI, too."

"That's me," I said.

"Your old man was a hell of a detective, lady. Shame about him getting sick like that. What's it been, six weeks or so?"

"Two weeks," I said, feeling a fresh surge of pain well up inside me.

The man shook his head. "Seems like longer ago than that

since I read about the funeral. I'm sorry, Ms. Bailey."

Quinn came hurrying over then. He put a hand on my arm and asked, "Are you all right, Laura? The officer who called me said that you had a fight with the killer."

"I'm okay," I told him. "I'll have a pretty good bruise on my back, but the paramedics have already checked me out. It won't amount to anything."

He rubbed a shaking hand over his face. "God, I never expected anything like this! I . . . I can't believe Jayne is . . . is . . . "

"We'll get whoever did it, sir," the detective I had been talking to assured him. But all three of us knew there was a good chance the murderer would never be caught. The cops would work the case until the file on it was maybe an inch thick, but I had a feeling they wouldn't be any closer to the killer.

The police let me call Aaron, since I was too shaken up to drive home. He exploded, "What!" when I told him I had walked into a murder, but he promised to be there as soon as he could. While I waited for him, I watched Quinn check over the store with the detectives. As I expected, nothing was missing.

Whatever Quinn's mysterious visitor had been up to, he didn't want it interrupted. Jayne had walked in at the wrong time.

I cast my mind back over the details of the encounter. The killer hadn't said anything, and I had never struck anything except glancing blows. I couldn't be sure that it had been a man fighting with me in the dark. A woman could have stabbed Jayne and clouted me with an antique brass spittoon. It had been lying close by me on the floor, and the cops had decided it was the weapon the killer had used on me.

The dagger had come from the wall of antique weapons. Quinn had recognized it right away. The leather-wrapped handle probably wouldn't have taken any usable prints, but the killer had paused long enough before I came in to wipe it clean anyway.

The uniformed officer at the door of the shop stopped Aaron when he arrived. I saw him gesturing frantically as he argued with the cop. One of the detectives signalled for him to be let in. He came hurrying over to me, his dark face set in worried lines.

"Are you all right?" he asked as he gripped my shoulders.

"I'm fine," I said, and then I let him pull me into an embrace. It hurt my back a little, but I figured the pain was worth it.

A few minutes later, they let us go home. I was more than willing. I wanted to take some aspirin and stretch out in bed, but I had a feeling sleep would not come easily.

I was right.

The next morning brought bleary eyes, a stiff, very sore back, and several surprises.

There was no way I was going in to work. Aaron got me set up on the sofa before he left, leaving me with plenty of pillows, a pot of hot tea, and the new Larry Niven novel. The phone was beside me, and once Aaron was gone, I called the office. No doubt Kenneth Owens had already heard about what had happened, but I wanted to give him my version.

His secretary put me right through to him. Sounding more cheerful than usual, he said, "Good morning, Laura. How do you feel?"

"I've been better," I told him honestly. "I wanted to explain to you why I won't be in today—"

"No need," Owens cut in. "Mr. Quinn is sitting here in my office right now, and he's told me the whole story."

"What?" I couldn't keep the amazement out of my voice.

"Yes, that's right. We're going to be investigating the death of Mr. Quinn's partner. I plan to take charge of the investigation personally."

Owens sounded properly solemn when he mentioned Jayne's

death, but I could hear an undercurrent in his voice that was almost gleeful. I understood completely now. What had promised to be a pointless, small-time case was now a murder, complete with posh surroundings and an exotic murder weapon. Just the kind of case to get a lot of press coverage for the man who solved it. Owens never liked getting involved in cases that were under police investigation, but I had a feeling he was going to make an exception this time. Those thoughts raced through my mind, but before I could say anything, Owens went on, "Mr. Quinn wants to talk to you. Is that all right?"

"Sure," I said tiredly. "Put him on."

A moment later, Quinn said, "Hello, Laura. I'm glad to hear that you're recovering from that awful experience."

"I'm fine," I told him, my voice curt. He sounded more like himself this morning; obviously, he had gotten over some of the shock of Jayne's death.

"I hope you don't mind that I came to see Mr. Owens. The more I thought about it, the more I realized you wouldn't want to continue with the case. You've been through too much already."

It would have been nice for him to ask me if I wanted to go on with the investigation, I thought, rather than deciding for me. Keeping a tight rein on my temper, I said, "Fine, if that's what you want. I'm sure Mr. Owens and National will do a good job for you. Unless the police find the killer themselves, of course."

"I don't really care who finds the man," Quinn said. "Just so he's found and punished." He paused and sighed, then went on, "I believe Mr. Owens wants to talk to you again."

Owens took back the phone and said, "Laura, I want you to take it easy and get some rest. Take as much time off as you need. In fact, why don't you just consider yourself on a leave of absence for right now?"

There was a grating edge behind the surface concern in his tone. I knew what he was getting at. He was angry at me for

taking the original case behind his back, even though he had made
it plain that he wanted no part of it. And now that it had turned
into something much more important, he was taking over.

"Why don't we just make that leave of absence permanent?"
I asked. Even as I said it, the cautious part of my brain was crying
out a warning not to burn my bridges, but I was too mad to listen
to it. I had seen the agency my father and I had worked so hard
to build up turn into just another division of some faceless
conglomerate, and I was damned tired of trying to cope with it.

"Are you sure that's what you want?" Owens asked.

"I'm sure."

He hesitated, then said, "All right. I'm sure that can be
arranged. We'll be in touch later." He was talking around it, not
wanting Quinn to know that I had just quit.

"I'm sure we will," I said, then put down the phone. I closed
my eyes, leaned back against the cushions of the sofa. I had a sore
back and I was out of a job—and I didn't have the slightest idea
what I was going to do next.

The answer came as another surprise. Aaron came hurrying
in at lunchtime, something he almost never did. He said, "Do you
feel up to getting dressed and going somewhere with me?"

I frowned. "Where?"

"A friend of mine called me at work this morning. She wants
to meet you."

I was puzzled by the request, but he seemed to think it was
important so I got dressed in jeans and a blue chambray work
shirt. Aaron had to help me into the shirt, and he winced when he
saw the big ugly bruise on my back. It was too sore for me to wear
a bra. Going out without one made me a little uncomfortable, but
it was better than hurting even worse.

We drove into north Dallas, to a fashionable residential

neighborhood. This was a wealthy part of town, and I was a little surprised that Aaron had friends living here. I didn't know all of his acquaintances, but none of the ones I did know had this kind of money. He parked in front of a large stone house set behind an impressive stretch of lawn.

He hurried around the car and helped me out. We went up a long, curving flagstone walk to the front porch of the house. Aaron pressed the doorbell, and a moment later the heavy door opened slowly.

"Hello, Aaron. I'm so glad you could come over. And you must be Laura."

The woman who greeted us was probably seventy years old, tall, spare, and gray-haired. She looked rather severe at first glance, but she had a quick smile and her blue eyes were friendly. She ushered us into the house, which was just as impressive inside as out. The carpet was thick, the walls panelled in rich dark wood. The woman led us into a living room furnished with massive antique furniture. I started to have a glimmering of what this might be about.

"Please sit down, Laura," the woman told me. "I know you must still be shaken up from what happened last night. I read all about it in the paper this morning."

I sat down on a claw-footed divan with Aaron beside me and said, "I don't want to be rude, ma'am, but why did you want to see me?"

"Of course. Laura, my name is Zora Sims. I'm a customer of Damian Quinn's. Many of the furnishings in this house came from his shop, in fact. And that's where I met Aaron." Zora Sims smiled again. "That's quite a young man you have there. I never met anyone so young who was so interested in history."

Only in a certain area of history, I thought. I glanced at Aaron and saw that he looked uncomfortable, so I didn't make any comments that would make him feel worse. I asked, "What can I do for you, Mrs. Sims?"

"I want to hire you," she said. "I want you to find out who killed Jayne Pleshette."

I had sort of expected that, but to hear it was still a shock.

"Why?" I asked. "Just because you're one of Quinn's customers?"

Zora Sims pursed her lips slightly. "I have to admit that I never really cared for Jayne. But I do like Damian. He's such a charming young man, don't you think?"

I was sure that she would think so, given the way that Quinn naturally played up to every woman he encountered. I kept a noncommittal look on my face and waited for her to go on.

She continued, "But the real reason I want to hire you goes beyond my affection for Damian, my dear. It has to do with you."

"Me?"

"You see, I knew your father. He handled a rather delicate matter for me many years ago, not long after he came to Dallas. I was always very appreciative toward him. When I got to know Aaron from seeing him at Damian's store, he mentioned one day that he knew you. I hope you won't be offended, Laura, but I did a little investigating of my own."

I didn't much like the sound of that. The idea of this woman poking into my life didn't appeal to me.

She went on, "Your father told me he came to Texas looking for a better place to raise his children. I think he was always disappointed that your mother did not agree with the move. I know the divorce bothered him a great deal. He must have been very happy when you began working with him after you graduated from college."

"I never intended to," I said. It was none of this woman's business, but for some reason I felt like I had to explain myself to her. "His health was getting worse, so I pitched in just to help for a while. We had stayed close, even after my mother left him, but I never intended for the arrangement to be permanent."

"You were just too good at your job," Zora Sims said. "Jim couldn't afford to let you go. I know he could be a persuasive man; I don't imagine he had much trouble talking you into continuing in the agency with him."

I had to smile. "No, not too much."

Zora Sims leaned forward in her chair, fixing an intent gaze on me. "I know you must think I'm an old busybody, dear, meddling in things that are none of my business. But you see, your father did an enormous service for me, and I've wished for years that I could have done more to pay him back than simply paying his fee. Now I have a chance to do just that."

I shook my head. "I don't understand."

"I have a proposition for you, Laura. If you find Jayne Pleshette's killer, I'll help you open your own detective agency. I'll provide whatever financial help you need. And I do have quite a few influential contacts in this town, if I do say so myself."

The proposal stunned me. My own agency, handed to me just for solving the Pleshette killing? A case that was being investigated already by both the police and a large detective agency with plenty of money and manpower at its disposal. On the surface, Zora Sims' offer sounded generous, but I knew how hard it would be to compete with Owens and the cops.

And then I found myself extending my hand to her and heard myself saying, "Thank you. I'll do it."

There was no way I could pass this one up!

5

The decision had been made on the spur of the moment. After I thought it over, I realized what a big job I was letting myself in for. But at the same time, I was more excited about what I was doing than I had been in a long time. It had only been a year since my father's failing health had forced him to sell the agency to National, but it seemed a lot longer than that.

Now I was on my own, and it was scary. I was determined to beat Kenneth Owens to the killer, though.

Sore back or no sore back, I couldn't afford to sit around waiting to heal. Aaron drove me back to the apartment from Zora Sims' house. I stood under a hot shower for a long time, letting the heat soak some of the aches and pains out of my body. Then I got dressed in a skirt and a loose shirt, took some more aspirin, and went to work.

My first stop was the antique store. I was a little worried that the cops might still have it closed and barricaded off as a crime scene, but evidently the photographers and the forensics team had finished their work. The place was open for business, and as I stepped inside I saw that there were several customers there. Nothing like a murder to help a retail business. It brings out all the morbid shoppers.

Mark Howard hurried toward me as I came in. He looked a little harried. When he recognized me, he slowed down and grinned. "Hi, Laura," he said in a low voice. "For a second, I thought you were another customer. We've been swamped today."

"Maybe I am a customer," I told him. "I've been fired from the investigation."

"What?" he stared. "I knew Damian went to see your boss, but I just assumed—"

I shook my head. "I don't work for National Security Services anymore, as of this morning, or Damian Quinn. But I do have a client who's interested in finding out who killed Jayne Pleshette."

Mark cast a quick glance around. "Come on into the back," he said. "I want to hear about this, but I've got to keep an eye on the customers. We have a lady who works part-time here, but she called this morning and quit. Said she couldn't work in a place where someone was killed."

"Maybe she's afraid of ghosts."

He grinned again. "I had forgotten about that. I guess what happened last night takes care of my poltergeist theory."

We walked past the staircase. I had to repress a little shudder as we passed the place where I had had my scuffle with the killer. I said, "You don't sound too upset by Jayne's death."

"Don't get me wrong," he said solemnly. "I was pretty shaken up when I found out about it. I'm sorry it happened. But Jayne and I were never very close."

"You and she didn't get along?"

"We got along fine. I think Jayne appreciated how much I helped out around here. That gave Damian more time for her. But we weren't really what you could call friends."

I nodded. What he said made sense. "Jayne was Quinn's partner. I know I asked you this yesterday, but it could be more important now. Do you have any idea how much money she had sunk into this place?"

Instead of answering my question, he asked one of his own. "You said you have another client. Who?"

"I can't tell you that, Mark. It's what they call privileged information."

"You're not working for Eve Rogers, are you?"

The question surprised me. I said, "No, I'm not. I can tell you that much. Why would I be working for her?"

He shrugged. "The way I've got it figured, if Eve was behind what's been going on around here, she might want to cover it up. She could have hired you to find out how close she is to being caught." That infectious grin broke out again on his freckled face. "But if you're not working for her, then you'll be going after her."

"I'm after the killer, whoever it turns out to be," I corrected him. "Now, about Jayne's financial involvement in this place . . . ?"

"Sure, I'll tell you what I know, but it's not much. I don't know any of the numbers, but from things that Damian has said, I think Jayne put up most of the money to start this place. The same holds true for the new store. But for all I know, Damian's been paying her back all along."

"They've been having an affair for a long time?"

"I know they've been friends for at least five years. I can't tell you anything about an affair."

I nodded. If he didn't want to put it into words, that was all rightÔ We both knew what had been going on between Quinn and Jayne. I asked, "Did Caroline Quinn know about them?"

"I don't know," Mark answered with a shake of his head. "She must have suspected, but I don't know anything for sure. See, I told you I wasn't going to be much help."

I wasn't sure about that. Mark had confirmed some of my suspicions and given more weight to the nebulous theories that were trying to form in my brain.

Mark had to go help a customer then. I stayed where I was, mulling over what he had told me. My eyes kept straying to the alcove. Jayne Pleshette's body was long gone, of course, and the chalk outline on the floor had been cleaned up. But I still seemed to see her there.

I knew from the line of questioning the cops had taken that they thought the murderer was whoever had been breaking in here. Plenty of killings were done by startled burglars who were interrupted at their work. But what if the motive for Jayne's death had nothing to do with the break-ins?

Caroline Quinn certainly had a reason for wanting Jayne dead—if, that is, she wanted to preserve her marriage to Quinn. And as far as I was concerned, Damian Quinn himself had to be considered a suspect. Jayne had obviously been quite jealous, too. Maybe she had issued an ultimatum to Quinn: leave his wife and marry her, or she would pull out of their partnership and take her financial backing with her. That would deal a death blow to Quinn's plans for expansion and maybe even threaten this store.

I wondered if Quinn and Jayne had the usual partners' life insurance policies. Quinn might emerge from this in a much better position financially, not to mention being rid of a nagging problem.

If Quinn was the killer, going to Owens and hiring National could be a smokescreen on his part, I thought. I wasn't sure he was that devious, but it was at least a possibility.

I was going to have to try to find out if Quinn and Caroline—and Eve Rogers, for that matter; might as well include everyone, I thought—had alibis for the night before. That was going to be harder to do, now that I was working on my own. Even in the old days, I had always had my father backing me up, giving me suggestions, calling in old favors. Now there was no one to rely on but myself. And I was starting to worry about being able to do it. I had big shoes to fill and a difficult case as a starting point.

I drove into downtown Dallas and found a place to park a couple of blocks from the police station. I wasn't expecting very much cooperation from the detectives in charge of the case, but I had to at least try to talk to them.

A lieutenant named Harkness was in charge of the investigation into Jayne Pleshette's death. He was a fairly young man with a drooping moustache. He wore cowboy clothes and looked more like a ranch hand than a cop, but he was friendly enough and willing to talk to me. He just wasn't willing to give me any useful information. I left Harkness's office not knowing any more than when I went in. He had refused to tell me if Quinn, Caroline, and Eve Rogers had alibis for the night before. That information was part of an ongoing police investigation, according to Detective Harkness.

Back in the car, I tried to think of what to do next. The pain from my bruised back, the lack of sleep the night before, and the brain-dulling effects of the aspirin I had taken all conspired to make it hard to think. What I wanted to do was go home and crawl back into bed.

Instead, I pulled a small notebook out of my purse. As I ran my fingertips over the black leather of its cover, my mind went back to all the times I had seen my father pull it out of his shirt pocket to make a note or look up a telephone number. Inside it were all the contacts he had made over the years of operating as a PI in the Dallas area, plus the names of a few people he had kept in touch with in New York.

It was part of Jim Bailey's legacy to me, and for the first time, I was going to get the chance to use it.

I got plenty of strange looks that afternoon as I talked to people in all sorts of places, from pool halls to executive offices. I was familiar with some of the cases my father had handled for them, which helped to convince them that I was who I said I was. It was a little harder to make them believe that I was serious in the questions I was asking, but in the end, I got some of what I needed.

From a banker, I got a credit report on Damian Quinn and discovered that he had never had the kind of money it would have taken to open up his shop. That meant that someone else had provided the financing for it. Jayne Pleshette? That was the obvious answer, and while a credit report on her provided no proof that she had backed Quinn, it did indicate that she had enough assets to have done so. Quinn, despite his success, had kept spending more and more and borrowing more and more from various banks. He was still not on solid ground, even though his operation was growing.

From some less respectable sources, I learned that no one was willing to admit to being hired to break into Quinn's store. That was no surprise. But I was able to put out the word that I was looking for whoever might have been responsible. I didn't expect too much from that. Professional burglars rarely commits acts of violence, even when caught in the act. But I had to pay some attention to all the possible angles of the case.

Kenneth Owens would be doing much the same thing, I thought, although I doubted he would investigate Quinn, who was, after all, the agency's client. And you almost have to start from the assumption that the client is innocent.

I didn't have that liability. I could suspect everybody.

By evening, I was plenty tired, and my back was hurting worse. I didn't want to take anything else for it, so I went home, soaked under the shower again, and got out just as Aaron was coming in from work.

"Did you find out anything?" he asked anxiously.

"I'm fine, thanks, and you?" I replied sarcastically.

He waved off the comment. "Sorry, Laura. I just thought you might have, I don't know, solved the case or something?"

Even though I was working for Zora Sims now, I could tell he hoped that I would solve the case and that Quinn would somehow wind up in his eternal debt. I said, "That's placing an awful lot of faith in my abilities, Aaron. I don't know a whole lot more than I did. But I'm working on it."

"Okay," he nodded. "That's fine." He moved closer to me. "Could I rub something on your back for you?"

   I took a tube of analgesic cream from the medicine cabinet
and handed it to him. "That would be nice," I admitted.
   And it was, bad back and all.

   The next day was more of the same. I had originally approached this case knowing it was going to take a lot of legwork
and surveillance. The surveillance had gotten me an encounter
with a murderer; now the legwork was giving me more sore
muscles.I was starting to feel human again. My back was better
and I had slept fairly well the night before, which helped.
   The lack of success I was having made me think it was time
to change tacks. If the person who had been slipping into Quinn's
was not the killer, there was a possibility that the intruder would
come back. Keeping an eye on the place might yet pay some
dividends.
   I got hold of Aaron on the phone at Los Colinas and told him
I wouldn't be home until late. I didn't explain what I had in mind,
and he didn't ask. Once I told him it had to do with the case, it
was fine with him. I hung up wondering just how much he would
have worried if I hadn't called to let him know not to expect me.
   The killer had come in through the back door at Quinn's. The
police hadn't told me that, but I had heard the door slam when he
was making his escape, and later, after the cops got there, I had
seen one of them try it and find it unlocked. I hadn't gotten a
close-up look, but I hadn't spotted any signs of forced entry.
   That meant the killer had had a key. Obviously, there were
more of them floating around than the ones Quinn and Jayne had.
That thought told me that Quinn must have an alibi for the time
of the killing, or he would have been arrested and charged by
now. The fact that he hadn't been meant the cops were operating
on the theory that the killer had his own key.
   And if the killer had a key, whoever had been sneaking into

the place might have one, too.

What all that convoluted thinking amounted to was that when night fell, I was parked on a side street off Greenville Avenue where I could watch down an alley and see the back door of Quinn's shop. This time there was a gun in my purse.

I had stopped by the apartment to pick up the little Colt .32. I had owned it for several years but had never fired it except on a firing range, had never even carried it on a job until now. But the memory of that desperate struggle in the dark was just too strong. I did not want to be trapped in a situation like that again.

Maybe I should have just brought one of Aaron's maces or broadswords, I thought wryly. The PI as barbarian warrior. A strange concept, that one.

Nobody bothered me. Nobody showed up and tried to get into the building. I sat there waiting, and my back began to stiffen up and hurt again by ten o'clock. It was time to call it a night and go home. I was reaching for the key to start my Dodge when I saw the car turn in at the other end of the alley. Its lights went black as soon as it was off the street.

I stayed where I was, sitting frozen in the darkness as my instincts told me something was about to happen.

The other car eased to a stop behind Quinn's. I couldn't tell too much about it, parked in the deep shadows of the alley as it was. It was fairly small but not a compact. I lifted the binoculars and focused in on it just as the driver opened his door to slip out. He was moving fast, but the dome light still came on for a few seconds before he could get the door closed.

An amateur, all right. Any professional would have just taken the light bulb out.

The car was a Mercedes, I decided.

What the hell kind of burglar drove a Mercedes?

The driver went to the back door of Quinn's. His shoulders were hunched as he worked with the door. It swung open a moment later, and the man disappeared inside. He had to have a key, I knew; no amateur could have gotten past the lock that fast.

I reached up, pulled off the plastic cover, and popped the bulb out of my own dome light. I got out and quietly closed the door behind me. The top of my purse was open so that I could reach in and get the gun in a hurry. I had forgotten all about the pain in my back as I started down the alley, my pulse racing.

I was going to get the son of a bitch.

This was stupid, the rational part of my brain was yelling as I approached the back door. Call the cops, it was demanding. Call the cops and stay out of it!"

I reached for the doorknob.

The door flew open, slamming against my arm. I let out a yelp and fell backward, losing my balance. Someone ran into me, knocking me the rest of the way off my feet. I sprawled in the alley, the purse skittering away from me on the dirty asphalt. I lunged after it, knowing that I had better get hold of that pistol in a hurry.

The door of the Mercedes slammed and its engine tried to cough to life. The driver had to be cursing diesel engines at the moment. The engine roared up as I finally scrabbled on hands and knees over to my purse. My hand dove into it and came out with the .32. I tried to come up into a crouch as I whirled to face the Mercedes, but my balance deserted me again.

I sat down hard on my rear end as the lights of the car lanced out and blinded me. I heard the scréech of tires as it took off. Panic made me move with frantic speed. I rolled toward the wall of the building, letting out an involuntary shriek as the Mercedes flashed by only a foot or so away from my shoulder. The driver seemed to be as panic-stricken as I was. I gazed after the fleeing vehicle as I tried to drag air back into my lungs.

The light over the license plate was lit up, revealing a vanity plate that read 2RICH. That wouldn't be hard to remember. But

I wasn't ready to let the bastard get away yet. I got onto my feet and started to run after him, lifting the gun to try for his rear tires.

Somebody else came out of the back door of Quinn's and smashed right into me.

I went down again, the thought racing through my brain that I was going to be black and blue all over before this case was finished. I rolled over and tried to locate the man who had just run into me. Could the driver of the Mercedes have had an accomplice already inside the store?

"Hold it!" a voice yelled at me. "Don't move or I'll shoot!"

I had already spotted the shadowy shape a foot away and was lifting my gun to aim at it. I froze, the barrel of the .32 lined on the figure and my finger tight on the trigger. There had been something horribly familiar about the voice that had shouted the warning at me.

"Hold your fire," I said, forcing my voice to stay calm. "It's me."

"Oh my God," Kenneth Owens said, staring at me over the barrel of his gun. "Laura?"

I lowered my Colt and slipped the safety back on. "That's right," I said as I stood up and started to brush myself off. "You were staked out inside Quinn's, weren't you?"

"I thought the killer might come back." He was on his feet now, and his tone was aggrieved as he went on, "I would have had him if you hadn't gotten in the way. What are you doing here, anyway?"

"Working, just like you," I answered. "And I might have had the guy if you hadn't come bulling out into the way." Now that I wasn't working for him anymore, I could speak my mind. It felt good.

He jammed his pistol back into the holster under his coat. "I guess we'd better call the cops," he said disgustedly.

I shook my head, enjoying the fact that I was suddenly on

equal footing with him, maybe even a little ahead. "Don't you want to catch that guy?"

"Of course." Enough light came out the back door of the shop for me to see the shrewd expression on his face. "Do you have any ideas on that subject?"

"Are we working together for the moment?"

He hesitated, then said, "I guess so."

"Then how hard can it be to find someone driving a Mercedes with the license plate 2RICH?"

He looked so happy that I thought for a second he was going to try to hug me. I was glad I still had my own gun out.

6

Owens' car was parked a block away on Greenville Avenue. There was a cellular phone in it, so we decided that Owens would use it to call a friend of his in the Dallas PD. We would probably have the name and address of the man who owned the Mercedes within a matter of minutes.

My arm was hurting a little where the door had hit it. I had gotten knocked around more on this case than any of the others I had worked on. I hoped it wasn't the start of a trend.

Owens was clearly uncomfortable working with me on an equal basis, but he didn't have much choice. If he didn't cooperate, I could call the cops and give them the story, including the license number of the Mercedes. That would kill any chance of Owens solving the case, or more importantly, getting the credit for solving the case. As we walked toward his car, he said, "I thought you were supposed to be home resting and recuperating."

"I decided I'd rather work."

He glanced suspiciously at me. "Work for who? I thought you meant to quit National."

"My license is in my own name, not the agency's. There's nothing stopping me from taking on a client of my own."

His expression became even more dubious. We reached his car, and he had his keys out and in the door lock when I suddenly hissed, "Wait a minute!"

Owens looked up at me in surprise. "What's wrong?"

"Look down there." I pointed down the block.

Owens looked and saw the same thing that I had just spotted. There was a Mercedes parked just outside Eve Rogers' gallery. It was well after business hours, but there were lights inside the building.

"Oh, no," Owens said softly. "He couldn't be that stupid."

"Well, if he is, let's not give him time to wise up," I said as I started toward Eve's.

The Mercedes was the right one. I glanced at the 2RICH plate and nodded to Owens. I felt a little shiver go through me as I glanced at the smooth hard surface of its fender and thought about how close it had come to running over me. The gun was back in my purse, but my hand was on the butt of it and my fingers clenched as I started toward the door of the gallery.

Owens pressed ahead of me and tried the door. It was locked. We looked through the glass and saw that most of the light inside was coming through an open door in the rear of the big room. The door had to lead into Eve Rogers' office, I thought.

"Is there a back door into this place?" Owens asked.

"I don't know. I was only here once, and I didn't get that good a look around."

"All right," he nodded. "I'll get out of sight, you bang on the glass."

I frowned at him. "You think she'll let me in?"

"Think of a good story," he growled at me as he retreated out of sight of anyone inside the gallery. He crouched in the shadows at the corner of the building. I hoped someone passing by on the street wouldn't see him and call the cops, thinking he was a burglar.

I took a deep breath and rapped hard on the glass of the door. After a moment, I knocked again. Someone emerged from the office then, the light from within casting a long shadow toward the front of the building. I saw the red hair, the quick lithe walk, and knew it was Eve Rogers.

She came to the door but didn't unlock it. There was a frown on her face as she studied me through the glass. "Ms. Rogers?" I called. "Remember me, Laura Bailey? From the insurance company?"

"What are you doing here at this time of night?" she demanded. There was a distracted look on her face, and I had a pretty good idea what was causing it.

"There's been another break-in at Quinn's," I said, telling her the truth. "I was wondering if I could ask you some questions before the police get here." My voice was loud enough for Owens to hear me.

Eve looked more disturbed. "The police are coming?"

"They should be here any minute," I nodded.

I could see her brain working. She had to get rid of the man from the Mercedes before the police arrived, and to do that she had to get rid of me first. The quickest way would be to listen to my questions, deny seeing or knowing anything, and send me on my way. She reached her decision and jabbed the key into the door lock.

"I thought you sold insurance," she said as she opened the door just enough for me to slip through.

"I do a little investigating, too," I said. I stayed between her and the door so that she couldn't lock it behind me. "Have you seen anything suspicious this evening?"

Eve shook her head. "Not a thing. I've been back in the office, trying to catch up on some paperwork—" She broke off suddenly, and I had a feeling I knew what had just occurred to her. Less than five minutes had passed since the Mercedes had peeled out of the alley behind Quinn's. The only way I could have known this quickly about the incident was if I had been there, which meant that I had probably seen the Mercedes—

I slid the gun out of my purse as her face hardened and she started toward me. "You bitch!" she snapped. "Get out of here!"

"Just hold on," I said quickly. "Don't do anything foolish, Ms. Rogers."

There was a quick patter of footsteps behind her as a man emerged from the office. I glanced past Eve Rogers and got a fairly good look at him. He was short, several inches below medium height, and young, maybe twenty-two. He would have been handsome if he hadn't looked so panicky.

"Dammit, Eve!" he said. "Get rid of her. She knows who I am!"

I didn't have the slightest idea who he was, other than the guy who had been sneaking into Quinn's shop and the maniac who had nearly run me down—and maybe the person who had murdered Jayne Pleshette. As he hurried toward us, I swung the barrel of the gun toward him and snapped, "Slow down, mister!"

He may have been an amateur, but he accidentally accomplished the thing I had been afraid of. I had to take my attention off of Eve to cover him, and in that moment the redhead sprang toward me. Her hand closed over the cylinder of the .32 and wrenched it aside. Eve's other hand struck at me, glancing off my shoulder. The man yelled, "Hang on to her!"

I twisted and snapped a side kick at Eve. It took her in the thigh, spinning her halfway around. She didn't fall, though. She recovered her balance and charged at me at the same time as the young man did. I couldn't handle both of them at once, I knew.

Eve by herself would be a handful.

The door of the gallery banged open behind me. Kenneth Owens ran in, leveling his gun at the man from the Mercedes. Owens yelled, "Hold it!" At the same time, Eve froze as she stared down the barrel of my pistol. It hadn't been much of a fight, but it was over now. Breathing heavily from exertion and anger, Eve said, "I don't know who you people are, but I'm calling the police! You can't come busting in here like this—"

"Go ahead," Owens said calmly. "All you'll be doing is saving a little time, because I intend to call the cops myself. I'm sure they'll be interested in talking to your friend here. They've got a murder case to clear up, after all."

"I didn't kill anybody!" the young man yelped. "I didn't even steal anything. I never could find it—"

"Shut up, Arnie," Eve grated. "You don't have to tell these people anything."

Owens grinned. "No, but you will have to talk to the police. Ms. Bailey and I will both testify that we saw you gain unauthorized entrance to Damian Quinn's place of business tonight. Your fingerprints are probably all over the back door, too, so it won't be just our word against yours. I think you'll make a fine suspect in the Pleshette murder, my friend."

Arnie shook his head vehemently. "I tell you, I didn't have anything to do with that."

I halfway believed him. I had already been playing with the idea that the killer and the person who had been getting into Quinn's shop were two different people. But I wasn't prepared for what Owens said next.

"All right, if that's the case, then you won't mind telling us about 'Ladies in the Cathedral'."

I took my eyes off Eve Rogers long enough to stare at Owens for an instant. Ladies in the Cathedral? What the hell was he talking about? When I glanced back at Eve, though, I saw a weary resignation on her face that told me she knew all too well what he was referring to.

She said, "I still don't know who you are, but you don't strike me as the type to be that familiar with modern art."

"My name is Kenneth Owens, Ms. Rogers. I'm a private detective, like Ms. Bailey here."

She gave me an icy glare. "You said you were with an insurance company."

"I said I did some work for them," I told her, equally coldly. To Owens, I said, "What's this about ladies?"

Eve Rogers answered for him. "'Ladies in the Cathedral,' Ms. Bailey. A set of small paintings by an Italian artist named Giacomo Giordano. Their whereabouts have been unknown for years, ever since they were stolen from a museum in Salerno, Italy following the war."

"And they're also quite valuable, aren't they, Ms. Rogers?" Owens asked.

"Their value has been going up ever since Giordano died. I wouldn't want to have to put a price on them," she admitted.

"But you hoped to set the price for one of them, didn't you? Once you had this kid steal it for you from Quinn, you could ask just about whatever you wanted." Owens grinned humorlessly. "It's definitely worth killing for, isn't it?"

The young man called Arnie started to say, "I told you—"

Eve cut him off. "You might be able to talk the police into filing criminal trespass charges against Arnie," she said with a slight smile playing around her mouth. "But I happen to know that he has a solid alibi for the night Jayne Pleshette was killed. I do, too, for that matter. So I'll tell you honestly that we were trying to get our hands on the painting. There have been several rumors in art circles in the area that one painting of the series was about to surface. I think Damian Quinn has it." She shrugged. "I didn't see any reason why I shouldn't have it instead."

"So you admit that your friend here has been sneaking into Quinn's and looking for it?" Owens asked.

"I'll admit that to you, but not to the police."

Owens switched his gaze to Arnie. "What about you, kid? Are you willing to stand up to being the primary suspect in a murder investigation just because this lady says so?"

Arnie lifted his hand and wiped the back of it across his mouth. He looked plenty nervous, but he seemed to have gained a little strength from Eve's growing calmness. "I don't think I want to say anything," he declared.

I had been trying to follow all of this and figure out how in the world Owens had discovered what Eve was after. I hadn't even heard of this missing Italian art treasure before.

"Suit yourself," Owens said. "Laura, these two aren't going to try anything else. Why don't you call the police?"

"All right." I spotted a telephone on a table near the office door. Letting the police sort things out sounded like a good idea to me, too.

But I had a feeling that the things which had happened tonight would not mean the end of this case. There was still something out there tugging at my brain, telling me that it wasn't over yet.

Lieutenant Harkness wasn't very glad to see either me or Owens, but he got over his aggravation enough to have a cup of coffee with us after he got through talking to Eve and Arnie.

"The kid's name is Arnie Weston," he told us. "Typical yuppie, doing fine until the company he worked for went out of business. Now he figures out how much money he really owes and realizes ain't no way he's going to be able to keep up the payments. So he goes to this Rogers lady, who's been selling him paintings for his condo and spins his sob story for her. She has some dirty work she needs done—namely getting into Quinn's and trying to find that little painting you told me about, Owens— and she figures Arnie to be a good choice for it. Arnie wants to keep all of his stuff, including that fancy German car, so he goes along with her. She gives him the key to Quinn's back door and he starts making his little nighttime visits."

"Where did Eve Rogers get the key?" I asked.

Harkness shook his head. "The lady's not saying, and to tell you the truth, I'm not sure we can force her to. Both of them are on their way down to the station for some more questioning." He glanced at his watch. "I want 'em to think on it a little; that's the only reason I'm taking the time to talk to you two."

"You think the Pleshette woman surprised Weston while he was there and he grabbed the dagger to stab her?" Owens asked.

Once again, Harkness shook his head. "They both have what sound like good alibis. We'll try to break 'em, of course, but I don't have much hope of doing that. And neither one of them strike me as the type, anyway. The kid's a greedy little sucker, and Rogers is, too, but they ain't killers."

"Which still leaves you with an unsolved murder," I said.

Harkness shrugged his shoulders. "Wouldn't be the first. I don't like it, but I never was one for railroadin' an innocent man, either." He stood up, settled his cowboy hat on his head, and gave us a stern look. "You folks best stay out of police business in the future, you hear?"

When he was gone, I looked across the coffee shop table at Owens and said, "What the hell is going on here?"

He sighed. "I'm afraid I haven't been totally honest with you, Laura. I got a call a few days ago from a PI in New York named Carlucci. He was looking for your father, and didn't know the agency had changed hands, so naturally I took the call."

I frowned, my mind flashing back to that notebook of my father's. I remembered seeing the name Carlucci in it. Salvatore

Carlucci, that was it. Then anger welled up inside me as I realized what Owens had said.

"Naturally," I snapped sarcastically. "What did this Carlucci have to say?"

Owens told me. And it was quite a story.

Salvatore Carlucci was working for a representative of the Italian government, trying to quietly track down Giordano's paintings, "Ladies in the Cathedral." He had tried to call my father to ask him to take on the job of recovering a painting in the series that was supposed to be in Texas. Obviously, Carlucci had been out of touch with my father and did not know about his selling the agency to National, let alone about his recent death.

I looked across the table at Owens when he finished. "So you were just guessing and running a bluff when you threw this business about the painting in Eve Rogers' face," I said to him.

"It seemed likely enough," he said. "That Weston kid was looking for something small, or he would have found it before now. He was too nervous or inexperienced or both to give the place a thorough search, so he kept having to come back. He would have been better off to take his time and make one trip do the job."

I nodded. My insides were still knotted up with emotion. "So you thought after you heard about this that you'd do the job for Carlucci instead of passing it on to me."

"I didn't know you were working on your own," he replied. "I'm still not sure it's a good idea."

"Get used to it," I told him.

Because now I not only had a killer to find, I had another job to finish, one last job for the agency which had been started by Jim Bailey . . . my father.

7

I didn't sleep well that night. My mind was too busy trying to puzzle out all the twists and turns of this case. I was doing some tossing and turning of my own, too, enough so that Aaron finally got up and went to the sofa in the living room to sleep. Listening to his grumbling as he left the bedroom didn't make things any easier for me.

The next day, I got up tired but determined. The first thing to do, I decided, would be to talk to Damian Quinn and find out what he knew about "Ladies in the Cathedral." I started calling early, knowing that Kenneth Owens would have had the same idea.

The only problem was that I couldn't get hold of Quinn.

When the phone at the antique store was finally answered, I got a woman, young by the sound of her voice, who told me this was her first day on the job. Damian Quinn had met her there, opened the store for her, then vanished somewhere. When I asked for Mark Howard, she told me that this was his day off.

That was the way my luck was running these days, I thought bitterly. I left my name and number with the girl at the antique store and asked her to have Quinn call me when he came in, but I didn't really expect him to. Even in the brief time I had known him, I had realized that he was an expert at ducking people he didn't want to talk to.

I called Zora Sims and filled her in on what had happened. She was encouraging, at least. "I know you'll get to the bottom of this, Laura," she told me. "Your father was the kind of man who just kept digging until he found the facts he needed to figure out his problems. I know you'll be just as successful."

I appreciated the kind words and told her so. Lieutenant Harkness wasn't as pleasant when I finally got hold of him.

"The kid's been charged with criminal trespass, like Rogers figured," Harkness told me. "We can't even make a burglary charge stick, since he never took anything from the place. Rogers paid his bail, no big surprise there."

"What about Eve?" I asked. "Surely there's something you can charge her with."

Harkness sighed tiredly. "Conspiracy, maybe, but the DA won't go for it. Too much trouble and not a good enough chance of a conviction, he says. So she walked, and the Weston kid won't ever do time. He'll just get probation, more'n likely."

"What about their alibis for the time of Jayne Pleshette's murder?"

"Solid enough. Weston was at a party with a couple dozen other people; Rogers was having a late supper with a few of her customers, all of them respectable folks. Those two didn't kill anybody."

"So who does that leave?" I asked.

"Quinn and his wife alibi each other," Harkness said thoughtfully. "Could be one of 'em's lying to protect the other. Might even be possible that they were in it together. I figure Quinn was fooling around with the Pleshette woman—"

I laughed shortly. "I'm sure of it."

"Yeah, he struck me as pretty much of a tomcat, too. Not too bright this day and age, but I guess some fellas just can't help themselves." Harkness paused, then said, "I don't mind talking to you about this case, Laura, but I don't want you pokin' around in it anymore, understand?"

I wasn't willing to commit to that, so I said evasively, "I don't see any other leads I can follow. It looks like you've got everything covered."

"Okay. I just didn't want to be trippin' over you again, or that Owens fella."

"You'll have to talk to him about that. Our partnership was strictly temporary."

After I hung up, I thought about what I had told Harkness and realized it was true. There was nothing left for me to investigate, at least not until I could talk to Quinn again. I was at a dead end for the moment, and that fact was frustrating enough to keep me pacing angrily for most of the day. Finally, I put the nervous energy to good use and started cleaning the apartment. My back was still a little sore, but it didn't bother me much anymore. There was a small bruise on my arm where Arnie Weston had banged the door into it the night before, but it was no problem.

I was in the bathroom, wearing cut-offs and one of Aaron's SCA pullovers and cleaning the tub, when he came in late that afternoon. I was putting plenty of energy into my scrubbing, taking out the anger I felt at Damian Quinn. I had called his store a few minutes earlier, only to be told that he had still not come in.

Aaron stopped just inside the bathroom door and looked at me in surprise. "How come you're not working?" he asked.

I held up the sponge I was using. "Does this look like fun to you?" I snapped.

"I mean working on the case."

"I solved the case, remember?" I had told him about the connection between Eve Rogers and Arnie Weston the night before when I got home.

"You don't know who killed Jayne yet. You just found out who was breaking into Damian's store."

"That was all he wanted to know at first."

"Yeah, but the cops may think he killed Jayne. If you don't find the real killer, Damian may go to jail!"

I tossed the sponge into the sink and stood up. As I reached out for a towel to dry my hands, I said, "Did it ever occur to you that your precious Damian might be guilty?"

Aaron's face tightened. "I don't like the way you said that, Laura."

"Well, I don't like a lot of things!" I snapped back, letting the frustration get the better of me. "I don't like the way you roped me into this thing just so that you could impress Damian Quinn. All you seem to care about is getting on his good side."

"He's an important man—" Aaron began.

"What about me?" I broke in. "Aren't I important? Doesn't my career—my life!—mean as much as some piece of medieval junk you've got the hots for!"

I was yelling. I knew it. I didn't like it, but there wasn't anything I could do about it. Aaron's features got cold and disdainful, and he spat, "You don't know what the hell you're talking about."

Then he turned and stalked out of the bathroom. A moment later, I heard the front door of the apartment slam behind him.

I sat down on the toilet, my fingers trembling slightly, mad at him, mad at myself, mad at the whole damn world.

That's the way I was two minutes later when the telephone rang.

I took a deep breath and listened to two more rings, then stood up and walked into the living room to answer. I never was the type who could ignore a ringing phone. I said, "Hello," leaving unsaid the thought *Whoever this is, you'd better make it good.*

"Laura?" a man's voice asked. It was familiar, but I didn't place it at first. He went on, "This is Mark Howard."

"Oh. Hello, Mark." I didn't know why he was calling, but I realized I should ask him about Quinn while I had the chance. "You haven't seen your boss today, have you?"

"Damian? No, I didn't have to work today. He finally hired someone else to help us out, a girl named Susie Ross. Have you been trying to get hold of him?"

"I wanted to ask him a couple of questions. Nothing that can't wait, I suppose. What can I do for you?"

"I heard about Eve Rogers and that Weston guy. Quite a story. I was wondering if you'd like to go out to dinner with me and tell me all the details."

I sighed. "Mark, I told you—" I stopped what I was about to say. He took my pause for something else. "Don't get mad, Laura. I know what you told me, but I'm not the kind of guy who gives up easy. Not when there's a girl like you around."

I hesitated a moment longer, then said, "I accept."

"You do?" He sounded surprised, despite his claim of being persistent.

"Sure. Why not? It sounds like fun."

And it did. Aaron had stomped out of here in a huff. There was no reason in the world I shouldn't go out with Mark Howard, I told myself. He had struck me as a nice guy, and there are too few of those around.

"Well, all right. That's great. When should I pick you up?"

"Give me an hour," I told him. I would need to clean up after spending the afternoon in a housecleaning frenzy.

"Fine," he said after I had given him the address. "I'll see you then. Goodbye, Laura."

"Goodbye, Mark." I hung up and headed back to the bathroom, to take a shower this time. A part of me felt guilty, like I was about to do something wrong by going out with Mark, but the part of me that was looking forward to the evening with anticipation outweighed it.

I was in the shower, my hair full of shampoo, when the whole thing clicked into place in my brain. I stared at the tile for long minutes, almost forgetting where I was as I went over all the pieces. And they fit together just fine.

I couldn't prove it yet, but I knew who had killed Jayne Pleshette.

Mark's freckled face broke out in a grin as he stepped into the apartment. "You look lovely," he said.

I didn't look bad. I was wearing a dark green dress with long sleeves. I only wear jewelry occasionally, but I had put on a plain gold necklace and earrings.

I put a smile on my face and said, "Why don't you come in for a few minutes?"

"Sure," Mark replied.

"Can I get you a drink?"

"That would be great."

"Scotch all right?"

"Sure."

I poured the drink and handed it to him. He took a sip as he looked around the apartment.

"You've got quite a few unusual pieces here," he said, nodding toward the weapons hung on the wall.

"They're not mine," I told him. "Remember I said I was involved with someone else? The weapons are his."

A quick frown crossed Mark's face. I knew what he had to be thinking. Maybe it hadn't been such a good idea to pursue me if I was mixed up with a guy who collected ancient weapons. No doubt Mark was acquainted with Aaron, but he probably didn't realize that Aaron and I were living together.

"Don't worry about it," I told him. "You just finish your drink and we'll go on to dinner."

"Okay," he nodded. But he still looked a little nervous.

"You must know quite a bit about antiques and art," I said as I sat down on the sofa and motioned for him to join me. "Your job must be fascinating."

He sat down. "I enjoy it. And I guess I do pick up a lot about the kind of thing that Damian handles."

"What about 'Ladies in the Cathedral'? What have you heard about it?"

The question made him frown again. "I'm not sure what you're talking about."

"Surely Quinn showed the painting to you before he hid it. He probably did that after hours, when you weren't around. I don't imagine he trusted even you with its whereabouts."

"I'm afraid I don't know—"

I stood up and moved away from the sofa, leaving him sitting there. "I finally got to talk to him," I lied without turning around. "He told me all about it. There wasn't any point in lying once he found out that Eve Rogers already knew he had it."

Mark said, "I thought this was going to be a date, not an interrogation."

I turned around to face him. "I'm sorry," I said, making my voice sincere. "I guess you just get in the habit of asking questions when you're a detective."

"Well . . . yeah, Damian showed the thing to me, but I don't know what he did with it. He was so paranoid that somebody would find out he had it before he was good and ready. He likes to have his little secrets. And he was trying to set up some sort of a deal with a collector so that the whole thing could stay quiet. He wanted to get his money without anybody knowing—especially Jayne." Mark chuckled. "He liked to keep secrets from her, too."

"The jealous mistress . . . " I mused. "He should have been more worried about you."

Mark drained his glass and put it down on the coffee table. "I'm not sure I like the sound of that."

"Then you won't like this, either. I know you told Eve Rogers about 'Ladies in the Cathedral.' You got hold of Quinn's key somehow and made copies of it. You passed one on to Eve so that she could have someone try to steal the painting, but you kept one yourself, just in case you ever needed to get into the store after hours. You didn't want to do Eve's dirty work because you were afraid you'd be suspected, but you didn't mind taking a payoff from her to help her steal the thing from Quinn."

He stared at me as the accusation tumbled out of me. He was obviously stunned by what I was saying, but I could see a flicker of panic far back in his eyes that told me I was right.

He tried to recover. With a grin, he said, "I think you've been working too hard on this case, Laura. You've got everything mixed up in your head."

"No, I've finally got everything straightened out. Jayne Pleshette found out that you were betraying Quinn and threatened to tell him. You met her at the antique store that night and tried to talk her out of it. She might have considered going along with you. I'm convinced that Quinn was having an affair with Eve Rogers, too, and Jayne had to hate that. That's why she didn't tell him right away when she found out what you were doing. She had to mull it over for a few days and decide how much loyalty she still felt for Quinn. But when you saw she finally made up her mind not to cooperate with you, you stopped her the only way you could—with that antique dagger."

His reaction was harsher this time. "You're crazy," he said as he got to his feet. "I came here to take you out—"

"You came here to pump me and find out how much the cops know," I said. "Well, they know about the painting, and they know Eve Rogers was after it. They'll put pressure on her until she tells them that you were her inside man at Quinn's. And then they'll start putting pressure on you. Oh, they'll find out all about it, Mark . . . "

My hands had clenched into fists. I saw the twisted look that jerked across his face as my accusations slapped into him. But then he seemed to grow suddenly calm, and he stared at me with expressionless eyes.

That was when I became truly frightened.

"You can't prove any of that nonsense," he said quietly. "But I won't allow you to spread such lies about me, either. I didn't let Jayne get away with that, and I won't let you, either."

He started toward me.

I took a step backward, thinking that I could talk him out of it or at least get to the door before he could stop me. But he suddenly moved faster than I had ever expected him to.

He lunged forward. I let out a startled cry and twisted away from him, but as he went past me I realized he hadn't been trying to grab me.

His hands fastened on the English war axe that was hung on the wall and wrenched it free from its hooks.

Mark Howard turned toward me, the medieval weapon clutched tightly in his hands. He said, "You should have just gone out to dinner with me, Laura." He sounded sad.

The ludicrousness of it was almost enough to make me laugh. He sounded like he was going to try to kill me because I had spoiled our date, not because I was a threat to expose him as a murderer.

But there was no laughter from either of us. He leaped toward me, whirling the axe. I screamed as I desperately dropped out of its path. The wicked spiked blade smacked into the wall, digging into the plaster. Mark wrenched it loose as I scrambled to the side. He whipped it down, and this time it thudded into the floor just behind my feet. I heard the carpet rip as he tore it free again.

His footsteps pounded after me. My brain was reeling with fear. I looked up, saw the German halberd leaning in the corner in front of me. It was similar to the weapon Mark held, only its spiked axe-like blade was at the end of a much longer pole. I reached out for it as a harsh cry tore from Mark's throat.

His hand closed on my ankle, dragged me back, my fingers

only inches from the shaft of the halberd. I twisted in his grasp, rolling over and throwing up my hands in what I knew would be a futile effort to fend off the next blow.

Something slammed into him before the axe could fall.

In the desperate struggle, I hadn't heard the door of the apartment open. But now, as he drove into Mark's back and knocked him aside, I saw Aaron, his face dark with fury. Mark caught his balance before he could fall and whipped around, slashing at Aaron's head with the axe. I cried, "Look out!"

Aaron dodged frantically out of the way. Mark came after him, his teeth gritted, wielding the war axe in savage back and forth swipes like some berserk Saxon warlord. Aaron lunged toward the wall, yanking at one of the ornate shields hung there. He got it loose just in time, spinning around to ward off a blow that would have caved in his skull if it had connected.

I felt tears of fear and anger rolling down my cheeks. Aaron had probably returned to the apartment to apologize to me—and now he was liable to get killed for his trouble.

I scrambled to my feet. There was an English short sword, a sort of glorified dagger, on the wall right behind me. I jerked it free and did the only thing I could think of. I yelled, "Aaron!" and tossed it in his direction.

He had to be acting on instinct, letting all the training he and his fellow SCA members had done come back to him as he reached out and snatched the hilt of the blade out of the air. Warding off another slash of the war axe, Aaron suddenly thrust out with the sword. The point of the blade caught Mark Howard in the side as he rushed in to strike again. I saw blood spurt, and then Mark seemed to freeze in his tracks. Aaron let go of the sword and backed up, staring at the growing crimson stain on Mark's coat. Aaron's eyes were wide.

The war axe slipped from Mark's hand and clattered to the floor. He let out a moan and followed it an instant later, clutching at the sword as he fell. He tried once to get to his feet, then gave it up and lay there curled around the sword, breathing harshly.

"Goddamn."

The exclamation made Aaron and I both jerk our heads around. Lieutenant Harkness stood in the doorway, staring grimly at us over the barrel of his drawn pistol. He took in the scene, lingering on Mark's bloody form, then lifting his gaze to Aaron and me.

"We'd best get some help for that fella," Harkness finally said. "Then it looks like you two have got some explaining to do."

That was fine with me. I was ready to explain the whole thing. I just didn't know if anyone would believe me.

8

It helped that under more intensive questioning Eve Rogers broke down and admitted Mark Howard was the one who had told her about "Ladies in the Cathedral" in the first place. She confessed that he had furnished her with a key to the store. That was all Harkness and the other detectives assigned to the case needed to get Mark to admit that he had killed Jayne Pleshette, once a hospital emergency room had kept him from bleeding to death.

That was quite a relief to me, because after I had given Harkness the story for the first time, there in my battle-scarred apartment, he had been completely convinced that I was crazy.

With Mark's confession on the record, though, Aaron and I were cleared of any charges in the melee, and Harkness had even invited me along when he paid a visit to Damian Quinn. Harkness had tracked him down to an apartment belonging to one Susie Ross, the good-looking young brunette who had just started working for him. It seemed that Jayne Pleshette had already been replaced in more ways than one.

And not so coincidentally, sitting on a table in Susie Ross's apartment had been what I considered a rather ugly painting called "Ladies in the Cathedral." Quinn had been pretty reluctant to part with it, but Harkness and I convinced him it would be the prudent thing to do. He didn't want any trouble with the Italian government, and as Harkness pointed out, a reputable antique dealer wouldn't want a reputation as somebody who dealt in stolen goods. Quinn handed it over.

I had talked to Carlucci on the phone and told him about the situation. He told me he was sorry about my father's death. He had been surprised to hear from me instead of Owens, but I had the painting and that was all Carlucci was interested in. Now, two days later, I found myself waiting at Dallas/Fort Worth International Airport to leave for New York.

I was taking the painting to Carlucci.

Kenneth Owens was waiting with me for my flight to be called. For the third or fourth time, he said, "I wish you'd reconsider, Laura. I know there were some harsh words between us, but nothing we can't both forgive and forget if you come back to work for National."

For the third or fourth time, I shook my head. "I'm afraid I'll be too busy setting up my own agency. I wouldn't want to disappoint Mrs. Sims."

Owens sighed. "What are you going to call the business? Don't forget we bought the Bailey Detective Agency. We can tie that name up in court if we choose to."

"Actually, I was thinking of Southwest Investigations."

"Not bad," he nodded. "But you know you're going to have trouble. The days of the small agency are over. You won't be able to afford to compete with the larger ones."

I was afraid he might be right, but I was not going to admit that to him. I just said confidently, "We'll see."

My attention wandered then. I kept looking around the terminal. It was starting to appear that Owens was going to be the only person to see me off.

Aaron had dropped out of sight. I hadn't seen him in almost two days.

He had been shaken up by the fight in the apartment. That was no surprise. I had had trouble accepting the violence myself. But I had work to do, and I wasn't going to let anything keep me from it. But I missed him, and I wondered if he would even be around when I got back from New York.

A voice over a loudspeaker called my flight, and I stood up and headed toward the gate where it would be boarding. Owens came with me. When we got there, he stopped and held out his hand to me.

"I don't think I mentioned this before, but that was good work, Laura," he said.

"Thanks." I shook his hand and smiled. I still didn't like him, but I didn't particularly want him for an enemy, either.

"I'll call you when you get back. Maybe you'll have changed your mind."

I shrugged and didn't say anything. Let him think whatever he wanted to.

I stepped through the gate, handed my boarding pass to the girl there, and started through the tunnel toward the plane.

"Laura!"

I didn't know how he found out where I was or when I was leaving. The important thing was that he found out. I turned around as he was stopped at the gate. He held out a hand toward me.

I hesitated a moment. There was time to go back and say goodbye to him, time to tell him that I would be back and ask him if he would still be there for me. I wondered if I really wanted to know the answer to that question.

But I was a detective, after all, and detectives always seem to be compelled to find out the answers, whether they hurt or not.

I went back to say goodbye to Aaron.

SUPERIOR'S DEAD

by
Loren D. Estleman

This is going to be pretty bad. I usually leave the reports to my assistant, a dumb cluck named Lee Wittenauer who washed out of the Dearborn Police Department when he fired a warning shot into a citizen's head while chasing a purse-snatcher through the parking lot of the Hyatt Regency; but since Lee has to chew over which end to shave in the morning, this one's beyond him.

A good report starts where it starts and ends where it ends, or so old Hardass Hardesty taught us during the twelve-week training course in Detroit, a hundred years ago. Here goes. The name is Riley Cooper, no middle initial or nickname, or at least none that I know about. I was born second to a truck driver and a waitress who got into an argument over the proper use of a butter knife shortly after I was born and didn't speak to each other for twenty-seven years afterwards, although that didn't stop them from having a third child. (It did stop my mother from serving butter.) Now my older sister Francine is the pain in the butt who writes the building codes for Wayne County and my younger brother Ernest is nobody knows where. He didn't come back from Vietnam with all his checkers, and since he didn't have that many going in, I suppose he's bumming or dead. Anyway I never knew him too well because I left home when I was sixteen.

I was with the Detroit Police Department for eighteen and a half years, working my way up from cadet-grey to plainclothes, where I made lieutenant the year before I quit. For a while I was with the old STRESS detail—Stop The Robberies, Enjoy Safe Streets—and those were high old times; wing-shooting muggers in railroad yards, kicking down safe-house doors in flak jackets, and spraying the rooms with double-ought buck—but all that came to an end when Mayor Young took office and disbanded the unit. Major Crimes was almost as much fun after that. Then I picked up my eleventh bullet wound during a drug raid—from another officer, no less—and the old ladies in charge at 1300 Beaubien got worried about the insurance costs and strapped me to a desk on the third floor. I threw in my shield eighteen months short of my twenty. If I wanted to stuff drawers and answer the phone I'd be a freaking secretary.

Believe it or not, there isn't a lot of call for middle-aged, out-of-work police officers. I tried security work, but that was as bad as piloting a desk, with none of the perks, like tripping the cops just in from mugging detail and seeing if they had their boxers on under their skirts, so I gave that up too. My brother-in-law offered me a junior partnership in his cement business; I was bored enough to consider accepting until I remembered that he's the kind of a twerp that would marry my sister and said no thanks. Then there was a spell where I gave up looking and sat around the house emptying six-packs and reading the funnies. One day I caught myself watching one of those home shopping shows and thinking seriously about ordering a Purple Chief Potato Atomizer, and that was when I put the place on the market and headed north.

Michigan is divided into two peninsulas, in case you didn't know, connected across the Straits of Mackinaw by a suspension bridge that was either the fifth or sixth largest in the world last time I checked. While the Lower Peninsula—the one that's shaped like a hand—is largely green and rolling, the Upper—the one that's shaped like an ink smear—is rocky and wooded and bears no small resemblance to the Pacific Northwest. I wasn't just wandering aimlessly the day I coaxed my tub of rusted guts across the bridge. About the only happy moments I had known as a kid were the times my old man got tired of the silence at home, loaded me and the tackle into his old Ford pick-up, and drove in a straight sixteen-hour shot to Iron Harbor, a clutter of ramshackle huts on the southern tip of Keweenaw Bay, to go fishing. Those trips weren't exactly jawfests themselves—Dad's conversational skills having atrophied through disuse to five words, all of them addressed as commands: "Beer," "Bait," "Sandwich," "Knife," and "Quiet"—but I never forgot the bracing winds off Lake Superior or the chill of the water even in the stupefying heat of July or the feelings of heroic solitude and absolute self-reliance. The old man had been dead a dozen years (I sometimes wondered how my mother had even noticed), but I tried to get back up every few summers for a vacation. Now I was going up there to find work.

Iron Harbor was founded, after a fashion, in the eighteenth century by a French missionary-explorer named Michel du Blacques, who had paddled a canoe up the St. Lawrence looking for the Northwest Passage and the chance to convert the heathen Chinee. What he found was a dose of the clap courtesy of an Iroquois woman he had tried to convert away from the Canadian trapper who had bought her downstate. When he found out what ailed him, du Blacques shot himself in the head. But he wasn't any better at finding his target than at locating China, and lingered on for almost a year in a lean-to his helpers built for him on the site of Iron Harbor. For a hundred and fifty years it was believed he was slain by hostile Indians—which he was, kind of, although she wasn't exactly hostile—and on the sesquicentennial of his death a saintly statue was unveiled on top of his grave showing the Jesuit seated on a log with an open Bible in his lap. By the time an unusually dedicated historian discovered the truth and published it, it was too late, and the locals had gotten used to having the statue around. However, the annual Father Mike Celebration of Faith was quietly rechristened Founders Day, and around graduation time some of the high school seniors could be counted on to scribble something clever on the statue's pedestal about what du Blacques was doing under the Bible. The Bible itself had become a repository for used condoms. The youth of Iron Harbor aren't awfully refined, but they're responsible.

When I came here to live—a thickish, fairly broad-shoul-dered forty-six, no longer the clumsy kid with his silent father—the place hadn't changed much, except for the blacktop on the state highway that runs through the center of town and the new McDonald's on the western end, which had finally forced Aunt Betty's Restaurant to board up its doors and windows (to the sorrow of no one who had ever ordered the meatloaf). There was a bait-and-tackle shop, a rock shop, a gift shop with a fancy French name on the outside and the usual miniature toilets made in Taiwan on the inside, a grocery, and a motel with a bar and a pool table in the lodge and four log bungalows in back of it. The Mobil station closed at nine in time for the nightly illegal crap game at nine-thirty, and if it was a slow night in Baraga you might be able to knock off a piece with one of the whores inhaling boilermakers in the bar, if her husband was in Marquette. All that has changed now—but that's for later. I'm talking about how I came to be Iron Harbor's chief of police.

2

I didn't know as I was registering at the motel that the village council was meeting at that very moment to discuss the problem of the current chief. It seems they'd recently signed Lee Wittenauer to a three-year contract on the basis of his resume without taking the trouble to find out the circumstances of his release from the Dearborn Police Department. Since then he'd shot three stray dogs, one of which belonged to Iron Harbor's wealthiest citizen, a professional animal lover named McNurr who'd agreed to include a donation in his will for the construction of a proper village hall; arrested a governor's aide for reckless driving on his way in to investigate a request for disaster relief following a catastrophic blizzard; stopped three escaped prisoners from the Michigan State Branch Penitentiary at Marquette for speeding in a car they'd stolen from the warden, then let them off with a warning; and remanded a popular local prostitute into the custody of state troopers on a bench warrant for unpaid traffic citations. She got six months at the Cassidy Lake facility downstate.

Depriving the village of its one good whore was the last straw. It had gone this long without a meeting hall and could conceivably go a lot longer; no blizzard could blow down anything in a place like Iron Harbor that couldn't be rebuilt out of pocket, assuming it was worth rebuilding to begin with; and as long as the convicts kept moving they were Marquette's problem. But during those long bitter evenings in the dead of winter, when the village population dipped below five hundred, the loss of a good sporting woman who didn't mind a little cold was a distinct blow—or rather the lack of one. The council voted six to one in favor of a new chief.

This solution posed two new problems: 1. Finding an acceptable replacement and 2. Getting around paying Wittenauer the $18,000 still owed him on his contract. Eighteen thousand dollars was not easily come by in a community that traced its past prosperity to an iron mine that had closed down in 1952, and now just barely survived on its flagging summer tourist trade. The president of the council himself held down three jobs in Marquette to support his wife and a mistress in Ishpeming; a portrait of the late Hon. Wilton F. Pickett, looking exhausted but happy, now hangs in the room behind the bait-and-tackle shop where the council still meets. (They never did get their hall, but then Old Man McNurr is still living in his mansion on Black Pine Road, stinking of dogs and cats and the occasional Bighorn sheep.)

Anyway, I wasn't exactly unknown locally, thanks to my fishing trips. When Skip Herbert behind the bar at the lodge took my drink order, he asked me how things were going on Detroit's mean streets. He actually said that, "mean streets"; Skip reads a lot of detective fiction. When he found out I'd left the department he didn't say anything, but the next morning old Wilton Pickett paid me a visit at my bungalow.

He was getting on seventy then and didn't look nearly as good as his portrait behind the bait-and-tackle shop. He had been bald for fifty years. His head above the colorless fringe was poreless and artificially shiny, as if Ariadne Kling at the grocery had buffed it with waxed paper, the way she did her apples and cucumbers. His eyeglasses were almost as bright, and when he nodded his head agitatedly—a habit—circles of light flew off him like reflections from one of those mirrored globes that hang from the ceilings of dance halls. Below the glasses his face fell away, flaps of gray spotted skin folding over his collar and characteristic bow tie.

"How are you, Riley?" he asked.

We had never spoken that I could remember, but once or twice in years past we had seen each other fishing, and names do get around.

"Fine," I said. As a matter of fact I felt stinking. I'd closed the bar only five hours previously.

"Good, good."

That ended the small talk. The best I can say about old Pickett, aside from commenting on his sexual stamina, was that he got to the point. He said he'd heard I was looking for work in my field, asked me about references, and took down some names in a pocket notebook. I figured he'd check them pretty thoroughly after what I'd overheard in the bar about the Wittenauer fiasco, so I told it straight. Then he brought up the matter of the contract.

"It says we have to keep him on or pay him off, but it doesn't say he has to be chief," he explained. "What we want to do is knock him down to assistant and hire a new chief."

"Makes sense."

"Thing is, we can't afford to pay two chiefs' salaries, so what we want to do is pay the chief what we'd normally pay his assistant."

"That doesn't."

He spread his hands. "Take it or don't. If we had money enough for two chiefs we could build a library, and we need a library a lot more than we need a chief of police."

"What are you going to do when the bad guys show up, throw books at them?"

"The baddest guy we ever had was the Thompson kid, who used to blow up mailboxes. He's in the navy now."

"Doing what, underwater demolitions?"

"You want the job or not? I'm late for work."

"How much is the assistant's pay?"

He told me. I laughed. Light flashed off his head. "Skip Herbert's offered to put you up here free gratis for an indefinite period. I think we can get Ariadne Kling to discount your groceries, and we'll pay your mileage. No squad car, sorry."

"I prefer my bucket anyway," I said. "When's Wittenauer's contract run out?"

"Two years."

I pretended to think about it. My head hurt and the three hundred and twelve dollars in my hip pocket was all that remained of my savings. My house was a white elephant on the Detroit market.

"We'll try it for two years," I said.

"Good. Uh, the council will need to meet with you before you can be officially appointed."

"Who's on the council?"

He counted on shaky fingers. "Me, Skip, Ariadne, Sherman Holloway from the bait-and-tackle, Doc Smeals, and the Slaughter twins, Earl and Dwayne. They run the gift shop. The decision to appoint you must be unanimous. Ariadne might be a hard sell. she's the one who voted against replacing Wittenauer."

"Figures. She'd be the only one not in need of a prostitute." I'd heard that story too. "When's the meet?"

"Seven-thirty tonight."

3

After he left I finished sleeping, caught McBreakfast, got some fishing in—no bites, hoped that wasn't an omen—and spent the afternoon brushing my one good suit and polishing my shoes. At suppertime I ordered pork chops and fries from the grill in the bar, thought about a beer, but decided against it under the scrutiny of Skip Herbert—no longer just a bartender, but a holder of my fate—and drank a club soda instead. Too late, I realized that might make me look like an alcoholic. I said to hell with it and chased the soda with a Pabst. The idle life will make you crazy.

The meeting room was spacious for the back of a store, with a yellow plank floor, painted plaster walls, and a distinct odor of fish despite the gallons of disinfectant and pine-scented air freshener that had been heaped on top of it. Skip, who had traded his apron for an old-plaid sportcoat and clip-on necktie, showed me to a chair placed directly in front of the long table where the council members sat. Pickett was in the middle with a gavel, flanked by Earl and Dwayne Slaughter, a hulking pair of identical twins in their late forties who looked like the truck drivers they had been before their mother died and left them the gift shop; Sherman Holloway, a fey type with a mop of carroty hair who looked a lot more like a poet than the owner of the bait-and-tackle and the council's landlord; old Doc Smeals, who looked exactly like a country physician with his white hair, old-fashioned half-glasses, and western bola tie on a white shirt—you wouldn't guess he'd once been deprived of his license to practice medicine for molesting his female patients—and seated at the left end, her gray-streaked brown hair brushed straight back and a thin blue sweater drawn over her shoulders and buttoned at the throat like a cape, Ariadne Kling. A not-unattractive woman of about fifty, she wore an expression that said she had come there straight from a romantic liaison with a pickle.

I knew them all by sight, and a few to talk to, so Pickett, who had to be at his second job by nine, didn't waste time with introductions. He announced that he'd checked out my references and found my qualifications impressive and opened the floor to the inquisition. From then on it was all Ariadne Kling.

"Our information is you killed six men while with the Detroit police," she told me. "Were those killings necessary?"

"I thought so at the time."

"Do you still think so?"

"I'm still breathing."

"That's no answer."

I leaned back, crossed my ankles, and laced my fingers over my stomach. "Miss Kling, I was wounded eleven times in the line of duty. I still have a slug in my back that bothers me on rainy days. Shouldn't you be asking that question of the men who shot me?"

"No one is questioning your valor. Iron Harbor is not Detroit. We don't want a chief of police who comes on like Dirty Harry. Are you wearing a gun at present?"

"I didn't think I needed one to attend a council meeting."

Skip Herbert laughed—and stopped when she glared at him. To me she said, "Our information says you moonlighted as a private detective when you were with the Detroit Police. Wasn't that a violation of department regulations?"

"Technically."

"And do you intend to continue as a private detective if we appoint you chief here?"

"I can't say."

"Indeed." She looked triumphant.

"My license is still valid," I said. "Miss Kling, none of the village offices in Iron Harbor is full-time. You sell groceries; Mr. Pickett has two other jobs; Dr. Smeals is an M.D.; Mr. Holloway deals in fishing equipment; Skip Herbert mixes drinks and runs the motel; and the Slaughters are in the gift business. If investigative work comes my way when I'm off duty and it doesn't make me gag, I'm going to take it."

"I don't like your attitude, Mr. Cooper."

"Neither did half the felons in Detroit."

It went on like that for a while. Nobody else had any questions, and finally I was sent out while the thing was put to a vote. Looking over the rods and reels in the shop, I wondered if Holloway could use a junior partner. Five minutes later I was summoned back in and told to report for duty Monday morning. There had not been a single negative ballot.

4

I knew Lee Wittenauer was trouble the second I laid eyes on him.

The police station occupied the defunct Aunt Betty's Restaurant, a narrow room with pine-paneled walls that had barely contained five tables and now offered a minimum of pacing space between two mismatched desks and an office copier. Citizens conducted their business over the counter where the cash register had stood. The griddle was still there, and from the looks of it no one had replaced the grease.

"You're Cooper." The former chief, a lanky thirty-year-old with a puppy moustache and amber glasses, sat behind the bigger of the two desks with his chair tilted back and one booted foot propped up on the typewriter leaf. His uniform was buff-colored with a tailored fit, not tight across the shoulders or sagging in the seat, like the one I'd drawn. He was cleaning his nails with a letter opener shaped like a naked woman.

"I'm Cooper." I unbuckled my gun belt and hung it on a peg. "I guess we're working together."

"What a brain. That's why you're chief."

I grunted. "Anything on?"

"The Taylor kid had his bicycle stolen yesterday. You want me to call SWAT?"

"What else?"

"*Nada.* I could put a cat up a tree if you're bored."

"Not necessary." I lifted the steaming glass carafe from a Mr. Coffee plugged in on the counter and filled the mug I'd brought. Wittenauer saw it.

"Got your name on it, I see. You make it yourself at cop camp?"

I smiled and shook my head. Sipping coffee I strolled past

his desk, getting the lay of the place. When I was behind him I hooked an ankle around the standard of his chair and jerked it out from under him. He hit the floor with a crash. Before he could scramble up I raised my right foot so he could see the steel taps on the sole of the black high-top.

"I caved in a pusher's skull with this shoe two years ago," I said. "I saw what brains he had and they weren't much, but I'm betting he had more than you. What do you call me?"

"Cooper." He didn't move.

"Try again."

"Chief."

"Better." I lowered my foot. "That smaller desk's yours. Throw away those newspapers on top. While you're at it, clean the griddle. I don't like the stink."

"Okay," he said.

"Okay what?"

"Okay, Chief."

"One more thing. From now on, clean your nails in the toilet. I'd rather watch you pet a snake."

"Okay, Chief."

That ended the rebellion. The only trouble I would have from Lee after that sprang from the basic fact that he should never have become a cop in the first place.

Police work is the same everywhere, boring as hell and too damn exciting by turns. In Iron Harbor my first year in office it was mostly boring. During the off season we broke up fights between natives in Skip's bar, occasionally arrested some local kid breaking into a vacation cabin and turned him over to the sheriff, and helped the township fire department pry the odd moron out of what was left of his car when he took an icy curve doing sixty and tried to move a one hundred-year-old pine. The tourist season brought the summer people and a more lively pace, but mostly it was more of the same, only the numbers were greater and we often had to borrow men from the sheriff to help batter the drunks into a more cooperative frame of mind. Once we thought we had an honest-to-God kidnapping, but when the state troopers finally ran the perp to ground it turned out he'd stolen the car while it was parked in front of the gas pumps at Ariadne Kling's store without realizing a six-year-old girl was asleep in the back seat. She was still asleep when the troopers returned her and the car to her parents.

The rest of the time it was sit around and wait for something to happen. Thanks to my investigator's license I sometimes killed a couple of days helping transport prisoners from Marquette to the main branch of the state penitentiary in Jackson, down in the Lower Peninsula; but those trips came a long way apart. Most of the time I sat around getting thicker through the middle and watching Lee not cleaning his nails.

Two months into my second year, the texture of the community changed drastically. A youngish chipmunk of a man named Dalrymple, who had made his first several hundred million selling tacos nationwide, bought two hundred acres of state land fronting on Superior a mile outside town, knocked down all the trees, and began construction on a convention center made up of hotels, condos, and an office building shaped not coincidentally like a gigantic taco. Immediately a string of rival fast-food chains started bidding on a strip along the state highway on the opposite side of Iron Harbor. Skip Herbert sold out to an Arab corporation with a string of motels across the continent and moved downstate, and the Slaughter brothers deeded over the gift shop to A & P for demolition and construction of a supermarket on the site. There was talk of a housing development and an airport.

Some of the old-timers and all of the sportsmen—myself included—protested, but planning and zoning was up to the township. Those officials caught the scent of new money and cut through the red tape like Leatherface on a binge. Some said the shock of so much unwelcome change was what killed Wilton Pickett. Since he died of cardiac arrest in the arms of his mistress, I had my doubts; but there was no getting around the fact that Iron Harbor was never going to be the same.

Police business picked up. There was a brawl every Saturday night at Skip's old bar, run by strangers now while the rest of the motel was undergoing renovation, and it was always locals versus members of the Dalrymple construction crew; there were thefts from the construction site, which became my business when some idiot from St. Ignace tried selling the stolen lumber and storm windows from the back of his truck on the village's main drag; and one day when the big iron ball swept through the condemned gift shop, kept going, and took out the east wall of Sherman Holloway's bait-and-tackle emporium, it took Lee and me ten minutes to pull Holloway off the hardhat at the controls. I would never again mistake him for a poet. It was about this time I found myself yearning for the quiet old days with STRESS.

Of course I didn't know then that I was about to be faced with Iron Harbor's first murder in thirty-six years.

5

They never did solve that old murder. Some old wheeze of a Scandinavian who had stayed on in town after the lumber business went bust was found one day with his head bashed in on the floor of his little room over the mill, which was destroyed by fire ten years later. He lived alone and didn't speak a word of English, so no one knew much about him or who might have wanted to brain him with the blunt side of his own axe. Eventually it was decided that someone had believed the rumors that grow up around strange old men who keep to themselves, that he had a lot of money hidden somewhere in his room, and killed him for it. Whether he ever had any money remained as much a mystery as the identity of his killer.

This one was different. Wobbling a little from having put down an unaccustomed mid-week donnybrook in the bar very early that morning, I plunked myself down behind my desk, hoping to catch a nap, when Lee hung up the phone and swung around in his chair. "We got driftwood."

"What?"

"A floater. On the beach."

I looked at him, waiting. He appeared eager, the way he had the day he arrested the state police commander's son because he kind of matched the description of the man who had stuck up the movie theater in Ahmeek a week earlier. "Are you trying to say there's a corpse washed up on the beach?" I asked.

"The Taylor kid found it a half hour ago. That was his mother on the phone."

"Did we ever find his bicycle?"

"The hell with the bicycle. We got driftwood."

"If you don't stop saying that I'll kick you in the head. Is it anybody we know?"

"Search me. The kid and Mrs. Taylor didn't recognize him anyway."

"Fisherman, probably. They're always getting drunk and falling overboard."

"Not in a blue suit and red tie."

I grunted. "Where is it?"

"Up by du Blacques' Landing."

"Damn it, Lee, that's outside the village limits. Give it to the sheriff."

"Shouldn't we go look?"

"I guess one of us has to." I got up, joints squawking. "Don't call County till I report back. It could be a hoax."

"The Taylor kid maybe. His mother's as level-headed as it gets. She's an Indian, an Ojibway. You sure you don't want me along?" He sounded as if he'd been asked to give up his chief's pay.

"A corpse I can handle alone. It's the live ones give me trouble."

I fired up my bucket— a green 1966 Ford Bronco, not much for power, but the gas mileage was lousy—and drove up to du Blacques' Landing, just the sort of rocky, inhospitable stretch of shore an idiot like the French missionary would choose to beach his canoe. A brisk April wind was chopping up the pencil-gray surface of the lake, a tame reminder of the November gales that had devoured the *Edmund Fitzgerald* and a hundred far more sea-worthy craft before it.

The only house in sight was a white Edwardian on a grassy knoll overlooking the landing, with a square roof and a widow's walk on top of it. This was the Taylor home. As I used the bell-pull it occurred to me I'd never seen Mrs. Taylor. That's how it is in places the size of Iron Harbor: You can get to know most of the citizens the first week and not happen to run into the others your whole time there.

Mark Taylor, whom I *had* seen before, answered the bell. He was about eleven and had on scuffed jeans and a sweatshirt with Daffy Duck on the front. He had fair hair and black eyes, thanks to the genes of his Anglo-Saxon father and American Indian mother. He took one look at me and yelled, "Ma!"

"Don't shout, Mark. Oh, hello."

Moving from the dim interior of the house into the sunlight, she was a sudden dose of blue-black hair caught behind her neck and olive features with the boy's black eyes and an athletic figure in a simple knit dress tied at the waist with a knotted belt. Her feet were bare.

I remembered my cap and took it off. "Mrs. Taylor?"

"I'm Laura Taylor."

"Riley Cooper. I'm the police chief."

"Yes, I've heard about you. How is it we haven't met?"

"I was just thinking about that. I guess you've done too good a job keeping order at the school." She taught—and ran—grade school in the one-room building that had been built for that purpose in 1849.

"They're all good kids. It's not like teaching in the city. come in."

I stepped inside and she closed the door behind me. In contrast to the turn-of-the century exterior, the ground floor was decorated along modern lines without clutter. It was a nice change from the breakfronts and tea sets that crowded most of the other homes in the area.

"Where's your gun?" demanded the boy.

I ignored him. "Lee Wittenauer said you found a body on the beach."

"She didn't. *I* did."

"Yes, it's out back. Let me put on shoes and a coat."

"It's my body. I saw it first."

But his mother had already left the room. I humored the little bastard. "When'd you find it?"

"Show me your gun first."

"Forget it. I know when you found it."

"Well, how come you asked?"

"It kept me from hitting you."

Laura Taylor returned a minute later. She had laced on a pair of half-boots and slipped into a hooded waterproof jacket with a blanket lining.

"Ma! The cop said he was going to hit me."

She hesitated for just a second. "I think if he were really going to hit you, he wouldn't have warned you first. This way, Mr. Cooper."

255

We went down a short papered hallway and through a stainless steel kitchen, where the boy took an insulated Windbreaker off a peg.

"You stay here, Mark," said his mother.

"Aw, Ma! It's my body."

"It was a human being. If it belongs to anyone it belongs to his family. Stay in the house."

A path that someone had started beating a hundred and fifty years ago led from the back door down to the beach, which was more jagged rocks than sand. We followed the beach for a hundred yards, frothy waves licking to within inches of our feet. A black shape that I had thought from a distance was a tree limb turned out to be a sodden overcoat with two legs sticking out from under it. The water washed over a pair of expensive-looking shoes with their toes buried in the sand.

"You covered it up?" I asked.

"Yes. The coat was barely clinging to one arm. I didn't want the gulls to get to it."

"That was the only reason?"

She shook her head. "My ancestors respected the dead. It's something I have to teach Mark."

I reached down and pulled the coat aside. It was heavy with water. The dead man lay on his chest with his head turned to the right. The end of a red silk tie, soaked almost black, trailed out onto the beach grotesquely, like a tongue. He was a white man in his early thirties with short brown hair and a surprised look. They always look surprised. No one ever really thinks it will happen to him.

"You don't know him?" I asked.

"No. I've lived around here all my life. He's a stranger."

"He hasn't been in the water long. A day, maybe."

"No more than two," she agreed.

I looked at her.

"My father was a commercial fisherman," she said. "I used to go out with him on his boat. Once we netted a corpse from an ore carrier that had broken up on Six Fathom Shoals. He'd been in the water three days."

"I thought Superior never gave up its dead."

"It does sometimes. If it gave up even ten percent we'd be up to our necks in cadavers."

I looked out across the water. A sickle of land curved around from the west, reaching a mile into the lake. "Isn't that part of Ernest Dalrymple's property?"

"Yes. do you think he might have fallen in off the peninsula?"

"Or a boat. He isn't dressed for boating."

"I did see the lights of a boat cruising past the end of the peninsula last night around ten. Pleasure craft, a big one."

"That would put it closer to twelve hours. Could you identify the boat?"

"Not definitely. I never saw one that big pass this close." She was looking at the corpse. "He wasn't used to this country, I can tell you that much."

"Why, because he isn't wearing a peaked cap or carrying a can of Skoal?"

"Nothing that obvious. You might wear a suit around here on occasion. You might even wear low shoes like those. But you wouldn't put on a wool overcoat, not if you were used to the weather around here. You'd wear something waterproof. The spray from the lake alone would've given him ten extra pounds to lug around after a while."

"Everyone's a detective."

"Don't forget, I'm an Ojibway. My people notice things."

"Maybe. I'm going to turn him over now."

"Do you need help?"

"No, I just thought I'd better warn you. Sometimes they

257

make a groaning noise when you move them, from the air escaping their lungs. It scares the hell out of some people."

"I know about the air."

"The stiff in the net," I said. "I forgot. Well, here goes."

The water in his clothes made him heavy. When I heaved he flopped onto his back with a noise like wet laundry landing at the bottom of a chute. He didn't groan, though. They hardly ever do when three bullets have pierced their vitals.

6

Lew Connable looked less like a country sheriff than any I'd ever known. A small man to begin with, he was fond of soft felt hats with wide brims that dwarfed him further and wore the same tight gray suit in all weather without a topcoat. He had a pinched face and bifocals with gold rims.

I heard the broken muffler of his unmarked gray Chevy station wagon from inside the house and went out to meet him. He left the car on the side of the road with its removable beacon flashing, stuck his hands in his pockets, and accompanied me through the damp grass and wet sand without heed to his saddleshoes. We stopped before the corpse.

"He's sure dead," he said. "This how you found him?"

"I turned him over. Kid found him an hour and a half ago. This is his mother, Laura Taylor." She had just joined us from the house.

"Sure, I know Mrs. Taylor." He touched his hat. "How's my kid doing?"

She smiled. "Okay in everything but algebra."

"How often you got to know what X is, anyway?" To me: "You ought to teach that dumbass assistant of yours a little plain

English. He kept telling me you had driftwood on the beach."

I shrugged. I'd called the station from the house and told Lee to call the sheriff.

Connable bent to examine the wounds. The water had washed away most of the blood, leaving three neat holes in the dead man's white shirt and three corresponding blue-black punctures in the flesh beneath. After a moment he straightened. "Thirty-eights anyway. Nice grou ." He pushed his glasses up his nose and gazed out toward the point.

"Mrs. Taylor says a big pleasure boat went past about ten last night," I said.

"How big? he asked her.

"As big as they come."

"Doesn't Ernest Dalrymple keep a yacht?" I said.

"Worth asking him about, I guess. I don't hardly think he'd shoot a man and dump the body this close to home, but if rich folks made any sense to me I guess I'd be one myself."

"Do you really suspect him?" asked the woman.

"Of putting snouts and tongues in his tacos, maybe. Check his pockets?" He was looking at me.

"I thought I'd leave that for you."

He fished a pair of disposable gloves from a pocket of his suitcoat, put them on, and squatted beside the corpse. He was quick and thorough. When it was over he had forty-one cents in change and a fold of wet paper. "Piece of luck," he said, peeling it open. It had been torn unevenly from a hotel pad. Only the letters ERY had come away with it at the top, printed in green. On the page someone had scribbled in ink:

3:00 DO

"Mean anything to you?" Connable asked me. I shook my head. He looked at Mrs. Taylor. She said no. with his free hand the sheriff patted his own pockets, dug out a glassine evidence bag, and slid the sheet inside. "Not that there'll be any prints on it after it's been in the water."

I watched him get to his feet. He had ten years on me easy and didn't vocalize half as much doing it as I would have; but then he managed to have a kid in grade school at an age when most people are grandparents. "What's your gut say?" I asked.

"You're the big-time Detroit detective. You tell me. Drugs, maybe. Hell, for all we know somebody pitched him out of a plane coming down from Canada. He ain't wearing nobody's idea of a yachting outfit."

In a little while we were joined by Doc Smeals, who was county coroner that year. He conducted a quick examination and declared the man had been in the water between ten and twenty-four hours.

"We knew that before you came," Connable said. "When can you have the slugs for me?"

"Sometime this afternoon." Smeals held up a hand. After a moment the sheriff caught on and grasped it and helped him up. I could smell the liquor coming out of the doctor's pores at ten paces; he set back the country practitioner sterotype thirty years. While he was collecting his instruments, Connable put his palm on my back and we walked a little way down the beach.

"I'm new to murder," he said. "What would you do?"

"Have the corpse printed and send the prints and the slugs to the FBI office in Marquette. While you're waiting to hear back, talk to Dalrymple like you said. If the boat wasn't his, call all the docks and marinas in the area and find out who put out with an ocean-going yacht last night."

He still looked doubtful. "You hiring out these days?"

"You don't need me, Lew."

"I wish I agreed with you."

"A year ago I might've taken the job," I said. "Right now

I've got all I can do to keep a lid on Iron Harbor."

"Times change."

"I'd like to know why."

We went back just as the county wagon pulled up behind the sheriff's car and two attendants came down the beach with a stretcher. They bagged the corpse and left. Smeals weaved his way back to his Continental Mark IV and Connable followed him, probably to make sure the old soak didn't run over any pedestrians on his way back to town. Laura Taylor had gone inside to fix lunch for young Mark. I couldn't remember if she'd said good-bye. I wondered why it mattered.

Alone on the beach, I noticed the woolen overcoat the dead man had been wearing lying on the sand. It had been overlooked in the crowd. I picked it up to carry to my heap and remembered that no one had been through its pockets. Well, what the hell.

There was a key in the right slash pocket with a plastic tag on it reading The Marquette Hostlery in the same shade of green as the printing on the sheet from the hotel pad.

The case meant nothing to me; although I admit, standing there holding the key, that I felt some of the old tingle. I replaced the key, threw the sodden coat onto the deck of the Bronco, and drove back to town to see what was happening at the station. Afterward I would call Lew Connable and tell him what I'd found.

Sherman Holloway was waiting for me, hopping mad because while he was at lunch someone had kicked loose the sheet of plywood he'd nailed over the hole the wrecking ball had made and run off with six graphite fishing rods and a case of spoon lures. Lee Wittenauer, who was as good a typist as he was a policeman, wasn't helping matters by stopping every few letters to erase an error in Holloway's statement. I took over at the old Royal. By the time I finished and schmoozed him out the door I had missed my own lunch by an hour. I gave the report to Lee to follow up on, ignoring his questions about the mysterious corpse, and went to McDonald's. Knowing the efficiency of the town grapevine, I ate in the Bronco to avoid more questions still. The sun warmed me through the windshield.

The mildewy smell coming from the back reminded me I still had the overcoat. I reached over the seat to push the coat out of nose-range and discovered that it was nearly dry on the exposed side. It was also stiff.

I got into the back and groped it like a suspect. I'd never heard of a coat being reinforced with cardboard. I turned it inside out and examined the lining. It had been machine-stitched along the top and sides and hand-stitched at the bottom, by someone who didn't know a great deal about sewing, in thread of a different shade. I unfolded my pocket knife, popped several of the stitches, got a hold of the loose flap, and pulled the lining away from the coat along the bottom. I reached up inside and worked a one-by-two foot square of damp canvas out through the opening I'd made. It was a painting.

7

It had been done in oils, in a cold modern style without much detail, and showed a gowned woman in a Gothic hall of some kind without furniture or windows, throwing a long black shadow across the floor in the moonlight from some mysterious source. Despite the darkening from the water, the painting had a disquieting quality, as if from some vague horror lurking outside the borders. It bore no signature. The edges were slightly uneven and one of the corners was ragged, as if the canvas had been cut out of a frame.

I let it roll itself up, as it wanted to do, put it in a patch of sunlight on the deck to finish drying, locked up the truck, and went into the restaurant to use the public telephone. Information gave me Laura Taylor's number. For some reason I was happy to learn she was listed under that name and not her husband's, whoever he might be.

"Hello?"

"Mrs. Taylor, this is Chief Cooper."

"Oh. I tried to reach you at the station a minute ago. You left before I could say good-bye."

"Thanks for caring." I got away from it quickly. "Do you teach art?"

"Art appreciation, mostly. I can't draw a straight line with a ruler."

"I wonder if you could look at a painting and tell me who did it."

"I'd have to see the painting before I could answer that."

"Are you going to be home for a while?"

"Yes. I'm playing hooky today. Come on over."

I called the station next. "Lee, I've got some business out of town. I'll be back in half an hour."

"Okay, Chief," he said. "Hey, what about that stiff? Scuttlebutt is someone plugged him."

"Tell you later." I hung up. Hanging up on Lee is one of the perks of the job.

8

"Where's Mark?"

"Playing with the Peterson boy." She looked at the rolled

canvas in my hands. "Is that it?"

"No, it's the floor plan of a bank in Marquette. I thought I'd take up robbery in my spare time."

"Well, excuse me."

"Sorry. If you had to work with my assistant, you'd lose patience with obvious questions too." I spread it out on the sleek table in the dining room. It had been cleared of its centerpiece since my last visit. I held down the corners of the canvas while she studied it.

"Neo-Romantic," she said. "Not quite surreal—the proportions are too precise—but the effect is similar. European, I think. Between the wars."

"Can you tell me who did it?"

"It's reminiscent of Diego Rivera, but the style is different. I'm afraid I can't help you."

"It was a longshot." I rolled it up again.

"Did it get wet?"

"I found it in the lining of the dead man's overcoat."

She took it in like a movie Indian, without changing expression. "Do you think it's why he was killed?"

"Maybe. If so, whoever did it was careless or he'd have searched him. It wouldn't have been hard to find dry. When it got wet with the overcoat it wasn't so obvious."

"Does the sheriff know about it?"

"Not yet."

"Are you going to tell him?"

"Sure. I've got enough to worry about in town without taking in other people's laundry."

"So why'd you come here?"

"I'm not sure."

We looked at each other for a while.

"Mark's father lives in Mount Pleasant," she said. "We're divorced."

"Sorry to hear it." I felt myself grinning.

She smiled too. "Can I get you something? A cup of coffee?"

"No, I really should be getting back. I have to call the sheriff, and we've got a crime wave in town. We're looking for a desperado who gets off on fishing rods and spoon lures."

She laughed then. "I can't help you with that, but you might ask Professor Groman about the painting. Ted Groman. He's the head of the art department at the University of Marquette. I had him in once to speak to my sixth graders. Tell him I gave you his name."

"I'll recommend him to the sheriff." I stood there tapping my left hand with the rolled canvas in my right.

"Is there something else I can do for you, Chief?"

"To begin with, you can stop calling me Chief. My name's Riley."

She thought about it. "A corpse is a real ice-breaker, isn't it?"

"I'm trying to be charming," I said. "There's a new Italian restaurant in Baraga. Would you like to try it out tonight?"

"I don't know."

"It's safe. I'm a cop." I hooked a thumb behind my badge.

"Someone has to watch Mark. The last time I left him alone he almost burned the house down."

"I know the Peterson kid's parents. They're nice people."

She touched her hair. "It wouldn't be the first time he ate at their table. I'll call them."

"You like Italian?"

"I hate it," she said. "Pick me up at seven."

9

Lee stopped cleaning his nails with the letter opener when I came in. "What's that, wallpaper?" He pointed at the rolled canvas I was carrying.

"Any calls?" I tossed it on the desk and sat down.

"Some guy named Carlucci in Brooklyn, New York." He made it sound like far Cathay. "He wants you to call him back."

"He say what about?"

"Only that it's important. He left his number."

"I'll call him later. You can go to lunch."

"I've been waiting all day to hear about that stiff."

I dialed Lew Connable's office number. "You've probably heard as much as anybody knows by now. This guy bought three slugs and went body-surfing into Laura Taylor's backyard."

"What do you think, drugs?"

"No, thanks. I just had lunch." I waved good-bye. He got up, squared his cap over his eyes, and left. The door slammed.

"Sheriff," said Lew's voice in my ear.

"Lew, this is Riley. Did you talk to Dalrymple?"

"Just got back from that big house he had a couple of million Egyptian slaves build for him. Hasn't had the boat out in a week, he said. I stopped at his dock on the way back. The crew had the deck stripped down to the teak. They said the same thing."

"What about the autopsy?"

"One of those slugs sliced his ticker like a hunk of cheese. The other two were just a formality. Thirty-eight special. I'm shipping the slugs and prints to Marquette like you said. Change your mind about that offer?"

"I'm thinking about it. You know anything about a guy named Groman that teaches art at the University of Marquette?"

"Oh, sure. Every time I plug a perp on the run I look up some egghead and talk about Rembrandt to unwind. I never heard of him, why?"

"Probably nothing. I just wanted to see if I needed an angle to ask him some questions."

"What's he got to do with anything?"

"I didn't say he had anything to do with anything. Listen, let me poke around for a day or two. If I turn anything I'll send you a bill."

"What's changed?"

"Maybe I'm getting tired of dusting bait-and-tackle shops for fingerprints. I'll be in touch."

When I finished talking to him, I unrolled the painting for another look. I wondered what went through an artist's head when he painted a thing like that. More than that I wondered who would buy it, unless he didn't like visitors. Whoever did it must have been voted the man most likely to have his work wrapped around a case of rigor.

I had no idea why I hadn't mentioned the picture to Lew, or for that matter dumped the whole business in his lap where it belonged. Maybe I really was getting bored, or maybe Laura Taylor had me doing cartwheels, showing off like a kid with a crush.

I called the University of Marquette, spoke to a couple of secretaries, and got Professor Groman finally. He remembered Laura. He agreed to see me at four o'clock and look at the painting.

Carlucci, whoever he was, could wait. I rolled up the canvas, wrote a note for Lee to say I'd be out the rest of the afternoon, and took my mid-life crisis to my room at the motel to change clothes. Nobody in Marquette was likely to be impressed by an Iron Harbor police uniform.

1 0

Ted Groman had a corner office on the fourth floor of the
Arts and Sciences Building on the Marquette campus. A secretary old enough to have gotten dust in her hair when the place was
built directed me down a rabbit warren of cramped corridors lined
with bulletin boards advertising for nude male models. I kept it
in mind in case the council fired me for investigating county
murders on village time.

"Come in, Mr. Cooper. Clear yourself a seat."

His age had been hard to determine from his voice on the
phone. I'd been expecting a great shock of white hair, a prune
face, a fluorescent-light complexion, and stooped shoulders
under a corduroy jacket with patches on the elbows. I got a man
not much more than half my age in mottled jeans and a T-shirt that
read Artists Do It On Canvas. He had shoulder-length red hair
parted in the middle and handlebars with waxed tips.

Every level surface in the office—desk, chairs, windowsills,
floor—was stacked high with books, manuscripts, and rolls of
paper and canvas like the one I had brought. The bookshelves that
covered all but the two windows were jammed with old leather-
bound art volumes and thumb-smeared paperbacks and pottery
almost as ancient as the secretary outside. Groman didn't get up,
but remained behind his desk pecking away at a venerable Oliver
typewriter balanced precariously on top of a pile of file folders on
a stand.

I set aside the painting, transferred a heap of paper and
buckram from a plastic scoop chair to the only clear section of
floor, and sat down. While he typed I admired his view of
Superior. It was slate-blue now and cold as a pump handle.
Groman struck one last key with a flourish and pivoted to face me,
smiling.

"I'm writing a book on forgeries," he said. "I've established that the Venus de Milo is a fake."

"The arms, too?"

"Never had any. The real one is in pieces at the bottom of the harbor in Istanbul. The statue in the Louvre was done by a Turkish sculptor in 1820."

"So?"

"So"—he blinked several times, rapidly—"one hundred and sixty-eight years of learned adoration and something over a million words of scholarship have been wasted on a phony."

"Who says they're wasted?

"Good God, man, an entire school of study has been founded on that chunk of marble! A hundred art historians have made their reputations on its significance to the Hellenic Movement. A discovery like this is tantamount to a revelation that George Washington bribed Lord Cornwallis to take a dive at Yorktown."

"It's still a pretty statue."

"What's that got to do with anything?"

"Excuse me, I don't know anything about art. I thought it was important."

He blinked some more. "What do you do, Mr. Cooper?"

"Chief Cooper." I showed him the folder with the badge in it. "I run the police department in Iron Harbor. Laura Taylor said you were the man to see when it comes to paintings."

"How is Laura?"

"Fine." I handed him the canvas.

He cleared some space on his desk, switched on the lamp, and unrolled the painting. He looked at it for a long time. Then he took a big magnifying glass from the top drawer of the desk and spent some more time studying the brushwork or something. He put down the glass and looked at me. "How did this come into your possession?"

"Do you know who painted it?"

"Certainly. It's a Giordano."

I got out my notebook.

"Giacomo Giordano." He spelled it. "He had a vogue in Italy during the twenties, but the Cubists overtook him. I really would like to know where you got the painting."

"A dead man washed ashore with it just outside Iron Harbor late last night or early this morning. He'd been murdered."

"There's water damage. I'll give you two thousand for it."

"It's worth that much?"

"According to legend, Mussolini had Giordano's entire twenties output seized and burned. Some scholars believe a handful of his paintings survived, only to disappear along with an art collection owned by occupied Italy when it was stolen out from under U.S. military guard after the Second World War."

Something kicked me in the stomach. "Was one of the guards killed?"

"As a matter of fact, yes. You heard about it?"

"A man I knew told me he'd lost a friend in an art robbery in Italy. He called me today. I wasn't there to take the call." I shut up.

He shrugged. "I'd need to conduct tests, but from its style I'm willing to gamble that this painting is from that period. It's worth rather more, but without a provenance—"

"This is a stolen painting?"

"Possibly."

"Isn't it kind of not too smart to offer to buy stolen merchandise from a cop?"

"Unless the present Italian government has put in a claim— something I'm not aware of—it's salable goods, at least until the State Department becomes involved. Meanwhile I can think of two collectors who would buy it sight unseen."

"Is this Giordano still living?"

"He died more than forty years ago."

"When an artist dies, doesn't his work increase in value?"

He smiled behind the handlebars. "You do know something about art. I'll give you five thousand."

"Sounds like bad news for Signor Giordano." I rolled up the painting. "It's not mine to sell. Who were those two collectors you mentioned?"

"So you can go to them and cut me out?" He was still smiling. I wasn't. He stopped smiling and touched one of his waxed tips. "One of them is named Vincenzo DeFiore and lives in Florida. I understand he's connected with the Mafia, if there is still such an organization by that name."

"There is. I've heard of Big Vinnie."

"The other one is in your own backyard."

"Don't tell me." I felt the tingle.

"Ernest Dalrymple," he said. "The Taco King."

1 1

I dropped some change into a public telephone on the ground floor of the Arts and Sciences Building and called Lew Connable for Ernest Dalrymple's telephone number. A deputy told me the sheriff was out, but after I convinced him I wasn't an assassin working for Taco Bell he gave me the number from Lew's Rolodex. I used it and introduced myself to the butler or male secretary or paid companion or whoever it was who answered on Dalrymple's end.

"May I ask your business?" he inquired.

"It's about the murder. Mr. Dalrymple will know which one I mean."

"One moment." Music came on the line. After a moment I

recognized it as a full orchestration of the taco company's commercial jingle.

"This is Ernest Dalrymple."

He sounded younger than I knew he was. I introduced myself all over again and asked if I might interview him in person.

"I've already spoken with Sheriff Connable," he said. "I don't know what I can add to what I told him. My boat wasn't out last night and I didn't know the man in the morgue photograph he showed me."

"There's been a new development. I'd rather not discuss it over the phone."

"I see." It sounded like he didn't. "I can spare you a few minutes tonight at eight."

I thought about dinner with Laura. "I was thinking of tomorrow morning."

"Tomorrow morning I'm flying to New Orleans for a convention. I won't be back until Monday. I don't suppose it can wait until then."

"No," I agreed. "Eight o'clock is fine. Thank you, Mr. Dalrymple."

"We deliver." He hung up.

I dialed Salvatore Carlucci's number in Brooklyn, charging the call to Iron Harbor.

"Black Moon," answered a voice like a mechanical dumpster.

"Is this Salvatore Carlucci?"

"Yes."

"This is Riley Cooper. Sorry I didn't get back to you before."

"I hope so."

"I'm kind of busy right now. What is it you need?"

He told me and damned if it wasn't all about Giacomo Giordano.

"Do you believe in coincidence?" I asked.

"They make me uncomfortable, but what've you got?"

I told him part of the story. I heard heavy breathing on his end.

"Can you send me the picture, or better yet bring it yourself?" he asked. "I got a standing assignment from the Italian government to recover those paintings. There's a reward in it, and I'll go your expenses."

"I need the painting for a little while yet. It's evidence in a homicide."

"One of the bastards is dead?"

"He's too young to have pulled off a forty-year-old heist, but he was in something up to his elbows. I'll be in touch."

"You'd damn well better."

Finally I called Laura. She didn't sound as disappointed about missing dinner as I'd have liked. "What about tomorrow night?" I asked.

"Tomorrow night's PTA."

"Isn't that over at ten?"

"I don't guess a late dinner will kill me," she said. "It means asking the Petersons to put Mark up overnight."

"I'll pick you up at the school."

"I'll be hungry."

The wind off the lake had stiffened when I left the building. I turned up my coat collar and stuck my hands in my pockets. One of them closed around the hotel key I had removed from the dead man's overcoat. I'd forgotten about it after transferring it to my civilian clothes.

"The Marquette Hostlery was an old hotel with a new facade and a lake view. I showed the key to the security man at the elevators and he let me go up. The number on the key was 612.

Nobody hit me over the head or shot at me when I unlocked the door. I hadn't expected trouble, but just in case I checked inside the bathroom and under the bed before returning my

revolver to the shoulder rig I'd bought when I was with Detroit
plainclothers. The room was a comfortable enough shoebox
looking out on a piece of the lake. The bed had been made and
the wastebaskets emptied by housekeeping. A gray suit and a
plaid sportcoat hung in the closet. I found a comb in one of the
pockets, nothing else. The dresser drawers contained shirts and
underwear, department store stuff; no weapons or pirate treasure.
A toilet kit stood on top of the dresser with the standard parapher-
nalia inside. I sniffed at the talcum and didn't feel like going out
and wrestling an alligator, so chances were he wasn't using. The
loose coins on the nightstand didn't come apart and spill out
microfilm. It was the dullest hotel room I'd broken into in a long
time.

The missing piece of the page of stationery the sheriff had
found on the dead man still clung to the pad on the nightstand. I
picked up the pad and turned it this way and that in the light until
I could read the indentation on the next page:

3:00 DO

It didn't mean any more to me now than it had the first time.
I put down the pad and lifted the receiver off the telephone.

"Desk."

"This is six-twelve," I said. "I found a message under my
door addressed to this room number, but the name was wrong.
Could you check and tell me how I'm registered?"

"One moment, sir." The young man came back on a beat
later. "We have you registered under the name William Whitelaw,
from Detroit. Is that correct?"

"Yes. Thank you."

As I cradled the receiver, a corner of shiny blue paper peeped
out from beneath the standard. I took hold of it and pulled out a
vacation brochure the size and shape of a legal envelope, doubled

over. The lettering was bright yellow on photographed blue sky:

WHILE YOU'RE IN CALUMET—
WELCOME ABOARD THE HISTORIC
ORE CARRIER
DONALD OLMSTED

Under the legend was the blunt black prow of the old carrier. It seemed to me that the D and O in the name painted on the sides were larger than the other letters.

1 2

Dusk was thickening when I got back to Iron Harbor. I parked the Bronco in front of the station and went inside. Lee looked up brightly from his typewriter. "Found the stuff from Sherm Holloway's shop," he said. "One of Dalrymple's construction crew got drunk at lunch, stole the tackle, and took his buddies fishing. I caught them dipping their lines in Keweenaw Bay."

"How many of 'em did you shoot?"

"The guy confessed on the spot. I called Holloway and he agreed not to press charges provided the stuff is returned and the crew helps him repair his wall."

"Good work, Lee. You're getting to be worth *my* salary anyway."

He looked me up and down. "Where'd you go in your civvies?"

"Marquette. What do you know about the Donald Olmsted?"

"Who's he?"

"It's not a who, it's a what." I tossed the brochure on his desk.

"Oh, that. Just some old bucket someone bought for scrap and turned into a tourist attraction. You can go aboard, peek into the bridge and the crew's quarters, walk around the hold. It's for the rubes from downstate. You got the tourist bug?"

"Kind of crowded for a meet, wouldn't you say?"

"Only during summer. It's probably closed for the season now. What kind of a meet?"

"The three o'clock kind," I said. "I'm starting to think it was three A.M. What's it to Calumet from here, thirty minutes?"

"More like forty-five. Who you meeting there at three A.M.?"

"Nobody. You know anyone named William Whitelaw?"

He shook his head. "You ask a lot of questions without giving out any answers. You've been acting hincty ever since that stiff washed up on du Blacques' Landing. Are you working on that? You said yourself it's out of our jurisdiction."

"I always did stink at geography." I opened the door. "Lock up, will you? I've got an appointment with Ernest Dalrymple at his place in twenty minutes."

"Well, la-de-da. Bring me back a taco."

1 3 ·

The man who brought heartburn to North America lived in a house he had had built from a dead architect's plans on a rocky promontory with a stand of virgin pine on one side and Superior on the other, far enough away from where his convention center was going up that the gulls drowned out the sounds of construction. It was all stone with a slate roof and windows all around, said to be made of bulletproof glass because he feared kidnapping above all other things. The man at the gate, a flinty-eyed ex-Marine type with a brush cut, read the fine print on my badge and ID, used the telephone in his booth, and opened the gate for me by hand.

"I'm surprised it isn't electric," I said.

"Up here he likes to rough it. Drive on up, but stay in the truck till somebody comes for you. We set the dogs loose after dark."

The winding composition drive was illuminated by lights set at ground level. Once a pair of eyes shone emerald-green in my headlights and I stopped until the dog, a two-hundred pound mastiff, decided to get out of my way, slabbed muscles rippling. In front of the circular porch I cut the engine and waited. A carbon copy of the squarehead at the gate came out in a black turtleneck and gray suit and opened my door.

"I got to check you for weapons," he said when I climbed down.

I shrugged and assumed the position with my hands on the Bronco's roof. "There's a Smith & Wesson Police Special under my arm and a Colt derringer in a holster on my right ankle."

He collected those, patted me down for others, and stepped back. I got the rolled canvas from the passenger's seat and held it so he could look down the inside. He nodded, motioned me to walk ahead of him.

The entry hall had a parquet floor, a suit of armor inside the curve of the staircase, and plenty of echoes. The Marine pointed down a hall that ran next to the stairs. "There's a door at the end. Knock first. Mr. Dalrymple has a camera crew in there with him. You'll get your guns back when you leave."

"Thanks. You enjoy *your* evening too."

The door at the end of the hall was opened by yet another crewcut; the John Birch Society was going to find it tough making quorum that night.

The room was a museum, with paintings and sketches hung all over the walls in expensive frames and pots and vases balanced on mahogany pedestals. The carpet was deeper than some rivers I'd fished and there was a big clean desk in front of a double window with the obligatory lake view. Behind the desk sat a man in a five-hundred dollar suit and a baseball cap. The insignia on the cap belonged to a major league team he'd bought recently.

The man who admitted me placed a finger to his lips and pointed to a vacant overstuffed leather chair. I sank into it and watched as Ernest Dalrymple fielded questions by a hyper sportscaster I recognized vaguely from one of the local TV stations. The sportscaster, an ex-linebacker type in a yellow-and-black-checked sportcoat and a toupee two shades too light for the rest of his hair, dwarfed the little Taco King, who looked twenty years younger than he was in his chipmunk cheeks and big glasses.

They wrapped after five minutes. The sound man, the light man, and the cameraman packed their equipment into travelworn cases, the sportscaster shook Dalrymple's hand and accepted an autographed baseball and a book of taco coupons, and Marine number three escorted them out. As soon as the door was shut the boyish smile dropped from Dalrymple's face. He whipped off the baseball cap and tossed it into a drawer. His eyes nailed me through an eighth of an inch of prescription glass. "You're Cooper?"

I said I was and got up and went over to shake his hand. He didn't rise, but he took the hand in his small hard one. Everything about him seemed harder since the camera crew had left. He indicated a chair closer to the desk. I took it.

"That doesn't look like a subpoena." He was looking at the rolled canvas.

"No. I'm told you collect art."

"Have you come to sell me something?"

"Specifically, I hear you're interested in the works of Giacomo Giordano."

He raised and resettled his glasses and sat back. "Where did you hear it?"

"Ted Groman at the University of Marquette. He said you and a man in Florida are the biggest collectors around."

"DeFiore. We meet at all the auctions. What's this to do with your murder?"

"Everyone owns murder," I said. "It's in public domain."

"I still can't help you. I didn't know the man."

"His name was William Whitelaw."

I was watching him closely. He didn't curse or go pale or reach for his pills. But he reacted, inasmuch as a veteran of board meetings and media coverage allows himself to react. I think his scalp moved slightly. I pressed him. "You know the name?"

"He was an assistant curator at the Detroit Institute of Arts. We never met, although I spoke to him on the telephone once or twice. He was eventually let go."

"What for?"

"It's not my place to blacken a dead man's reputation."

I passed it for now. "What was your business with him at the DIA?"

"It never was with him, actually. I merely went through him to get to the curator. He helped me, the curator helped me, to authenticate a painting on occasion before I bought it. Now, what's this about Giordano?" His eyes wandered to the canvas.

"Professor Groman said you were mainly interested in the pictures Giordano painted in the twenties."

He laughed shortly. "Who wouldn't be? They were all destroyed."

"I don't know much about collecting," I said. "All I ever collected was bullets. But the collectors I've known were all just a little bit crazy. As long as there was the slightest possibility the thing they wanted most still existed, they wouldn't give up hope. According to Groman, there's some belief a few of the paintings were among a collection stolen from the Italian government after World War Two."

"I've heard the rumor."

He was still looking at the canvas. I rolled it up and down the arm of my chair with my palm. "Let's try this. Suppose Whitelaw, in his capacity as assistant curator with the Detroit Institute of Arts, stumbled on one of the stolen pictures and told you he had it. Would you kill for it?"

"Sheriff Connable has established my boat was in drydock last night. You're going to have to do better than that if you're looking to frame me for Whitelaw's murder."

"The fact that a big boat passed close to shore last night could have been a coincidence. You might have dumped the body off the penisula without ever leaving dry land. It's on your property."

"Why would I dispose of him so close to my own land?"

"I didn't say you did. Just that you might have."

He sat back farther. Now he was deliberately not looking at the canvas. "I think you'll acknowledge I'm not a stupid man, Cooper. Backwoods cops aren't necessarily hicks anymore. I'd hardly expect them to overlook a corpse on my back steps. Besides, I was entertaining here late into the night. Would you consider a state supreme court justice a reliable witness?"

"Men in your position hardly ever do their own killing. They usually hire it done."

"Now you're mixing me up with DeFiore. Why don't you question him?"

"He doesn't live here. May I unroll this?" I held up the canvas.

"Do what you like." He didn't even drool.

I stood and spread it on top of his desk. He came forward eagerly, abandoning the phony indifference at last. After thirty seconds he made a sound of disgust and sat back. "It's a damn forgery."

"It's been in the water."

"That wouldn't change the brushwork or the choppy style. I've seen photographs of his other twenties work. He never painted like this."

"Huh." I let it roll itself back up. "You could be saying that to cover yourself."

"I could be, but I'm not. I'll tell you now why Whitelaw was fired. He was caught selling forgeries of French Impressionists to gullible collectors, using his position with the DIA to win their confidence. They got rid of him and bought the victims' silence to avoid a scandal. Check with them; and while you're at it, have them look at the painting. Any expert can tell you it's a fake."

"I already had an expert look at it," I said.

1 4

A lonely ore carrier inched along the line where black sky met the blacker surface of the lake, its running lights pinpoints in a clammy shroud. It might have been the ghost of the uninhabited shell that rose before me on a patch of grass. TRESPASSERS WILL BE PROSECUTED read the rusty sign swinging from the chain across the opening in the cyclone fence surrounding it. I ducked under the chain and trained my flashlight on the scuttle-shaped prow:

DONALD OLMSTED

Blocks away, Calumet's town clock chimed the first strokes of midnight.

I snapped off the light and felt my way up the gangplank. There was no moon and a low cloudbank obscured the stars. I smelled rusty metal and rotting wood.

I started at the bridge, dark oak trimmed with brass, and worked my way back down to the deck, risking the light in brief flashes and shielding it with my body. I didn't know what I was looking for. I inspected the crew's quarters—cramped berths stacked one atop another with checked mattresses and pillow-cases to hide the dirt—and the heads fore and aft. I shone the light inside the deck vents. When I was through there I went below, down a steep flight of iron steps into the hold. More rust, and stale oil from pistons long silent. And black as a coffin.

It seemed I walked a long time, casting the beam around, before it reflected back from something; the carrier was as long as a football field and almost its entire lower half was for cargo. The something was the inside of the hull at the bow end. I turned and walked back the other way. My footsteps rang.

The light caught something on the inside of the hull near the stern and darted away. It took me a moment to find the spot again. At first I thought the little shiny points were rivets, but they stood alone. There were two of them several inches apart, one higher than the other. Keeping the light on them I went up to them and probed them with a finger. They were concave dimples the size of my fingertip, punched through the rusty surface to the brighter metal beneath.

I smelled it then, or maybe it was just my imagination: the faint acrid residue of spent powder. I knew now where William Whitelaw had died.

The deck above me creaked slightly. When it creaked a second time and then a third I snapped off the light. I was in complete darkness now, maybe for the first time in my life.

It seemed I waited for hours, tracking his progress by the thumps and squeaks he made as he searched the ship. I had the patience for it. I knew he'd make his way down to the hold eventually.

His first steps on the iron stairs were tentative. He paused as if listening. I caught my breath. He came down a few more steps, and then a light sprang on and the smoky shaft of his flash swung around 360 degrees, poking up and down randomly. It fell short of where I stood near the stern. The light went off and he came down the rest of the way—quickly, without a false step, as if he'd been there before. Which of course he had.

He reached the bottom and moved away to my right. He stopped, and after a moment started to whistle, air hissing through his teeth tunelessly. Something clicked—a familiar sound—his flash came on briefly, falling on an exposed cylinder loaded with brass cartridges. He swung the cylinder back into the revolver and snapped off the light. Went on whistling.

"It won't work," I said then. "I'm not Whitelaw."

He sucked in air. "Who is it?"

I flicked on my own flash. He blinked. In the glare his long hair and handlebars looked black. "Riley Cooper, Groman. The same Riley Cooper who called you to meet me here tonight. If I'd known you were such a rotten shot I wouldn't have been so cautious. You missed Whitelaw twice. I saw the dents."

"What's this about, Cooper?" He was standing with the revolver at his side and a little behind his hip, hiding it. I kept my attention on that hand.

"You shouldn't have steered me to Dalrymple so soon," I said. "But then you'd have to have told me about him sometime or it would've looked bad. He took one look at the painting and knew it was a forgery. Why didn't you? You were writing a book on that subject. I'm a working-class guy, Professor. When an expert makes a mistake I wonder why."

"I'm not an authority on Giordano."

"Drop it, Groman. If you were innocent you wouldn't have come here. You knew the painting was a phony, but you didn't say anything. Instead you offered me five grand for it. Why? Because you didn't want anyone else to see it.

"Whitelaw was blackmailing you, wasn't he? You were in on the scheme to sell forgeries under the auspices of his position with the Detroit Institute of Arts. When he was fired he tried to sell one of the fakes to you in return for keeping his mouth shut about your involvement. You couldn't afford that, not with a book in the works that would make your reputation in the art world. So you lured him here and killed him. The trail might've ended right here, but you had to get cute. You took the body to the end of the peninsula on Ernest Dalrymple's property and dropped it into the lake, knowing it would wash ashore, implicate Dalrymple, and confuse the investigation. That was one mistake. The other was failing to search him. You could've had the painting for free."

"I painted it," he said.

I said nothing. He was smiling in the light of my flash. The gun was still out of sight.

"To hell with my reputation," he went on. "If it got out I did a little forging of my own, my book would have sold twice as well. That wasn't the reason I killed Whitelaw. I painted two Giordanos. The idiot sold one of them to Big Vinnie DeFiore."

"The Mafioso."

"His eye isn't as good as Dalrymple's; nevertheless it's only a matter of time before he finds out he was screwed. Whitelaw realized that and came up here for a getaway stake. If I didn't come across with ten thousand, he said, he'd call DeFiore and tell him I was behind the fakes. The rest you know."

"What about the other painting?"

"He never mentioned it. If I know Whitelaw, he was going to hedge his bet by peddling it to Dalrymple; I mean, as long as he was in the neighborhood. After I shot him I took his wallet to slow down the identification process. There was no reason to search him further. I had no way of knowing he had the other canvas on him."

He laughed shortly. "You want to hear something funny? I've got the original Giordano I copied that one from. I bought it in an auction lot from a collector's widow who didn't know what she had. He was too old even at the end of World War Two to have been one of the thieves, so one of them must've gotten hard up and sold it to him. I figured I could make a lot more money making copies and selling the same painting over and over again. You saw it lying around my office with the others, but you never knew what it was." As he spoke, he raised the revolver and fired point-blank at the flashlight.

By then I was nowhere near it. While he was talking I'd laid it on one of the steel steps and moved away. His bullet ricocheted off the rear of the hull shrilly and I put four into him from the .38 I'd been holding since I'd heard his first footsteps overhead.

His face contorted and he slid below the circle of light. His gun hit the floor with a clang. He followed it with a dull thud. I barely heard that. My ears were ringing as if I'd been standing inside a church bell at High Mass.

It was a moment before I realized I was bleeding. I reached behind my left shoulder and brought my hand away wet. I knew then where Groman's bullet had gone after it bounced off the hull. The hold got a little blacker then, and that was the last thing I was aware of for a while.

1 5

"Riley, is that you?" Laura Taylor sounded sleepy. "It's four o'clock in the morning!"

"I know. Sorry I woke you up."

"Are you all right?"

"I'm swell. I just wanted to hear your voice." I kept mine down. Lew Connable, wearing a pajama top under his gray suitcoat, was in conversation with a nurse and two Calumet cops inside the door of my hospital room. The telephone receiver felt heavy in my hand. I was still dopy from the anesthetic.

"That's nice," she said dreamily. "Oh, that big boat came by again about dusk. I got its number."

"Forget it. The killer didn't use a boat."

There was a short pause. "Did you get him?"

"Yeah."

"You sound strange. Are you sure nothing's wrong?"

"Nothing that didn't happen eleven times before."

I told her then. I'd come to in the ambulance on the way to the hospital in Calumet and again when they were wheeling me into the operating room. When I came out of the anesthetic, Lew told me someone had heard the shots and called the cops.

"You were shot?"

"Just in the meaty part of my arm. The slug was almost spent after hitting the hull. You should see the other guy." According to Lew I'd put them all in Groman's breadbasket. He died of shock.

"I can't believe it," Laura said. "Ted seemed like such a nice man."

"Artists. Go figure."

"I'm coming over."

"Don't bother. They're letting me go tomorrow. I just wanted to tell you I won't be able to make dinner."

Another pause. "You're not just lying to make me feel better."

"I swear."

"Well, we won't have any more of this."

I breathed some air. "I understand. It was nice knowing you, Laura."

"I didn't mean that. I mean we'll have no more of you standing in front of bullets."

"And how do you plan to do that?" I felt myself grinning.

"With delicacy and finesse."

The nurse approached the bed. "Put down the phone, Chief. You're not out of the woods yet."

"Like hell I'm not," I said.

CARLUCCI'S WAY

by
Robert J. Randisi

The stitches hurt like hell when I moved a certain way, so I tried not to move that way. It wasn't easy, though, because that way happened to be *breathing*, and I couldn't very well stop that.

The morning after the incident with the punks I dressed as slowly as I could and went to the Black Moon, after phoning the PIs in the other cities. I hadn't planned to open that day, but I needed some time to recover from the fight. In a day or so maybe the stitches wouldn't hurt that much.

Over the next two days I heard from Hawkins and Edward. Hawkins called first, the afternoon of the first day, the same day I talked to Luciano and my "operatives." Actually, I'd only talked to Parnell and the fella in Texas who had taken over for Bailey. Jacoby had given me a name in Lake Superior—Riley Cooper— but I had only been able to leave him a message. I was waiting for Andy's call to discuss my idea with him of "planting" something in another computer.

"What have you got for me, Andy?"

"Not a heck of a lot," Andy said. "In fact, nothing. All I could find out from the computers was that your man Luciano is some kind of minor official at the Italian Consulate. Hell, I can't even get a title."

"That's all right, Andy," I said. "You've ID'd him as a member of the consulate. That's enough for me."

"I wish I could've done more, Sal."

"That's okay, kid. Listen, there's something else you could for me."

"What?" he asked, putting a lot of caution into the one word.

I explained my idea and asked him if it should be done.

"Sure, I can do it, Sal—"

"*Will* you?"

There was a moments hesitation and then he said, "Sure. Just tell me what you want planted."

I did and he took it all down.

"How soon will they have it?" I asked.

"Within a couple of hours."

That was good. I'd be able to follow up with a phone call before the day was out.

"Listen, thanks, kid. I'll see ya, huh?"

"See ya," he said, and hung up.

The fact that he couldn't get much, even from his computer, could've meant a couple of things. It could've meant that Luciano was actually a *high* ranking official, and any information on him was classified. Or, he *was* actually a low ranking official who was using this case to try and elevate himself.

Either way I stood to make a lot of money and that was the main reason I had taken the case.

Wasn't it?

The next day I got the call from Edward.

"Well, you were right," Edward said. "I can't believe it, but you were."

"It's here?" I asked. "In New York?"

"It's here."

"Where, Edward?"

"I don't know exactly where it is now, Sal, but I know where it was."

"All right, where?"

"Joliet House."

"What is Joliet House?"

"You've heard of Sotheby's?"

"That's where they hold all those high-priced auctions, isn't it?"

"That's right," he said. "Joliet is the same thing, only they're not as open about it as Sotheby's and some of the others. They cater to private collectors, people who don't want it generally known that they've purchased a particularly high priced article."

"Where is this place, Edward?"

"It's on Broadway, near Twelfth Street, right near the Strand."

"What's the Strand?"

"A book store."

"I don't read many books, Edward. Thanks for the info, though."

"You going over there?"

"Yep."

"They know me there. I'll call ahead and tell them you're coming, otherwise they wouldn't talk to you."

"I appreciate it, Edward."

"Ask for Jesse Marlowe—"

"Thanks, Edward," I said and hung up before he could invite me to his next art show.

I would have felt obliged to go.

2

When I awoke the next morning the stitches didn't really hurt any less, I had simply gotten used to the pain, so I hopped the subway to Manhattan.

Joliet House was on Broadway, between Eleventh and Twelfth Streets. On the northeast corner of Twelfth was the bookstore Edward had mentioned, the Strand. Supposedly there were "Eight Miles of Books" inside. I wondered if there was enough time in someone's life to read eight miles of books.

I approached Joliet House. It was right next to a place that sold pool tables. Both establishments handled merchandise beyond my means. I paused a moment to look at myself in the plate glass window of Joliet House. I'd worn a sports jacket and tie, and tried sucking in my belly, but it would have taken more suck than I had to disguise it. I also needed a haircut. Luckily, I wasn't going inside to do any more than ask a few questions.

I entered and stopped just inside the door. There were antique items everywhere, and to my unpracticed eye some of them looked like no more than knickknacks. They must have been expensive, though, because there was plenty of aisle space between each item, so that there was no danger of knocking anything over unless you were extremely big and clumsy—like me.

The floor of the aisles was made of some sort of material that looked like brick, which seemed odd to me. They were taking a chance of someone stubbing a toe and tripping. The tables that the items were set on stood on carpeted spaces.

I was looking at a piece of sculpture without any understanding at all when a man approached me. He was tall, slender, in his early forties, well dressed and very well kept. His cologne was rather strong and I almost backed away as he came near.

"May I help you?"

"Yes," I said, "I'd like to see Jesse Marlowe."

This eyebrows raised and he asked, "Do you have an appointment?"

"Not exactly."

"I beg your pardon?"

"Edward Wells may have called to say I was coming, but he wouldn't have said when."

"I see," he said, raising his eyebrows again. I couldn't tell if he was silently commenting on something, or if the raising of the eyebrows was just an idiosyncrasy of some sort. "Wait here, please."

"Sure."

He went to the back of the store to a desk and picked up a phone. I turned my head to look out the window. At that moment a young woman was walking by. She was about twenty with long, blonde hair, dark eyebrows and very red lipstick on her full lips. She was wearing tight jeans and a white T-shirt. Her breasts were large and firm, as round as I've ever seen. Her legs were long, and her ass shapely and taut. She was the kind of art I *could* understand—but which was still beyond my means.

My stitches started to hurt.

"Excuse me."

I turned and found the man staring at me. I smiled and said, "Just admiring the scenery."

"You can go upstairs," he said. "We're setting up for a . . . private auction, and you'll have to talk to Jesse up there."

"That's fine. How do I get up there?"

"This way."

I followed the man to the back of the room, past the desk, to a closed door. He opened it, revealing a stairway going up.

"Thanks," I said, and climbed the stairs. There was a doorway at the top, but no door, and I walked right through.

293

I found myself in a a cavernous room that was alive with activity. Chairs were being set up—noisily—and pedestals were being placed according to the instructions of a woman holding a clipboard. She was about thirty or so, with red hair worn behind her head. The suit she was wearing was severe, but I could see that she had all the equipment. I wondered how she'd look in tight jeans and a T-shirt.

I looked around the room but I couldn't see anyone else up there other than a half dozen workmen and the woman who was giving them orders.

"Hey, excuse me," I said to one of the men passing me. He had an armful of chairs but he stopped and gave me an impatient look.

"Yeah?"

"Can you tell me where I can find Jesse Marlowe?"

"Sure," he said, jerking his chin, "up front, there."

"Where?" I said, looking towards the front of the room. The woman was berating one of the men for knocking over a pedestal. I didn't see anyone else.

"Right there, man," the workmen said. "The broad who thinks that clipboard is a sign of power, or something."

"That's Jesse Marlowe."

"The woman?"

"The tyrant," he said and moved on.

Approximately half the room was filled with chairs, with aisles on each side and the center. I moved to the center aisle and walked to the front of the room, towards Jesse Marlowe, the tyrant.

Up close she looked a little older than I had first thought, but not much. Thirty-five was still a year or so off. As I approached she looked at me with an impatient look that was already a few hours old.

"Are you from the gallery—no," she said, catching herself,

"you wouldn't be from the gallery." She glanced up from the clipboard briefly. "You're the detective Edward called about."

"That's right."

"I told Edward I didn't have anything to tell you."

Edward hadn't told me that.

"Well, I'd like to ask you a few questions, anyway . . . if you don't mind."

"No, I don't mind," she said with a shrug, "but I can't stop doing what I'm doing . . . if you don't mind."

"No, that's fine."

"Be careful with that!" she shouted at some workman. "So, what would you like to ask me?"

"I'd like to ask about the 'Ladies in the Cathedral.'"

"What about them?"

"You know what they are, right?"

"No," she said, but she wasn't talking to me, "that goes over on the other side!" She looked at me then and said, "Of course I know what they are."

"I understand they've begun to surface, separately."

"I hadn't heard that."

"Edward didn't mention it?"

"Not to me."

How had Edward found out that one of the ladies had been here if he hadn't spoken to Jesse Marlowe about it?

"Can I ask what your position is here?" I asked.

"I'm the assistant director," she said. "You! No, you there! Move that one a little to the left. That's it, right there."

"And you don't know anything about one of the ladies passing through here, being purchased from you?"

She turned now and gave me all of her attention. I noticed that her eyes were a startling clear green and very large. It was the first time she'd looked up from the clipboard for more than a split second.

"Mr. . . ."

"Carlucci."

"Mr. Carlucci, don't you think if one of the "Ladies of the Cathedral" showed up here I'd know about it?"

"I don't know," I said. "Would you?"

"Of course I would."

"What about the director, here?"

"What about him?"

"Isn't it possible that he might know something about it—"

"If he knew," she said, "I'd know."

"Is he around?" I asked. "I'd like to talk to him."

"He's away."

"For how long?"

"He won't be back un il Friday."

This was Wednesday.

"All right," I said, "I'll try him then."

"You'll be wasting your time, Mr. Carlucci," she said. "I assure you none of the ladies have passed through here. If they had, they would have caused a sensation."

"I thought all of your auctions were private?"

"Not all of them," she said, "although we do conduct many private purchases and auctions."

"And you don't think this could have been one of them?"

"No," she said, "definitely not."

"Why not?"

"Because I know about all purchases," she said, "public or otherwise."

"I see. Well, thank you for your time, Miss Marlowe. I'll come back Friday to talk to your boss. What's his name?"

"Andrew Maynard, but he won't be able to tell you a thing more than I have. Oh, excuse me," she said, and hurried away to chastise some hapless workman.

I went back down the stairs and out the front door. I stood there for a few moments, wondering why Edward had sent me to Joliet House if Jesse Marlowe knew nothing about the "Ladies in the Cathedral." After all, he had given me her name. The other side of the coin was that she did know about it, but was protecting her client. Maybe I'd get more from Andrew Maynard on Friday.

I started towards Fourteenth Street, to catch the subway. When I was directly across the street from the Strand Bookstore I saw the same young woman I had seen pass in front of Joliet House. She was coming out of the store, carrying a large bag of books.

My stitches started to hurt.

3

I went back to Greenpoint and opened the Black Moon. Fifteen minutes later there were six people sitting at the bar: Harry the Map, Ben Simmons, Mad Myra and some other familiar faces.

After I was opened two hours Carl Devlin walked in and sat at the end of the bar. I drew a cold one and brought it over to him.

"I came by earlier," he said, accepting the beer. "You weren't open."

"I don't need you to tell me that," I said, leaning on the bar. "Why were you looking for me?"

Devlin shrugged.

"Wanted to see if you had anything else to say about the other night."

"Let me think a minute," I said. "No, I can't think of anything I didn't tell you."

"No?" he said. "How about 'why?'"

"Why what?"

"Why those punks jumped you."

"I don't know why," I said. "I thought that was your job."

"No," he said, "my job is to find them, if I can, but if I knew why they did what they did, maybe that would make my job easier." He leaned a little closer and said, "Wouldn't you like to make my job easier?"

"I'd love to make your job easier, Carl," I said, "but I can't. I didn't know them, and I don't know who sent them."

"You'd tell me if you knew, right?" he asked. "I mean, you wouldn't try to . . . do something on your own, would you?"

"Do I look like I just stepped out of a private eye movie?"

"Not unless they get Brian Dennehy to play the part."

"Brian who?"

"Never mind," Devlin said. He drank half his beer and left the rest. "If you think of anything I should know, give me a call, huh?"

"You'll be the first, Carl."

"Yeah," he said, and left.

Harry the Map was the last person I had to clear out that night before I could close.

"Come on, Harry," I said, "finish up. I want to go home."

"Hey, Sallie," Harry said, "are you workin'?"

"What does it look like I'm doing?" I asked, raising the two glasses I was washing.

"Naw, I mean on a case," he said. "Are ya workin' on a case."

I hesitated, then said, "I might be looking into something, Harry. Why?"

"Well, you might need someone to cover the bar for you," he

said. "You know, maybe open up for ya? Like today?"

"I'll let you know, Harry," I said. "Finish that beer, will ya?"

"Sure, Sal, sure."

He guzzled the last of his beer and navigated toward the door. Harry could drink more beer without keeling over than anyone I knew. I rarely worried about his getting home safely.

It helped that he lived right around the corner.

I closed up and left by the front door. I didn't want to give anyone else a chance to jump me in the alley, even if I was wearing my old off duty revolver on my hip.

Outside I found somebody waiting for me, waiting to jump me, but not the way I had been thinking.

It was Mad Myra.

"Myra," I said, "I thought you went home."

"I left, Sal," she said, sadly, "but I didn't go home."

I seemed to remember that she had left with a man, not one of the regulars. I guess they never got where they were going—together.

"Well, why don't you go home now, Myra?"

"I can't," she said, "not alone."

"Myra—"

"Can I go home with you, Sal?" she asked, moving closer. She put her hand on my arm and pressed one firm breast against me. As usual, she was wearing too much perfume, but tonight it didn't bother me as much.

Maybe it had something to do with the two women I had seen that day—the one in the T-shirt, and Jesse Marlowe—but I almost said yes to Mad Myra.

"Myra, come on—"

"Sal," she said, trying to sound sexy, "Sallie, you don't know how good I can be—"

"Myra, no."

She looked at me and in the light cast by the corner lamp she looked older to me tonight. Her face seemed to have been ravaged by the years, and the booze . . . . she started crying. Not bawling out loud, but big tears starting rolling down her cheeks.

"I can't go home alone, Sal," she said. "I just can't!"

"Myra—"

"We don't have to do anything, Sal," she said, squeezing my arm urgently. "I just . . . can't be alone, not tonight. I'll . . . I'll die!"

I stared at her then and saw that she really believed that. She believed it enough that if it *didn't* happen, she might *make* it happen.

"All right, Myra," I said. "Come on."

My house was five blocks away and we walked. Myra was a little unsteady on her feet and leaned on me for support. To anyone watching we might have looked like a slightly over the hill couple returning home from a night at the neighborhood bar.

What a thought.

As we approached my house I spotted some movement further down the block. When we reached the walk leading to my door I saw that there was someone trying to break into a car.

"Oh, shit," I said.

"What?" Myra asked sharply, as if I had just woken her.

"Nothing, Myra," I said, slipping my hand into my pocket. "Look, here's the key. Go inside and wait for me."

"Where are you going?" she asked, sounding alarmed.

"Don't worry," I said. "I'll just be a few seconds. Go on."

Hesitantly she started toward the door, looking back at me over her shoulder.

"Go," I said, softly, and then started down the block.

I could have called out to whoever was breaking into one of my neighbor's cars, but maybe I needed to get my hands on somebody. Anyway, I started down the block, hoping to reach him before he heard me coming, and that's when the explosion came.

I turned and saw the front of my house blow out. The blast lit up the night and I looked back at the car thief. He was about seventeen, and there was a shocked look on his face as he looked past me at the source of the blast. He turned and ran, and I let him go.

I knew there wasn't much of a chance, but I had to go and see if Myra was still alive.

4

I opened the front door of the Black Moon and hit the light switch on the way in. Carl Devlin entered behind me and closed the door.

"You want a drink?" I asked, heading for the bar.

"Yeah, sure."

I went behind the bar and pulled down a bottle of Irish whiskey and poured us each a stiff one. He sat on a stool and I pushed his drink over to him and leaned on the bar.

"Jesus," I said, wrinkling my nose and running my right forefinger under it, "I can still smell her."

"The smell of charred human flesh stays with you for a while."

That's all that was left of Mad Myra—charred flesh.

"You got someplace to stay?" Devlin asked.

"Here," I said, tapping the bar.

"I got a couch—"

"Here's fine," I said. "I got a cot in the back."

He hesitated a moment, then said, "They might try for you here, Sal."

"Yeah."

I drained my drink and poured myself another.

"I could put a radio car out front," he said, "or I could put a man inside—"

I waved him off.

"Just have a car pay special attention to the bar, Carl. That'll be enough."

Special attention. When I was on the job that was what we told people when there was nothing else we could do. We'll pay special attention to the area.

"Sal," Devlin said, leaning forward as if to add emphasis to the point he was about to make, "somebody's trying to kill you."

"No shit, Sherlock."

"Well, you don't act like you know that."

"I know it," I snapped back. "I got a barbecued customer and a house with three walls to prove it."

"Is that all she was?" he asked. "A customer?"

"That's all," I said, roughly.

"I mean, she was going home with you—"

"That doesn't mean anything," I said. "She just didn't want to be alone tonight. She was terrified of being alone, especially when she was drunk."

"Well, she won't have to worry about that, anymore."

"What the hell is that supposed to mean?" I said, exploding. "The woman's dead, dammit!"

"Well, better her than you!" he snapped back. "Shit, she saved you life by opening that door instead of you. Why *was* she opening your front door, Sal?"

"I gave her the key."

"Why?"

I looked at him, and for a moment I couldn't remember why.

"Uh, there was a kid trying to break into a car down the block. I told her to go inside while I took a look."

"What happened to the kid?"

"I don't know," I said, shrugging and pouring myself another Irish, "he took off, I guess."

"Did you know him?"

I shook my head.

"Sal, think! If we can find that kid, maybe he saw something. Maybe he saw someone coming out of your house. Think, man!"

"Not tonight," I said. "Tonight I just want to drink, I don't want to think. Hey, that rhymes, don't it?"

"If you're looking to get drunk," he said, pushing his own unfinished drink away, "you've got yourself a running start."

He slid off the stool and headed for the front door. When he got there he turned around again.

"If you think of anything, give me a call."

"Sure, sure," I said, pouring myself a fourth drink. This time instead of just decorating the bottom of the glass I filled it halfway. It was a highball glass.

"And lock this door behind me!"

"Yeah . . ."

"Jesus . . ." he said, and left.

Between the fifth and sixth drink I remembered to lock the door.

Between the eighth and ninth I tried to set up the cot in the back room.

I went to bed with the tenth.

5

When I woke the next morning my ears were still ringing. The doctor had warned me about that. To tell the truth I hadn't noticed it so much the night before. A little ringing in the ears had seemed a small price to pay for one's life, at the time.

In addition to ringing ears my stitches hurt, my back was killing me from the damned army cot I'd slept on, and my head was killing me from all the drinking I'd done. I know I own a bar, but I can count on one hand the times I've gone to bed as drunk as I had last night.

At least, I *used* to be able to . . .

I put the coffee on and took a cold shower, trying to wake myself up in more ways than one. Under the tepid spray given off by the cheap shower head I tried *not* to think of Mad Myra, but I wasn't having any luck. I toweled myself off and put a fresh bandage over the stitches, took four Tylenols with a cup of coffee, then poured a second cup and dialed my client's phone number.

"Mr. Carlucci," Luciano asked excitedly, "have you found out something?"

"I sure have," I said, adding to myself, *you lying scumbag!* "We have to talk."

"This is wonderful," Luciano said, barely able to contain his glee. "Can we meet somewhere?"

"Sure," I said, "if you don't mind coming into Brooklyn."

"Uh, not to Greenpoint again—"

"No," I said, "that won't be necessary. Do you know where the Promenade is?"

"But of course," he said, "it is right across the river from the World Trade Center. When I first came to this country I made an effort to see the sights—"

"That's right," I said. "Meet me there at noon and I'll give you what I've got."

"Excellent!" Luciano said, sounding like a kid on Christmas morning. "I can't tell you how pleased I am."

"Tell me at noon," I said.

The Promenade was a small walkway overlooking the East River and the Brooklyn Queens Expressway in downtown

Brooklyn, spitting distance from most of the law offices and all of the Brooklyn court buildings.

I had a special reason for wanting to meet Luciano on the Promenade. There was a hotdog vendor there who had the best hotdogs in New York.

Also, if Luciano didn't come clean with me, I was going to throw him off of it!

6

I got to the Promenade first, as I planned. I'd already had one hotdog and was working on a second when Luciano pulled up in a cab. Only a fucking foreigner would have taken a cab and not the subway.

"That the guy you're waiting for, Sal?" Jake, the hotdog vender, asked.

"Yep."

"Looks like a fuckin' faggot."

"I wouldn't know about that, Jake."

"I'll betcha he don't take no onions on his hotdog," Jake said.

"No bet."

Jake ran his hotdog stand here on the Promenade nine months out of the year and spent the other three months at his condo in Florida. He was built like a fire hydrant and his face was seamed, defying you to guess his age. He had fingers like the hotdogs and sausages he sold, but when they were working, laying your dog on a bun and dressing it, they moved like a dancer's legs.

Luciano approached and I said, "How do you like your hotdog?"

The Italian actually looked happy to answer the question.

"Hotdogs," he said. "One of your country's delicacies that has touched my heart. Mustard and, uh, kraut, please," he said to Jake.

Jake built it up and then asked, "How about some onions?"

"Oh, no," Luciano said, "no onions."

Jake gave me a triumphant look and handed Luciano the dog. I made myself a bet he'd ask for club soda or Perrier.

"Something to drink?" I asked.

"Do you have Perrier?"

"Hell, no," Jake said, wrinkling up his already wrinkled face.

"Club soda?"

Jake shook his head.

"Have some ginger ale," I said, and Luciano agreed. It didn't matter, he wasn't going to get a chance to finish either the dog or the soda.

"Cream soda, Jack," I said, and when I had it turned to Luciano, saying, "This way."

I walked to the railing and looked at the river and at Manhattan, across the way, listening the cars go by underneath. "A marvelous city," Luciano said, also looking across the river. He was chewing on a bite of hotdog, a dab of mustard staining the corner of his mouth. I waited for him to take another big bite, then dropped mine and grabbed him by the throat. The sudden move made my stitches pull, but I ignored the pain.

"Mmph," he said, trying to breath around the mangled hotdog in his mouth.

"I want the truth, you sonofabitch," I snarled into his mottled face, "and if I don't get it, I'm going to throw you into the river."

I saw his throat working and let him go, stepping back just in time to avoid the torrent that rushed from his mouth. I waited until he was done puking up what little hot dog he'd eaten, plus his breakfast, then grabbed him by the back of his jacket. The front was stained with his vomit.

"Talk, you little weasel," I said, shaking him. Jake was studiously looking the other way.

"I can't—" he said, but I shook him until his eyes rolled.

"Wait, wait!" he cried. "Tell me what you want."

I let him go and he staggered, stepping into the puddle of his vomit. His feet almost went out from under him, but he grabbed the railing and kept his feet.

"What do you want?" he asked again, his voice a harsh rasp.

"I want to know why someone blew up my house last night," I said. "I want to know why an innocent woman had to die last night. I want to know why three punks tried to carve me up. I want to know what you're not telling me, Luciano, and I better hear it damned soon."

"I don't know—" he started, but he stopped when I started towards him. "Wait, wait, let me finish!"

I stopped, giving him a chance to speak. When he was done if I didn't like what he said I could still toss him over.

"Undoubtedly someone is trying to kill you to keep you from finding the paintings, but I do not know who it is, I swear!"

"What's so damned important about the paintings?"

"They are valuable—"

"How does anyone know I'm looking for them, Luciano?" I asked. "You hired me. Who else did you tell about me?"

"No one, I swear," he said. "You have been asking questions—"

"I was attacked by those four punks before I even spoke to anyone," I said. "You had to have told someone, Luciano. Someone at the embassy, a friend, a lover. Think!"

"I am trying," he said, rubbing his throat. He looked down at himself, saw the stains on his jacket, took it off and hung it over the railing. "I cannot think of anyone. I was very careful—"

"Not careful enough," I said. "Somebody's trying to kill me, and I'm not going to stand still for it, even if I have to go to your embassy—"

"No!" he said, quickly. "Do not do that!"

"Why not?"

"I told you, I do not want anyone to know—"

"Wake up, man!" I said. "Someone already knows!"

"Give me time," he said, "let me find out."

"And meanwhile what do I do?"

"Continue to look for the paintings."

"With someone trying to fry my ass—"

"I will double your fee," he said. "Please, you must continue. My country needs those paintings."

I didn't think Italy was going to sink from sight without them, but since he was doubling my fee . . .

"All right," I said, "I'll keep looking, but I want to know where the damn leak is. If there's another attempt on my life you're going to be the first to know."

"Yes, yes, I understand," Luciano said, "believe me, I will find out for you."

"Get out of here," I said. "Get started, already."

"I am going," he said. He looked at his jacket, wrinkled his nose, and for a moment I thought he was going to leave it there, but in the end he took it and carried it gingerly with him as he went in search of another cab.

I was disgusted with him and I was disgusted with myself. He'd waved a few more bucks in my face and I'd gone for them. Still, looking for the paintings was maybe the only way I was going to find out who killed Jim Wyman, and who was trying to kill me.

I walked over to Jake's stand to get another hotdog.

7

From Brooklyn I hopped the subway to Manhattan. It occurred to me that I hadn't asked as many questions about the damned paintings as I should have. My damn mistake. I never claimed that I was a *great* detective.

When I got to the Manhattan side I got off at Fourteenth Street and Union Square and found a pay phone. You can get anywhere from Union Square, and what trains it doesn't give access to are available a few blocks away on Seventh Avenue.

I called Edward's gallery, but his "friend" told me he wasn't in. I decided to believe him. He didn't have any reason to lie to me.

Maybe he was one of the few people I'd talked to lately who didn't.

I must have figured I'd get nothing from Edward and subconsciously decided to get off the train at Fourteenth Street, two blocks from Joliet House.

At the corner of Twelfth and Broadway I stopped and looked across the street at the Strand. Maybe I was hoping that same girl would come walking out and need help carrying her books. I was about to start walking again when something else occurred to me.

Eight miles of books . . . they must have had some art books.

I crossed Broadway and walked into the Strand. The floors were bare wood and the rest of the place was made of books, old and new. You couldn't tell from the smell which were which, but it wasn't a bad smell. "Old" things usually smell bad. The fact that old books didn't made me think that maybe I'd neglected reading for much too long—aside from *Playboy* and wrestling magazines, that is.

The one thing the Strand did have was rather odd-looking

employees. A girl with short orange hair and long green earrings
was walked by. She was wearing a Strand T-shirt over a flat chest
and a pair of khaki pants. I stopped her and asked her where the
art books were.

"Downstairs," she said sullenly, and kept walking.

I traversed a narrow set of stairs to the basement and found
much the same conditions: bare floors, lots of books and an odd
assortment of employees with variety of hair colors, earrings—
women *and* men—and sullen looks. There were about a half-
dozen desks and some of the workers seemed to be taking phone
orders, or just fielding questions. I decided to try and find the art
books myself. It wasn't hard. On my right were a couple of aisles
of books marked "Art."

I didn't know exactly what I was looking for, but I stopped
everytime I came to a book that had the word "Italian" in it. When
I had three I found a corner of the store where hopefully no one
would bother me and began leafing through them. All three
books had entries on Giacomo Giordano and on the "Ladies in the
Cathedral," but one book in particular had more than the others.
I set the other two aside and started reading.

It was interesting stuff, some of which I already knew. Apparently the "Ladies in the Cathedral" were five separate paintings, but all of one lady in particular. Each painting seemed to
depict the woman differently, ranging from a rather serene pose
to the fourth painting, in which she looked highly distressed.

And then there was the fifth painting.

According to the text no one knew exactly what the fifth
painting showed. Obviously, it was the same woman, but there
was no description of exactly how she looked.

I put the book down and did some thinking. It was a logical
assumption that if 'he first painting showed her to be serene and
in each successive painting her expression changed until, in the
fourth, she appeared distressed—or "agitated,"—then the fifth

painting would show her in a state that succeeded distressed.

What? Frightened? Terrified? And why was it such a secret?

I opened all four books to see if there were any photos of the paintings. There were not. I opened the third book again and read the final paragraph, which I had not yet read.

According to the final paragraph there were rumors and/or beliefs that the woman who was the subject of the paintings was the artist's wife. There were also rumors and/or beliefs that the fifth painting did not actually exist at all.

The last sentence gave the date of the artist's death, 1949—the year the painting were stolen from beneath Wyman's, Parnell's and my noses.

Undoubtedly, they went up in value moments after the artist took his last breath.

Nice business.

8

When I left the Strand I figured I was too close to Joliet not to stop in and see Jesse Marlowe and Andrew Maynard.

When I entered, the same man who greeted me last time did so again.

"Miss Marlowe, please."

"Mrs. Marlowe," he said, taking delight in correcting me.

"*Jesse* Marlowe, please."

"I'll call. Wait here, please."

While he went to make his call I stared out the window. A pretty brunette in red shorts and a blue top walked by. She wasn't like the blonde from yesterday, but she had long, lean legs and tight breasts, and she had a neat little butt. New York was like that, no matter what part of Manhattan you were in. There just wasn't very much foot traffic like that in Greenpoint.

"Mrs. Marlowe will see you now," the man said, drawing my attention from the window.

"Admiring the scenery," I said. I thought I had said the same thing yesterday. "Do you ever get lost looking out the window?"

"I never look out the window," he said, and turned and walked away, towards the back of the store. I followed.

"Is she upstairs?"

"Yes," he said, turning to face me.

"I know the way," I said, and brushed past him.

I went up the stairs to the second floor and into the cavernous room. It was all set up now, with row upon row of chairs, easels and pedestals for the art works, and a rostrum for the auctioneer. Jesse Marlowe was sitting in a chair in the first row on the left, with her back to me. Her hair was caught behind her with a green ribbon, and cascaded down her back in a wavy column. I wondered how it would look loose and fanned out behind her.

I walked to the center aisle and walked down to join her.

"Mrs. Marlowe," I said, announcing my presence.

"Mr. Carlucci," she said. She stopped writing and folded her hands over her clipboard, looking up at me with those big green eyes. "What can I do for you today?"

I sat next to her, less one chair, and said, "For one thing you can call me Sal."

She looked surprised, but said, "All right, Sal."

"Things look a bit less hectic here today."

"Oh, they are," she said. She looked more relaxed than she had the day before, and maybe that was why she looked younger. I was revising my age estimate again, down a few years. "Mr. Maynard isn't here, you know. I told you Friday."

"I know you did," I said. "I came to see you."

"Oh? Why?"

"Because I knew you'd be hungry," I said. "You haven't had lunch today, have you?"

"How did you know that?" she asked, a tiny line forming between her eyes.

"I'm a detective, remember. Come on, I'll buy you lunch."

She looked down at her watch, a gold thing with a tiny face. "It's a little late for lunch."

"Then an early dinner. Come on, it isn't often I spring for a meal."

"Oh?" she asked, cocking her head one side prettily. "And what makes me so lucky?"

"I'm into redheads today."

She stared at me for a few seconds, then said, "You have a way with you, you know."

I shook my head and said, "It's all a front."

"Are you going to ask me a lot of questions?"

I nodded and said, "A *lot* of questions."

She smiled widely now and said, "Wait for me downstairs."

I went downstairs and waited by the front window, taking in the sights.

"Girl watching?" she asked, coming up from behind me.

I turned to answer and stopped short. She had let her hair loose so that it tumbled down around her shoulders, and she had freshened her lipstick, which was a sort of orange color.

"Not any more," I said, and she rewarded me with a smile.

On the street I said, "You work around here. Where can we eat and talk?"

"On University Place," she said. "Do you like Mexican food?"

"Sure," I said, although it wasn't one of my favorites.

"Have you ever had it?"

"Once or twice."

"Let's go to Viva Pancho's."

We went to Viva Pancho's and she introduced me to something called a fajita. The place was narrow, with rows of tables against each of the brick walls. The ambience was simple, and it was cool and quiet. Aside from us, only two other tables were taken. She asked for the window table, which was pretty isolated.

They started us off with some taco chips and hot sauce, and I ordered two Dos Equis, dark.

"I thought you didn't know much about Mexican food?" she asked, sipping her beer.

"I know about beer," I said, "all kinds of beer."

"Why is that?"

"I own a bar."

"Really? I thought you were a private eye."

I winced.

"What?" she asked.

"I hate that term, private eye."

"What *should* I call you? A private detective?"

"Detective is a police rank," I said, "and I'm not a policeman anymore—and I was never a detective, anyway. No, I'm a private investigator."

"Oh," she said, dipping into the beer again. "I seem to remember you telling me you were a detective."

I smiled and said, "Caught. I should have said investigator."

"I didn't know private eyes—I mean, private investigators—were so sensitive."

"Well, that's something I've never been accused of."

The waiter came with the fajitas, and they were sizzling. I had opted for beef, while she had ordered shrimp.

"Watch," she said.

She put some of it in the soft, flat bread—*tortillas*—they gave us, rolled it up and bit into it, like a sandwich. I did the same, and it was delicious.

Over the fajitas we talked—or rather, I asked questions and she answered them. I started with personal things, finding out how she got interested in art while in college, how she had worked in several different uptown art galleries before meeting Andrew Maynard and being hired by him to work at Joliet House, where she had eventually worked her way up to assistant director. Along the way she'd married twice and divorced once. The math didn't escape me. She was still married, but she never mentioned her present husband, and I didn't ask about him—the lucky sonofabitch.

"And you?" she asked after finishing her story.

"My life's boring," I said, and then went in to tell her how I had used my brother's ID to join the army after the war.

"What did you do in Italy?" she asked. "Chase the Italian girls?"

"I guarded the 'Ladies in the Cathedral.'"

"What?"

"You didn't know the ladies and I went back that far, did you?"

"What happened?"

"I had a friend named Jim Wyman. He was one of the few men I got along with in the army. I had a thing about authority, and I had a thing about people."

"What about them?"

"I didn't like them much, back then. I was a loner."

"Oh, and you're not a loner now?"

"Now, I'm still pretty much a loner—but I like classy, redheaded ladies."

She grinned and said, "Go on with your story."

I toyed with the side order of rice and said, "Wyman was a little older than I was, and took me under his wing. He did the same to another man, named Parnell, who was closer to my age than Wyman's. When the detail to guard a Salerno museum came up, Wyman grabbed it and brought us in on it. Parnell and I didn't like each other much—I think we were jealous of each other, to tell the truth—but we both liked Wyman, so we made an effort to get along.

"Anyway, Wyman took the inside of the museum and we took the outside. We never thought anything would really happen, we had just been put there to keep relations friendly between our government and the Italians. You know, we were doing them a favor, guarding the national treasures, and all."

"And?"

"And the museum got hit," I said. "They stole the 'Ladies in the Cathedral' and killed Jim Wyman. They shot him. We heard the shots, but by the time we got inside, they were gone."

"Oh," she said, solemnly. "I'm sorry."

"Then after all these years the ladies resurfaced, and maybe I've got a chance to find out who killed Wyman."

She picked up her beer glass, then put it down and said, "How can I help?"

"Did one of the ladies come through Joliet House?"

She bit her bottom lip, picked up her glass again and began to swirl what was left in it. I let her alone, gave her time to think it over.

"If Mr. Maynard ever finds out I talked to you," she said. "He's very strict—"

"I'll never tell him, Jesse," I promised.

"One painting came into our possession."

"Which one?"

"The fifth."

"I thought there was some doubt as to whether a fifth painting really existed or not?"

"It exists."

"Did you see it?"

"Well, no—but Mr. Maynard said—"

"Who bought it, Jesse."

"That I don't know, Carlucci," she said. "I really don't."

"Could you find out?"

"Well . . . Mr. Maynard wouldn't tell me—"

"There are records of the sale somewhere, aren't there?"

"Somewhere . . . but if I get caught . . ."

"I understand," I said. "Fajitas just aren't worth that kind of risk. I mean, after all, it's your job . . ."

"I'd like to help you, Carlucci," she said, "I really would like to help you learn who killed your friend, but . . . does it really matter after all this time?"

"Maybe not to anyone else, Jesse," I admitted, "but it matters to me. Like I said, I'm pretty much a loner. I can't afford to have someone kill a friend of mine and get away with it. I just don't have enough of them to be able to afford that luxury."

She got a pained look on her face and drank the rest of the beer in her glass.

"Take a guess," I said.

"What?"

"You must know most of the large collectors in the city," I said. "Most of them must have bought something from Joliet House at sometime or other. Take a guess for me. Who'd be able to afford the 'Ladies?' Who would *want* one or all of them?"

"Give me a minute," she said, and honestly looked like she was wracking her brain for names.

"*Señor*?" the waiter said, appearing at our table. "I can get you something else?"

"No," I said, "I think we're finished. Just bring the check."

"*Si, Señor.*"

"All right," she said. "You're right, there are a lot of collectors in New York, but there are only five that I can think of who might be interested in the 'Ladies.'"

I took a small notebook out of my pocket and handed it to her, with a pen.

"Write the names down, and addresses, if you know them."

She took the pen and pad and wrote down the five names.

"I don't know any addresses off hand, but I can get them for you when I get back to work."

I wrote my phone number on a piece of paper and tore it from the pad.

"This is my business number. Call me there when you get the addresses—or any other information."

"What about your home number?" she asked, innocently.

I tucked the notebook back into my pocket and simply told her, "It's out of order."

9

When I got to the Black Moon, Harry "the Map" was waiting in front for me.

"I heard what happened to your house, Sal," he said as I unlocked the front door. "Pretty shitty."

"What happened to your house, Harry?" I asked, pushing the door open.

"My house? This is more home to me than my house is, Sal, you know that, especially since Lucille died."

Lucille had been Harry's grown daughter, with whom he'd lived—or vice versa—and who had died last year of cancer. Until then he had been a frequent customer in the Black Moon. After she died he spent more time in the saloon then anyone but me.

"Come on in, Harry," I said.

"Thanks, Sal."

We went inside and Harry hit the lights for me.

"You staying here until your house is fixed, Sal?" he asked, taking a stool at the bar.

I laughed.

"I don't even know if my house *can* be fixed, Harry."

I went around behind the bar and got us both a Budweiser.

He sucked half of it down and wiped his mouth with the back of his hand.

"You hear of this new Canadian beer they got's named after a bear?"

"You mean Grizzly?"

"Yeah, that's the one. You gonna get that in, Sal?"

"I might try it, Harry."

"I volunteer to be your guinea pig, Sal."

"I'll keep that in mind, Harry."

The phone rang then and I wondered if it was Jesse Marlowe calling so soon.

"Harry, get around behind the bar, will you? In case a customer comes in. I'm gonna get that in the back."

"All right!"

I went into the back and grabbed the phone up off my desk on the fourth ring.

"Where have you been?" Carl Devlin demanded. "I been calling you all day."

"I didn't know I was supposed to check in."

"Shit, you don't, I was just . . . wondering if you were all right, is all."

"I'm fine, Carl."

"How's the damage to your house?"

"I haven't had a chance to go back there, yet."

"You been working?"

"Yeah."

"Well, so have I. Those four punks who jumped you the other night?"

"What about them? You get a line on them?"

"Just on the one with that tattoo. His name's Sammy Rosa and I've got an alarm out on him right now. His record is pretty colorful."

"Like how?"

"Like he once worked for Nicholas DiMonte."

I whistled softly and said, *"Don* Nicholas?"

"Retired Don Nicholas, yeah. He was a punk for Fruit Salad Nicky a year and a half ago."

Nicholas DiMonte had to suffer the nick name "Fruit Salad" because his name sounded so much like *Del* Monte. I guess he was lucky they didn't call him Canned Peaches, or something.

"And then what?"

"Nick retired, and I guess all but his closest soldiers either went freelance, or joined some other family."

"Didn't he name somebody to take over his operation?"

"No, when he retired he did it all the way, disbanded operations and got out."

"For real?"

"As near as we can tell."

"Where's the kid live?"

"Going visiting?"

"I'd just like the address for my files."

"Wait a minute," he said. He was shuffling papers and said, "This bum better not show up dead, Carlucci."

"You know me better than that, Carl."

"Yeah," he said. "Here it is. Fourteen Twenty-Four Van Dam. He wasn't there when I had some of the locals check it out, but maybe you'll get lucky—or he'll get unlucky."

"What about Don Nicholas?"

"Him too, huh? Hold on." More papers shuffling. "Central Park South, Sal. Two-twenty."

"Thanks, Carl."

"I'd better hear if you get anything, Sal."

"You will."

"Watch your step."

I hung up, sat back in my chair and took out my note pad. I opened it and looked at the five names. It had struck me odd on the train home when I saw it, and now the coincidence was too much to accept.

The third name on the list was Nicholas DiMonte.

I was about to get up when the phone rang again. This time it was Jesse Marlowe.

"I could lose my job for this, Salvatore," she said by way of greeting.

"I'll hire you as a barmaid."

She laughed and said, "Would I get to wear one of those low-cut peasant blouses?"

"The lower the better," I said, reminding myself that she was married.

Maybe she remembered, too, because she got down to business, then.

"The painting we had *was* the fifth painting, and it *was* bought by Mr. DiMonte."

"Fruit Salad Nicky!" I said, triumphantly punching the air.

"What?"

"Do you know DiMonte's background?"

"I know that he's reputed to be some kind of mobster."

"Yeah," I said, "reputed. It seems kind of odd to me that Nicky would be an art lover."

"He's not."

"What? I thought you said he bought—"

"He bought it, but he bought it for his wife, Inez."

"Inez?"

"She's about twenty years younger than he is. They've been married for about five years."

"I guess I'd better go see Mr. and Mrs. DiMonte," I said. "They're in possession of a hot painting."

"There's one more thing you should know, Sal," she said. "I got this from reading the society pages."

"What's that?"

"Mrs. DiMonte's maiden name," Jesse said. "It's Giordano."

                              1 0

I went back to my house to get some clothes. The bedroom was in the back, and only the front of the house had been destroyed. Most of the front wall had been blown out, and I knew it was going to cost more than I had to fix it. I'd have to worry about that later.

I took the clothes back to the Black Moon—where I had left Harry the Map in charge—and stored them in a closet in the back room. I made sure my one suit was hanging up, because I'd be wearing it the next day, when I went to see Don Nicholas DiMonte.

First, though, I had to make an appointment.

When I was stationed in Italy I had met a young man named Luigi Caboletti. This was after the death of Jim Wyman, and even after Wyman's death Parnell and I didn't become the best of friends, so I became friends with Luigi. What I didn't know was that the Caboletti family was Mafioso. When I did find out Luigi told me that he would be going to the United States someday, where he would become *Capo di tutti capo*, or perhaps even a *Don* himself.

Well, Luigi Caboletti went to the United States and became Louie the Cab Driver, and later Louis Caboletti, *Capo di tutti capo* to Don Pietro Frazzini, known in his early days as Petey the Ice Man. The Ice Man—once the most feared of Mafioso hit men—had worked his way up to be a *Don*, and had taken Luigi as his *Capo*.

Luigi and I still kept in touch, and it was him I called to get me an appointment with Don Nicholas DiMonte.

When I got through his front men Luigi came on the line and said, *"Salvatore*, my friend. Long time."

"Long time, Luigi. Too long, I think, to only be calling to ask a favor."

"Don't let that worry you, my friend. Just ask. We go back a very long way, together."

"I need you to make an appointment for me . . ."

1 1

I had to admit to some nervousness.

To people on the outside looking in, Nicholas DiMonte was a "reputed" mob figure. To people like me, cops and private operators, people on the inside, he was Don Nicholas. To the best of my knowledge he was in his sixties and had stepped down just two years ago, but he was a legend in my business—the crime business, not the bar business.

I wiped my palms on the pants of my only suit and pressed the penthouse buzzer at 220 Central Park South.

When the elevator came down two men stepped out. They were impeccably dressed, and to my practiced eye both were armed.

"Hands above your head," one of them said. I obeyed and they frisked me and came up empty.

"ID," the other one said.

I handed one of them my whole wallet and let him find the photostat of my PI ticket and my driver's license. That satisfied him and he handed it back.

"Let's go," he said.

We rode up in the tiny elevator in total silence, and when the door opened we stepped out into a small hallway. One of them moved to the door and knocked. When it was opened he said, "Salvatore Carlucci."

He motioned me to enter, and he and his double came in behind me.

The door had been opened by a handsome-looking woman in her late thirties. She was wearing a white silk blouse, a gray skirt, and a stern expression. I didn't know if it was me she disapproved of, or the Gold Dust Twins.

"Mrs. DiMonte."

"My husband will be out shortly," she said.

"Well, actually, I'd rather talk to you, Ma'am."

"About what?"

"About a painting you bought."

She looked past me and said, "Eddie, you and Tony go get something to drink."

"Mrs. DiMonte—"

"Go ahead."

The two of them exchanged glances and then Eddie said, "We'll be in the hall."

"Fine."

I waited until they left and closed the door behind them.

"My husband is dressing," she said. "We have a few minutes."

"About this painting, Mr. DiMonte," I said. "It's one of five in a series called the 'Ladies in the Cathedral.' Do you know it?"

"I know them, yes," she said. "As you can see, I have a small art collection."

I looked around the large living room and the walls were covered with paintings. I didn't see one that fit the descriptions I'd heard of the ladies.

"What makes you think I have one of the ladies?"

"Oh, it was just something I heard."

"Well, you heard wrong."

"I also heard that your maiden name is Giordano," I said. "Kind of a coincidence, isn't it, that you have the same name as the artist?"

"There are a lot of Giordanos." She said it without much conviction, and averted her eyes. It was then that I knew I was in the right place. She *had* to be related to Giacomo Giordano, but how did that explain what had been going on?

"Mrs. DiMonte," I said, "how were you related to the artist?"

She turned her back this time, shoulders hunched.

"Inez?"

I turned at the sound of the voice and saw him. He was tall and solid, white-haired, and I recognized him right away, even though I'd only seen him once, ten years ago, when he was testifying before a grand jury that failed to indict him.

"Inez," he said again, then looked at me. "Are you Carlucci?"

"Yes, sir."

"Mr. Carlucci, I've only suffered your intrusion on our lives at the behest of a friend." That friend being Don Angelo, at the further request of my friend, Luigi Caboletti. "However, I will not have you upsetting my wife."

"I'm sorry to upset her, Don Nicholas—"

I stopped when he made a chopping motion in the air with his right hand.

"Do not call me that," he said. "Not anymore."

"I'm sorry—"

"What is it you want here, sir?"

"I've been hired to find some paintings, Don—uh, sir. They

were stolen from a museum in Italy almost forty years ago."

"What is your business?" he asked. "Are you a policeman?"

"I was, once," I said. "Now I'm private."

"And you're looking for these paintings now?" he asked. "Isn't that trail a little cold, sir?"

"Perhaps," I said, "but I was there when they were stolen, and a friend of mine was killed."

"Ah," he said, "I see. You are seeking to avenge your friend."

"I'd like to find out who killed him."

"Well, I assure you it wasn't me, or my wife. In fact, my wife wasn't even born then."

"I know that, sir," I said, "but I believe that one of the paintings has found its way into your hands."

"And?"

"And I would have to lay claim to it for the Italian government."

Don Nicholas folded his arms and looked amused. I knew he was over sixty, but aside from the white hair he could have been ten years younger.

"Where were you born, Mr. Carlucci?"

"Here," I said, "in New York."

"And your father?"

"Here."

"And his father?"

"Sicily."

"Ah," he said, "but you feel allegiance to Italy?"

"No," I said, "I'm doing a job."

"With a personal slant, eh?"

"Yes," I said.

He stared at me for a few moments before speaking again.

"If I had bought the painting you speak of for my wife—and I am saying *if* I had—it would have been because I love her. I would not just hand the painting over to you because you ask for it."

"That's all right," I said. "As long as I knew you had it I could inform the Italian government, and they would get in touch with you. *You* were born in Sicily, weren't you, Don Nicholas."

"Yes, I was," he said, "and as a boy I knew a Carlucci. He ran a small grocery store. His name was Guido Carlucci."

I nodded and said, "That would have been my grandfather."

He nodded, as if he'd known that all along.

"You give your information to the Italian Government," Don Nicholas said, "then we will see."

"Then you have it?"

He didn't answer, but suddenly Mrs. DiMonte spoke without turning around.

"Yes, I have it."

"Inez—" he said, but she turned and shushed him.

"I want him to know, Nicholas."

She looked at me and waited until he had moved alongside her. He put arm around her waist and I could see her take strength from that. Suddenly, I envied them both having someone to take strength from.

"The artist was my grandfather, Mr. Carlucci," she said, softly. "And the ladies in the paintings are all the same lady, my grandmother."

"I see."

"No, you do not see. If you return the painting to the Italian Government, they will put it on display for everyone to see. I can't allow that."

"Why not? I mean, they're supposed to be such incredible works—"

"Oh, I don't care if the first four are seen, but the fifth—" She stopped moment and leaned against her husband for support, lowering her eyes. "My grandmother was not a well woman. The fifth painting does not . . . show her in a good light."

I remembered what I had read about the paintings, and the sequence that they displayed. I recalled wondering what the fifth one would show.

"Mrs. DiMonte—"

"The fifth painting shows my grandmother—you see, my grandmother was judged . . . insane when she died. Why my grandfather painted that fifth painting I don't know, but it shows her . . . it *clearly* shows her insanity etched on her face, reflected in her eyes." She looked at me and I saw something reflected in *her* eyes. "I can't allow that painting to be seen. That was why when I heard it had surfaced I asked my husband to buy it for me. I want to keep it safe, Mr. Carlucci."

"Mrs. DiMonte," I said, "you haven't destroyed the painting, have you?"

Her eyes widened and she said, "Oh, I could never do that. You see, I'm stuck in something of a quandary. I can't destroy it, and I can't let it be seen. All I can do is keep it safe, Mr. Carlucci. Do you understand?"

"I'm afraid I do, Mrs. DiMonte."

I had only to look at her face to know that she was telling the truth.

"My dear," DiMonte said to her, patting her shoulder, "go inside and lie down. I'd like to speak to Mr. Carlucci alone."

"Yes," she said, "yes, all right."

As she started to leave the room I said, "Mrs. DiMonte."

She turned and looked at me.

"Thank you for your honesty."

She nodded, and went through the doorway that DiMonte had entered by, leaving me alone with Don Nicholas.

Suddenly, I was even more nervous than before.

"If that painting were to go on public display, Mr. Carlucci, it would break my wife's heart."

"I realize that, sir."

"I hope you do."

I waited for him to say more, but he didn't, and I turned to leave.

"Uh, Don Nicholas," I said at the door.

"Yes?"

"There have been some attempts on my life since I started looking for the painting," I said. "Sammy Rosa and some punks tried to kill me. You remember Sammy?"

He frowned, trying to remember.

"He's got a tattoo on his wrist—"

That prodded his memory.

"Yes, yes. He worked for me once."

"And somebody put a bomb in my house, blew up a friend of mine."

"Mr. Carlucci," he said, sounding suddenly fatigued, "if I wanted you dead, you would be dead. All I'd have to do now would be to call in those two young men who are waiting outside, and they would kill you. The fact of the matter is, I never heard of you until I got a call from my friend saying that you wanted to see me. I had no reason to kill you before I knew you, Carlucci, and I have no reason now . . . do I?"

Well, it was my call. Was I going to give him a reason to kill me? Hell no!

"No, sir," I said, "you don't."

I put my hand on the doorknob and opened the door.

"Mr. Carlucci?"

"Yes."

"The other four paintings . . ."

"I have a line on them."

"Good," he said. "I hope you find them."

"Thank you, sir."

I was shown to the street and left there with my confusion. What was I to do now? Tell Luciano about the painting and risk Don Nicholas DiMonte's wrath? Or keep quiet about it and lie to Luciano?

I decided that the first thing I was going to have to do was see how the search for the other four paintings was coming.

Maybe I could get Luciano and the Italian government to settle for four out of five.

1 . 2

I made a stop before heading back to Greenpoint, and when I got there I made a bunch of phone calls. I had instructed all of my out-of-town help to wait until I called them, rather than calling me, because I knew I'd be in and out and I hadn't quite gotten myself to the point where I'd buy an answering machine. I still hated talking to the damned things, myself, and besides even if I had one, it would have gotten blown up with the front of my house.

During the course of the past couple of days I had talked to each of them. Mack was a little pissed, but that didn't keep him from continuing to work on the case. As for Cooper, as it turned out he had already become involved in a search for the painting, by coincidence.

I was a little surprised to find that everything had gone well out of town. Of course, I wasn't filled in on the gory details, but Parnell, Mack and Riley Cooper all seemed to have laid their hands on one of the paintings. As for Texas, I found out that there was a *Laura* Bailey, Jim's daughter, and she was the one who had found the painting there. Apparently the man who now owned her father's agency, Kenneth Owens, had not been up front with her about my call. I knew the guy had sounded like an asshole. I managed to convince everyone that it would be worth their while to hand deliver the paintings to me, at the Black Moon Saloon.

Satisfied that four of the paintings had been recovered, I still had to decide what I was going to do about the fifth one. There was this belief in some circles that there was no fifth painting; maybe I could use that as my out.

I wondered if I was considering lying about the fifth painting to help Inez Giordano DiMonte, or because I was afraid of Don Nicholas DiMonte.

Instead of pondering that question I went to the front door and opened for business.

At closing time I still hadn't quite made up my mind what I was going to tell Victor Luciano.

As usual, Harry the Map was the last customer, and I left him alone to finish his beer, locking the door to keep anyone else from entering. I'd let him out when he was finished.

I went into the back room and felt the breeze on my face too late. There was no breeze back there unless the back door was open, and by the time I realized that it was there was a gun pressing against my right temple.

"Take it easy," I said.

"You take it easy, fucker," a man's voice said. "Put your hand out."

"What?"

"You heard me."

I put my left hand out and he removed the gun from my head long enough to bring the barrel down painfully on my wrist. I howled, more to warn Harry in the front room than from the pain, although the pain was considerable.

"How do *you* like it, you scummer!" the voice said, and then I knew who it was.

"You should have closed the back door, Sammy."

"Can't," Sammy Rosa said, "I busted it. Move."

"Where?"

"Go sit at your desk. I took your gun out, anyway."

Holding my wrist—exaggerating the damage he'd done to it, although it *could* have been broken—I moved to the desk and sat down.

"Turn on the light."

I turned on the desk lamp and looked at him. His right wrist was in a cast, and in his left he held a mean looking .45. My back door was being opened and closed about an inch by the breeze in the alley. I hoped Harry had gotten the hell out.

"What's the story, Sammy?" I asked. "Where are your friends?"

"How do you know my name?" Sammy Rosa asked.

He wasn't as young as I had thought that night in the alley. He looked to be about thirty. His hair was still as white-blond as I remembered, and it was a mess. He was wearing an old trench coat, and his injured arm was held inside rather than through the sleeve.

"You've got a distinctive tattoo on your wrist," I said. "I know your name and the cops know your name. You didn't bring any help this time?"

"I don't need help killin' an old scumbag like you."

"Oh, you're here to kill me this time?"

"You bet."

"Change of orders?"

"That's right."

"From who?"

"Never mind."

"I talked to Don Nicholas today," I said. "He remembers you."

"Oh, yeah?" he asked, licking his lips. Punks like Sammy

Rosa usually got nervous when they heard a name like Don Nicholas DiMonte.

"We came to an agreement, Sammy," I said. "If I show up dead he's going to be real upset."

He frowned and said, "I don't know nothing about no agreement."

"Maybe you'd better talk to him again."

"I don't talk to him—" he started to say, and then he stopped. "Never mind all that. I got my orders."

I sat back in my seat, as far back as I could, and braced my foot against the bottom of the desk.

"What are you doin'?" he demanded, extending his hand as far as his arm would let him.

"Don't get nervous, Sammy," I said. "I'm getting comfortable. If you're going to kill me I want to be comfortable."

"You're pretty cool for a man who's gonna die."

"Not really," I said, aware of how hard my heart was beating. "As a matter of fact, I'm pretty scared."

"You should be," he said. "I'd like to pick you apart with this thing—"

"I know you would," I said, "but one shot might go unnoticed, right? Two or three would bring trouble."

"One shot's all I need, Carlucci," he said, cocking the hammer on the gun.

I braced myself, but before I could move the back door slammed open, harder than if the wind had been responsible. A uniformed cop appeared in the doorway, his gun drawn, and Sammy turned real fast and fired. The cop yelled and disappeared from view.

I straightened my right leg with all the strength I could muster and my desk went sliding across the floor, hitting Sammy Rosa in the hips.

"Jesus!" he shouted and staggered backwards, trying to keep

his balance. I was thankful at that moment that all I'd ever been able to afford was a cheap desk, and not an expensive, heavy one.

Sammy went down, landing on his broken wrist, and cried out in pain. A second cop—the first one's partner—appeared in the doorway from the bar and from the floor Sammy tried to bring his gun around.

"Sammy, no!" I shouted.

The cop, aware that a shot had been fired, didn't take an chances. He fired three times, Sammy's body jerking under the impact of each bullet.

"Christ!" I said, rushing to Sammy's side, but he was already dead, far beyond answering any questions about who had sent him to kill me.

As much as I hate coincidence, that's what saved me. A radio car was driving by just as Harry the Map went running out of the Black Moon. He knew where I kept the keys and when he heard me yell he grabbed them and ran outside. He flagged down a passing car and told them what was happening, and the two cops split front and back. The one who had come in the back had been shot in the shoulder and was on his way to the hospital. His partner was still in the back room with me and Carl Devlin.

"What the fuck," Devlin said.

"That's what I say."

"Did you talk to Nicky today?" he asked.

"I did," I said. "I was going to call you tomorrow and tell you about it."

"Sure you were."

We moved aside so the coroner's men could get by with Sammy Rosa's body.

"Tell me about it now."

I did.

"And you believed him?" he asked. "That he wasn't behind trying to kill you?"

"I did."

"And what about now?"

"I still do."

"Even after this?"

"Don Nicholas didn't lie."

"You know," he said, "you always had more respect for these guinea bastards than I did."

"Maybe that's because I'm a guinea bastard, too."

"I keep forgetting that. Okay, hot shot, who sent Sammy over here to ice you, then?"

"I can only think of one person," I said, and when I named the name he whistled softly.

"Prove it."

"That's just what I intend to do."

1 3

This time I didn't call Luigi to make the appointment for me, I made it myself early the next morning. Don Nicholas took the call, and agreed that I could come right over.

I didn't tell him that I was bringing Devlin, and when we got there and his boys tried to frisk him Devlin showed his tin.

"Hands off, boys," he said.

"You can't go up there with a piece," one of them said.

"Try and stop me."

At that moment the front doors opened and four uniformed cops entered, along with two men in plain clothes. Devlin had called ahead for assistance from the local precinct, and this was it.

"Stand aside, boys," Devlin said, and we went into the elevator while the other cops entertained the twins.

"Let me do the talking, Devlin," I said, in the elevator.

"You afraid I'm gonna be disrespectful to the bum?"

"No," I said, "I *know* you would be, but this is my show, remember?"

"All right, Sal," he said. "It's your show."

When we got to the top floor I knocked on the door and it was opened by Don Nicholas himself.

"*Salvatore*," he said, as if I were his nephew, or something. "And who is this gentleman?"

"This is Detective Carl Devlin, Don Nicholas," I said.

"A policeman?" he said, frowning. "You bring a policeman to see me?"

"If we could come in, Don Nicholas, I will explain."

He hesitated a moment, the stepped back and allowed us to enter.

"Don Nicholas—" I began, but the old man held up his hand to stop me.

"Please," he said, "the title . . ."

"Mr. DiMonte—"

"Please, a friend of my friend may call me Nicholas."

I caught Devlin giving me a sidelong glance, but I ignored it. I also swallowed hard, because it was a singular honor the man was presenting me with, and I was about to abuse it.

"Nicholas," I said, "Sammy Rosa is dead. He tried to kill me last night."

"That's terrible," he said. "And you killed him?"

"The police did."

"How fortunate for you."

"Nicholas—Mr. DiMonte, I believe I know who sent him, this time and last time. I also think he put the bomb in my house."

"On my orders, Salvatore?" he asked, "I thought we had

settled that yesterday."

"We did, sir," I said. "I don't think you did it, but judging from Sammy's reactions when I mentioned your name, and because of his past association, I think his orders had to have come from this apartment."

"This apartment?" he said. "That's ridiculous. I gave no such orders."

"I know you didn't."

We stood in silence for a while, the only sound being Devlin clearing his throat. He was dying to say something, and I admired his restraint.

"Do you realize what you are saying?" DiMonte finally said, with ice in his voice.

"Yes, sir, I am afraid that I do."

"I must ask you to leave," he said, "both of you."

"We can't do that, Nick—Mr. DiMonte," Devlin said, finally speaking. "I have to talk to your wife."

"My wife had nothing to do with this!"

"Nicholas . . ."

We all turned our heads at the sound of her voice. She was standing in a doorway, wearing a green silk robe that was knotted tightly at her waist. In fact, her hands were knotting even tighter at the moment, and her knuckles were turning white.

"Inez, go back to bed—"

"Nicholas, I can't," she said, and started crying. He went to her and put his arms around her. "I have abused your name—"

"Shh," he said, "say nothing, *cara*."

"Mr. DiMonte—" Devlin said, but I put my hand on his arm to stop him.

I walked over to where the DiMontes stood.

"Mrs. DiMonte," I said. "Sammy was working for you, wasn't he?"

She pulled her face from her husband's chest and was about

to answer—she was about to say "yes,"—when DiMonte said, "She will not speak to you."

I barely heard him. I saw something in Inez DiMonte's eyes that captured my attention, and for a fleeting moment I thought I knew what that fifth painting would look like.

"Mr. DiMonte—" Devlin began, but DiMonte turned his head and snapped, "Nor to you! Please leave, now."

"DiMonte," Devlin said, harshly, "she's gonna *have* to talk to us—"

"You will speak with my attorneys," he said. "That is all. Leave now!"

I turned and walked back to Devlin.

"Let's go," I said.

"Sal, this bum's—"

"Carl," I said, "what can we prove? Sammy's dead."

I opened the door and we stepped outside and rang for the elevator.

"I *hate* backing down—" he started to say.

"Carl, if you can find any of the other three punks who jumped me, they might be able to definitely tie Inez DiMonte to this. Without that, all we've got is what I believe."

"Well, for what it's worth," he said, "I believe it, too. She was gonna *confess!*"

"Yes, she was," I said, "but we have to remember who she's married to. He'll do whatever he can to protect her."

"Which will be a lot," Devlin said. "I doubt we'll ever be able to touch her."

"Maybe not," I said, "but I doubt I have anything to fear from her, anymore."

"You don't think she'll try to have you killed after this?"

I shook my head.

"I don't think he'll let her."

The elevator came and we stepped in.

"You know," he said, on the way down, "you never did tell me what started this whole thing."

"You're right," I said, "I never did."

1 4

Three days later I was getting the Black Moon ready for a private party. I needed a hostess/barmaid for the party, and Jesse had volunteered.

Well actually, I didn't *need* a hostess, and she didn't really *volunteer*, I asked her, and she accepted on one condition.

"I get to wear one of those peasant blouses," she said, with a twinkle in her eye.

"You'll have to buy it yourself."

"Done!" she said, clapping her hands, happily. It took a concerted effort on my part not to ask her what her husband would think of the idea.

The other reason I asked her to come was because she'd been a big help to me, and I figured she'd like to be in on the ending.

Tony Mack was the first to arrive. I felt badly about the way I had roped Tony into this. We hadn't exactly been friends when we were both with NYPD, and I wasn't sure how he'd take hearing from me. I'd called in another favor from the computer whiz and had him tap into the computers of the Florida insurance company Mack did a lot of work for. From then on he thought he was working for them—hell, *they* thought he was working for them—until he caught on. By then he was hooked, and stayed on the case.

"You're a scumball, Carlucci," he said as he entered, but at least he shook my hand.

"Nice to see you, too, Tony."

Ralph Parnell was the next in. It was an awkward moment when I met him at the door. I guess we were both trying to remember what it was we had disliked about each other forty years ago.

When he finally spoke all he said was, "Did we get him?"

I knew he was talking about the man who had killed Jim Wyman.

"We'll get him," I said.

Parnell was just getting a beer from my barmaid—it was all Jesse knew how to serve—when another man walked in. He was about forty-eight or so, six foot maybe more, thick and solid, especially around the middle.

"Riley Cooper?" I asked.

"That's right," he said, taking the hand I offered.

"I appreciate you coming."

He just nodded and said, "Is there a beer around?"

"If there wasn't I'd be running a pretty poor imitation of a saloon."

He went to the bar to get one, and the door opened to admit a pretty woman in her twenties who looked as if she wasn't sure she was in the right place.

"You Laura Bailey?" I asked.

"Yes, I am."

"Then you're in the right place," I said. "I'm Carlucci."

"Hello," she said, and we shook hands. She had a good, solid handshake, and I liked her immediately. I had liked her father, too.

"I'm . . . sorry about your father . . ." I said, lamely. She could have asked me why, since I hadn't exactly stayed in contact with him, and hadn't even heard when he died.

She had grace, though, this one and she simply gave me a smile and said, "Thank you."

"Come to the bar and I'll get you a drink," I said, and walked her to the bar.

Luckily she wanted a white wine, and I was able to coach Jesse. As Laura took her wine the door opened and a man walked in—a man I hadn't invited to this little party.

"Uh, excuse me," I said, and hurried to the door. "Harry, no—"

"Doin' a brisk afternoon business, eh, Sal?" Harry the Map asked, looking around happily.

"Harry, this is a private party—"

"Private?" he asked, frowning.

"Yeah . . . it has something to do with the case I was working on. They all helped me with it."

He thought for a moment, and then brightened and said, "Well, what about me. Didn't I help you, too?"

I stared at his seamed face and thought, damned if he hadn't. As a matter of fact, he'd probably saved my life.

"Yeah, that's right, Harry," I said, clapping him on the shoulder, "you did. Come on, I'll get you a drink."

"All right!"

And so everyone was there—except for one last person, and he wasn't due for an hour.

I introduced everyone around—including Jesse and *ex* - cluding Harry—made sure they all had fresh drinks, and then began my meeting. Before I did, though, Ralph Parnell raised his hand and said, "I've got a question."

"What's that?" I asked.

He pointed to Harry the Map and asked, "Who's he?"

"That's Harry," I said. "He's a friend of the family."

I turned to the others without giving him a chance to comment.

"I guess you're all wondering why I—okay, okay, wait," I said, holding up my hand. "No jokes. For the past week or so you've all been working on the same case for me. Some of you did it as a favor, some of you I roped into it, but all of you will be paid, and paid well—and you'll all have my thanks, for whatever that's worth to you. We're waiting for one last person to arrive, but before he does I think you're all entitled to know every detail about what you got yourselves involved in. If none of you mind, I'll explain how some of this all started, and then I'd like each of you to give as long or short a report as you like on what you had to go through to accomplish your end of this. When you're done, I'll explain what happened on my end."

"When do we hear the end of this story?" Ralph Parnell asked. Of course, he had more personal interest in that than the others did.

"I won't tell you how it ends," I said, "because you're here, and you'll all see it."

None of them seemed to object to that.

I went ahead and explained how Victor Luciano had first entered the Black Moon to hire me, and went on up to the point where I, er, drafted all of them.

From then on they each spoke in turn, and while one talked the others all listened intently. When they were done I picked up my story and held nothing back. When I got to the part about Mrs. DiMonte possibly walking away from her part in it, there were some glances exchanged, but no one said anything.

"And now," I said, looking at my watch, "the grand finale."

At that point the door opened and Victor Luciano walked in. He stopped short when he saw all the people present, and I had to laugh at his timing.

"Right on cue, Lucky."

"What is all this?" he asked. "Who are all these people?"

I walked up to him and said, "Did you bring what we talked

about on the phone?" I had called him the day before and asked him to come to the saloon at five p.m. I had also told him what the rest of my fee was to be. He had argued a bit, but finally agreed to bring it—in cash.

"This is highly irregular," he said, "but yes, I have brought it." He lifted his left hand, which was holding an attache case, and I took it from him. One peek told me that he had brought the cash.

"Thank you."

I walked to the bar and gave Jesse the case, which she put down underneath.

I turned back to Luciano and said, "Come on over and sit here on the last barstool, Signor Luciano. These are the operatives I used in locating the paintings. Allow me to introduce you to them."

When I save my introductions and then said,"Lucky, I've got good news and bad news for you."

"W-what?"

He ruined it. He didn't say, "What's the good news?" like most people would have.

"You'll be happy to know that each of these people arrived here with one of the 'Ladies in the Cathedral.'"

Indeed, each of them had arrived with the painting rolled up under their arm, and each of them had leaned it against the bar at their feet.

"How wonderful!"

"That's the good news."

He ruined it again. He simply frowned at me instead of asking, "What's the bad news?"

"The bad news is, I'm not giving any of them to you."

That really startled him.

"What? I do not understand."

"I do," I said, "finally. You see, I checked with your consulate, and they informed me—"

"I specifically asked you not to do that!"

"—that you are not now nor have you ever been a representative of the Italian government."

The others suddenly became very interested in what was going on between Luciano and me.

"I— I—" Luciano said.

"So what was his interest?" Riley Cooper asked when it became obvious that Luciano was having a problem forming his thoughts into words.

"His interest?" I said. "Well, I'm guessing now, but Mr. Luciano here knew where one of the original thieves was, and he knew what one of the original thieves had said, and he knew so much *about* the original theft that my guess is—and you'll tell me if I'm wrong, won't you, Signor Luciano—he was one . . . of . . . the . . . original . . . thieves!" I used my forefinger to punctuate each word—in his chest.

"That—" he said, backing away from me, "that is . . . preposterous!"

"Well," I said, "I guess you're telling me that I'm wrong, but somehow I don't think I am."

"You mean he's one of the men who killed Wyman and stole the paintings?" Ralph Parnell said, getting up from his stool. Parnell is a big man, and Luciano did not like the idea of Ralph possibly poking his chest, so he backed away even more.

My guess was that Parnell was playing good-cop/bad-cop, and was being the bad cop.

Tony Mack, being an ex-cop himself, caught on and played along.

"Easy, Parnell," he said, taking hold of Parnell's arm. "Let Carlucci finish."

"You're in big trouble, Lucky," I said.

"You cannot prove anything," Luciano said, warily.

"I can prove that you illegally represented yourself to be a representative of the Italian government," I said. Jesus, it sounded like a mouthful to me; what must it have sounded like to the others? "Now I'm not too clear on the law in this area, but I'm sure you've broken one or two—at least."

Luciano suddenly developed shifty eyes and couldn't look at me.

"Three men break into a museum in Italy," I said, looking at my colleagues at the bar, "kill a guard, and make off with a series of five valuable paintings, all of which stand to increase in value because the artist is on his deathbed. Now, obviously these three geniuses managed to sell the paintings but one of them—maybe the smartest one—somehow keeps track of them. Forty years later this same man is dying in prison, and he decides to confess, so he tells somebody what city each of the paintings are in."

"I guess he wasn't so smart after all," Laura Bailey said, watching Luciano.

"Maybe not so smart," I said, "but the smartest of the three of *them*."

"Wait a minute," Riley Cooper said, "if he knew what cities the paintings were in, why didn't he go after them himself?"

"Well, since this isn't *Murder She Wrote,*" I said, "we may never know that. He's dead, and we can't ask him. What's important here, though, is that one of his partners is still alive, and gets a hold of this information."

"How?" Parnell asked.

"He kept tabs on the man, knew he was in prison. Maybe he bought himself a guard . . . hm, Lucky?"

"I do not know—"

"Sure, that's it," I said, "he buys himself a guard because he knows those paintings are worth five times what they were forty years ago—and probably twenty times more than what he and his friends dumped them for. He's been waiting a long time to get them back, and this was his chance."

345

"So he hires you?" Ralph Parnell asked.

I looked at him to see if he was passing judgment on my abilities as a detective, but he stared back at me blankly.

"Yeah, well, he can't be in five places at once, and he doesn't want to take a chance on going for one of the paintings and having the news get out. It might make the other four harder to find."

"And was it a coincidence that he picked you?" Parnell asked.

"No, obviously not. When he came to me *he* told *me* that I was one of the guards back then."

"Wasn't he taking a chance coming to you?" Tony Mack asked.

"My guess is he felt I'd take the job faster because I had a personal interest, or maybe he figured I'd go that extra mile. If we want the real reason we'll have to ask him." I looked at Luciano and said, "Well?"

"You are mad!"

"No, not mad," I said, closing the distance between him and me, "maybe a little pissed, but not mad."

He took a step back, but by now he was so close to the front door that he bumped into it.

"I don't like being used, Luciano, especially when it leads to a couple of attempts on my life, and the death of a friend. That makes two friends that I've lost because of these paintings. That pisses me off!"

"Look," Luciano said, "give me back the money I paid you and I will leave."

"No, no, it doesn't work that way," I said. "We performed a service and we were paid for it."

"But—but you refuse to turn the paintings over—"

"I'll turn them over, all right," I said, "but to the proper authorities. I'll turn them over to a true representative of the Italian government."

"But . . . you can't!"

"Sure I can. Watch me."

"Wait—" Luciano said, looking as if he was going into a panic, "—now wait. We must talk."

"So talk."

"No, no, I mean alone, you and I. We must—"

"You want to cut a deal with me, Luciano? Offer it to all of us."

He looked around then, from face to face, the last being Harry the Map, who was halfway to being soaked and who was totally confused. He grinned at Luciano and raised his glass to him.

"Those paintings are *priceless* !" he finally said. "There is plenty of money for all of us."

As far as I was concerned, that constituted a confession of some sort.

"As far as I'm concerned, no deal," I said. "I don't know about the rest of these people."

"Will you bow to the majority, Carlucci?" Luciano asked. "Will you?"

"Why don't we first find out if there is a majority?" I suggested, and I looked at the others.

Tony Mack shook his head.

Parnell said, "No deals."

Riley Cooper said, "No."

Laura Bailey simply shook her head.

"I vote no!" Harry the Map said, and then said to Jesse, "Can I have another drink, honey?"

I turned to Luciano and said, "It seems there *is* a majority, Luciano, and I'm in it. You've fallen in with a den of honest people."

"No," he said, "no, it can't— "

The others must have thought I had it covered, because none

of them moved when Luciano reached into his pocket and came out with a gun, a small, foreign looking-automatic.

Lucky for them he pointed it at me.

"I want those paintings!" he said.

"What about your money?"

"Keep the money," he said. "I want the paintings. I have gone through too much to get them."

"What have you gone through, Lucky?"

"Years," he said, "years of waiting. We were young men when we stole them. We sold them *cheaply*! We were fools. Years later I heard from Bagetta. He had actually kept track of me. He knew I had become interested in art later in my life and that I had a gallery in Italy. He wrote to me and told me he was in prison. He wanted me to help him."

"So you didn't. You just left him there and bought yourself a guard."

"No, I went to see him, to see if he knew anything about the paintings. He told me no, but I didn't believe him. That was when I bribed a guard to keep an eye on him, in case he let something slip. It took years! I tried to track the paintings myself, but I never had any success. I had given up when I heard that Bagetta had died, and that he had spoken of the paintings. This was my chance, do you see that?"

"Oh, I see it, Lucky," I said, "but I also know that you've got no chances left, so put down the gun."

"No!" he said. "I want those paintings! I will kill you all, if I have to."

"Do you have enough bullets for that, Lucky?"

His hand tightened on the gun and he shouted, "Stop calling me that!"

I moved towards him and he straightened his arm and pointed the gun right at me.

"Do not move! I *will* kill you."

"You don't have enough bullets to kill everyone, Luciano."

"This clip holds nine shots."

I grinned and said, "Still not enough. Devlin!"

Everyone was surprised when I called out Devlin's name, and even more surprised when he came out of the back room with two uniformed cops. They had gotten in through the back door.

And then there were ten.

1 5

When Luciano saw the cops I thought he was going to shoot me. His hand steadied suddenly and I think he actually started to squeeze the trigger.

"One shot and you're a dead man!" Devlin called out.

Luciano was staring at me and I waited. When his eyes shifted to look at Devlin I darted in and slapped his hand aside, then clipped him with as hard a right as I've ever thrown.

Devlin came up next to me and looked down at the unconscious Luciano.

"I've never seen you move that fast."

"I hope I never have to again."

He slapped me on the back and opened the door.

"Uh, before I leave," he said.

"What?"

He pointed to Harry the Map and asked, "Who's he?"

"He's my partner," I said, "the brains of the outfit."

After Devlin and his men had taken Luciano away I bought another round of drinks for everyone.

"I have a question," Laura Bailey said.

"What?"

"What's he going to get for this? I mean, impersonating a government official. I mean, whatever it is, it certainly won't be what he deserves for murder—even a forty-year-old murder."

"There's no statute of limitations on murder," I said. "I'm sure the United States will let him be extradited to Italy."

"But . . . how can they prove anything?" she asked.

"Fingerprints."

"Fingerprints?" Mack said. "After all this time?"

"Oh, they have the fingerprints that were left behind at the museum, they just couldn't match them up with anyone's prints that were on file at the time. Obviously, the three young men had never been fingerprinted."

"So now they dig out the old prints," Parnell said, "take Luciano's, and match them up."

"Right."

"You think they'll match," Cooper said. It wasn't a question.

"That's my guess."

"A lot of guesses," Tony Mack said.

"Looks like most of them paid off, though," Parnell said. "Good job, Carlucci."

Somehow, it meant more to me that he was the one who said it.

"We all did a good job," I said, looking at them all. "I guess the chemistry was right, huh?"

"I guess so," Parnell said, and the others nodded.

"Well," Laura said, "here's my painting."

She handed me hers, which was rolled up and stuffed into a cardboard tube. The others followed her lead. They were all rolled up and protected by something. I took them around behind the bar and took out Luciano's attache case so I could pay everyone off.

"What about the fifth painting?" Laura Bailey asked.

I leaned on the attache case and looked at each of them in turn.

"As far as I'm concerned," I said, "there is no fifth painting."

"And that's what you'll tell the Italian government?" Tony Mack asked.

I nodded.

"Unless someone objects."

No one did.

After they had all gone Jesse made a pot of coffee. She and I sat at one end of the bar and drank it while Harry the Map dozed at the other end, his head down on the bar.

"I have a question now," Jesse said. She had remained admirably silent throughout the whole thing. "*Was* Luciano a member of the Italian consulate or not?"

"He was not,' I said. "He must have done the same thing I did with Mack's insurance company, he had himself put into their computers on a very low level, where no one would notice him unless they were looking. That makes me feel *real* smart."

"What do you mean?"

"If I had simply called the consulate instead of fooling around with computers, I could have saved myself some trouble."

"Well," she said, "that's past. My next question is this: You said that Mrs. DiMonte sent those punks to hurt you."

"That's right."

"How did she know so soon that you'd been hired? Did Luciano tell her?"

"No," I said, "I cleared that up with a phone call yesterday."

"To whom?"

"Edward Wells."

"But . . . he's your friend? Why would he call Mrs. DiMonte?"

"He didn't. He called your boss, Maynard."

"Andrew?"

"They're friends, aren't they?"

"Well, yes, but—"

"Edward felt a duty to both of us, Jess," I said. "He had to give me the information, but he had to warn Maynard."

"And Mrs. DiMonte?"

"It's fairly obvious, isn't it? Maynard sold her the painting, so he called her and told her about me. I guess I understand the kind of loyalty that was involved all the way around."

"And she sent those men to . . . to hurt you or kill you."

"I don't think they were supposed to kill me," I said. "At least, not that time."

"You're thinking about your friend? Myra?"

"Yeah . . ." I said. "Yeah, I am."

"Was she a close friend?"

I pointed down to the end of the bar and said, "As close as Harry there, I guess."

"Oh," she said, and unless I was reading too much into one two letter word, my answer had pleased her.

"Well," she said, "thanks for the chance to play barmaid. It was . . . interesting."

I walked her to the front door.

"If you ever have another case involving art," she said, "and need an expert, give me a call."

"I will, Jesse," I said. "Thanks for your help."

I thought she had something else on her mind, but she simply smiled and left. Maybe she was thinking the same thing I was, that I *could* call her even if I didn't need an art expert for a case.

Maybe.

"Come on, Harry," I said, jostling him awake.

"Hmm, what? Party over?"

"The party," I said, "is definitely over."